The

Custodian

By

C S Quilly

ISBN 978-1-0682222-1-4

Cover illustration by Zoe Beardsley of Greatstone Art. www.greatstone-art.com

To my family and friends with thanks for their support and encouragement.

Table of Contents

1968 Redemption

The old house seemed to sigh as it settled for the night and Rob heard the familiar creaks and moans of the beams and floorboards as he gazed down at his family. His wife Susie slept at last, her face still wearing the tired smile with which she had greeted the fruits of her labour. As he looked down into the crib, tears of wonder and happiness filled his eyes and he felt encompassed by the house's warm embrace.

Two tiny, dark eyes opened momentarily and stared intently at him.

"Hello, my beautiful girl," he smiled down at his tiny daughter as he gently stroked the soft down that covered her head.   A soft mewling from her companion made Rob chuckle.

"Hello to you too my son," he said proudly, "Think I would leave you out?" he said as he reached out a finger that was instantly grabbed by a tiny hand.

"And to think that we might never have met you," he whispered and the tears began to fall.

Susie woke with a start, a look of panic on her face.

"It's alright sweetheart." Rob said softly, "They are quite safe here in the crib."

Susie smiled. "It was not a dream then," she said sleepily and then, more sharply, "She... er.... they are here at last. ... and well?" Rob nodded.

"No dream sweetheart. See, they are both safe and whole, though small. Our prayers have been answered at last.   You go back to sleep and I will sit watch over you all."

Susie smiled again and, as her eyes closed once more, she whispered softly, "Thank you Nell."

As he kept watch Rob sighed with contentment. That he and Susie had a daughter was a miracle. Something they had longed for but had thought was to be denied to them.   That she had been accompanied by a brother had been nothing short of a miracle. His tiny son gave a small hiccup and Rob smiled.

"You gave us quite a scare my boy," he said softly, "though small, your determination and will to live will be a lesson to us all."

"Thank you my dearest Nell," he smiled towards his friend who shared his vigil. "Your faith and strength brought us these precious little ones."

He sat back in his chair, his offspring snoring gently in their crib. He felt so blessed and could barely contain his excitement at becoming a father but the impact of the day's events and strain of the past few months caught up with him and his eyes closed.

Nell looked across at her sleeping friend and his new family and a sense of peace and fulfilment washed over her.

"You have done well Mistress Jenkins," came a gentle voice. "Your work is done. Come."

"Can I not say goodbye to my friend?" she pleaded but could already feel herself drifting away.

"Come," the voice repeated and the room began to fade from her sight.

"Farewell Rob," she cried out, "Thank you for your love and companionship."

Rob sighed in his sleep and nestled further into the surrounding cushions, oblivious to her cries.

"God bless you my precious boy," she called as she disappeared from the room but Rob slept on, his dreams filled with the strain of the past months during which he and Susie had faced a most harrowing decision regarding their unborn children.

After several early miscarriages it had seemed that he and Susie had been destined never to be parents and then, as Susie had reached the second trimester of a pregnancy for the first time, they had dared to hope but disaster had once again struck. Susie had contracted whooping cough and had experienced severe symptoms, with vicious episodes of coughing and gasping for breath that had continued for several weeks. During this period she had been barely able to eat and became frail and weak.

Her parents, Stephen and Della, a GP and nurse respectively, had feared for their daughter's health and for the viability of her baby. They had called in professional colleagues for advice and Susie and Rob had been told bluntly that their baby, should it even survive to full term, would likely be mentally or physically disabled, possibly both. Physical examination had indicated a confusion of limbs and the doctors had advised that the birth would be dangerous for both Susie and the baby.

Susie and he had been devastated; even more so when the doctors had recommended that as their case fell within the parameters of the newly initiated Abortion Act, they were recommending that Susie undergo a termination on the grounds that her life would be in danger if she were to proceed with the pregnancy. They were inconsolable. How could they kill their baby?

Fierce debate ensued, with Susie's parents advocating in favour of the termination. Susie was adamant that she would not countenance the killing of her baby but Rob was torn. Although aghast at the thought of getting rid of their baby, he selfishly admitted to being equally concerned at the risks facing his beloved wife.

"How could I live without you my darling?" he had reasoned. "If I am to be denied the opportunity to become a father must I also face the rest of my life alone?"

"You are young yet," his wife had stated bluntly, "and could find love again with another."

At his shaking head she added sadly, "Do not add to my burden my love."

Chastened, Rob had tried so hard to be brave and supportive in front of Susie but when he was at his lowest ebb and could no longer control his tears, his friend of many years Nell, had come to comfort him. With her extensive knowledge as a midwife and healer, she expressed concern at the physicians recommendations. She had witnessed many innovations in the world of medicine over the years but was shocked to learn that today's Physicians could only offer a termination as the best solution to Susie's predicament. She asked to examine Susie so that she could assess the situation for herself.

Rob had known Nell since he was a small child, an evacuee from London who had come to this lovely old house with his four siblings when their home in the east end had been bombed and their parents killed. Of all the Lee children, he alone had been able to communicate with Nell and had been enthralled to learn of her life and long association with the house. He trusted her completely and had not hesitated to ask Susie to allow Nell's examination. Though she could neither see nor hear Nell, Susie, whose family had resided in Mulberry House for generations, had been told of Nell's existence and was happy to allow the examination. Her mother Della, who had known and enjoyed a pleasant friendship with Nell all her life, though siding with the professional experts due to the perceived risk to her daughter, was present during the examination and she watched with interest as her friend conducted a thorough examination of her daughter's abdomen.

"My instinct and examination indicate that your babe is healthy and whole," Nell later advised Rob who repeated her words to Susie. Their eyes shone with unshed tears but before they could comment, Nell held up her hand.

"I was also aware of a second, albeit much fainter heartbeat," she added slowly, "The presence of a second babe might explain the 'confusion of limbs' as described by the physicians."

"Twins?" Rob and Susie said in unison once Nell's words had been repeated.

Again Nell held up a hand.

"The second heartbeat is much weaker and I must advise that the babe might not survive the pregnancy, let alone the delivery, but yes, at present my examination would indicate that Susie is carrying twins."

As Rob passed on Nell's words to his wife, Della, who shared a quite remarkable bond with her own twin, Charlie, took her friend's hand.

"Thank you dearest Nell for your honesty."

Following Nell's examination and revelation, Rob and Susie had needed no further discussion with regard the proposed termination. That Susie was carrying at least one healthy baby was indication enough for them to   advise the professional clinicians that Susie intended to continue with the pregnancy.

The babies stirred in their crib, disturbing their father's dreams. He stood and stretched as he gazed down at his children. "To think that you might have been taken from us."

"You are Eleanor Adelaide, my darling daughter," he said in a whisper, "and you, littlest one," he turned to his son, "are Christopher Charles. You are named after four of the most kind and wisest people I have known.

I apologise to you my son, for the ignominious way in which you were treated at your birth." He whispered. "We had steeled ourselves for the disappointment that you had would either not survive the pregnancy or your delivery and were little surprised therefore that you did not breath or show any signs of life when you arrived some ten minutes after your sister. That you were put in a shoebox and tucked under the bed out of sight was to spare your dear Mama the pain of seeing your lifeless form."

Rob sighed as he remembered his disappointment at his son's demise and then smiled as he recalled Nell's sudden agitation at the feeble noises she could hear emanating from beneath the bed.

Nell had grabbed Rob's arm and pulled him away from his adoration of his new daughter. She had bade him pull out the small box in which his son lay.

"See how he has bubbles around his nose," she had shrieked. 'He is attempting to breath" she had continued. "Wipe the area gently with some cotton and ask Della to fetch a syringe quickly'

He had done as instructed and Della had quickly arrived to complete the clearance of mucus that was blocking the tiny baby's nose. Rob watched in amazement as the bubbles quickly disappeared and his son's little chest started to rise and fall in a steady pattern.

"Oh the poor little mite has his tongue attached to the roof of his mouth," Della had exclaimed. "Pass me the surgical scissors Rob."

A tray of sterile surgical tools lay on a nearby table and Rob reached for the scissors and was transfixed as his mother-in-law quickly snipped each side of the child's little tongue and released it from its confinement. Whether from the discomfort or the indignity of the occasion Rob was unable to say but when his son let out an almighty wail, he would later confirm that it was one of the most wonderful sounds he had ever heard but was one that he prayed he would never hear again. He had quickly picked his son out of the box and taken him across to the bed to meet his mother and be reunited with his sister.

In keeping with the family tradition initiated by Sophie's late and much missed grandpa Kit, her grandma Lexie, brandishing her husband's favourite camera had taken a snap of the new arrivals and their parents.

Della and Nell stood to one side beaming with pride.

"Thank you my friend," Della said quietly whilst Nell offered up her own silent prayer of thanks.

The following days were filled with the joy of getting to know their children and introducing them to the wider world, with little time to ponder on Nell's disappearance. However, it was Della who later mentioned with relief and delight that it appeared that the twin's arrival had served to win the redemption that dear Nell had so long awaited.

"Though we will miss her greatly, I pray that she is able to rest in peace at last," she said with a smile.

Rob, however, who had felt that his relationship with Nell had been so much closer than that she had enjoyed with anyone else, felt slightly cheated that she had failed to say goodbye to him, although he reluctantly acknowledged that her departure had perhaps been beyond her control and he recalled a vague dream in which she had made her farewell. Nevertheless, one morning he ventured up to her customary haunt in the attic, in the faint hope that she had managed to leave him one final message.

Sure enough, as he reached the top of the stairs and stood on the small landing that had been Nell's particular sanctuary, a package fell from a high beam. As he picked it up he saw that it bore his name, written in an unsteady script. He opened the outer layer carefully and found a letter from his friend wrapped around several bundles of papers and artefacts. He slumped into a lumpy, dusty old chair and started to read his old friend's words, grateful that she had managed to leave him something with which he could remember her.

Tears of surprise and love fell as he read...

My dear, dear Robbie,

As you read this be reassured that I am gone to a better place and that you and yours have helped me achieve my freedom at last. Please forgive the rudimentary writings of an ignorant old woman. Learning to read and write was one of the greatest pleasures of my time in this dear house but though I read at every opportunity, writing was a skill that I had scant occasion to practice. It has taken many months to compile this history for you but, being hopeful that my time here was at last coming to an end, I could think of none better with whom to pass on the secrets and treasures for which I have been the custodian over the centuries.

I was born in the small town of Rye in the year of our Lord 1309. As you already know, like my mother before me, I learned the skills that enabled me to work in the service of the town as a midwife and healer. In respect for my services to the town, on my death at the age of 56, my body was laid to rest in the churchyard, alongside my dear husband Arthur who had died in the service of the Cinque Ports Fleet. However, for my sins, the greatest of which I will reveal in due course, my soul was not permitted to enter Heaven to be reunited with Arthur and I was condemned to purgatory to await the opportunity for redemption. I was confined to the house and grounds of Capel House on Middle Street, the home of the wealthy Alard family and site of my greatest sin, that later became the location of the lovely home you know as Mulberry House.

I had assumed that any potential for redemption would directly involve those against whom I had sinned but it appeared that God had other plans for me.

Following a number of defeats at the hands of the French and a subsequent downward turn in the town's prosperity, the Alards of Capel House lost the favour and support of the town and they left Rye to take up residence in one of their other properties. Capel House was thus abandoned and I was left alone.

Over the ensuing years, as other families took up residence and then left my house it became clear to me that one of the chief lessons of my purgatory was to be that of patience. Some of those who lived in the old house were completely unaware of my presence amongst them and some, perhaps fearful of being thought possessed, chose to ignore my presence. Of these people I feel no need to comment except to say that despite my best attempts to interact with them, I remained isolated and frustrated and the years passed extremely slow.

Eventually though I was able to make contact with some of my fellow residents and there were several, like your good self, with whom I gained enormous pleasure in conversing and, I hope, assisting through the years. The first of these was Meggie, your dear Susie's many-greats grandmother from long ago. She, along with several others of these much-loved friends, entrusted me with their secrets and treasures and it is these that I now leave in your care. Will you take on this onerous responsibility?

On the face of things, some of these items may appear to have little value, save their survival over so many years, but they have inordinate sentimental value to me and, being an historian, you will I am sure, recognise the enormous significance and financial worth of some but also the intrinsic value of the rest. I know you will use them wisely.

I have faithfully maintained the secrets over the centuries and have never felt the need to share them with anyone during this period. Nobody, that is, until your good self. When you first arrived at Mulberry House, a small, rather grubby but warm-hearted, clever and inquisitive boy, I sensed a connection with you and was delighted that you were able to both see and hear me. We spent many a happy hour together and your interest in this old house and its former residents drew you ever deeper into my affections. It came to light that you were the relative of one who I had helped many years earlier, a very young, misused girl named Ivy who, with her brother Tom had sought refuge in this place when she was on the run from a life of abuse. I was touched to learn that my actions had been so fondly remembered by the young runaways and that my history and involvement in their care had been passed down through their descendants. When the war ended and you returned to your former life I was distraught, as I had felt, as I had never felt with another, that your presence here would directly lead to my salvation. That you later returned, the same honest, kind and intelligent person, was confirmation enough for me to accept I had been correct in my assumptions about you and that the time for my redemption was approaching. I thus began to compile the enclosed documents that would enable you to understand their import in my time here.

I give thanks for your companionship and affection these last years and for the faith you bestowed on me when those around you with greater expertise than I, advocated a different course. As you start a new chapter in your life, I give thanks to the Lord that I was able to assist you, and darling Susie, through this most challenging of episodes. May you continue to be strong for those who love you.

Use the knowledge and artefacts you are soon to uncover, with respect. I know them to be in safe hands.

With my deep affection

Your friend

Nell Jenkins

Rob sat back in the chair and whispered a heartfelt thanks to his friend. He gazed at the weighty package that accompanied his letter. The historian in him wanted to rip open the outer wrapping and plunge straight in but he held back. Nell had taken months, perhaps years, to compile the contents and he felt compelled to show due respect to her efforts. He therefore carefully unwrapped the package but took out only the first of the folded bundles therein. He would savour each revelation slowly and methodically as time allowed and not make any decision on their future until all had been read and enjoyed.

The First hundred years

Meggie

Capel House fell into disrepair once the Alard family had left Rye but, when the French sacked the town in 1377 even that poor shelter was taken from me. Doubts began to cloud my thoughts and prayers. Without even a house to offer shelter to one in need, how would I ever be able to offer my assistance and gain redemption.   Doubt and despair overwhelmed me as I sat amongst the ruins of the old town.   Had God forsaken me?

It was several decades before this current house, Mulberry House, as it is now known, was built in the second decade of the fifteenth century.   I took a keen interest in the construction of what was to become a large, impressive half brick/half-timbered family home that straddled the sites of both Capel House and its former neighbour.   The owner of the new building, that was to be named Oak House, was one Edward Pope, a prosperous timber merchant, who spared no expense in the creation of his new family home.   I lovingly watched as every brick and beam was carefully positioned by the craftsmen who created it.

 The building and furnishing of the house took nearly two years during which time I wandered around the busy site, enjoying the camaraderie and fine craftsmanship of those employed in the construction and internal finishings. Having spent many frustrating years awaiting the rebuilding of my home, Oak House, was everything I could ever have hoped for and, as I moved from room to room, admiring the well-appointed kitchens and caressing each beam and carved panel, the house seemed to welcome and embrace me as it's chatelaine.

When Master Pope eventually took up residence with his wife and young family, I was intrigued to hear him mention to his wife that his great grandmother Isabella had been born in a fine house on Middle Street which was why he had been so keen to build their new home there.   I remembered that prior to his abandonment of Capel House, Sir Gerald Alard had been keen to find appropriate husbands for his eldest daughters amongst the prosperous merchants and businessmen of Rye and Isabella Alard had been betrothed to the son of a successful local timber merchant. I was therefore pleased to consider that if it were indeed this Isabella who was Edward's grandmother, the family connection could mean that my chance to make amends might be imminent.

The Popes soon settled into their beautiful home and were a happy, loving family although, sadly, none of the household seemed to be aware of my presence in the house. Having learned to be more patient over the years however, I was content to watch over them, to keep them safe, and await whatever God had in store for us all. They were a god-fearing family who treated their staff well and, as the years passed, I watched with interest as the local midwives assisted in the deliveries of subsequent generations of the family. I became very fond of them all and, though it meant a prolonged purgatory, each time a new babe was born I was relieved that there had been no need for any intervention on my part.

The house, with its frontage edging the street, comprised a central door that led into a large welcoming hallway with a grand staircase leading to the floors above where a fine room that looked out over the gardens, occupied a similar position to that of Lady Mathilde's chamber. It was in here that I spent much of my time, admiring the fine gardens that were being recreated outside.   As well as large leaded windows that, as the sun set each evening, allowed the room to be bathed in a gloriously warm glow, there was a door that led directly into the garden and it was in this room that the ladies and the children of the house spent many contented hours, sewing, gossiping and playing games.

The years passed slowly and I had almost given up hope of ever achieving direct contact with any of the residents, when, towards the middle of the fifteenth century, on Edward Pope's demise, his grandson William inherited the family timber business and became master of Oak House. With his wife Margaret and their three young children, twin boys and a younger daughter, all of whom I had watched being born, I sensed that my prayers might at last be answered as the little girl, then aged eight years, named Margaret for her mother but known fondly as Meggie, would occasionally stare directly at me and seem to want to speak.

Meggie had deep auburn hair and twinkling blue eyes and could be as demure as any young maid when pressed to be so but was firmly the boss of her two older brothers and was usually the victor during the regular bouts of rough and tumble that she and the boys engaged in. During her silent observations I became aware of an occasional half-glance in my direction or sometimes the hint of a shy smile. I was desperate to speak to her but did not want to frighten her so held back, sensing that it had to be she who took the first step towards communication. However, I contrived every opportunity that I could to be alone with her.

One afternoon, as I sat in the garden room,   Meggie entered and settled down to mend some stockings. As she sought out the right colour wool from the basket, I leant forward and tipped the basket over.

"I saw that, you wicked woman," Meggie had shrieked before clamping her hand over her mouth, her blue eyes wide with fear.

I smiled warmly, "So you can see me then," I said gently. "My name is Nell, and I mean you no harm."

Meggie snatched up the fallen skeins of wool and the basket and ran from the room. However, confident that having at last made contact, Meggie would overcome her fear and her natural curiosity would lead to further such encounters, I was content to bide my time. Sure enough, it took only a few days before Meggie's curiosity overcame her fear and she actively sought me out as I sat in the pretty rose garden enjoying the intoxicating scents and the humming of the bees. Meggie came close to me and reached out to try to touch my arm. When her hand passed straight through she quickly withdrew her own as if burnt but this time she did not run. After ensuring that there was nobody else nearby she had asked timidly, "Are you a ghost?"

I had smiled and nodded, "I am a poor sinner awaiting entry to heaven," I explained simply, "I am tied to this place until I am able to atone for my earthly sins. Only then will I be allowed to assume my place in heaven. I mean you no harm and would be pleased to call you my friend."

Meggie nodded as if my explanation was completely normal, and then she asked, "Were you very evil?" Her eyes grew large and she reddened, embarrassed at her rudeness, but could not contain her curiosity and she added, "Why is it only I who can see you?"   I had shrugged my shoulders.

"I was not very evil, I promise you." I reassured, "In fact, I was a midwife and healer so I brought both life and better health to many but I made a grave mistake for which I must atone before I can leave this place."

I sighed, " I cannot explain why it is only you who are able to see or hear me. I have been here for nigh on one hundred years and though I have sensed that several have been aware of my presence, you are the first to admit to being able to do so, and I am very glad that you can," I had added with a warm smile.

Having overcome her fear, Meggie contrived many opportunities to sit with me and learn of my life. So long had it been that I had communicated with anyone, that I too had many questions about the happenings in the town and beyond and we spent many a pleasurable afternoon in deep conversation. Meggie was thrilled and proud to be the first to communicate with me and I gave thanks to the Lord that he had enabled me to get to know this bonny, bright and curious child.

Meggie had an unbridled need to learn and was equally disappointed and angry when she learned that her gender excluded her from joining her brothers in their lessons at the new monastery that had been built on Conduit Street. The subject became the source of much conflict between the young lady and her father who, like her mother and I, tried to explain that it was not just she that was excluded. Girls were simply not required or indeed allowed to attend such lessons; it was sufficient that they learn how to run a godly home and raise a family. Meggie ranted and raved about the unfairness of this situation, particularly as her brothers were completely ambivalent towards their lessons, and her poor mother despaired of ever being able to persuade her of the importance of her domestic duties.

In an attempt to assuage Meggie's frustrations I offered to teach her about the use of medicinal herbs and how to prepare simple remedies. She mentioned her interest in the art of healing to her mother and Margaret, pleased that Meggie had found a channel for her energies, took pleasure in discussing remedies and treatments with her daughter, not seeming to recognise that the child's knowledge quickly outstripped her own.

Meggie was an avid student and over the ensuing years absorbed everything that I could teach her. By the time she was fourteen years of age she began to ask questions that far exceeded my knowledge and I encouraged her to ask her parents if she might be permitted to assist at the monastery infirmary so that her knowledge could be put to good use. Her mother was not a little surprised at her daughter's request but recognised that her daughter needed a channel for her boundless energy. She was also very proud that her precious girl wished to serve those in need. Margaret persuaded her husband to approach the Abbot and ask if Meggie might work alongside the nuns who assisted the monks in the infirmary. At first William had not been keen on the idea of his daughter attending the infirmary where, he advised, the monks tended to those who were suffering from 'who knows what conditions' and who could not afford the attendance of a 'proper physician.' However, Margaret assured him that the monks would not allow Meggie near anyone suffering from any dangerous or contagious condition and stressed how useful and economically sensible it would be to have someone in the household who could administer treatments and remedies to the family and their staff, thereby saving him the cost of calling for a 'proper physician.' Margaret also suggested that giving Meggie an outlet for her energies would help calm her and perhaps make her more marriageable when the time came. Seeing the sense in these arguments, William gave his permission and, having gained reassurances from the Abbot that Meggie would be protected from any 'unsavoury' situations, she was allowed to present herself at the monastery infirmary.

Once there, her existing knowledge, energy and enthusiasm for learning, not to mention her charm and caring nature with the patients, was heartily welcomed and she was quickly taken under the wing of Brother Anselm who was in charge of the infirmary. He was happy to pass on his extensive knowledge to such a responsive student and it became a common sight for the two heads, one tonsured and greying and the other with unruly auburn locks escaping from a starched white coif, almost conjoined as they pored over a physic book, garden herb or patient, keenly discussing the benefits or otherwise of certain treatments and remedies. With his encouragement and help, Meggie secretly learnt to read and write so as to further aid her learning. As the years passed and her knowledge increased, even the nuns turned to her for advice and she became an integral member of the staff. At home too, it was to Meggie that all turned if they had any sort of health concern, and the efficacy of her remedies soon became quite renown amongst their friends and neighbours.

By the time she was nineteen, with my encouragement and teaching, Meggie had also achieved a sound reputation as a midwife and I was justly proud of my young protégée. I listened with interest as she described certain conditions and illnesses she had learned to treat, and she had brought home many cuttings of plants and herbs from the monastery physic garden, that Brother Anselm recommended she grow and use for her own patients.

As was her nature, however, Meggie hungered for more knowledge and was again disappointed that she was not able to undertake any more formal medical training. Her earlier frustrations rose to the fore once again. Her brothers had shown no interest in academic pursuits, both being happy to work alongside their father in the family timber business. She, however, being a woman, despite having the ability and the enthusiasm for higher education, was denied the opportunity. I must admit that I shared her frustrations as during my administrations as a midwife and healer, I had often felt slighted by the professional Physicians, some of whom had been complete charlatans in my opinion but could offer the girl little in the way of hope that things would change. Nevertheless, I prayed most ardently that one day women would be accorded the same opportunities as their menfolk.

One afternoon Meggie returned home in a rare state of high dudgeon. She quickly sought me out in the garden and let forth a tirade of frustration and anger at how one of the Physicians had humiliated her. It became clear that a Master William Ashworth, who occasionally condescended to offer his services in the infirmary, had looked down his nose at her and practically laughed as he watched her apply a lungwort poultice to a patient's chest to help ease his breathing. Adding to his rudeness but not wishing to 'soil' his hands with her 'witchery,' he had, with the aid of a long quill, flicked the poultice onto the floor and pushed past her. He had then sought out the Abbot to whom he complained long and loud, so that many within the precincts could hear, about the monastery practice of allowing a chit of a girl to 'play' Physician. She had barely been able to control her fury at his rudeness and lack of professional courtesy and had turned to Brother Anselm for support. The embarrassed monk had quickly ushered her from the room, not because he approved of the man's behaviour but to spare her from any further backlash should she vocalise her displeasure. Leaving her in the care of one of the senior nuns, he had returned to the main room to calm the distressed patient who had also been much upset by the Physician's words.

Meggie, hurt at what she saw as a lack of support from Brother Anselm, and unable to curb her anger, had stormed out of the building to return home, but not before careering into James Southerden, one of the other, younger and more affable, of the visiting Physicians.

James, the youngest son of a successful local ship builder, had, like her, shown an interesting in the healing arts and had initially trained under Brother Anselm. He had recently completed his studies in medicine at Oxford university and, having returned to his hometown, was fast establishing himself as an efficient, reliable and caring Physician.   He had not however forgotten the source of his expertise and he was a regular attendee at the monastery infirmary. Clutching at the wall to avoid being bowled over, he watched in surprise as Meggie, with eyes still blazing, had stormed past him with only the merest muttered apology and continued apace up the hill.

Now, seated in the garden beside me as she related her tale, her heartbeat began to slow and the flush left her cheeks.

"How can I ever continue to care for others if I am so publicly undermined and humiliated?" she cried and the tears, so long suppressed, began to fall. "I can never return to the infirmary now, having been so ill-used. That is if Brother Anselm does not bar me from continuing my studies, given my behaviour," she added sadly, despair replacing her former anger, "and what of Master Southerden? He of all the attending Physicians has always offered me courtesy and respect and I all but felled him in my haste to escape. He will likely think me ill-mannered as well as unladylike in my demeanour."

I had been relieved to see Meggie's normal humours being slowly restored and had offered comfort and reassurances that her skills would never be dismissed by the brothers at the Monastery. "I have oft heard your dear father comment on Brother Anslem's high regard for you, dear girl," I reminded her, "He prizes your skills and efforts for his poor patients and I am sure he will have been as embarrassed by Master Ashworth's behaviour as you were distressed. I am confident that he would be most upset if you were to turn your back on them. Act not in haste my dear, take a while to restore yourself before you make any rash decisions."

I then turned the conversations towards the young Master Southerden, remembering well a young Henry Southerden who had ardently courted me in my youth. So keenly had he pursued me that it had taken a bloodied nose from my beau Arthur to convince young Henry that I was already spoken for. Henry had soon married another bonny girl of the parish and had appeared to hold no grudge, as they had repeatedly called on my professional services as their family grew and grew. Smiling at my memories, I sighed, "I knew of a family of ship makers named Southerden in my time," I said. " Helped bring several of their babes into the world – large strapping babes if I recall correctly. Their father was a big, handsome man, with a shock of blonde hair and bright blue eyes; a real charmer, though a kind man who, with his dear wife, was a charitable soul who helped many of the poorer families of the town. I wonder if your Master James is of the same family?"

"He is not my Master James," Meggie retorted with a blush, "but he is very tall and blonde, with sparkling blue eyes, so he could well be their descendant. He has never shown me any disdain, indeed, he has sometimes sought me out and asked for my assistance or advice and does seem to have a caring manner, no matter how lowly the patient," she paused and smiled briefly at the thought of the young man she described, but the smile quickly changed to a grimace as she remembered her earlier embarrassment and added, "unlike some of his professional colleagues." Once again I changed the subject, and we spent the next hour or so discussing the thriving herb garden and what new salves and tinctures Meggie could create.

Several days later and Meggie, yet to return to the infirmary, received a visitor. Young Master

Southerden had called enquiring after her wellbeing. Margaret, after settling him in the front parlour, called for her daughter and sent her to 'tidy herself to receive her visitor' whilst she organised refreshments. Keen to ascertain if he was indeed a member of the family I had known previously, I had entered the parlour and gasped with delight when I beheld the open countenance and good looks of an earlier generation. Most assuredly was this young man a descendant of that young Henry who had pursued me so passionately and the thought instantly warmed me to him. If he were half as kind and loving as his forebears, Meggie could do a lot worse. As Meggie entered, looking neat and demure, she looked enquiringly towards me and I nodded.

James stood quickly as Meggie entered the room. He seemed a little flustered but bowed towards her and said,

"Miss Pope, I am glad to see you looking well. You had seemed to be in some distress when we last encountered one another and I was concerned that you were unwell." He blushed and continued quickly,

"I have missed your friendly and invaluable presence at the infirmary and hope you will not think me too forward in calling to enquire after you."

Meggie had bobbed a curtsey and indicated that he should sit. "I am quite well sir," she reassured him, "and I apologise for my unladylike behaviour. I had felt slighted by one of your professional colleagues, but my behaviour was most inappropriate. My mother is always telling me that my pride is likely to result in my downfall...." she faltered as her mother entered bearing a jug of beer and some bread and cheese.

As the refreshments were served and enjoyed, James had looked compassionately towards Meggie, "Brother Anselm informed me of the events at the infirmary," he admitted, "and asked that I visit you to reassure you that he was most anxious that you might have thought him complicit in the conduct of my colleague Master Ashworth."

Meggie and her mother sat quietly and nodded as James continued.

"He was most aggrieved by Master Ashworth's behaviour however, the affronted Physician was not easily placated and, rather than be calmed by Brother Anselm's gentle words, seemed to become more agitated, bandying words such as witchery and devilish practices in relation to your activities at the hospital and further afield. I am afraid that to defuse the situation Brother Anselm was forced to insist that you were merely following his own instructions. He further added that many of his treatments and remedies had been passed down to him from his sainted mother, daring Master Ashworth to suggest that she might have been a witch.   After much pontificating at the respect due to a Physician such as he, Master Ashworth seemed to calm, suggesting as he left that he would consider withdrawing his assistance to the hospital if certain people, by which he meant your good self, did not mend their ways."

He paused and shook his head slowly.

"I fear that you have made a dangerous enemy of the gentleman and, despite having his full support, Brother Anselm suggests that you do not return to the hospital for a while to allow things settle. Many were able to hear Master Ashworth's harsh words and insinuations of witchcraft and you must be aware how dangerous such accusations can be. I personally think it unlikely that he will show his face at the infirmary again and frankly, he will not be missed. I am here to offer you a heartfelt apology on behalf of the brothers and nursing sisters and some of my fellow physicians, not to mention most of the patients, and to beg you to take care.   Though, if I may dare add without causing offence, your extensive knowledge and skill, not to mention your smiles and constant sunny disposition which are as good as any tonic will be missed by us all, we wish no harm to come to you as a result of Master Ashworth's venom."

Margaret had been horrified at the accusations hurled at her daughter but, after several minutes of heated discussion, it was agreed that Meggie would remain at home for a while to enable the unfortunate issue to dissipate. Meggie also begged her mother not to mention the unfortunate event to her father who would most assuredly act in defence of his daughter and risk further publicising and exacerbating the whole unpleasant situation. So it was agreed.

As he left, Master Southerden had reassured Margaret that none who knew her daughter would give any credence to the words of Master Ashworth and it was purely as a precaution that they advised that Meggie remain at home for a while. He had promised to return as soon as Brother Anselm felt it safe for Meggie to resume her work at the infirmary.

Meggie had been most touched by James' comments and her mother was most appreciative of his concern. Once the young physician had left Oak House, she had smiled at her daughter and suggested that there had appeared to be more than just professional courtesy in his demeanour. Meggie had blushed and I could that see that she was not displeased by this idea.

Not one to sit idle, Meggie had become increasingly frustrated at the inactivity that had been imposed on her. She had bustled around the house in search of anything that would satisfy her need to be useful, with her anger mostly targeted at her brothers and her poor mother.

In despair Margaret had paid a visit to the infirmary and engaged in a lengthy discussion with Brother Anselm. On her return to Oak House she had arranged for refreshments to be served in the garden room and sent for Meggie.

Once they had partaken of the refreshments, Margaret had presented Meggie with a small parcel.

"I have spoken with Brother Anselm with regard your obvious frustration at not being able to return to the infirmary. He advises that it would be inadvisable at present but he has come up with a solution for you that he thinks will help challenge your energies."

Meggie sat quietly, keen to learn what Brother Anselm" had suggested.

"He has sent you this parcel," her mother continued, "with the suggestion that you might compile a compendium of common herbs and their medicinal uses."

Meggie's face lit up as her mother quickly continued. "I suppose I should not have been surprised to learn that you are able to read and write a fair hand," she said, with a hint of sadness but not a little pride, " You were always one to challenge convention."

She smiled across at her daughter and sighed. "If only your brothers had half of your drive."

"They have talents in other ways, mother," Meggie had proffered.

"Be that as it may, it is your talents we are discussing now," her mother reminded her. "I understand your frustrations but am so proud when I hear others praising your achievements. What do you think of Brother Anselm's idea? He offered to have one of the young novices help with illustrations but I assured him that drawing was one of the few ladylike pastimes that you actually enjoyed and so I felt sure you would be able to manage the illustrations for yourself. I hope that was correct."

"Oh mother, I do not deserve your praise, but yes, you are correct. I am happy to embark on this task but would wish it to be all my own work."

"Which brings us to a point on which Brother Anselm was most insistent. He has sent you a supply of parchment, ink and quills with which you can commence the work but imposes one crucial condition – one that you might find difficult to accept but one that he feels is imperative if you are to protect yourself - the source of the compendium must remain a secret. Your name must not appear on any page lest you open yourself to further accusations of witchcraft in the future."

Meggie sat back in her chair, although disappointed that her name would not be associated with the herbal compendium, she recognised the sense of Brother Anselm's condition. She nodded, "He is right as always, I understand and accept his condition. I will write him a short note of thanks and will then start my work."

Seeing the light in her daughter's face, Margaret was happy but, without wishing to cause Meggie any further distress, she said quietly but firmly, "and nobody else may be aware of your endeavour, my dear. Nobody. This must remain a closely guarded secret."

"I understand, mother," came the sad response.

Later that evening, in the privacy of her bedroom, Meggie unwrapped the precious parcel of writing equipment and hid them in a chest.

Before she commenced the work she and I had much debate on which herbs to feature and how best to organise them so as to make the compendium easy to use. Finally agreeing to group the herbs in terms of the conditions for which they were most commonly used, Meggie commenced her compendium, working secretly in her room in the evenings. It was therefore several months before she declared it finished.

When she finally resumed her work at the infirmary and was able to present the precious pages to Brother Anselm. She was barely able to hide her pride when she later told me of the monk's praise for her work.

"He is arranging for the precious pages to be carefully bound and with a front cover that is to read:

'A Compendium of Herbs and their Uses'

dedicated to Mistress Nell Jenkins

whose input has been most invaluable.

You will be famous Nell!   What do you think of that?" she sat back and clapped her hands.

"Brother Anselm asked who Mistress Jenkins was and I was able to advise, in all honesty that you were an old family friend without whom I could not have produced such a work," Meggie had said with an angelic expression on her face. "I reassured him that you were a very old lady and unlikely to be affected by any slanderous accusations in the future," she laughed.

The final pamphlet had been much admired by all who saw it and Brother Anselm arranged for several copies to be produced, one of which was keenly acquired by James Southerden who remained ignorant of its authorship.

Meggie had understood the need to retain her anonymity, however, when the original pages were returned to her she compiled her own cover for them to which she added

Compiled by and illustrated by

Miss Margaret Pope

She whispered for me to join her as she retired later that evening and presented me with the newly covered pamphlet.

"I give you this dear Nell," she began, "it is dedicated to you as without your support and knowledge, so generously shared over the years, it would not have existed. I pray that you hide it away so that it may never cause me or mine any harm. Its existence in this house fills me with pride and fulfilment such as I never hoped to achieve."

I was much moved by her words and promised to keep the precious pamphlet safely hidden.

Meggie had been delighted to return to the infirmary and, as the months passed she was pleased to report to me that no mention was made of the reason for her long absence. On the rare occasions that she and Master Ashworth were both present in the infirmary, he ignored her completely and she in turn learned to keep out of his way. She had resigned herself to a changed role at the infirmary in light of the accusations made against her but was happy to report that things were, if anything, better than before the unfortunate incident. She was pleased to advise that James and the remaining Physicians seemed so keen to make amends for their colleague's assault on her reputation, that they often made a point to seek her out and openly ask her advice on a particular remedy or treatment, and, when appropriate, they also began to instruct her in areas where her knowledge was lacking.

It became customary practice for Master James to escort Meggie to and from the monastery and he was often invited to join Meggie for supper if they arrived home later than usual. Her demand as a midwife and healer increased as well and I was pleased to note a renewed sense of personal fulfilment within my young protégée.

It did not take long before it became clear to all that the handsome young physician and the beautiful young healer were becoming more than just colleagues and thus, it was no surprise to the family, when James asked William's permission to marry his daughter. They were married in St Mary's on a glorious June day and, though I marvelled at the glorious peal of the bells that rang out for the young couple and wished them every happiness, I could not but be a little sad as I knew that Meggie would no longer reside at Oak House and be my companion.

I need not have worried however, as Meggie's new home, a gift from James' father and only a short walk away near The Mint, had only a very small garden and she continued to visit Oak House to raid its abundant herb garden and thus we were able to maintain our friendship.

Meggie continued her work as a healer and midwife and also assisted her husband in his thriving medical practice and helping at the monastery infirmary when time allowed.   She and James were blessed with two healthy sons but sadly, when Meggie brought them to visit Oak House, neither appeared to share their mother's ability to see or communicate with me. After a number of years Meggie finally gave birth to a daughter, named Eleanor Margaret, as a tribute to the two women who had been so important in her life. I was touched and delighted by her gesture, even more so when Meggie brought her new daughter to Oak House, to introduce her to me and, whilst we were sitting in our usual spot in the garden, the babe stared intently at me and held out a hand in my direction.

Eleanor and Ned

Meggie's family soon outgrew the little house in the Mint and she and James moved to a larger and grander house a few yards further up Middle Street from Oak House making it easier for Meggie to visit her family home on a more regular basis. The older of her twin brothers, named William like their father, had taken over the running of the family business and, with his family, had moved into Oak House with their aging father. It was there, whilst her parents were busy tending to the sick and needy of the town and her brothers attended their lessons, that little Eleanor spent much of her time. She was a quiet, thoughtful girl who found her much older cousins rather too boisterous, preferring instead to spend time with her grandfather. As the youngest grandchild, she was indulged by everyone in the family but was by no means spoiled by all the attention. She had curiously dark and dreamy blue eyes and often seemed to be off in another place. We spent many an afternoon conversing in her room or in the garden and, like her mother, she had a thirst for knowledge and was keen to learn of my life as a midwife and healer.

Her older cousins thought her odd and sometimes made disparaging comments about her talking to herself around the house or in the garden, but she had only to turn and give them a long stare and their criticisms ceased. Even at a young age she seemed to realise that her relationship with me was unusual and was not to be discussed with anyone but her mother.

William senior, since the death of his beloved wife Margaret a few years' earlier, loved spending time with his young granddaughter, and they enjoyed nothing more than watching the hustle and bustle of the traders, seafarers and local townsfolk passing up and down Middle Street and, to facilitate this, he installed a fine bench below the large leaded windows at the front of Oak House. Seated there, protected from all but the most inclement weather by the projecting first floor, he would spend many an hour, with Eleanor at his side and myself listening at the window above them, greeting and conversing with former business associates, friends and strangers alike and telling of the Kings and heroes of old.

Having lived through the seemingly endless wars with neighbouring countries, most notably France, I had never before taken much interest in the fates and fortunes of those beyond my small world. However now, the tales and news I overheard helped pass the time and I became intrigued about life beyond our walls.

As she got older and much to my disappointment, following the death of her grandfather, Eleanor spent less and less time at Oak House. Her father James, now enjoying significant standing within the community, was hopeful of becoming the town mayor one day. Thus his boys were being educated as befitted the family's status, in the hope that they would be able to take up such professions as the Law or Medicine. James hoped to marry Eleanor into one of the eminent families of the area and thus enabling her, one day, to attend the Royal Court. To this end therefore Eleanor was being educated in music, dancing, embroidery and poetry but James rejected any notion of his daughter learning of midwifery and healing, despite Meggie's insistence that this would prove useful when Eleanor was a fine Lady in charge of a large country estate. I had to be content with only an occasional visit from Eleanor or Meggie when they came to collect herbs.

Sadly, as the century slipped slowly towards its close, Meggie made what proved to be her last visit to the old house. She and I sat in our favourite spot in the garden, not speaking but simply enjoying the gentle warmth of the spring sun, and the chirping of birds in the trees.

Eventually Meggie spoke. "You and I both know that my time is close, dearest Nell," she said softly as she struggled to breath. "You have been my companion over the last forty years or so, and I will make sure that your support and kindnesses are remembered forever within my family." A fit of coughing prevented her from talking and I felt helpless as she fought for breath. When she could speak again she said, "and I will put in a good word for you in heaven if I am permitted entry. You must not be sad at my passing, I have had a good life, which was enriched by your friendship and affection. I hope I have been able to help you to better endure your purgatory and I pray that another such friend will join you soon and take over my role."

Sadness overwhelmed me at the thought of losing my dear friend.

"You will never realise how much you helped pass the time and enrich my existence over the time we have spent together." I insisted, "The early decades after my demise, with none of the light, humour and intelligence you brought to lift my spirits, passed exceedingly slow. I will pray for you dearest Meggie and have no doubt that you will soon join our dear Lord in heaven. I thank you for your kind words and would welcome the opportunity to help your descendants in the future, should they have need."

Meggie smiled.

"Rest assured dear friend that your existence in this fine house, not to mention the skills and knowledge you have shared with me, will be passed down and used to the benefit of all my family through the generations to come. I would have written of our friendship were I not wary of such an admission being used against my family in the future. I repeat my earlier gratitude for your friendship over the years and assure you that your name will always be remembered fondly within my family."

I raised my eyes and looked into the loving eyes of my friend for the last time. We both smiled.

Meggie looked across the garden and said, "Now, here is Sam come to escort me home. "Take good care of my secret pamphlet. It is my hope that one day you will be able to safely pass it on to any future protégée you may encounter in this glorious house."

Racked by a further bout of coughing, Meggie reached for her grandson's hand.

"Let our parting not be one of sorrow. I will pray for your soul and hope that one day we will be reunited in heaven," and with that, leaning heavily on Sam, Meggie slowly left the garden, and I was once again alone.

Meggie died soon after our emotional meeting and a day or so after her funeral, Eleanor, now a mature matron and looking sad but as beautiful as ever, visited Oak Hall accompanied by a very handsome young man. Seeking me out in the garden, she greeted me most warmly and confirmed that the young gentleman was her beloved husband, Ned. She went on to describe her mother's funeral in detail, aware of how precious our friendship had been and, whilst she spoke, her husband feigned interest in the lovely flowers that surrounded us. However, I became aware that he often stared directly at me and showed no surprise at his wife's engagement in a conversation nor concern at our obvious close relationship.

He turned to join us as Eleanor explained, "Ned my dearest, will you come and meet dear Nell."

She turned back to me, "I have told Ned all about you dear Nell, and he is very keen to make your acquaintance. He encountered similar lost souls when he was a young boy and has high hopes of being able to see you."

Ned bowed low, "Mistress Jenkins, I am honoured to finally meet you."

I stood and bobbed a courtesy. "Welcome to my home, sir," I said a little coyly, for he was obviously a gentleman. "You are the first gentleman who has acknowledged my existence here and for that I give thanks. My name is Nell if it please you."

Ned turned to his wife, "Eleanor my dear, will you allow me a short private chat with Mistress Nell. I have a favour to ask of her."

Eleanor, though intrigued, nodded and duly wandered off to visit the top level of the garden, leaving me with Ned amongst the colours and heady scent of the rose garden.

Ned turned toward me and whispered softly, "During my life I have often been aware of the presence of unfortunate souls such as yourself and was intrigued to learn of your presence in this place and that dear Eleanor was able to communicate with you directly. I was most keen to make your acquaintance as I have an urgent need of your assistance. There is nobody else with whom I can entrust my secret and I wondered if you would hear my confession?"

I was excited and curious and nodded at the troubled young man.

"Eleanor is aware that I am the adopted son of Sir Hugh de L'Isle. My brother Dickon and I were taken in by him when we were young boys and he has since been our protector and mentor. We received a sound education and were formally adopted by him some years ago. However, our true identities remained a secret, known to only Sir Hugh, his wife Lady Alice and his most trusted steward, Gerald Gasson.

On my marriage to my dear Eleanor, I was named as Sir Hugh's heir, and my brother, younger than me by two years, and more adversely affected by the experiences of our early years, turned his back on the cruelties of this world and committed his life to God. He resides in a monastery in France where I hope he has found peace.

Once established as his heir, Sir Hugh made me promise that I would commit my true origins in writing so that history might one day be set straight."

Ned reached inside his jerkin and produced a roll of parchment and a ring which he held out towards me.

"This I have now done. As will become obvious to you shortly, for the foreseeable future there can be no benefit in making the contents of my declaration public. Even Eleanor must remain ignorant of its content and existence. Indeed, should it fall into the wrong hands, my whole family would be in danger. I would leave it with you for safekeeping if you would accept the responsibility.

I ask that you to keep these well-hidden if you value the safety and security of dear Eleanor and our daughters. If the items were to be found at this time, I fear that all our lives and of those who care for us, would be forfeit."

I gasped.

"I would not ask you to safeguard my declaration in ignorance of its contents, dear Mistress Nell. If you consent, I will make my confession to you, as affirmed in this document. You will then understand why it is so necessary that its contents remain secret."   He coughed and I nodded my assent.

"As I have mentioned, my brother and I were taken into the household of Sir Hugh de L'Isle of Shrubsford Manor in mid Kent when we were but boys. Introduced as the sons of Sir Hugh's late cousin who had resided in Normandy, there were none who questioned our formal adoption a few years' later." He paused.

"But we are not blood kin of the kind-hearted Sir Hugh." He became overcome by emotion.
"Oh Mistress Nell, you will never know how much I have wished to broadcast that which I am about to reveal. It is only the love and respect I hold for Sir Hugh and his good wife Lady Alice, and for fear of the potential repercussions on them and my own sweet family that I have kept silent."

"I lived a long and full life, Sir," I said hoping to comfort him, "and during my time in this place I have heard a great many things. I too bear my own secret and am in no position to pass judgement on anything you wish to confide in me."

I gestured for him to continue and, after he had cleared his throat and taken a deep breath, he began his story. Exactly what I was expecting to hear I could not have said but I almost fell to the ground with surprise as he began.

"You may well have been aware of the decades of battles, primarily in the north of our blessed country, between the Houses of York and Lancaster both of which had roots within the Plantagenet line and who thus claimed the right to rule England and Wales."

"I have only limited knowledge of such things, sir." I admitted.

"Well, it was a time of great turbulence and bloodshed and the throne passed backwards and forwards between the two Houses for many years. Ultimately, it was hoped, peace was achieved when Edward IV of the House of York, wrested the throne from the Lancastrian Henry VI. Despite ongoing skirmishes and intrigues led by the supporters of Henry, Edward was a charismatic and strong young king and many hoped that his reign would herald a level of peace and stability not seen for decades. Sadly however, he died prematurely after a sudden illness and his eldest son, Edward, being only twelve year's old, was named king, with Edward IV's brother Richard, Duke of Gloucester named as Lord Protector.

The death of Edward IV led to a resurgence of hope for those of the Lancastrian persuasion who, together with some on the Yorkist side who feared further bloodshed until such time as the boy king attained his majority and who insisted that the crown should pass to the late king's brother Richard, challenged the legitimacy of Edward's marriage to a young widow, Elizabeth Woodville, and thereby the legitimacy of their children. Elizabeth was not without her own supporters who, fearing a loss of their status at Court, vociferously challenged the Duke of Gloucester's right to act as Protector for the young king. Thus, for their safety, the child king, Edward V, and his brother, also called Richard, were taken to reside with their uncle in the Tower of London. There they lived in sumptuous chambers, as befitted their status, and their uncle oversaw their education in the world of politicking and diplomacy thus ensuring that Edward would have the skills to securely hold his throne when he reached his majority.

The Tower of London was a bustling, thriving community in which it was believed the boys could live and learn safely and securely. Sadly, however, despite its stout walls, several attempts to abduct or kill the young princes were made and their uncle feared for the long-term safety of his young nephews. Under pressure from his Yorkist supporters, he was ultimately persuaded to denounce Edward IV's marriage to Elizabeth Woodville as illegal, due to Edward's prior betrothal to another. This rendered Edward V and his siblings as illegitimate and as such they were not entitled to sit on the throne. Very soon after the boys' illegitimacy was declared, Richard was encouraged to take the crown and a hasty coronation took place. The protector thus became King Richard III."

Ned paused to gather his thoughts and I commented,

"Frightening times for those poor little boys, sir." I suggested.

"Indeed, indeed," he agreed and then continued with his tale.

"Sadly, the boys' public loss of legitimacy did not result in a new period of safety and there were yet further attempts to either remove them from the Tower or to kill them once and for all. After moving them several times from their splendid chambers to less salubrious apartments that were easier to guard, Richard realised that the only way to truly keep his precious nephews safe, was for them to disappear once and for all.

Calling his nephews to him one evening, Richard explained his plan to take them from the Tower to a place where they could live secretly in comfort and safety. He bade them remain patient and to live quietly and unobtrusively until such time as he was safely able to send for them. He further advised that though he had his own son, their cousin, also called Edward, he was a sickly child and unlikely to see his majority. He therefore planned that when his nephew, the erstwhile Edward V, reached his majority, he would legally adopt him, marry him to one of the Lancastrian princesses, thereby uniting the two warring factions, and name him as his heir in the hope that the senseless warring between the two royal houses would finally come to an end.

The princes were terrified at the thought of leaving the Tower where, despite the attempts on their lives, they had felt safe and loved under their uncle's protection. However, Edward recognised the sense in his uncle's plan and where he led, his younger brother was happy to follow.

Thus it was that, over a period of several months the two boys became less and less visible within the confines of their apartments, taking exercise outside mostly after dark when there were fewer spectators. Two young boys, of similar height and age to the royal princes, were taken secretly into the closely guarded apartments and thereafter 'became' the so-called Princes in the Tower.

Then, when all plans for their security were in place, the two princes were removed from the Tower of London. They were tall for their age but still with the faces of children and, much to their chagrin, were disguised as two of the Queen's maids who were to escort their Mistress to her estates in the north where her son lay ill. After travelling north for a few days, the 'young maids' changed carriages and, whilst the Queen continued north, were taken to the Shrubsford estate of Sir Hugh de L'Isle, a minor noble in Kent, and from there by fishing boat, to northern France where, finally able to abandon their feminine disguises, they joined the household of their aunt, Margaret of Burgundy, where they were introduced as the illegitimate sons of a distant cousin of the Duchess.

The Burgundy household, like most of the ruling houses in France at that time, was full of intrigue and the boys' identities soon began a subject of much conjecture, particularly when rumours of the English princes' disappearance from the Tower of London started to emanate. Richard, fearful that his nephews might yet be at risk of kidnap or used by the French as pawns to undermine the English crown, arranged for them to be brought back to Shrubsford where they 'became' the orphaned sons of Sir Hugh's late cousin newly arrived from Normandy."

Realising what Ned was about to reveal, I gasped. "Then you are….?"

"Yes Mistress Nell, I was born Edward of York, son of King Edward IV, and was, on the death of my father, briefly heralded as King Edward V. My brother Richard, known as Dickon, and I were placed under the protection of Sir Hugh and his wife Lady Alice, who had once been a much-loved nursemaid to our uncle Richard's lady wife, Queen Anne. They lived quietly, away from the eyes and ears of the Court, and, under their care at Shrubsford, our new identities were readily accepted and we enjoyed a family life of safety and security such as we had never before experienced, so insecure and disjointed had been our childhood years. Sir Hugh and Lady Alice could not have loved us more had we indeed been their own kin.

It was after the sudden victory of the Lancastrians and the death of our Uncle Richard at Bosworth Field that Sir Hugh and Lady Alice formally adopted their two orphaned 'nephews.'

The new king, Henry VII, having further cemented his claim to the throne by marrying our sister Elizabeth, wasted no time in sending out agents to look for evidence of our continued existence so that, if such were found, we could be disposed of and thus present no further threat to the new ruling house of Tudor.

Over the years, there were a number of bogus claimants to my name, each suppressed with a firmness that left no doubt as to King Henry's determination to consolidate his own position and that of his heirs. Indeed, knowing of our successful escape from the Tower, although thankfully not of our current location or aliases, our aunt, Lady Margaret, supported and assisted a couple of the ill-advised pretenders, who were arrested and, unsurprisingly, put to death as traitors on the orders of the King. When no evidence of our ongoing existence was found, the King's supporters invented the story that we had been killed at the hand of our wicked Uncle Richard and this calumny has gained widespread acceptance throughout the land and beyond.

We continued to live safely and quietly in Kent where Sir Hugh considered my marrying into a minor aristocratic household, as had been my uncle's plan, to enable me to perhaps attend court and enjoy something akin to the life I had been born to. Lady Alice however, had warned against this option, fearful that my close resemblance to my father would likely raise suspicion amongst some at court who might delve more closely into my lineage and thus endanger them all.

I admit that there were occasions when I may once have courted the notion of making my existence known and challenging Henry Tudor's rights to the throne. However, I accepted the wisdom of Lady Alice's advice and, in time, came to accept and enjoy the security that my role as heir to Shrubsford and other lands in Normandy afforded me. I pray that my brother has found a similar peace in his monastery.

Though we both turned our backs on our birthright, do not think badly of us for this. My own choice was not simply a matter of self-preservation but was also due to a desire to prevent any further bloodshed across our blessed land. I also admit that following my marriage to sweet Eleanor, for whom I have developed such a deep and wondrous love, and having become a father to our three beautiful daughters, I feel that my decision to remain hidden was the right one. I could not bear the thought that any action of mine could put their lives in danger, not to mention the lives of my adopted parents and their steward who had so diligently maintained my secret over the years. Having spent the first twelve years of my life being buffeted from all too brief periods of peace to periods of extreme turmoil, confinement and fear for my life, I would not wish any such experiences for my current family. Had the dear Lord blessed us with a son I might have felt differently but I am content with my life and would wish nothing to threaten it.

Sir Hugh and Lady Alice, like many of their associates who knew and respected my uncle Richard, were distressed that his reputation had been so besmirched under the Tudors. Uncle Richard had, both before our father's death and afterwards, acted towards my brother and I with kindness and concern for our security and welfare, with the full intent that I would ultimately take up the crown. That history now portrays him as our murderer weighs heavy on my mind.

As I promised Sir Hugh, I have authored a true report of our treatment at the hands of our uncle and it is this that I now entrust to your care, together with my father, King Edward IV's ring to further endorse my claim. One day, many years in the future, when none survive who currently harbour ill will towards me and mine, and the monarchy of this great land is secure and unchallenged, I would ask that you enable the document to be placed in the hands of those who will allow the facts to be made public and thereby clear our dear uncle Richard's name as our murderer."

I was dumbfounded and stared intently at Ned who smiled and nodded.

" 'Tis true Mistress, and none but Sir Hugh, Lady Alice, Steward Gasson and now your good self, know my secret. Not even my dearest Eleanor knows, nor must she.   Will you keep my secret and hide this document?" I took the scroll and tucked it inside my shawl.

"I will Sire."

"Then I will die content in the knowledge that the record will one day be set straight. You have my deepest respect and thanks dear lady."

Ned rose and crossed the garden to join his wife. "Come my dearest, we have spent too long away from our girls. Let us return home to Shrubsford."

They bade me farewell and left me ruminating in the garden. What a responsibility had been placed on me. That one of my special girls, my own namesake Eleanor, could be Queen of England! Even though the situation could not be broadcast, it was a wondrous thought all the same.

I returned to the house and secreted the precious items behind the old beam in the attic alongside dear Meggie's herbal compendium.

I had waited long and not always patiently, to communicate and interact with the residents of this place and now gave a heartfelt prayer of thanks to God. Firstly, for his generosity in enabling Meggie and Eleanor to enter my life and fill me with their love, and secondly, for allowing me to be entrusted with such an historic secret.

"Let me prove worthy of that trust, Lord," I had prayed.

Though I realised that this new responsibility would likely involve a prolonged existence in purgatory, I looked forward to the challenges ahead and the opportunities to care for and assist any other such residents that might have need of me.

The sixteenth century

Jane

With Meggie gone and Eleanor living so far away, the time passed slowly for me.   Meggie's brother William also passed away and, with his twin brother already deceased and his widow desirous of living with their eldest son who was continuing the family timber company but who resided in a fine house in Winchelsea, Oak House passed to William's youngest son Andrew. As a serving officer on the flagship of the Cinque Ports' Fleet, as yet unwed and spending many months away at sea, Andrew had little need of a large family house. He therefore decided to turn the premises into a lodging house for the many merchants and his fellow naval officers who frequented the port. The expansion of trade around the continent due to the relative peace amongst the previously warring nations meant that there was a constant stream of ships coming in and out of the port at the bottom of Middle Street and as such, despite the proximity of an inn across the street, there was still a need for comfortable accommodation. Andrew had arranged for a small team of staff to be engaged to manage the boarding house, now renamed The Merchants' Arms, and it proved a great success.

I had been initially saddened at the thought of sharing my home with a selection of transient strangers but, having come to realise that close interaction with the residents of my house had made time pass much more quickly and pleasurably, I had no wish to return to a life of solitude. I therefore spent much time simply sitting in the front parlour, now a comfortable sitting room for the residents, listening to their tales of the world beyond my little town. Once or twice I was aware of an odd glance in my direction, but none made any attempt to converse with me.

To my shame I had been thrilled to learn of the death of King Henry VII, in my mind always thought of as 'the Usurper', and the accession of the new king, his son, another Henry. My thoughts at once dwelt on the declaration hidden in my attic and I fully expected Ned to appear at my door in order to act upon it before the new young king had time to cement his hold on the throne. No such visit transpired however and I had given thanks for the ongoing safety of dear Eleanor and her girls.

Life in the boarding house continued relatively uneventfully and the guests' stories of the young king's exuberance and lust for life enthralled and entertained me.

Decades passed until one evening Andrew Pope arrived home unexpectedly; his ship having required urgent repairs after a skirmish in the channel. He brought with him an aristocratic-looking gentleman, Sir Francis Mansford, and a shy, awkward young girl, his ward, Mistress Jane St John, who was heavily pregnant. They had sought safe passage across the channel to Calais where the young Jane was to join her husband. She did not look at all well, although whether that was due to her condition or the skirmish at sea, I could not determine. My midwifery instinct instantly came to the fore and I decided to keep an eye on her and, once she had been made comfortable upstairs and had been supplied with refreshments, I entered her room. To my intense pleasure, she turned and look straight at me.

"Good evening Mistress. I hope you have not been overly troubled by your experiences this day?" I asked pleasantly.

She had looked rather askance at me and tried to affect a haughty "Who pray are you?" but managed only a rather timid whisper.

I introduced myself and explained my presence in the house and that I meant only to assist her should the need arise. To my surprise, rather than be afraid of me, the poor young thing had seemed quite overcome at my gentle voice and kind words and dissolved into tears.

"Oh Mistress Nell, I am undone. You must help me," she had pleaded.

In between her sobs she revealed her story.

It transpired that at the age of eight years, her father, a minor noble, her mother and her brother had died during an episode of the plague that so regularly hit our shores, and she had been placed under the care of her mother's cousin, Sir Francis Mansford. He spent much of his time at the king's court and Jane had lived happily enough in his large house in Oxfordshire under the tender care of his steward and housekeeper, Master Harding and his wife Mary. Jane had been schooled in the ways of a lady and, when she was but fifteen years of age, Sir Francis had decided that he would introduce her at court so that he might better his status via her marriage.

Always shy and timid, Jane had been taken into the household of the Queen as a junior lady-in-waiting to the Princess Mary. Jane and the princess were of similar age and demeanour and soon became close friends, although Mary had inherited her father's short temper and this was often most keenly felt by her friend Jane. On one such occasion, Jane had been sitting crying in a corner of the palace garden when who should have come across her but the King and members of his close council. Sensing her distress, the sensitive King had dismissed his entourage and sat with Jane, trying to cheer her. Not wanting to complain of his daughter's harshness towards her, Jane had advised the king that his kindness, and that of Queen Catherine and the princess, along with the other members of the household, made her only too aware of the loss of her own family and that this occasionally overwhelmed her. He had thanked her most warmly for her words of appreciation and affection for his family, insisting that she should think of them as her own, and thereafter he had often sought her out for a private chat or publicly praise her for her ladylike manners and fine singing voice.

As she had matured, the King's attentions had become somewhat more amorous than befitted his role as father-figure. Although she was aware of his reputation for affairs with ladies of the court and beyond, she had at first dismissed his actions towards her as her own fanciful notions but gradually, as he contrived evermore occasions to be alone with her, she had admitted, to her shame, that she enjoyed his attentions and token gifts and indeed, came to enjoy his caresses and desired him in a way that belied her maiden status. Had she been sensible, she acknowledged, she should have sought the protection of the Queen but she did not and, when at last the King had tired of her and turned his attentions elsewhere, she was already with child. Confessing her condition to the Queen, albeit without mention of the babe's father, Jane had been dismissed from court and sent back to her uncle's estates in Oxfordshire in disgrace.

Sir Francis had been aghast at her behaviour and insisted that she name her seducer so that the dastardly fellow could be brought to book and marry her forthwith. Jane had initially refused to name the babe's father, knowing that marriage was out of the question, but her resolve ultimately failed her and she had named the King.

Under other circumstances, Sir Francis might have simply sent Jane off to a nunnery to await the birth of her child and, once the said offspring had been given over to some worthy couple to raise, she would have been forced to live out the rest of her life in seclusion. However, he was never one to overlook an opportunity to profit from someone else's misfortune and had recognised that should the child be a boy, the raising of the king's illegitimate son might further enhance his own credentials at court. He had therefore decided, without any consultation with his young ward, that he would marry her off as soon as the babe was born and, if it were indeed a boy, would raise the child himself. Jane would be married off to anyone who would take her, although to none of the high-born English families who might find out about her child and wish to use him for their own benefit. Thus he was taking her to France to await the birth of her child, following which her marriage had been arranged to an elderly widower, a wealthy merchant who resided in Calais.

"You must help me Mistress Nell," she had wailed, "I cannot countenance the idea of my child being taken from me, nor of marrying this elderly merchant but my guardian is a most determined man and has virtually kept me under lock and key lest I harm myself or the babe or, at worst, escape from his control. What can I do?"

I tried to calm the poor girl who was close to becoming quite hysterical.

"You must try to stay calm for the sake of your babe." I instructed firmly. "You must let me think on your situation."

After much questioning it became clear that the young innocent had little or no real understanding of what pregnancy actually entailed. She could not be certain as to how many moons had passed since she had last bled and, following my limited examination, seemed incredulous and terrified when I described how the babe would emerge. Nevertheless, scared or not, she remained defiant that she would not relinquish her child.

Leaving her to rest I resumed my usual place in the attics and prayed for guidance. All at once, Ned's parchment and ring fell to the floor, though I knew they had been securely hidden away. I snatched them up quickly and restored them to the niche behind the beam and then an idea came to me.

Thanking the house for directing my thoughts to the one person on whom I could rely to assist young Jane, I returned to her chamber and gently woke her.

"Can you write my dear?" I had asked eagerly. At her nod, I fetched parchment and ink from the guests' parlour and bade her write to my dictation. The letter was addressed to my dear friend Eleanor, advising that a young maid had come to the house and was in urgent need of assistance on a highly secret and serious matter.   I asked that she, and Ned if he so wished, come to the house with all haste.

When the maid later came to bring the young guest some hot water for her ablutions, Jane passed her the letter, together with some coins, and bade her arrange for it to be despatched straight away, without the knowledge of her guardian. The maid, who was much of an age with Jane and seemed empathetic toward her, had promised to find someone trustworthy to deliver the letter, which she tucked securely into the pocket of her apron.

"Eleanor will help you my dear Mistress Jane," I had said with as much conviction as I could muster.   "In the meantime, we must contrive to prevent you continuing your journey."

The next morning we learned that the repairs to Andrew's vessel would take but a few days and under my guidance, Jane insisted that she was experiencing occasional pains that indicated that her time was near and that she could therefore not countenance travelling any further.   Sir Francis, not wanting any harm to come to the babe, called on the services of a local midwife who, without any examination of her patient and who, in my professional opinion, seemed lacking in any real midwifery skills, had obviously appreciated the opportunity to earn a pretty penny and advised that the young lady should not be moved as the babe would likely be born very soon.

Jane's presence in the house having been secured, at least for a while, she and I could only wait.

As I had hoped, three days later, Eleanor and Ned, now looking much older but still as handsome, arrived at the house in a state of some agitation. At her cousin Andrew's surprise at their arrival, Eleanor had implied that she had had a dream in which he had appeared to her and seemed desperately unwell. So real had been the dream that she had insisted to her husband that they travel to Rye in all haste so that she could help in her cousin's care.   Andrew,   who had been accustomed to Eleanor's odd ways when they were children, seemed to accept her 'premonition' but reassured his cousin that he was entirely well. Eleanor had declared herself happy and relieved at his obvious good health and announced that they would nevertheless remain in the house for a few days so as to recover from their frantic journey from Shrubsford and to pay a visit to her other cousins who still lived locally.   Andrew had apologised to his cousin and explained that the best chambers were currently occupied, by a member of the king's court and his ward who had been enroute to France when the young lady in question had become unwell, due to the latter stages of her pregnancy. Eleanor instantly reminded him that her mother had long been the town midwife and that she herself had learned some of her mother's skill. Without further ado she made her way to the garden chamber to offer her services to the young lady, leaving Ned downstairs with the men to reassure Sir Francis, who had been trying most vehemently to keep his ward's presence and identity a secret, that his wife had experience of midwifery, not least having had three beautiful daughters herself, and that his ward would be in safe hands. Indeed, he had stressed that the young lady would perhaps fare better under the care of another lady rather than the less salubrious offices of the local midwife and Sir Francis had had little option but to accept Eleanor's help. I had smiled warmly at Ned as he had skilfully outmanoeuvred the poor man.

I quickly made my way upstairs and found Eleanor and Jane deep in conversation in the garden chamber. Once Jane had completed her sorry tale, excluding the precise paternity of her babe but inferring that it was someone high-born at the court, Eleanor was quick to reassure the girl that she would do all she could to assist her.

"It is of no import to me as to the identity of the father," she had stressed. "Why it could be the King of England himself and I would still counter no forced removal of any babe from its mother." At Jane's face, Eleanor had smiled.

"You are not the first my dear young lady, and, if things at court continue as we are led to believe, you will not be the last. In fact we recently heard tell that the king is currently seeking an annulment of his marriage to Queen Catherine, as he has another young maid in his sights, Anne Boleyn, the younger sister of one of his former inamorata, who has not as yet given herself to him but is teasing him and holding out for marriage. I would suggest that it is good that you are away from that environment. You are young yet and still have the potential for a good life if we are able to keep you out of the hands of your guardian. I will tell your tale to my husband and together we will ascertain how best to help you. Rest now and think only of your babe, who despite your previous midwife's assertions, will not make an appearance for several weeks."

Leaving Jane, now looking more relaxed about her situation, Eleanor and I ascended to my attic room to discuss things. Eleanor had expressed her concern at the machinations of men and the harm that they often inflicted on those women they professed to protect. She gave thanks to God for her own sweet Ned and prayed that their daughters, now apparently in happy and loving marriages, would ensure that their offspring, both boys and girls, would show appropriate respect towards their own spouses.

The following day, as with several that followed, Ned persuaded Sir Francis and Andrew to accompany him out and about the town and its environs, in the guise of needing to escape the unfathomable 'women's world' that was threatening to take over the Merchants' Arms. It was after they had returned from a sumptuous meal at Andrew's brother's house in Winchelsea that Eleanor, in an apparent state of high anxiety greeted them with the news that Jane had become unwell and was running a high fever. She had probed both her cousin Andrew and Sir Francis about the possibility of Jane having come into contact with some contagious disease, either before or during her journey on land or ship, and although the word plague was not voiced, fear was etched on their faces and Sir Francis, as had been predicted by Eleanor, declined her suggestion that he visit his ward. Thus the young girl was left in peace.

Over the next couple of days, reports of Jane's unchanged condition were encountered with barely veiled apathy on the part of her guardian and, when news reached the house that the king had fallen from his horse and was gravely ill, Sir Francis, with barely a thought to his ward's ongoing care, had arranged to leave for London so as to be in the thick of things should the worst come to pass. Eleanor, seizing on the opportunity to rescue Jane from her uncle's control, had assured him that his niece and her babe would likely not remain long at the Merchants' Arms but that she would continue to care for the poor girl for as long as was required. He had, as planned, assumed that Eleanor had meant that Jane was at death's door and she was appalled to see a look of relief on his face which served to further endorse the rightness of their actions. He had thanked her for her kindness and proffered a small purse with which he asked that she and Ned make all necessary arrangements when the time came, thereby completely washing his hands of any further responsibility for the poor girl. He then took his leave without so much as a glance back towards the house.

The following morning Andrew Pope, whose ship had been fully repaired, was called back to duty and it was with visible relief that he took his leave of his cousin and her husband.

All those who remained at the Merchants' Arms were delighted when Jane made a 'wondrous recovery' and Eleanor was pleased to reassure the staff that her condition had been due to her pregnancy rather than anything more sinister. A few days later Eleanor, Ned and Jane left for Shrubsford and, if any assumed that they were returning Jane to her guardian's care, Eleanor and Ned made no attempt to suggest otherwise. When we made our goodbyes, they promised me that safe in the knowledge that her guardian was unlikely to check on her demise, Jane and her babe could reside in their household for as long as she wished to remain there. They also solemnly pledged that they would never reveal the secret of the babe's paternity.

Before she left, Jane had handed me a fine amethyst bracelet that had been a gift to her from King Henry.

"I have no wish to keep this Nell," she said sadly. "It will only serve to remind me of my weakness and folly. My uncle's parting purse will be adequate for my needs for a goodly while and I would rather my child live simply than avail myself of the bracelet's worth. I therefore leave it in your safekeeping until such time as another may have need of it." With the bracelet she had included a note in which she told of its previous owner, though not to whom it had been given or why.

So it was that I had another treasure to add to my cache. Who would have thought that purgatory could have proven so fascinating. Although always mindful of my ultimate goal of atoning for my sin, I was also eager to encounter my next 'friend' and wondered if they too would have some interesting secret or treasure with which I might be entrusted. The anticipation of such interaction helped me endure the long years of solitude as I waited for a random glance or word that would once again lighten my existence.

Jennie

Andrew Pope retired from a life at sea and married Hannah, a local widow who had a grown-up daughter, Mary. Andrew and Hannah, desirous of a quiet life together, chose to live in a modest little house on Watchbell Street from where Andrew could watch the comings and goings of ships up the river and out at sea. The running of the Merchants' Arms was therefore given over to Mary who took her stepfather's name and moved into the house to better manage the day-to-day administration of the boarding house.

Neither Mary nor her staff in the Merchant's Arms acknowledged my existence and I had to content myself with once again being simply a spectator within the house. Sometimes reference was made to the 'resident ghost,' but I felt that these comments were usually said in jest rather than because anyone could actually see or hear me.

Rye's prosperity as a trading centre waxed and waned for several decades and by the end of the fifteenth century Mary was finding it hard to compete with the newly refurbished and enlarged inn across the street. The Mermaid Inn's success was due in part to the landlord's close involvement with local smugglers which enabled him to offer his customers a wide range of spirits and other goods at prices with which Mary was unable to compete. Also, the Merchants' Arms, with its emphasis on fine and comfortable chambers, could, at best, only accommodate about six residents at a time and, despite employing an excellent cook and offering a superior menu, the business simply did not bring in enough income to ensure its survival. It became clear that Mary would have to change course if they were to remain in business.

Over the years, Mrs Waite the cook, and her son Peter, who had assisted her, had developed a wide repertoire of excellent dishes that kept a few of their guests returning on a regular basis and it was to them that Mary turned for help. During a period of increased prosperity, a series of shops had been built along the Strand at the bottom of Middle Street and Mary had suggested to Peter and his mother that they form a partnership and take a short lease on one of the new shops where they could sell their fare to a wider clientele. The wholesome and tasty dishes took the local populace and visiting seafarers by storm and business became so good that they were quickly encouraged to expand to a larger premises on the Strand and to take stalls at the weekly markets held near the local courthouse. Indeed, so successful was the venture that Mary decided to close the failing boarding house and concentrate all their energies on their new business. To mark the end of the Merchant's Arms as a boarding house, she changed the name of the premises back to Oak House.

When Andrew and Hannah died within months of each other, Mary sold the house in Watchbell Street and set about modernising and improving the facilities at Oak House. The kitchens in particular were extended, enabling Peter and his mother to offer an even wider range of dishes in their shops. Mary proved to be an astute businesswoman and became respected as such with her fellow traders who were soon lining up to do business with her. Several offers of marriage ensued but Mary remained unwed and enjoyed the independence that the lack of a husband afforded her.

She was rightly proud of her flourishing businesses, adamant that she had no need for a husband's assistance or interference.

All this while I remained an invisible and silent presence in the house, praying daily that I would soon be permitted to enjoy a close interaction with one of my residents. Loneliness often overwhelmed me and I would seek out my treasures in the attic in order to remind myself of those I had loved. You will imagine my excitement when I learned that, as a result of the expanding business and the demise of Peter's mother, Mary had taken on two young people: one to aid Peter in the kitchen and the other to undertake the deliveries of food around the town. Annie Jenkins, the youngest daughter of a local fisherman, and Ted, her younger brother, were taken on as apprentice cook and delivery boy. My own dear boy had had two young sons and, despite the episodes of disease that had oft swept through the town, I wondered, might these young Jenkins siblings be my own kin and, if so, might they be able to communicate with me?

Contriving to be present in the kitchen whenever Annie was assisting Peter or Ted was being loaded up with provisions for the shop or market stall, I was disappointed when neither seemed to be aware of my presence. However, one afternoon their older sister, Jennie, visited the house to offer Peter some particularly large crabs that her brothers had caught down near the harbour mouth. As Jennie entered the kitchen she had looked directly at me and paled, obviously taken aback at my presence. Once the deal was completed I had followed the girl out of the kitchen and into the hallway.

Jennie had looked at me with fear in her eyes.

"Who are you?" she had asked stretching out a hand which passed straight through my arm. "Are you a ghost?"

"I mean you no harm," I had assured her.

Jennie had given a half-hearted smile of relief that I was not merely a figment of her imagination. "You gave me quite a start," she said, "you look just like my old Grannie."

I quickly explained my situation to Jennie, without actually mentioning what my 'great sin' had been, and that my name had been Jenkins, so it was possible that we were distantly related. I became even more convinced of that when Jennie mentioned that her old Grannie, named Agnes, had been a 'wise woman' and a midwife, and that Jennie had taken over this role when her Grannie had become too frail. Though she seemed keen to find out more about my previous life in Rye and why I was resident in Oak House, Jennie had had to return to her chores elsewhere. I was also keen to find out more about Jennie and her forebears but explained that I was unable to leave the house. I therefore begged her to return so that we could discuss our possible familial connection. I suggested that the gardens, that had remained largely unchanged since dear Meggie's time, could offer Jennie a good supply of herbs and other medicinal plants that she could use in her work. I also offered to teach her some of my old receipts and persuaded her to ask Mary if she could collect the necessary herbs from the gardens at Oak House. Thus, she would have a reason to visit the house regularly, giving us the opportunity for further discussion.

Mary had been delighted to allow Jennie access to the gardens for her work and even suggested that if the medicaments proved efficacious, she would consider selling them in her shops and market stall.

Jennie proved to be an avid student, and it did not take long for her simple treatments to be in demand. Some of her basic treatments such as a lavender and petitgrain balm for chapped hands, a thyme and willow bark infusion to help ease muscle aches and pains and a peppermint and honey tea to allay coughs and sneezes, were offered for sale in Mary's shops and market stall and proved to be remarkably successful.

Despite lengthy discussions about her family, Jennie had little knowledge of her antecedents beyond her grandmother Agnes, apart from the fact that her great grandmother had been named Eleanor. These names, together with the history of midwifery and healing skills being passed down the generations, was enough for me to believe that Jennie, Annie and Ted were indeed my descendants and that my family line continued. However, whilst I was happy to sit with Jennie and pass on my knowledge, I was still all too aware that I was no nearer achieving my goal of atonement.

With my encouragement, Jennie was happy to discuss her patients with me, describing in detail any pregnancy that she felt was not proceeding well and we discussed possible actions and treatments that might help the mother to be. I was delighted that my skills were being put to good use and prayed that perhaps by proxy, I might have a positive effect on the outcome of a delivery and thus achieve redemption. If not however, I admit that I was pleased to feel useful once more.

Time passed slowly despite my ongoing friendship with young Jennie who, along wither sister Annie, had, on the death of Peter Waite, been offered a partnership in the business by Mary. Mary herself, mindful of her own aches and pains and approaching mortality had also suggested that Annie and Jennie move into Oak House which, she advised, she intended to bequeath to them when the time came.

Annie and Jennie were both surprised and delighted to be asked to move into the lovely old house with Mary of whom they had become very fond. Jennie's husband, Jacob Capsey, a talented cabinet maker, and their three young sons, were also happy to move into Oak House. The two sisters worked well together and, with the younger women taking over much of the day-to-day responsibilities from Mary, the business continued to thrive.

When Mary ultimately died at the age of 58 the sisters were formally confirmed as the owners of Oak House, with the proviso that they continue the business of which Mary had been so proud. You can understand how delighted I was at this news, proud that these two fine young women, who I wholeheartedly believed to be my own kin, were the proprietors of my fine house and successful businesswomen to boot. Annie, with a small team of assistants, continued to offer good wholesome food to the townsfolk and port visitors and Jennie was still able to perform her duties as a midwife as well as producing the medications that were proving as popular as ever in their shops.

Jennie and I were able to spend many happy hours together and both expressed our disappointment that Jennie's young sons seemed as unaware of my existence as their father and aunt. Nevertheless, I found great comfort watching the little family as they went about their lives. I would sit quietly in the parlour in the evenings, listening to their chatter and occasional songs but most of all I enjoyed listening to Jacob as he told of his travels to London where his work was much sought after. After a commission to build a grand bureau for the king himself, Jacob had returned to Oak Hall and presented Jennie with a fine pearl necklace, presented to Jacob as a mark of the king's appreciation of his fine craftsmanship. Similar commissions by wealthy courtiers and merchants followed and Jennie soon acquired an assortment of very fine jewels and trinkets. Not having the self-confidence to adorn herself with these items of jewellery and wary of keeping such valuable items in the house, particularly given that Jacob was so often away, Jennie begged her husband to hide them away. Jacob, though keen for his family to enjoy the fruits of his work and to be seen to enjoy the status that their combined businesses talents accorded, recognised the sense in his wife's words and agreed that their treasures should be kept secret.

Rather than fashion a secret compartment within a piece of furniture, a talent for which he had become quite renowned, Jacob decided to construct a secret chamber within the house itself, which he felt would be even more secure. Oak House had been built across two former houses on the steep hill that was Middle Street and thus the western end of the front parlour extended over a substantial empty space as the ground below dropped away downhill.   Jacob contrived a secret access to this space via a panel in the rear dining room, the floor of which was at the level of the rear courtyard and several steps lower than the floors of the kitchen and parlour.

Not content with a simple sliding panel, Jacob designed an elaborate combination of moving knobs and devices hidden within intricate carvings, that would, only if moved in a certain sequence and with the insertion of a small innocuous looking wooden peg, allow access to the secret storeroom and the treasures deposited within. When it was completed I watched with interest as he showed Jennie how to open the storeroom and I duly memorised the sequence of moves. Not that locked rooms were a barrier to me, I could access the storeroom easily without recourse to any clever mechanism, but I felt that access to the hidden storeroom might be useful to future residents of my house and I thus contrived to hide one of the spare 'key pegs' in my secret attic store.

Jacob continued his trips to London and around the south of England and the treasure trove hidden in the secret storeroom grew and grew. Jennie, despite being able to wear finer garments and be accorded the respect due to her as a business woman, did not flaunt their newfound wealth   or forget her humble beginnings and would not turn her back on those less fortunate. With the consent and assistance of her sister Annie, they arranged that at the close of business each day a simple but wholesome meal could be offered from their shop - free of charge to those in need.

Years passed and the residents of Oak House prospered and were happy. Their ongoing wealth was a reflection of the stability and prosperity of the nation and I wondered if England was ready to learn of Ned's secret. He had likely passed away by now, as perhaps had Eleanor, and their girls securely married and settled. There could be few people alive who could remember the turmoil of the years of civil war and still wish the Yorkist prince and his family ill, nor indeed any who would wish to overthrow the popular Henry VIII.

I determined to bring Ned's declaration to Jennie's attention but, as is so often the way, fate determined otherwise. Jacob returned from one of his London trips and advised that the king, Henry VIII, was said to be dying and that there was much debate and politicking about the succession.

I listened with interest but little surprise when I learned that King Henry VIII, obsessed with the desire for a son, an obsession that I had witnessed before and which had so blighted my own life, had divorced or executed four of his six wives. One had died whilst giving birth to the much-desired son, and the sixth wife was likely to outlive her husband.

Even more shocking to me was the information that his divorce from his first wife, Queen Catherine who had so kindly befriended young Jane on her arrival at court, had caused a rift with the pope, and that the king had been excommunicated. Unperturbed by this, the king had merely appointed himself Head of the Church of England and many of the previous 'popish' practices had been abandoned in favour of simpler, English services. My faith was my bedrock, on which my entire life and subsequent existence in purgatory was based. I was afraid. If the English congregation were being turned away from His anointed representative in Rome? What would become of me if God then turned His back on this new English church?

I shared my fears with Jennie who, like many of the local population preferred the new, simpler, less ritualised services in St Mary's and did her best to reassure me that God was just the same benevolent being as always and that I had nothing to fear. He saw all and would welcome all who believed in Him to heaven when the time came. She was confident that He would never abandon me or any of his flock, regardless of how they worshiped Him.

Of more concern to Jacob and his family and many like him around the country, was that the long-awaited prince, the offspring of wife number three, had proved a sickly child. With his father's death imminent and the prince being young yet, many feared that life would likely become quite unstable as different factions at court vied for control of the boy.

Not knowing if Ned and Eleanor had a strong, healthy grandson who might be able to garner support and lay claim to the throne and not wishing to involve their descendants in any political turmoil or danger, I decided to stay my hand and continue to keep Ned's declaration hidden.

I shed no tears when the king passed away and was glad to recognise that Jacob and Jennie were luckier than most, as their individual skills remained in demand, albeit without Jacob's constant commissions at court where other matters predominated. Their hidden storeroom under the parlour was near full of treasure and would see them through any economic turmoil. However, instability at home meant changing relationships abroad and the subsequent drop in trade saw the port of Rye, like many of the southern ports, once again suffering as a result.   Jennie's free soup kitchen experienced a surge in demand and I was enormously proud of my family who continued to offer help to their less fortunate neighbours.   Jacob, with more time on his hands, set up a new workshop in the town and offered training in basic carpentry to the poorest boys of the town.   Once their training was completed he presented each boy with a set of basic tools thereby giving them the means of supporting themselves and their families around the town and beyond.

Sadly the boy king, Edward VI died at the tender age of fifteen and his elder sister, Mary, the daughter of Henry's first wife and a staunch adherent of the church of Rome, acceded to the throne and the country was thrown into an era of unprecedented religious crisis and instability. Like so many in the nation, the people of Rye had welcomed the new Anglicised practices of the church, and they became anxious at the attempts to reinstate the Roman church across the country. Likewise, as international alliances changed with the religion of the monarch, so too did the opportunities for trade and prosperity fluctuate.

After about five years of intense turmoil and violent religious persecution, the younger daughter of Henry VII, Elizabeth, succeeded her sister and Jacob was proud to confide in his wife that the new queen seemed to be proving to be every inch her father's daughter. Though young and inexperienced, she showed great energy and wisdom and a shrewdness of which her father would have been justly proud. These talents she used to advantageous effect and, by retaining advisors from both sides of the religious divide into her court circle, she managed to address the dreadful excesses of her sister's reign . Gradually the extreme acts of Queen Mary's reign were repealed and, though several of those Catholics who vehemently opposed the new Queen's right to the throne, were tried and executed, Jacob and Jennie were pleased that England entered into an era of stability.

During the middle of the century, with the security of the nation as a protestant state widely accepted and recognised abroad, life returned to normal and Jacob was called back to London to undertake commissions for the great and the good. However, as trade improved and with more people moving betwixt city and town for work, London and the south of England was once again hit by plague. If the bells' tolling and the sight of carts trundling daily up and down Middle Street were anything to go by, this episode of plague hit Rye harder than any I had previously witnessed. Jennie, as committed to helping her neighbours as ever, went out day after day to offer what little assistance she could to her friends and neighbours but was able to do much to stem the spread of the disease. She returned home each day exhausted and frustrated, bemoaning her inability to offer a cure and afraid for the future of her family and her town. Sadly, I could offer no words of hope and I watched in despair as one by one, she and Jacob, their three children and then Annie succumbed to the disease. Like so many others after the plague, Oak House was boarded up and left unloved and I was once again alone.

With the population decimated and coastal erosion causing the accelerated silting up of the river the viability of the port of Rye diminished and Oak House remained empty for several years.

Though we had not discussed it prior to her untimely death, I felt confident that Jennie would have wanted the contents of the hidden storeroom to be used for the good of her remaining family or, failing that, the poor of our town. In her memory I pledged to enable any future resident of the house, at time of great personal need or the desire to offer succour to the poor, to avail themselves of the treasures hidden so cleverly under the parlour floor.

Once more alone, my faith and patience were put to the test. People's lives had certainly become more varied and interesting over the past century. Time that had for centuries been measured by the seasons, had become measured by the month, sometimes even by the week, but now dragged by slowly once more. So accustomed had I become to watching and occasionally contributing to the lives of my residents, not to mention the excitement experienced when one or more of them were able to see and communicate with me, the years of solitude stretched before me in my empty house and I was once more despondent.

The intermittent partial conversations overheard in the street or the irregular calling of the local town criers, did little to entertain or lift my spirits. I filled my days and nights with prayer but occasionally, when despair threatened to turn me from God, I stalked the house and gardens, wailing and moaning, little knowing or caring that some in the neighbouring houses or who passed in the street, might hear my inhuman cries. The house too, sensing my mood, groaned and creaked in harmony with my ill moods and thus Oak House attained quite a reputation as a place haunted by an unhappy and malevolent spirit.

A gift fit for a Queen

Ultimately those townsfolk who survived the plague began to rebuild their lives as the threat of the disease abated. It was recognised that fresh blood was required if the town were to fully recover and prosper and the town gates, closed and so fiercely guarded to protect the town from new plague-carriers, were opened. The flood of people seeking sanctuary in the town included many groups of refugees fleeing political and religious persecution in Europe. These groups, most notably Huguenots from France, not only swelled the diminished population but also brought new skills and ideas with them.

For many of the refugees Rye was just a temporary stop until they were able to return home. For others it was merely a short-term break in their journey until they were able to travel on to join relatives who had settled elsewhere. However, for some, Rye became their home, and they were welcomed and encouraged to settle and establish their businesses to help boost the town's economy. Slowly, the fishing and timber businesses ceased to be paramount to the prosperity of the town and, with the systematic reclamation of land to the east of Rye that offered good pasture, it was wool that brought newfound wealth to the area.

Soon sheep outnumbered people out on the marshes and the burgeoning wool trade proved beneficial to some of the newly arrived Huguenot migrants, many of whom were skilled weavers. One such was Henri Le Roux who took over the deserted Oak House in the 1550s. The upstairs, garden room, with its large windows and fine southern outlook over the garden, was ideal for Monsieur Le Roux to set up his loom and the substantial, albeit overrun garden, proved to be a valuable source of plants and flowers for the dyes he used in his work. He and his wife, Collette, their two sons and their household staff quickly settled into the house and began to restore it to its former glory as a fine family home. I was entranced by the new residents who filled my house and garden with new life, light and colour, although, not having any knowledge of French, I despaired of ever being able to communicate with them even if they were able to see me. Between themselves, the family spoke only

French, although I had heard Henri and Collette speaking in a heavily accented English when dealing with some of Henri's customers and their neighbours.

I very much enjoyed watching Henri at work at his loom. His brow would furrow over a particularly intricate design whilst his fingers flew deftly across the threads. I was fascinated by the process of weaving and would have loved to be able to wrap myself in the exquisitely soft shawls he produced. Once or twice he seemed to look up at me and smile, as if inviting me to compliment him on his work, but he remained silent and I too held my tongue, unsure if he would understand my uneducated English. I had no real knowledge of the beliefs of the Huguenots but was sure they would not understand or indeed approve of my status in purgatory. Their faith seemed to be based on much simpler lines; what would Henri think of me if he discovered my dreadful sin?

Apart from Henri there was one other member of the household who seemed aware of my presence. Young Jacques Gill, the son of the cook, who often stared at me open mouthed, sometimes winning for himself a smack on the hand with a ladle from his mother for his lack of attention.   One afternoon, whilst most in the house rested, Jacques entered the kitchen where I was sitting by the hearth half-heartedly turning the empty spit, and said boldly, "What is your name Mistress Ghost?"

I was quite taken aback at his perfect English, directness and lack of fear.

"My name is Nell, and I have resided here for many a year." I said simply, "Few people in that time have been able to see and converse with me and you are only the second young man who has openly admitted to doing so."

"Perhaps you are too scary," Jacques suggested cheekily and this idea had made us both laugh heartily. He advised that several of the young lads who lived in the area had warned him that his new home was notorious for housing a particularly malevolent ghost.

"You don't seem a bit scary to me," he reassured and we had laughed once more.

When his mother returned to the kitchen to commence preparations for the family's evening meal, she had frowned at her son's apparent groundless giggles, which were further exacerbated by her fierce looks and sighs.

Whenever he could, Jacques enjoyed talking to me and was keen to learn of my history and that of the previous occupants of this fine house. Over time I learned that his father, an English protestant who had fled England during the reign of Bloody Mary, had found work with the Le Roux family in Paris, where he had met and later married Jacques' mother, then an assistant cook. Jacques had very few memories of his father apart from his determination that his son should speak English in the hope that one day he and his family could return to England. However, as a protestant and an Englishman, he had fallen foul of a gang of thugs, one of many that roamed the streets of Paris causing disruption and fear amongst the law-abiding citizens and he had been abducted, tortured and left for dead a few miles from the Le Roux house. That he made it home at all was thanks to the kindness of the priest from a nearby church, but in spite of the best of medical care the Le Roux family provided, he had died of his injuries within a few days. Jacques was extremely grateful to Henri and Collette for keeping him and his mother safe and for allowing them to accompany the family to England.

Encouraged by Jacques' willingness to converse with me, I decided that when the next opportunity arose to communicate with Henri, I would put aside my fear of rejection or misunderstanding. There would be no need to be explicit with the details of the cause for my penance and if he were not happy about my presence in the house there was little he or I could do to ease his discomfort.

A few weeks later, as I watched him scratching out a new design in his pattern book, I coughed quietly and said slowly, "Good day to you Sir. That is a fine design."

Henri had looked up with a smile, "Ah, you speak to me at last. I was beginning to doubt your existence and my sanity."

"My apologies sir, but I was not sure that my coarse speech would be comprehensible to a foreign gentleman such as yourself."

Henri threw back his head and laughed loudly. "My dear lady, your words are perfectly clear to me, and frankly I would welcome the opportunity to learn more of your language if you would be so kind as to teach me." I drew closer to his desk and introduced myself with a curtsey.

"My name is Nell, and I am very pleased to make your acquaintance, although I am not sure that a poor ignorant woman such as myself could teach anything to an educated man like yourself, sir. "

Thereafter, as he worked, Henri was happy to relate his story to me and I in turn told him of some of the previous occupants of my house. He was a master weaver whose exceptionally fine designs had been much admired back in France and he and his family had moved from Bordeaux to Paris where he had built up a successful business. However, the King's tolerance of the Huguenots' beliefs was changeable according to the whims of his advisers and it had become obvious to Henri and his associates that this instability was dangerous for them all, hence their decision to leave France before they were ultimately expelled or worse.

Apart from his apparent skill at fine weaving, he was a man of great ambition and was determined to improve the weaving tradition in his newly adopted country. He had brought with him a small and very costly blend of merino wool, imported from Spain. So fine was this wool that it was said that a lady's shawl made from it could pass easily through a finger ring. Henri had many contacts around Europe, both licit and otherwise, and he hoped to ultimately obtain some merino sheep from Spain and establish a merino wool industry in England. Thus far, the sale of these sheep outside Spain was prohibited as the Spanish crown was determined to maintain its monopoly and the ongoing war between England and Spain made even the legal purchase of any merino wool difficult, although Henri was prepared to pay handsomely for it. He was nevertheless hopeful that one day his plan would come to fruition.

He also had a desire to obtain some live silkworms or moths from China, again a tightly controlled commodity, and establish a home-produced silk industry England. Current silk weaving, based mainly in the northern towns of Macclesfield and Congleton, relied on the pricey import of raw silk thread from China but Henri yearned to establish a colony of silkworms and moths in England to enable a more cost-efficient industry. There was no legal trade in these precious worms, but Henri had contacts amongst the Flemish merchants who regularly visited Rye and who dealt in goods from the far east, and he had high hopes that they would one day be able to obtain a supply for him. To this end he had designed and had built a special warehouse alongside the stables at the rear end of the top garden, backing on to the watch tower and bell that guarded the south-western approaches to the town. The warehouse had double walls, the cavity between which was stuffed with straw and wool to provide insulation, and, with a large central stove to ensure a constant warm temperature, he hoped the facility would provide the right conditions in which he could establish and nurture a colony of silk moths.   He also needed to acquire some mulberry trees as it was on the leaves of these trees alone that the silkworms fed. However, he had been disappointed to learn that the growing and planting of these trees was controlled by the Queen of England herself and none could furnish him with the said trees.

I was sad to learn of Henri's self-imposed exile from his homeland (unable to imagine what it would be like to have to make such a drastic decision, even for the safety of one's family) but was impressed at his strength of purpose and excited at his energy and ambition. When I summoned the inner strength to advise of my own history, without revealing the exact nature of my sin, he had nodded wisely and sympathetically.

"When you have encountered people from around the world, as I have my dear lady, and learned of the many different faiths and religious practices that abound, you soon realise that there is much about man's relationship with his God that is inexplicable. I will remember you in my prayers, Mistress Nell."

Henri was delighted to learn that young Jacques could also converse with me and both he and Jacques enjoyed discussing their good fortune, which they both held to be a special gift. I too was grateful for their companionship, and very much enjoyed instructing Henri in some of the more common expressions and words of the area and he reciprocated by teaching me a few simple words in French. Jacques, already fascinated by the history of his new hometown, also asked that I share my knowledge of healing with him. I proudly showed him Meggie's Herbal compendium and he was rightly impressed by its contents, handling each fragile page with care and respect. As time went by I recognised that he, as had Meggie been before him, was capable of learning far more than I could ever teach and I encouraged him to ask his mother if she would allow him to make enquiries of Monsieur Le Roux with regard a possible apprenticeship with one of the local apothecaries or barber surgeons who had businesses in the town. I had also mentioned Jacques' interest and capabilities to Henri who, as a great advocate of social equity and opportunity for all, was delighted to assist Jacques when his mother made her subsequent request.

So it was that Jacques left Oak House and took up residence in the house of Master Edward Jenkinson, a noted barber-surgeon and apothecary who lived in the former home of the Friars of the Sack. Before he left, I was pleased to allow him to make a copy of Meggie's precious compendium so that he and others could benefit from my dear friend's knowledge.

Jacques' visits to Oak Hall were thereafter all too brief and infrequent and Madame Gill and I both missed him greatly but had to be content in the knowledge that he was being given an opportunity to forge a worthy profession for himself.

I continued to spend hours closely watching the intricate work of Henri and his two sons who were learning their father's craft. One afternoon they were joined in the garden room by Collette and there was great excitement as they poured over Henri's pattern book. Henri had learned that the Queen herself was to visit Rye and Henri had determined to produce a fine merino shawl to present to the monarch.   If he were able to bring his fine work to the attention of Queen Elizabeth, he had hopes that he would then be able to persuade her to support his efforts to establish England as a centre for merino wool or silk production.

Despite the Huguenots' preference for subdued colours and understated elegance, albeit using the finest quality of materials, Henry had no qualms about creating beautiful and colourful designs for his patrons. However, the family decided that none of his previous designs were fitting for the Queen of England. Henry later sought me out and asked for my guidance on how best to impress Queen Elizabeth. Despite never having had the pleasure of seeing or meeting the lady in question, I had heard tell of her vanity and sense of duty towards her realm. I therefore suggested that the shawl should be full of imagery to flatter her sensibilities and should comprise strong, rich colours to reflect the power and prosperity of her nation. Henri excitedly started to scribble out his design and, late into the night he showed me what he had devised. I was amazed at his clever interpretation of my simple suggestions when I beheld a design that incorporated a rich, creamy-white background, to reflect the queen's purity, with a border of intricate Tudor roses entwined with oak leaves and other native flowers. In the centre stood a proud, flame-haired lioness surrounded by common English woodland animals who gambolled around her, safe in her presence and majesty. It was an intricate and bold design and Henri was adamant that only his finest work would be appropriate as a token of his gratitude for the benevolence of England's monarch in opening her country and welcoming his family and all his Huguenot compatriots.

The rest of Henri's family were equally impressed with his design for the shawl and they worked on it tirelessly, using only the finest of dyes and softest blend of merino and local lambswool. When at last it was finished to Henri's satisfaction, he showed it to me and I could only gasp in awe at its beauty. I assured him that the Queen could not fail to admire it and appreciate its quality and beauty, not to mention the symbolism, and added that I was enormously proud of my newly adopted French family. Henri, by way of thanks for my support with the venture, then presented me with the first prototype of the precious shawl.

"I give you this, Mistress Nell, in gratitude for your help in its design, and for the love and support you have shown me and my family. I have also penned a note that you should keep with the shawl, referencing its production within this dear house, naming you as co-designer, and confirming that it is identical to that which I intend to present to her majesty, Queen Elizabeth. Keep it safe my dear and perhaps one day some other resident of this house may benefit from its provenance."

I was completely overwhelmed. To be given such a gift – one indeed fit for a queen! There were no words that I could offer him to fully express my thanks but he had only to look at my face to recognise my pleasure at the gift. I later took the precious parcel, to which I added a sachet of rosemary and lavender leaves to ward off moths and hid it away behind the beam in my attic. I thanked the dear house for providing me with the space in which to hide my treasures intrigued that the hidden space seemed to grow as my need for a safe repository increased.

On the day of the Queen's visit Henri and his family, whilst not invited to join the local dignitaries in St Mary's, managed to attain places near to the entrance to the church so that they could watch the great procession arrive and join their friends and neighbours in their cheers for the popular monarch. Even from my house I was able to hear the people's cheers and share the excitement of the occasion. After a service of welcome and thanksgiving the Mayor, Master Gaymer, invited a select group of local dignitaries and wealthy merchants to his nearby home and gardens where the Queen was to dine and be entertained. It was to this event that Henri and Collette had been invited and at which he intended to present the Queen with the fabulous shawl.

Once the exchange of gifts and feasting was over Henri returned home and retired to his office where he told me of the events of the day. His descriptions were so vivid that I could picture the fine attire of Queen Elizabeth and her courtiers, not to mention the many sumptuous dishes that had been created for the occasion. Even Madame Gill had been asked to contribute to the feast and had obliged with a rich marchpane which she shaped and coloured to resemble fruits. Queen Elizabeth, who was well known for her particular love of sweet things, had very much enjoyed Madame Gill's 'fruits' but had been even more delighted with the beautiful shawl. She had fully appreciated the workmanship and symbolism of the images, as had several members of her entourage, and she had commissioned several other comparable items from Henri that she might offer as gifts to her favourites. Henri was ecstatic at her patronage, however, what excited him even more was that, for the short while he had managed to converse with the Queen, she had enquired as to the treatment of the Huguenots in France and had stated how happy she had been to open her borders and offer sanctuary to them. Henri had been pleased to be able to offer his heartfelt thanks for her benevolence and her country's welcome on behalf of his family and compatriots.

He had also taken the opportunity to convey his wish to establish silk production in England and she in turn had confided to him that she was of a like mind and had commissioned several of her more daring seafaring subjects to try to obtain live silkworms from China on her behalf. To this end she had also initiated the planting of mulberry trees in many of her palace gardens. When Henri explained that he had tried to obtain some mulberry trees for the same purpose, she had called her private secretary to her and instructed that three mulberry trees were to be brought to Rye and planted under Monsieur Le Roux's instructions. Henri expressed his enormous gratitude for this generous gift, astute enough to realise that by providing the means by which any future silkworms that he might be able to obtain from China would be appropriately fed and nurtured, the Queen would be able to claim a share in any subsequent silk production. This prospect filled Henri with even greater hopes of long-term royal patronage.

His audience ended all too quickly, but when Henri and Collette later left the festivities he was satisfied that he had made a good impression on England's charming and shrewd monarch.

As had been promised, a few weeks after the Queen's visit, three mulberry trees were delivered to Oak House and planted with great aplomb and ceremony. One was planted in the top garden of Oak House, near to the future silkworms' accommodation, another was planted in the grounds of the old hospital, down and across Middle Street, and the third was planted about one hundred yards up the same street, in the gardens of Master Gaymer's grand house at the corner of church square and West Street.

To mark the auspicious occasion Oak House was renamed Mulberry House.

Following his gift to the Queen and her subsequent gift of the trees, Henry enjoyed much local favour and received many commissions for his work. Business was good and as his sons grew up and joined him as partners in the business, they soon came to appreciate that Rye and its environs offered only limited opportunities for their combined talents, particularly as its importance as a trading port continued to wane.

They realised that they would need to move to a larger town if their business were to further expand and support them all, and it was to London that they turned, confident of being able to take advantage of Henri's dealings with the Queen and also to place him firmly within her reach should her agents be successful in obtaining the precious worms from China.

I was saddened at their removal from Mulberry House but wholeheartedly wished Henri well for his future ventures. He had mentioned that once the family were settled in their new home in London and if it proved feasible, he would arrange for the queen's precious mulberry tree to be carefully uprooted and transplanted in their new garden. I was disappointed that the tree, already established and starting to fruit well, would be removed from my garden. It stood tall and proud in the top garden, and I spent many hours seated at its base looking back at my grand old house. Happily, when the Le Roux family did establish themselves in the burgeoning Huguenot weaver's community in Spitalfields in London, there was precious little garden space available and thus the queen's tree remained at Mulberry House.

I was once again alone in my dear old house, with only the mice and the garden birds for company. Life in the town continued uneventfully and I wondered how long it would be before a new family took up residence.

One evening I had been alarmed when the beacon behind the stable block had been lit, along with its partners that were visible along the coast, and the bell had rung out to warn of an imminent invasion. I waited anxiously for the coming of a marauding hoard but our little town was spared. I learned later that a great Spanish fleet had been vanquished by the smaller but more deft English navy. For a while the town revelled in the euphoria that followed the English triumph but ultimately the victory did little to restore the town's role as a major coastal port.

Later, as Queen Elizabeth's reign approached its end and the question of the accession once again became the topic of conversation in the street, I pondered once more on the secret document hidden in my attic room.

When I heard the town crier announcing that the Queen was dead and that the new monarch was to be her cousin, James, currently King of Scotland, I was intrigued. Over recent decades I had witnessed how the whims and actions of the monarch could affect the lives of ordinary people, and I prayed, as never before, for stability and peace. The new King already had two sons and I was therefore hopeful that this new Stuart Dynasty would herald a period of stability for the newly joined nations of England and Scotland. Perhaps I would not have to wait much longer before bringing Ned's document to the country's attention and finally honouring my promise to restore the good name of his Uncle Richard.

I reflected on the changes that had been wrought over my little town and indeed the country, over the previous century. Despite not having an opportunity to make amends for my sin, the last hundred or so years had sped past as I had been immersed in the lives of my various residents.

The seventeenth century

Ivy

The new Stuart Regime heralded little change to the small town and Mulberry House remained empty for several years. I became much frustrated as time seemed to stand still when I was alone. My prayers, as always, included my request for His care of my past residents but now my pleas for an end to my purgatory began to take precedence.

One afternoon in the summer of 1605, whilst sitting in the herb garden enjoying the afternoon sun, I became aware of a faint smell of smoke. It was rather too early for the neighbour's fires to be stoked in preparation of their evening meals and, being only too aware of the vulnerability of the houses and the damage that fire could cause, I quickly gazed around to try to establish the source of the smoke. Surprisingly, there was a faint hint of smoke emanating from the roof of the hitherto unused silkworm house behind the mulberry tree. How could that be?

One of the guilty delights of my existence at Mulberry House was that closed windows and doors proved no barrier to me. I could pass easily between even the most securely locked rooms and thus it was of no issue for me to enter the worm house. Inside I was surprised to see a slight girl, with her back towards me, stirring a large pot that was precariously balanced atop the stove wherein there was a weak and smoky fire. It appeared that the chimney was blocked as the room was filled with smoke and, on the far side of the room a skylight window had been propped open to allow the smoke to escape. I coughed slightly and the girl spun around in fear. As she turned I could see that she was incredibly young and heavily pregnant.

"Where'd you come from?" the girl cried. She gazed beyond me at the firmly closed door, "This is my home and you've no business here."

"Really?" I began, "This is actually *my* house, and I could say the same of you. How ever did you get in here?"

As they stood staring at one another a chink of light appeared across the room and a small outer door from

Watchbell Street slowly opened and a young man entered.

"Got us some fish scraps and a few carrots, Ivy" he said gently as he secured the door behind him. He turned towards the girl and then stopped abruptly when he saw that she was standing scared and rigid and brandishing a spoon in front of her.

"Sorry Ivy. Did I startle you?" he laughed, "no need to crown me with that spoon, I've only been gone a short while." His laughter stopped abruptly as he saw the panic in the girl's eyes. "What's happened?"

Ivy screamed at him, "This old besom has found us and says it is *her* house," she cried, "you'd better run Tom, (*and yes, Robbie, this was indeed your antecedent*) no need for her to catch us both."

Tom's eyes peered around the smoky room, "I can't see any old besom sis, perhaps you've had a dream, you know you've not been sleeping good lately." He paused. "And what do you mean run away, you know I'll never leave you after what we've been through."

"She's right there by the other door," his sister had shrieked, "What do you mean you can't see her!"

Tom simply shook his head as he walked up to Ivy and removed the spoon from her hand. "Why don't you have a lie down, I'll fix us something to eat and then you'll feel better."

"But she's right there," Ivy said weakly, pointing straight at me as she sat down heavily on a pile of old sacks.

"Not everyone is able to see or hear me," I said gently. "I actually mean you no harm. My name is Nell Jenkins I have resided here for many centuries but you need have no fear of me."

"She's a ghost," Ivy said warily and pointed towards Nell, "Can you truly not see her Tom?"

He shook his head, "There is nobody else here Ivy," he had pleaded.

Ivy looked across at me and said,

"Do something to show him I'm not mad," she pleaded.

I strode across the room and managed to open the door that Tom had so securely closed behind him, though I closed it quickly as it was obvious that the young people were in hiding and I did not want to do anything that might attract any unwanted attention and place them in danger. I then closed and re-opened the skylight window and went to the fireplace and lifted a couple of badly dented cooking pots and clanged them together.

Tom's mouth opened and shut quickly, and he too looked frightened. His legs started to shake, and he sat down hard on the stone floor.

Ivy, who had enjoyed my show and seemed to accept that I meant them no harm, smiled reassuringly at him. " Her name is Nell Jenkins, and she says she means us no harm Tom."

Tom scuttled across the floor and sat warily beside Ivy on the sacks.

I decided to take charge. They both seemed so young and in need of assistance. I glanced at the girl's belly and gauged that she was probably only a few weeks from giving birth.

"Why don't you let Tom fix you both some supper and you can tell me how you came to my house whilst you rest by the fire," I suggested.

Ivy nodded and conveyed my instructions to Tom who moved towards the fire and did as he was bid. She then moved closer to the fire whilst she began her story.

She explained that Tom was her brother, and they had been born and raised in Lydd, a small town across the marshes. They had two older brothers who were away at sea and had lived comfortably enough with their fisherman father and their mother. Unfortunately, their poor mother had died slowly and painfully from a terrible sickness and Ivy had nursed her to the end. During this time, their father, who had often bullied and beaten his poor wife, turned his attention to his young daughter. Being too young and innocent of the ways of men and for fear of a beating, Ivy had not been able to avoid his advances. On the rare occasions that she had tried to stand up to him he had threatened to take his belt to young Tom, and she had acquiesced.

After their mother's death their father had become even more of a tyrant, physically using Ivy on a regular basis. When it became all too obvious that she was pregnant he had become incensed, accusing her being a wanton and entertaining men whilst he was away fishing. He had beaten her black and blue, saying that she would bring shame on his good name, and when Tom had tried to intervene, he too had been brutally beaten. One evening, when their father had been drinking heavily and had finally become overcome by his exertions, Ivy and Tom, fearful that their treatment at their father's hand would only end with their deaths, realised that they could no longer stay in their family home. They had gathered together some meagre blankets, a few old pots and pans, a little food and a few coins, and run from their cottage, to take refuge in the misty marshes.

For some nights they had been able to sleep under hedges and live off the wild plants they found in the meadows. Tom sometimes managed to snare the odd rabbit or gamebird at which time they would risk lighting a small fire and once or twice they were lucky enough to spend a night in one of the odd Looker's (shepherd's) huts that were dotted around the marsh. Unfortunately, on one particularly clear night when they had lit a fire and enjoyed a hot rabbit stew, they had been found by a gang of smugglers (locally known as Owlers) with whom their father did regular business. They had been recognised but, whilst the drunken smugglers had debated whether to return them to their father or take them across the sea and sell them as slaves, they had managed to escape along a dry dyke and had disappeared into the marshes.

Realising that Ivy was near her time, they had decided to come to Rye and see if any work and accommodation would be available to them. Sadly, they had been turned away at countless establishments as nobody wanted the responsibility of caring for Ivy and her child. Tom, despite some offers of menial work, had not been prepared to abandon his sister and they had been sleeping under a great yew tree in the churchyard until one day, as he passed the silkworm house, the door had silently opened, as if beckoning him inside.   After a couple of months living under the stars it had seemed like a palace.

"So here we are," Ivy had sighed, "awaiting the birth of my baby and whatever else fate throws our way."

Horrified at her tale I reassured Ivy that the house was currently unoccupied and they would thus be safe in the worm house. It seemed that the old house agreed with my reassurances and, having already granted the young runaways access to the worm house, the door to the garden that had been sealed for so long, suddenly swung open to facilitate the young runaways access to the overgrown but still fruitful garden. A plan was hatched that I would keep Ivy company whilst Tom was out seeking odd jobs and ward off any person who feigned interest in the old worm house. I asked Ivy pertinent questions about her pregnancy and explained that I had been a midwife for many years. I laid my hands on her belly and reassured her that the baby seemed healthy, with a strong heartbeat, although I did not add my concern that the stresses and privations of the last weeks had had an obvious effect on Ivy's own health.   She was undernourished and weak which did not bode well for her. I calculated that Ivy would go into labour within the next six weeks or so and endeavoured to reassure the young girl that all would be well. The real question, however, was that if she survived the delivery, what they would do once the baby arrived?

My prayers for assistance were rewarded when, less than a week after my encounter with Ivy and Tom, a new family moved into Mulberry House. To my surprise and intense pleasure I was sought out by the new proprietor, a Master Jack Gill, who, it transpired, was the grandson of my former friend Jacques and who was as delighted as I that he had inherited his grandfather's ability to see and communicate with me. Jack's grandfather had married his former employer's daughter and subsequently taken over the apothecary business from his father-in-law. He had been happy to train his son and grandson in the family business and had ensured that they were fully aware of the importance of his friendship with me and my guidance during his early years in Mulberry House. Jack's father had inherited the business from Jacques but had sadly died a few months earlier following a fall from his horse. Jack had been away completing his studies but had now returned to Rye ready to take over the family firm as an apothecary and barber surgeon in his own right. I was thrilled to meet young Jack who, having heard so much about Mulberry House and not wanting to 'live over the shop' had been excited to purchase it as a home for him and his new bride, Catherine, and, if possible, to renew his grandfather's acquaintance with me.

Catherine, who was much younger than her husband was a slight, quiet, shy girl who had been raised by a maiden aunt in Hastings, her own mother having died when she was born. Her father, a fellow apothecary and associate of Jack's father, had long known young Jack and, when his sister-in-law had died and his daughter had returned to his home, was delighted when love had blossomed between the two young people and they had married.

Jack quickly took control of Mulberry House, employing local tradesmen to make the house bright and comfortable for his new bride. He also engaged a bevy of staff so that his wife would not be burdened with the physical needs of running the household.

Jack took every opportunity he could to converse with me and I was pleased and proud to note the obvious deference shown to him by the craftsmen and the staff to whom he was likewise both civil and respectful in return.

I had wasted no time in advising Jack of the current residents of the worm house at the top of the garden, briefly outlining their history and asking for his help. Jack accompanied me to the shed and was horrified to see Ivy's pitiful state and hear firsthand of their father's abuse. He wasted no time in returning to the main house and advising Catherine of the plight of the two young people currently hiding in their garden. She shared his horror at their story and agreed that the two young people should be brought into their household and made safe.

Within minutes Jack had brought the runaways to the front door of the house and introduced the ragged pair to the household staff as Ivy and Thomas Lee, distant cousins of Catherine's who had walked to Rye from

Dorset where, having been orphaned, they had subsequently been left destitute after the death of Ivy's seafaring husband.

Tom, grateful for the generosity of Jack and Catherine, undertook whatever jobs he could around the house and in the garden until Catherine, recognising that he was a bright and intelligent lad, suggested that Jack might take him on as an apprentice. Jack thought this a splendid idea and decided to convert part of the old worm house into a laboratory within which he and Tom could work. Both Tom and Ivy were thrilled at this opportunity, promising that he would work hard and prove worthy of their kindness.

Most of the staff accepted their presence in the house without question and made the two youngsters welcome and it was only Mrs and Mr Fuller, the housekeeper and her husband the gardener, who appeared to resent and mistrust the new additions to the family. When I mentioned this to Jack one evening he had laughed.

"In all honesty my dear Nell, have you ever seen either of the Fullers show kindness or support to any in this house?   I sometimes wonder how I came to employ them, so mean-minded do they appear now. For now I do not want to cause my darling wife any extra strain as she believes she may also be pregnant, and I am therefore content to leave things be, but rest assured, I will act accordingly if they display any overt cruelty towards any in my care."

I was delighted at the news that Catherine might be pregnant and contrived to spend as much time with her as possible to ensure she was not overdoing things. Sadly, just a few days later, I came across the young woman sobbing quietly in the parlour.   Jack entered and seeing his wife's distress, knelt beside her and took her hand.

Catherine, her eyes filled with tears, gazed sadly at her husband.

"There is no baby my dearest," she sobbed as he took her into his arms.

I felt sad. How could she help these two who were so desperate for a child and who had so generously opened their home to Ivy, Tom, and Ivy's ill-conceived baby?

Any thoughts about helping Jack and Catherine achieve a successful pregnancy were summarily pushed to the back of my mind however, when, a week or so later, on a calm and balmy autumn evening, Ivy, with the minimal administrations of the resident midwife, was safely delivered of a son.

She took little interest in her son however and, given the circumstances of his conception, this apathy was of little surprise to me. In her weakened physical state, she was not able to suckle him and a wetnurse was therefore found.

Though she slowly regained her strength Ivy could hardly bear to look at her son and her lack of interest was shared by her brother. She could not even bring herself to name the poor wee thing and he was referred to simply as 'Baby.' By the time he was three months' old, after a brief discussion but without any prompting from me, Ivy suggested to Jack that she and Tom should leave the household as soon as possible so as to fully turn their backs on their troubled past. They proposed leaving the boy with Jack and Catherine to raise as their own son. Ivy was full of gratitude for Jack's kindness and support at a time when she had been on the brink of despair and likely death but affirmed that could not bear to look at the baby whose presence only reminded her of the abuse she had suffered.

When Jack had advised Catherine of Ivy's suggestion, she had at first been saddened by the lack of feeling between mother and child, although she understood the circumstances that gave rise to such feelings. She had then felt a glow at the thought of becoming a mother to the poor little boy who she had already come to love. Jack was gladdened to see the light in her eyes when she considered this possibility, as he too cherished the opportunity to become a father. Thus it was thus agreed.

I approved of the arrangement but asked that Jack try to help Ivy and Tom find suitable employment. With many contacts within his professional circle and, in line with Ivy and Tom's wishes to be as far away from their father as possible, Jack was able to secure them positions as housekeeper and apprentice to an apothecary friend, a Master Samuel Barnard, who had a thriving shop in the Blackfriars area of London.

The evening before they were due to leave for London, as I commenced my prayers in my little attic room, a small object fell from the great beam wherein lay my treasures. I picked up the item and found it to be the small peg with which the secret storeroom could be opened. I placed it back in its secure hiding place and resumed my prayers but the peg fell to the floor a second time. I picked it up and held it gently in my hand. Was the house suggesting I give some of Jennie's treasure to Ivy and Tom? It would seem so.

"Very well, dear house. I will do as you suggest."

Once all in the house were asleep I made my way downstairs and silently opened the secret room. I selected a pearl necklace and some small but exquisite silver candlesticks and then resealed the storeroom.

The next morning I passed the treasured items to Jack, explained their existence and advised of my wish to provide Ivy and Tom with the means to one day live independently if they so wished, as some recompense for their previous hardships. He was completely in agreement and thanked me for my generosity. He had the items added to the young people's meagre belongings and, lest there be any questions as to their ownership of such fine items, he had added a letter confirming that the items were family pieces that he had given to them in thanks for their gift to him and his wife. He had then accompanied the siblings to London in order to introduce them to their new employer.

He had returned to Mulberry House laden with gifts for his beloved wife and his new son who, it was decided after much debate, was to be named Henry, a reference to Jack's grandfather's former benefactor Monsieur Le Roux.

That night as I prayed in my attic I hoped for Jennie's approval of my gift from her cache and, as I concluded my prayers I believe I heard a faint whisper

"You have done well."

It was a pleasure to witness the happiness and love that now filled my beloved house. I was grateful to Jack for assisting Ivy and Tom and prayed that they would find security and love for themselves in the future. Jack had made discreet enquiries about their father and discovered that he had quickly remarried after the disappearance of his children but continued to have a reputation for a long memory and a short temper.

Jack often mentioned me to Catherine and stressed how supportive of his father I had been. Despite professing not to be able to see or hear her, I often caught her staring straight at me as if she wanted to address me and, on one such occasion I had simply smiled and said quietly, "I mean you no harm. I wish only to be your friend and help you should you ever have need of me." Catherine had not responded however, but I remained hopeful that if I were patient and the need arose in the future, the girl would ultimately approach me herself.

Catherine proved to be a good and kind mother to little Henry and her obvious adoration and admiration of

Jack further endeared her to me.   However, her gentleness, kind nature and obvious preoccupation with her new son, made it easy for the housekeeper Mistress Fuller, with the support of her husband the gardener, to take advantage of her and undermine in front of the other staff. I was appalled at the lack of respect shown towards Catherine, particularly when they openly criticised her for lavishing such affection on a mere 'pauper's bastard'   and determined to contrive a way to assist her.

One afternoon, as Catherine sat in the garden, young Henry lying quietly in a basket at her feet, her eyes closed and an air of contentment on her face, I sat beside her in the arbour and took her hand. She did not flinch at my touch and I smiled.

"Dear Catherine, it does me good to see you looking so content."

Perhaps thinking herself dreaming, she smiled and nodded. "Am I not the most fortunate of women?" she whispered.

"Fortunate indeed," I agreed, "although I have often witnessed you close to tears in your dealings with some in this household. I would help you resolve the unnecessary unkindness of the Fullers, if you will allow me."

"Would that you could," Catherine sighed.

Gently stroking her hand, I then outlined ways in which I could unsettle the Fullers, making them appear at best confused and perhaps even inept so that ultimately Catherine would be left with no alternative but to dismiss them.

"Initially, of course, you might ask the rest of the staff to offer them support and assistance during their period of 'ill-health,' thereby being seen as the firm but fair Mistress of your own home." I suggested. "Then, when the Fullers are ultimately dismissed you will have surely regained the respect and support of the entire household and will be able to appoint a new couple to take up the positions, perhaps a younger couple who will be more amenable to accepting guidance and instruction from you. Will you let me help you?"

Catherine opened her eyes, that threatened tears and turned toward me,

"My apologies for my previous ambivalence towards you Mistress Nell. I thank you for your patience and for your offer of help. I beg you not to mention your plan to Jack. He would be most upset if he realised how the Fullers have been behaving towards me. Let this be our secret. I would not have him feel guilty for employing them. After all, he had only my comfort in mind."

I was only too happy to agree to her terms and thereafter let my mischievous side have full rein. I advised Catherine of my antics in advance so that she could 'inadvertently' draw attention to the issues in front of the other staff.

Plants that were carefully planted by Mr Fuller by day 'disappeared' overnight. Water butts were tipped over and allowed to flood areas of the garden and several well-established rose bushes suddenly lost all their blooms. A barrow lost its wheel – later found high up in the mulberry tree – and tools were moved around the shed and hidden under sacks and boxes.

Unaware of my involvement, when Jack was advised of these mysterious happenings by a disgruntled Mr Fuller, he expressed his concern but suggested that perhaps the gardener was finding the work too strenuous for him and that he was mistaken and had simply forgotten what he had done or where he had put things. Jack had even, seemingly half-heartedly, suggested that if it was not Mr Fuller himself, perhaps the house and garden were haunted.

The poor man was dumbfounded but refused to take responsibility for the events himself, blaming other members of the staff for their incompetence. He had become quite belligerent, and Jack, who completely dismissed the notion that the other staff were to blame, had asked him firmly to compose himself. Jack reminded Mr Fuller that the staff were all busy with their own work and would have little time or indeed inclination to interfere with his.

In the kitchen I also subjected Mrs Fuller to some strange goings on. Large amounts of salt found their way into some of her stews and soups; pots and pans mysteriously disappeared, only to reappear later in the oddest of places; dishes of milk were upset in the dairy and cheeses managed to roll themselves into the meat safe or vegetable storeroom; the kitchen fire, always kept smoored at nights ready for rekindling in the mornings, was regularly found completely extinguished; cuts of meat hung to smoke in the large chimney disappeared and were found weeks later hidden behind barrels of beer in the pantry; cupboards were left open, and mice allowed to feast on the contents, and, on one occasion, a whole roast chicken simply vanished from the cold safe where it had been left to cool and a few bones were all that were later found in the garden, once the local cats had enjoyed an unexpected meal. On Mrs Fuller's exasperated rants about the goings on, Catherine had gently smiled and suggested that she was perhaps mistaken and needed a lie down. After her reports of further such mysterious events, Catherine had even asked if perhaps the work was becoming too much for her as she seemed to be continuously forgetting where she had put things. She too had jokingly suggested that the house was haunted, and that Mrs Fuller must have upset the resident ghost at some time. I was delighted.

As time wore on, Catherine called a meeting of all the staff and asked them to be extra vigilant and take the time to assist Master and Mistress Fuller in their respective duties as things seemed to be becoming too much for them. She also offered the Fullers her full support and offered to engage a Physician to help them with any problems, be they real or imagined. She also let it be known amongst the other staff that she was concerned about them and feared that she would have to 'let them go' should their work continue to suffer.

The house too seemed to assist me in my mischief. Doors and windows rattled without any reasonable cause or slammed shut just as either of the Fullers needed to pass through them. At night, more so than was usual, the house seemed to sigh and boards creak where nobody walked and on one occasion, a tile fell from the roof, breaking into many pieces and missing Mr Fuller by mere inches.

So much did I enjoyed interfering with the work and lives of the Fullers, I was quite disappointed when my mischief achieved the desired effect. With Catherine's blessings and best wishes, it was agreed that the Fullers would leave their employment at Mulberry House, described by Master Fuller to one of the other staff as an 'ungodly' house, with immediate effect. My disappointment was short-lived however when I beheld the look of relief on Catherine's face. The strain of the previous months was over, and she could at last start to enjoy her life in this wonderful house and with her loving husband and thriving son Henry who was fast approaching his first birthday.

Catherine was finally able to confide in Jack regarding the Fullers' hostility, particularly towards little Henry, and begged him to formally legalise their son's position in their family. So it was that Jack had papers drawn up legalising his adoption of the young 'foundling.'

"No one will ever be able to take him from us, dearest," he had reassured his wife.

However, lest the boy ever desire to know the real facts of his birth, he carefully recorded such facts as he knew and asked me to guard the precious paper so that none might use it to harm the boy but that it could offer him some enlightenment should he so desire it in the future.

(*This document will be of significant interest to you dear Robbie as it confirms your family's link with this dear house.*)

Within a few weeks I saw a visible change in Catherine who, with the recruitment of a new housekeeper and gardener and an appropriate shift in the attitudes of the remaining staff, showed a new confidence in her own abilities. There also seemed to be a difference in her relationship with Jack, an extra smile here or there, a new bounce to Jack's step and a secret glow in Catherine's eyes. I was therefore thrilled but not surprised to learn a month or so later that young Henry was to have a sibling. Jack and Catherine were of course delighted at the news, although Jack begged me to watch over his wife most astutely, reminding me that Catherine's mother had died in childbirth.

Catherine was happy for me to take over her care and, as the pregnancy proceeded, I was delighted to reassure them both that all was well.

For years I had prayed for the opportunity to atone for my sin but for Jack and Catherine I prayed that the pregnancy and delivery would be completely trouble free and that there would be no need for any intervention on my part. Sure enough, my prayers were answered when, after a long and exhausting labour, but requiring little more than encouragement from me, Edward Gill was born to the amazement and delight of both his parents and brother Henry. The two young boys filled their parents' hearts and lives with much happiness and I was content that my old house and garden were filled with much fun and laughter.

Jack and Catherine had always made light of the house's resident ghost following the departure of the Fullers, and the whole household had seemed to accept the presence of this usually benevolent spirit, sometimes even asking for the assistance of 'Master Ghost' with a particularly bothersome task. I obliged if I could and once again felt part of a family and experienced a sense of utter contentment. However, deep down, I had to acknowledge that this contentment could not last. Purgatory was surely intended as a period of testing and adversity through which a soul could atone for sins and achieve a sense of grace in order to ascend to heaven. It was surely not meant to be pleasurable. I prayed that my little household be spared any undue sadness and sure enough, over the next few decades life was calm and peaceful for all in Mulberry House. Despite the continuing decline of Rye as a port, Jack's ministrations were still in demand and, though he treated anyone, regardless of their ability to pay him, he and his family lived fairly comfortably.

Ultimately, however, things change and the boys Henry and Edward, neither of whom seemed aware of my presence in their lives, grew up and established new lives for themselves in London, Henry as a lawyer and Edward as a clockmaker. When Jack died after a short illness, Catherine, not wanting to remain alone, decided to sell Mulberry House and move to London to be nearer to her sons and their young families. I missed them all dreadfully and was once again plunged into loneliness and a deep depression which, I had to admit, was more in line with how I assumed purgatory was supposed to feel.

A Nation Divided Once More

Mulberry House was sold to a printer by the name of Master Thomas Boreham who took up residence in the house with his wife Bethany and their two grown-up daughters Patience and Prudence. They lived a simple life, being strictly adherent to Puritan doctrines and I despaired at the lack of mirth, music or any obvious show of affection within the dear old house. When the family were not engaged in their daily work or offering charity to the needy, they sat in the parlour taking it in turns to read from the bible. Though I might not have shared their simple faith, I was delighted to learn that the Puritans thought it fitting that both boys and girls should be taught to read and thereby learn from the good book.

Master Boreham quickly converted the old stables and laboratory at the top end of the garden into a printing workshop. With access from there to Watchbell street and thence down to the Strand, the house could be left as a simple family home, albeit free from any frivolous decoration or ornament. I watched in horror as the beautiful formal flower garden, ornate rather than functional, was ripped up and the land used for the production of basic fruit and vegetables for the family's needs. Only the prolific fruiting of the by then large, well-established and beautiful mulberry tree, ensured its survival in the garden. Goodwife Boreham and her daughters became proficient at turning any surplus vegetables and fruit into all manner of preserves, cordials and pies which they distributed to the poor and needy of the town.

If any of the new household were aware of my presence, it was not clear. Not that they were likely to admit to seeing me, as their faith seemed to reject the concept of purgatory. Their doctrine instructed that God would forgive all those who repented and welcome them into heaven. Thus they appeared to close their minds to that which could not be explained.

However, over time I sensed that perhaps the two young women, Patience and Prudence, could see me as they occasionally glanced in my direction and looked as if they would speak. I contrived to be on hand if either of them were alone, in the chance that I could speak to them and ere long, I confronted Patience whilst she worked in the garden.

"Good morrow, Miss Patience," I said quietly.

The poor girl looked terrified but did not run away.

"My name is Nell Jenkins." I persevered. "I would be your friend if you so wish it."

Patience gazed around the garden. There were none who could help or hear her.

"How do you come to be here?" she eventually enquired, "and how is it that only my sister and I can see you?"

I had given great thought as to how to respond to her enquiries and said simply,

"I am a lost soul who God has charged to fulfil a special task before He will admit me to heaven. I reside in this place until such time as He provides the means by which I will undertake this task."

Patience concentrated on her work whilst she mulled over my words. Eventually she looked up at me and smiled. "I bid you good morrow, Goodwife Jenkins and offer you any help you might require in pursuit of God's work."

Thereafter, Patience, Prudence and I spent many pleasant hours, mostly in the garden discussing the affairs of the old town and myself advising on simple herbal remedies that could help alleviate certain of the family's ailments and even showing them Meggie's precious herbal pamphlet. They proved able students and were keen to share their knowledge with family and those in need around the town.

They did not, however, take into consideration the widespread fear and distrust for some of the 'old ways,' and were therefore shocked when their father stormed into the kitchen one afternoon calling down hellfire on them for their witchcraft.

Bethany was justly horrified at the accusation levied against her daughters and Prudence and Patience sat slumped in chairs by the fire, ashen faced as they looked to me for assistance. As their father continued to rant whilst they each vehemently denied the charge of witchcraft, I hastened to my attic and quickly retrieved Meggie's pamphlet, having removed the front cover. Returning to the kitchen I slipped the papers into Patience's hand, saddened once more that my simple remedies were the source of trouble for the women who made use of them.

Patience showed her father the pamphlet, which, she claimed to have found in the house. She commented on the author's fine hand and exquisite drawings, adding that it must surely been written by an educated, Godfearing man who, like she and her sister, only wished to serve their community according to their strong Christian values; values that they had so earnestly learned from his goodly self. I nodded encouragingly at the young women. Surely he could not believe such charges against his girls.

Master Boreham snatched the pamphlet from his daughter's hand and glanced through it. He listened carefully to his daughter's words and their mother added that their daughters were good, honest girls, strict adherents of church doctrine and with never a thought to devilish inclinations or aspirations to witchery. The atmosphere eased slightly but then Bethany challenged her husband as to where he had heard such calumny. He shook his head and explained that one of his fellow elders at the church had questioned him as to his daughters' 'unholy' ministrations to people of the town and had gone on to question his control over what went on in his own household.

I smiled. So it was the suggestion that he could not control his women that had most incensed the indignant printer.

Bethany too recognised the truth behind his vehement assault on their daughters. She, who was so usually quiet and dignified, could not contain her anger. Clenching her fists, she banged furiously on the kitchen table and screeched at her husband.

"So you thought to accept this vicious and dangerous gossip rather than stand up for your daughters?" she exclaimed.

Looking duly chastened, Thomas mumbled his concerns for his family's reputation in the town.

"Your daughters' reputations or simply your own?" Bethany had countered loudly. "I would remind you that pride is a sin my *dear* husband. If you had cared for the reputations of your daughters you should have stood up to the gossipmongers, not run home in high dudgeon repeating their baseless accusations.

Come girls, let us to our prayers. God knows of your innocence and our adherence to His word, even if your poor sinful father does not."

Leaving Thomas to his thoughts, the women left the kitchen to pray.

After their prayers, Patience attended me in my attic and I sincerely apologised for having encouraged them in the art of herbal remedies and for being the cause of their current predicament. Wise beyond her years, Patience declared that there was no need for any apology on my part. She acknowledged that she and her sister should perhaps have been more circumspect about their treatments but she assured me that the fault lay with the ignorance and bigotry of those in the town, most particularly amongst the men, who feared what they could not understand or control. She thanked me for passing on my knowledge to them and assured me that she and her sister would continue to help those in need, albeit perhaps more subtly than before.

A day or so later, an abashed Thomas advised his wife and daughters that he had shown their pamphlet to a local Physician who had, with a few adaptations, endorsed the treatments recommended therein. Not one to miss an opportunity, Thomas had suggested that he print copies of the book under the Physician's name, so that members of their community could learn such remedies for themselves and thus it had been agreed. Master Nicholas Howard's Herbal became an overnight success in the town and beyond, bringing the aforementioned Master Howard and Master Boreham considerable wealth and status.

Patience and Prudence on returning the now rather tattered papers to my care, expressed outrage that her father should have so exploited the pamphlet.

However, I calmed them insisting that I was pleased that Meggie's knowledge was at last being circulated as she would have wished, albeit without her name being attributed to it.

Thereafter, my conversations with the girls centred on their hopes and aspirations for the future. From them I learned that King James had died and his son Charles had become king. They expressed concern that the king's marriage to a French princess had influenced him towards the old Catholic ways and feared that their protestant way of life was under threat. Although none still lived who had endured the religious backlash of Bloody Mary's reign, stories passed down within protestant families stirred up fear of the potential for another zealous upsurge in Catholicism. It would appear that the Stuart dynasty was falling far short of my hopes of a stable monarchy and I was saddened.

In light of the fears regarding their faith and way of life, Thomas Boreham, as an elder of the community, convened several meetings in his home, when like-minded men of the town would debate and discuss how they would react if they were ordered to abandon their strongly held beliefs.

As was my wont, I sat in on these meetings and was aghast to learn how divided the country had become. I had long been aware that there had often been friction between the King and Parliament. However, I was nevertheless shocked to learn that the current disagreements had resulted in a civil war, with those openly supporting the Parliament taking up arms against the King and his supporters. Rye stood steadfastly on the side of Parliament but the Borehams, who were pacifists and did not believe that war should be a means to an end, were pessimistic about the ultimate outcome. Having been brought up at a time when the absolute right of the monarch was never questioned, let alone challenged outright, I was also afeared that no good would come out of such conflict.

The Borehams carefully considered their options. With many able-bodied young Rye men away fighting for the Parliament, Thomas was concerned that despite his belated but very public challenge to the rumours of witchcraft levied at his daughters, the potential damage to their reputations and the shortage of suitable men, might make it difficult for him to find appropriately committed puritan husbands for the young women. There had also been talk that the French might invade in support of the English King and, Rye, given that its defences had been sadly neglected for decades, was thought vulnerable to such an attack. Thus, the Borehams also feared for their daughters' safety should the French turn their attention to the southern coast of England.

One of the many items that Master Boreham had been recently commissioned to produce was a poster that promoted the idea of migration to the New World. Such a move was keenly discussed at one of his regular meetings and I was surprised to learn that several prominent puritan families from Rye had taken this course earlier in the century and had now established new settlements, called Rye and Hastings, near the already well-established Dutch settlement of New Amsterdam. The heads of these communities were keen to encourage the further migration of like-minded individuals, and the poster stressed the enormous opportunities available to craftsmen, tradesmen and farmers alike in the new protestant lands where they would be free to live their lives in a Godly fashion, away from the vagaries and whims of monarch or parliament. There was apparently also a need for honest, industrious protestant women to travel to the new settlements to become the wives of the early settlers and mothers to the next generation, thereby ensuring the continued existence of their godly community in the New World.

The Borehams discussed this life-changing move and I could see that the idea of becoming the wives of the brave puritan pioneers, and the mothers of a whole new generation who would be free to practice their faith in peace, was extremely exciting to Patience and Prudence. Irrespective of the outcome of the civil war, they did not see that Rye would offer them such an opportunity. They prayed long and hard and managed to persuade their parents that it was their duty to follow this godly path. They had even suggested that if their parents were not sufficiently bold enough to undertake the challenge, they would travel without them. Master Boreham would not entertain the idea of his daughters travelling alone and thus, in 1644, he made plans to take his family to a better life in the Americas. Whilst he arranged to have their belongings packed, including his precious printing press, and sold anything they could not or would not take with them, I retrieved some silver coins from Jennie's secret cache, and gave Patience and Prudence each a small purse with which, I hoped, whether they married or not, they could ensure a secure future for themselves.

I wished them well in their adventure across the sea and prayed that the girls would find happiness and fulfilment but, I had to admit that I was not really sorry to see them all go. Praying also that the war would end and religious tolerance would soon prevail, I waited and hoped that the next family to inhabit my house would be less austere in their lifestyle and beliefs.

Though the war persisted, it was only a few weeks before another printer and former associate of Master Boreham's, one Adam Bacon, took over the workshops and house at Mulberry House. I was delighted to see that he, his wife and three young sons were much less dour than the former residents. Sadly, there did not appear to be any in the household who could see or hear me, but, whilst the Bacons also followed the protestant doctrine, they seemed less prone to quiet prayer and solitude, and I was happy to witness them playing games and enjoying spending time as a family.

In the absence of any direct contact with anyone in the household, I passed my time by simply watching and listening to the family going about their daily routine. I was captivated by Adam's work in the print shop and was impressed at the care with which he conducted his craft. The boys were normal, fun-loving children and their mother, Elizabeth, known as Beth, was a loving wife and mother who ran her household with a gentle hand. Like Master Boreham, Adam was keen that his children learn to read the scriptures for themselves and he engaged a tutor for the boys. Master Butcher, an elderly gentleman who had been Adam's teacher years earlier, attended the house regularly to tutor the boys. Having always been in awe of people who could read and write, I took advantage of the opportunity that was presented to me and took to sitting at the back of the room to learn alongside the children. It was a struggle for me but I was determined to succeed, even practising my letters in the dust that abounded in my attic.

When not at our lessons the boys and I spent much time in the garden, they participating in noisy games and I revelling in Beth's restoration of a small rose garden. The mulberry tree for which the house had been named, stood proudly at the top end of the garden, near the workshop, and the boys loved to climb the tree which seemed to embrace them in its sturdy branches. It continued to produce an abundance of fruit each year, some of which Beth sold at the town market and some of which she turned into pies, jellies, jams and a particularly potent cordial, which her family enjoyed.

After a few short years the lessons with Master Butcher came to an end. The boys (and I) were able to read and comprehend the bible and Adam and Beth were justly proud as one by one they were accepted as pupils at the new grammar school in Longer Street.

Determined to continue to expand on my newfound skills. I spent many nights in my attic reading Meggie's Herbal and a bible I had 'borrowed' from Adam's workshop and scratching my name on one of the old beams.   I also enjoyed spending time in Adam's workshop reading and learning about local events and the world beyond my hometown.   I really missed the lessons with Master Butcher and was most surprised when he subsequently resumed his visits to Mulberry House, although now he mostly attended at night. He spent many hours ensconced in the printing shop with Adam, discussing the benefits of different typefaces and paper/ink quality, as well as occasionally moving large heavy boxes to the house.

Adam, with a keen eye for detail, had quickly ascertained the potential for a storeroom beneath the parlour floor. He spent many an evening trying to contrive an entrance to the space and I, in turn, spent the time removing Jennie's cache from the storeroom and hiding it up in my attic. Once the treasures were secured upstairs, I 'enabled' Adam to find the little wooden peg, the key to the secret mechanism that unlocked the entrance to the secret storeroom, and between the house and I, we guided him through the procedure that enabled him to access the large hidden storeroom.   Thereafter, he and Master Butcher brought and stored many heavy boxes therein, further obscuring the entrance by placing a large, oak coffer full of the family pewter vessels and plate, afore it.

I was keen to find out what was in these hidden boxes, particularly as they did not remain long in their hidden sanctuary but were quickly collected and removed, again always at night, by gangs of somewhat disreputable-looking men, but try as I might the boxes remained securely locked.   Fearful that Adam was involved in something that could put his family and home in danger, I decided to oversee the night-time activities in the print shop to ascertain exactly what was being hidden in the boxes and why it involved such secrecy.

Imagine my surprise and shock when, during a night visit to the print shop, I found that Adam and Master Butcher were printing posters and pamphlets that openly supported the absolute rights of Kings.   The language used was rather more flowery than that used for Adam's daytime work and the actual type used was also more elaborate and was taken away each night and stored in the secret room. Some of the papers were beyond my rudimentary reading skills but as a result of my time spent with Henri Le Roux and my memories of a lifetime attendance at Catholic masses, I was able to make out a few familiar words that suggested that these papers were printed in French and Latin. Why was Adam Bacon, a seemingly good and honest Protestant, printing such material? I was confused. Were the Bacons secret Catholics, despite regularly attending the parish church of St Mary's and openly adhering to the protestant ways of life? Alternatively, just because they chose to follow a simpler doctrine and way of life, did being a protestant mean that you completely disregarded or abandoned the rights of hereditary positions and titles?

I had been aware that under Queen Elizabeth and King James, England had certainly become known as a protestant land, but that it had been accepted that some still adhered to the Catholic faith and they remained largely unchallenged, provided they appeared to adopt protestant practices and did not flaunt their Catholic beliefs in public. However, with the country now locked in a bitter civil war, religious differences were once again in the foreground.

Through my life and the centuries since, I had been aware of how the whims of Kings, and Queens, could adversely affect ordinary folk and cause dissent. However, when I discovered that the King had been captured by the Parliamentary forces, imprisoned, tried and executed, I had felt that the world had truly gone mad.

On later reflection however, I realised that the regicide paled into insignificance when compared to my own actions. Surely, mine was the more heinous crime. Poor little Alys Alard had died without being given the chance at life; her only 'crime' being that of her gender, whereas King Charles had experienced a life, one assuredly filled with luxury and self-indulgence. That he had ultimately been held to account for his errors of judgement, lack of empathy and flagrant dismissal of the needs of his country and his people, was perhaps an inevitable sign of the rapidly changing times - but to end in regicide? Only time would tell if this had been a sound decision.

With the execution of the King and the establishment of a Commonwealth under Oliver Cromwell, peace was restored. That the late king's children had fled to the continent, there to be supported by sympathetic royal houses pending a time when they might reclaim the throne, was of little consequence to the ordinary people who seemed happy to allow parliament to assume control over all aspects of their recently disrupted lives. One of the first acts of parliament was to make attendance at the protestant church compulsory. Severe penalties were imposed on anyone not complying with this law and the hitherto barely hidden practices of the Catholics were outlawed.

By day, much of Adam's work involved the printing of prayer books, pamphlets and posters that endorsed the work of Cromwell and his fellow parliamentarians and Adam and Beth openly approved of the Commonwealth, seeming hopeful that at last the needs of the common man would be met. Not once did I discern even a hint that their true feelings lay elsewhere. It was therefore even more of a mystery to me that Adam's secret work accelerated during this time. I was further intrigued when, after several months of almost frantic nightly activities, Master Butcher remained in the hidden store alongside the boxes. He remained there for four days and nights, only being let out at night by Adam to enable him to eat and stretch his legs. When that particular cache of boxes was collected later Master Butcher had accompanied them. Indeed, with his disappearance, the secret night work also ceased and Adam returned to his previous normal routine. He had even melted down some of the type that he had used for the secret papers and passed on the lead to the local militia to be used for shot, but not before I had taken a set, along with some of the inflammatory posters and leaflets, and secreted them in my cache in the attic.

I had certainly never witnessed any deviation from the protestant doctrine in Mulberry House and indeed, Beth Bacon had often been heard openly criticising the 'catholic' tastes of some of her wealthier neighbours up Middle Street, whose dress and behaviour she felt harked back to more frivolous, what she called 'popish,' times. Adam himself gave no indication of any royalist leanings and I wondered why he had participated in his clandestine activities.

One afternoon as I was sitting quietly in the garden room watching Beth at her mending, a neighbour had come rushing to the house with some shocking news. A Catholic priest had been found celebrating mass in one of the large manor houses in nearby Guestling. He had been travelling around the country, holding secret masses for those royalists who still followed the old faith. This particular errant priest, along with the head of the house, Sir Denny Ashburnham, MP for Hastings and whose father had been a renowned Royalist and friend of the former King Charles, had been arrested and taken away for trial. The priest was almost certain to face execution, but it was thought that Sir Denny still had enough friends in parliament to ensure that he would keep his head and that he would most probably be fined or face a short period of incarceration in the Tower of London.

Whilst it had been generally believed and feared that Catholic priests had continued to travel between the Catholic households in various disguises, and that special hidey-holes, or priest-holes as they became known, and even secret chapels had been established in these safe homes, Beth had been most scathing of the deviousness of the secretive Catholics and I was convinced that she had known nothing about her husband's clandestine activities.

I had neither seen or heard anything to suggest that Adam Bacon shared Sir Denny Ashburnham's faith and there was certainly no priest hole or hidden chapel in the house - but then I remembered the time that Adam had hidden Master Butcher in the secret storeroom and presumably facilitated his subsequent disappearance. Had Master Butcher been a Catholic priest posing as a teacher? As Adam's childhood teacher, there was certainly a bond of friendship between them, but might Master Butcher have influenced Adam's formative years towards Catholicism. This could perhaps explain why Adam had helped him hide evade capture.

I had become very fond of all the Bacon family and became obsessed with trying to find a rational explanation for Adam's clandestine activities. However, without direct contact with anyone it was proving difficult and very frustrating for me to establish the truth. Happily for my sanity, the town authorities became involved and the whole story was revealed.

Two of the mayor's henchmen arrived at Mulberry House and demanded to inspect the print shop. They explained that a group of French papists, disguised as wool merchants, had been intercepted near Tenterden and had been found to be in possession of a large quantity of posters and pamphlets in support of the so-called King in exile, Charles II, as well as a number of catholic catechisms. All print shops in the area were being searched for evidence of involvement in this criminal activity.

Adam had led the men to his workshop and I accompanied them through the garden and watched as they meticulously searched every pile of paper, box of inks and tray of type. When he had asked to see some of the offending pamphlets, suggesting that he might be able to identify a specific printer's style or layout, Adam had paled when some of his own work was presented to him. I, who had been holding my breath, gasped and was fearful that Adam's obvious discomfort would give him away. Happily, he had covered his reaction as that of shock at the content of the treasonable notices.

"You cannot believe that this is the work of any true Englishman," he had proclaimed. "Why even the font is so obviously foreign," he had added. "I am confident that this is not the work of any of my associates here in Rye."

The men had been thorough in their search and examination of his type faces and, finding none that matched the offending papers, had reassured him that all was well.

"We are just doing our duty, Sir" they had reassured. "The mayor is most keen to establish that nobody in his area has been involved in producing these abominable tracts. We must all be seen to be good members of God's Commonwealth here in Rye, Sir."

Adam had thanked them for their vigilance and stout work on behalf of the townsfolk and escorted them from the premises. On returning to the house, he had slumped in his usual chair by the fire in the front room and asked Beth to bring him a tot of brandy – ostensibly kept for medicinal use only. Beth was surprised but fetched the drink which Adam drank down in one go. He held out the glass for another, which Beth poured before she left the room, taking the brandy bottle with her.

Adam sat for some time just staring into the fire, perhaps realising that his covert activities could have had disastrous consequences for his family.

"Are you going to explain why you are so shaken my dear?" Beth had asked on her return.

Adam had seemed to age before her eyes and had eventually shaken his head and sighed. "Oh my dearest wife," he had said quietly, "You must be assured that all I have done has been for the overall benefit of you and the boys," he had stressed.

"You are alarming me now," Beth had said shakily. "What exactly have you been doing that has you so anxious?"

Sitting across the room, I could hardly contain my excitement. Now at last would I find out the truth behind his actions.

Adam had explained that the gradual decline of Rye as an important port had adversely affected all trade in the town, including his own, and he had been struggling to maintain sufficient income to run their home and keep the boys at school. Master Butcher, his old teacher and friend but known Catholic sympathiser if not open adherent, had been aware of Adam's dwindling income and had suggested he could earn substantial money if he were to print certain items in secret for unnamed interested parties. Adam had at first declined, declaring that he was an honest and upright protestant and would do nothing to jeopardise his family or his country. However, as the general situation in the country deteriorated into civil war and business almost evaporated, Adam had become desperate. With the proviso that none of his work would be distributed locally, he had agreed to print some simple posters and pamphlets in support of the King, which Master Butcher had translated from French into English for him, and he had certainly been paid most handsomely for his work. However, the commissions had soon become more frequent and overtly anti-parliament, and he had become scared. He had advised Master Butcher of his fears and stated that he was putting his family at too great a risk by his ongoing involvement with this work. He had wanted to cut his ties with them once and for all. Master Butcher had promised to pass on his concerns to his associates although he had suggested that they would not be pleased. Adam had not thought that Master Butcher would take up against him but was concerned that those who commissioned the work and who controlled the purse strings might not be so loyal, and so it transpired. Word was sent back to him that if he did not reconsider the withdrawal of his services, word of his involvement would reach some powerful people.

Adam had felt completely trapped and had continued the clandestine activities, ever fearful of being denounced as a traitor. His relationship with Master Butcher had changed irrevocably and it was some relief to Adam when his old tutor advised that he was to accompany the current batch of inflammatory papers when it was collected and that this would be Adam's last commission. Master Butcher had explained that as a peripatetic teacher he had good cause to visit a number of different households and had thus been able to distribute many of the dangerous pamphlets. However, he had recently been apprehended by a parliamentary patrol whilst on his return to Rye and had been taken for questioning and a search. Thankfully he had had no offending papers on his person, and no trappings of popery to suggest he was a disguised priest, and after an uncomfortable and scary night in a cell, he had been released. His superiors had subsequently decided that he should disappear for a while and that the printing work at Mulberry House would cease.

Adam explained about the secret store under the front room floor and took Beth to see the hidden door. She was rightly shocked at his treasonous endeavour, even when he showed her the amount of silver he had been able to squirrel away. They returned to the warmth of the fire and Beth sat on a stool by Adam's chair. He gently stroked her hand and reiterated that the episode was now closed. He gave a solemn oath that he would never again do anything so reckless and potentially harmful to his family and Beth had to be reassured at that. She stressed that their lives could never be so bad as to consider breaking the law and he had to promise to be honest with her should things become difficult in the future. Duly chastened by her support, Adam promised to never keep anything from her again.

I was relieved to finally hear the truth, though I had been sure that Adam was no real conspirator. A foolish man desperate to support his family perhaps, but no traitor. I felt exhausted by the strain of the last few years and could only imagine how physically drained Adam must have felt.

After Adam's shocking revelation, the Bacons lived simply and comfortably like the godly people they were. Enquiries into the identity of the treacherous printer were eventually abandoned and it was strongly believed that the pamphlets had been printed in France and brought across by one of the numerous smuggling bands who frequented the south coast.

As their sons grew up, John, the eldest went to London to study law; Thomas, the middle son remained at home and having been apprenticed to his father, gradually began to take on more and more responsibility for the work. His young wife Edith helped Beth with the household chores. The youngest son Samuel also remained at Mulberry House and had been appointed as a teacher at the grammar school. True to Adam's promise to Beth, the print shop took only commissions from worthy townsfolk, the church, or fellow craftsmen and traders and life for them all was simple but safe.

A few years later I was astonished to learn that the Commonwealth had fragmented after the death of Oliver Cromwell and things went full circle when the monarchy was restored, albeit with limitations on the range of power of the King.

The restoration of the monarchy had little effect on the Bacon household or indeed the town, although the lifting of some of the more austere laws of the Commonwealth, such as the banning of Christmas, did seem to raise the spirits of the people. Thomas and his new wife Edith completely took over the management of the business and Mulberry House household and Adam and Beth enjoyed a period of mutual contentment and peace in their retirement.

Once again my thoughts returned to Ned's secret document and the weight of its responsibility weighed heavy on me. Was there ever to be a time when the monarchy was so secure as to be able to withstand its dramatic contents? Perhaps this new constitutional monarchy would prove more stable in the future and I prayed that God or the house would guide me if the time came for Ned's revelation to be made public.

John

On his occasional visits to his parents at Mulberry House, John Bacon regaled his family with tales of the grand times he was witnessing in London. Known as the Merry Monarch, King Charles' reign heralded the restoration of many social activities that had been banned under the Commonwealth. Theatres and drinking houses reopened and colour seemed to fill the streets. Adam and Beth were concerned at the effect of all this on their boy but John, a sensible chap who had recently married Harriet, the daughter of a successful high court judge, appeared to be making a good life for himself and was content.

When subsequent news of a great fire that had destroyed much of the capital city reached Rye, Adam and Beth were distraught. How had John and his young bride fared? Young Samuel was despatched to London to get news of or offer assistance to his brother as required, and it was with much relief and great celebration that Samuel returned to Rye bringing his heavily pregnant sister-in-law Harriet to reside in Mulberry House. John, having lost his home and chambers in the fire had decided that, with the responsibility of becoming a father, he would leave the highly stressful life of a London lawyer behind him and return home to establish new chambers in Rye which he hoped would be more conducive to family life. He was finalising a few business matters and planned to follow soon.

Harriet was heartily welcomed by the Bacons who were excited at the imminent arrival of a new addition to the family. Harriet immediately fell in love with the lovely old house and spent many hours sitting in the garden room with Beth learning of life in the quaint old town. I was most excited to note that Harriet could obviously see me and did not appear to be surprised or alarmed by my presence. As soon as the opportunity arose, I introduced myself and reassured the young woman that I meant her no harm. Harriet was delighted to converse with me and explained that she had previously been aware of similar spirts in her old home in London but had never thought to converse with them. On hearing of my previous profession, she was happy for me to lay my hands on her vast abdomen and I in turn, was happy to confirm that all appeared to be well with her baby.

A few weeks later Harriet gave birth to a healthy son and the only thing that marred her pleasure at his arrival was that his father had yet to arrive in Rye. Once again Samuel was despatched to London but returned only a week or so later with the distressing news that John had left for Rye only days after he and Harriet had started their journey. Despite enquiries at the various inns on the route home, Samuel had been unable to find any trace of his brother. Harriet was distraught and even turned away from her new son, so lost was she in her own misery. Try as I may, I was unable to lift her out of her despair, and Adam, whose health had been failing for some time, also found it difficult to cope with the disappearance of his eldest son and it was left to poor Beth to manage things. A wetnurse was employed to care for the baby, named Matthew, and groups of friends and business associates of Adam's, together with Thomas and Samuel, continued the search for John.

After several weeks spent traversing the countryside between London and Rye, Thomas and Samuel , with a couple of friends, were staying the night at an inn near Tonbridge and learned of a gang who had been active in the area for a few months. This particular gang, not content to simply rob their victims, were reputedly taking able-bodied men away to be sold as slaves to the many disreputable merchants who traded with the powerful Ottoman empire.

Aghast at this news but having found not a single trace of their brother since he had left London, it was with heavy hearts that Samuel and Thomas returned home, suspecting that John had indeed been a victim of such a gang. They told their parents the likelihood that their brother had been abducted and sold into slavery, and they all agreed that this possibility should not be discussed with Harriet.   The shocking news that his son could have been a victim of such a gang caused Adam, already in a weakened state, to have an apoplexy from which he died a few days later. This loss and the fear that her darling husband might also be dead caused Harriet to fall further into a mire of despondency and Beth, burdened with her own grief at the loss of her beloved husband, was genuinely concerned for the future of their family.

A small private funeral service was held for Adam, at which prayers were also said for the soul of dear John. Friends and neighbours visited the house to express their sorrow at the family's losses and a month or so later, those same friends and neighbours joined the family at the christening of young Matthew, when all expressed the wish that his presence in the family would somehow compensate for their recent sadness. Many had noticed that Harriet appeared to be still in a state of shock, completely understandable considering the circumstances, but concern was expressed about her apparent apathy towards her son. She vehemently refused to accept that John might be dead and implored Thomas and Samuel to keep searching for news of their brother.

I was fearful that grief might completely consume the new mother and spent a lot of time encouraging her to take an interest in her baby. Weeks passed and it became obvious that kindness and encouragement were not going to have the desired effect. Thus, one afternoon as Harriet was lying languidly in the garden room, apparently oblivious to the cries of her son in the next room, I decided on a different course of action. I entered the room and confronted her.

"What would John say if he could see you thus?" I had shrieked, making Harriet shrink back on her bed. "He would not have wanted to see you turn your back on his precious son. I know you are grieving but how much longer will you wallow in this self-pity? You don't deserve to have a healthy baby and the love and support of this good family, if you are not willing to even try to take up your responsibilities as the mother of John's child. You are unworthy of such a gift."

I stopped my ranting and sat down, still glaring at the poor girl. Harriet, wide eyed and white faced, got up from her bed and walked to the door.

"Get out of my room," she said slowly and quietly as she opened the door, "How dare you speak to me thus."

Although a closed door was never a barrier to me, I left the room as instructed and Harriet closed the door firmly behind me.   I then heard her sob as she had never sobbed before, a long-overdue,   heart-wrenching sound that told of pent up pain and distress.

It seemed that my words had achieved the desired effect and the dam on Harriet's grief had finally been breached as she slowly began to resume an interest in life and her son. When Edith suggested that perhaps some of the other young mothers from the community could bring their young offspring to Mulberry House to help her through this difficult time,   she apprehensively agreed. So it was that Beth, Edith and Harriet hosted many pleasant afternoons with their friends and their young children. The old house rang once again with the joyous sounds of children playing and laughing and, sure enough, Harriet began to slowly return from the abyss of despair.

Matthew was a charming, easy-going child, happy to be petted and loved by all and despite their troubled start, he became extremely attached to his mother. Harriet too seemed to be pleased to make up for lost time and she sought him out from the nurse as often as she could, regaling him with tales of his beloved father. Although far too young to understand her words, Matthew lay quietly beside her, or later sat on her lap, appearing to be listening intently to her words. It was Harriet, with a long-absent twinkle in her eye, who held him towards me one afternoon and we were both charmed when he had smiled and held up his arms towards me as if for a cuddle. Oh, how I wished I could have obliged him but he seemed content with just my smile and gentle words of affection.

Time passed and the family gradually resigned themselves to John's loss. As the third anniversary of Matthew's birth and John's disappearance neared however, there was an increased sense of sadness throughout the house as Beth, who had started to decline some months earlier, passed away quietly and peacefully, with her family around her. Edith, at last pregnant with her first baby seemed to take Beth's death hard and I feared that her malaise would affect her baby. Normally such a strong woman, Edith lost weight and seemed apathetic towards her unborn child. Once, when Edith was resting, I endeavoured to ascertain the wellbeing of the child and was concerned at the very weak heartbeat and lack of activity I found.

I counselled Harriet to encourage Edith to take better care of herself and, getting little positive response from her sister-in-law, she spoke to Thomas who had needed little persuasion to enlist the services of the town's best midwife. She too seemed concerned at the size and apparently slow development of the babe and did her best to draw Edith out of her depression, but nothing seemed to have any effect.

Edith continued to decline, and Harriet had to assume much of the responsibility of running the household. Matthew, tall for his age and by now a very curious boy, followed his mother around the house, incessantly asking questions that usually began with the words 'Why' or 'How'. One afternoon, as Harriet, with Matthew in tow, was supervising things in the kitchen and Edith was slumped in her usual seat by the fire, she had almost tripped over her son in her haste to fetch some ingredients from the dairy. She had cried out in her anguish at the near accident and had picked up the child and briskly placed him on Edith's lap.

"Stay with Aunt Edith whilst mother sorts out our dinner," she admonished, and continued on to the dairy.

Edith instinctively placed her arms around her nephew's little body and he, though still so young, seemed all too aware of his aunt's sadness and simply sat still and put his little arms around the small mound of her belly. After a few minutes he put his head against the mound and appeared to listen intently.

"Why is your baby girl crying?" he asked solemnly, " Don't be sad little girl, *I* love you," he had promised.

Edith, looked down at her nephew and large tears began to cascade down her cheeks.

"A girl?" she enquired and Matthew nodded.

"Why do you not love her?" he had asked.

Edith continued to sit still and sad and Matthew, not expecting an answer from her and being bored of sitting still, had wriggled and squirmed to escape her lap. She did nothing to restrain him but his legs had become entangled in her skirts and as he attempted to descend he fell forward and launched headfirst towards the fire. Edith, stirred from her reverie by his panic throes, attempted to catch him but was too late and he fell onto the large, hot hearthstones near to the heart of the fire. I, who had been spellbound at Matthew's apparent communication with Edith's unborn child, was frustrated at not being able to prevent the accident and called for Harriet to come quickly.

As she ran back into the kitchen Harriet witnessed Edith, now on her hands and knees by the hearth, scrabbling amongst the burning embers and pulling Matthew clear of the hearth. Between them they managed to lift the inert little body onto the table and Edith ran to the scullery for buckets of water and cloths. They had soon stripped off Matthew's still smouldering clothes, bathed him in water and wrapped him in cold, wet cloths.

It was only when he eventually opened his eyes and said, "Hurt Mama," did the two women dare to breathe again. Matthew had slight burns to the right side of his face and right hand which had come into direct contact with the extremely hot hearthstones, and a large bump on his forehead which had borne the brunt of the impact. He had lesser burns down his body. Edith's hands however were much more severely burned as she had seemed unaware of any pain whilst she had frantically pushed the red-hot embers away from Matthew's body lest they caught his clothes aflame. I advised Harriet of which salves to apply to Matthew's and Edith's burns and, once they were duly anointed and bandaged, they were each given an infusion of willow bark to help relieve their pain. Matthew quickly drifted into an uneasy sleep and Harriet gently carried him upstairs and laid him carefully in his bed. As she sat by his bedside Edith joined her and they sat in silence, each giving private thanks that the accident had not been any worse.

Harriet reached for Edith's bandaged hands and held them gently in her own, "Thank you for saving my boy," she said simply, "I pray that your poor hands will not be overly damaged."

Tears filled Edith's eyes, "I was only distracted for a second, but he had become entangled in my skirts and fell before I realised what was happening," she had tried to explain. "He always seems so knowing for his age and I forget that he is still little more than a babe himself," she had added.

Harriet had gently patted Edith's poor hands, "This was nought but an accident my dear good sister, please do not berate yourself."

Edith had then turned to her sister-in-law and said quietly,

"He told me that my baby is a girl and that she was crying as I do not love her. That is why I was somewhat distracted."

Harriet nodded but did not seem unduly surprised by Edith's revelation,

"He certainly does seem to have an insight into things," she agreed, "He often tells me of stories relating to his father, even though they have never met. He means no malice by his words but merely wishes to give me comfort. However, let us not broadcast his revelations – you know how easily these things can be misconstrued.   A girl you say, how wonderful, what shall you call her?"

Edith's pondered for a while, "Of course, I have not yet discussed this with Thomas, but I think Elizabeth would be appropriate, for our dear mother-in-law who I loved as my own. She had been excited at the prospect of another baby in the house, and I was so distressed that she passed away before being able to meet her new grandchild. You must have all felt me so unfeeling."

"Sad yes but unfeeling, never," Harriet had reassured her, "and now you can put aside your sadness and plan for your new daughter's arrival."

Thomas,   at first concerned at his wife's damaged hands, was delighted that the accident had appeared to bring his poor wife out of her long malaise. He too agreed that if the child was a girl, she should be named Elizabeth and suggested Bartholomew, after Edith's father if it were a boy.

As with most young children, Matthew was soon up and about, seemingly unperturbed by his experience. His face and hand responded well to the salves and I reassured Harriet that there was unlikely to be any long-lasting damage or scarring. Edith's poor hands healed much more slowly but, by the time her daughter was safely delivered, she was able to hold her safely without any pain. The scarring remained unsightly however, and Harriet embroidered some fine soft gloves for Edith which she wore at all times and which she said made her feel like a grand lady. Elizabeth, though tiny at birth, was a contented baby and soon had her parents and all her family, wrapped around her little finger.

Matthew, who grew to be a fine lad, never tired of his cousin's constant demands on his time and even after he had followed his father and uncles to become a pupil at the grammar school where his uncle Samuel was now headmaster, still made time to spend with little Elizabeth and take an interest in her activities. He also managed to seek out moments alone with me and delighted in my tales of times past in their wonderful old home.   He intrigued me with fantastic tales of his father who, he was adamant, was still alive.

Life continued simply and quietly for the Bacon family and, like his father, Matthew did well at school and expressed a wish to attend university. He did not, however, want to study the law but preferred history and the classics. Thus he went up to Oxford where he revelled in the academic environment and enjoyed the interaction with like-minded students.   When he graduated and returned to Rye he was intent on becoming a writer.

When Matthew neared his twenty-first birthday Harriet was surprised to receive a letter from her father in London inviting them to visit him. She had regularly corresponded with her father, to keep him abreast of their ongoing attempts to obtain information on John's disappearance and to entertain him with tales of Matthews antics, but he had always blamed pressures of his work that prevented him from visiting Rye or from offering his daughter and grandson his hospitality in London. This time however, he extended a warm invitation to them to visit him and had sent sufficient funds for a comfortable journey, overnight accommodation in a reputable hostelry enroute, and with guards to protect them from brigands. Matthew, of course, was delighted at the prospect of meeting his hitherto unseen grandfather, but most of all he was excited to be visiting London.

"It will be a great adventure, Nell" he had said as I had sat with him whilst he stuffed his clothing into a travelling bag,

"We will only stay for a few weeks I am sure and I will come and tell you all about it on my return."

I was anxious however, afraid that the fascinations of the great city would entice my curious, lively and precious boy away from me.

Harriet and Matthew set off to London in a fine coach and with two stout guards in attendance. Along with their personal effects they took a fine array of fresh produce from the garden as well as some of Edith's finest preserves and one of the last bottles of Beth's special mulberry cordial as a gift for Harriet's father.

A day or so later a letter arrived from Lord Justice Balfour, confirming his daughter and grandson's safe arrival at the Inns of Court and offering thanks for the delicious gifts.

Some weeks later, Harriet had written to advise that her father did not appear to be in the best of health and she and Matthew would remain in London until such time as her father was fully restored.   How I missed my dear friends and Edith and Elizabeth offered little in the way of distraction.

Time passed slowly until one afternoon Thomas received a strange letter. He ran from the print shop calling for Edith and Elizabeth who hurried from the kitchens to join him in the front room.

"I have received a letter from someone purporting to be John," he exclaimed, "I have sent my lad to summon Samuel – he will surely know how to proceed."

Elizabeth had grabbed the letter from her father and slowly read the contents aloud.

Sir,

My name is John Bacon, former lawyer and son of Master Adam Bacon, printer of Rye.

I hope the recipient of this letter is my brother Thomas to whom I send my best wishes. After many years enforced exile, I am returned to England and am hopeful of being restored to my family. However, I am mindful that you may have believed me dead and that my dearest wife Harriet may have moved on and established a new life for herself. I would wish her a happy life and would offer no disruption of it. I therefore await your advice as to whether I should make my return known to her.

I am currently resting in Canterbury after an arduous journey across Europe during which I became ill. I am now sufficiently well and would welcome the opportunity to meet with you and our brother Samuel, should you both wish it.

I remain your loving brother.

John Bacon.

Like Edith, I had tears in my eyes at the news; perhaps Matthew's tales of his father had been based on real visions after all.

"You must go to him at once my dearest husband," Edith had stated. "You and Samuel must be sure that he is indeed your brother before we contact Harriet and Matthew. After twenty-two years he will be much changed, and we must be sure that his return does not cause them any further pain."

Samuel burst into the room just as Edith was speaking and after reading the letter for himself, nodded at her words.

"As ever, my dearest good sister, you are the wisest of us. My initial reaction was that we should in all haste send a rider to London to bring back our brother's family but, your advice is sound. Thomas and I must first ensure that the gentleman who wrote the letter is indeed our long-lost brother John. Brother are you agreed?" he turned to Thomas.

"Most certainly," his brother confirmed, and, with the minimum of fuss and bother, the pair were soon packed and heading off to avail themselves of a cart or other means to take them to Canterbury.

I sat quietly in the upstairs garden room deep in thought at what John's return would mean to the family. What hardships and adventures had he endured, and would he be the same kind man who had left for London all those years ago? I was joined by Edith and Elizabeth and whilst the latter, who had never known her uncle but who had heard mention of his supposed plight all her life, was excited at the prospect of his return, Edith cautioned her that they must refrain from such excitements until such time as his identity was confirmed by her father.

The wait at Mulberry House seemed interminable but after ten days, Thomas and Samuel returned, accompanied by their brother John, a haggard, weak and broken man. I shared the family's shock at his appearance but later, having heard something of his experiences in the intervening years, it became clear that he was lucky to have survived at all.

He had been moved to tears to learn that he had a fine son, and that Harriet had never ceased to believe that he was still alive. He pleaded with his brothers to refrain from alerting them to his presence until he had had time to more fully regain some of his former strength.

John's health gradually improved with the careful administrations of Edith and Elizabeth, although he still tired easily and regularly experienced severe headaches. He found intense pleasure in pottering around the lovely garden and sitting and dozing under the mulberry tree in the spring sunshine.

Two to three months after John's miraculous arrival, a letter arrived from Harriet stating that sadly, her father has passed away and that she would be returning home to Rye once the funeral had been held and her father's affairs settled. All was panic in Mulberry House. Should they write to Harriet and advise of John's return, thereby enabling her to prepare her emotions? And what of Matthew? She had made no mention of his return. It was Samuel who made the decision to write to Harriet, offering their condolences at the loss of her father but hoping that the news that her husband had at last been returned to them, would help her recover from her grief. He had also mentioned that John's health had suffered during his exile but that it was had been his desire to return to his beloved wife that had kept him going through all the arduous years. It was his wish that Matthew accompany his mother on her return to Rye, as he was keen to meet his son.

All in all it was to be another month before the family were fully reunited but when at last Harriet and Matthew arrived home, it was to a house full of much joy and celebration. Harriet had thought she might not recognise the man she had so loved but one look at his precious face and loving eyes had been enough, and she was soon enwrapped in his arms. Matthew, on the other hand, had had no such reserve. So confident had he been of his father's continued existence, that he showed no surprise at his return and, to John's overwhelming relief, welcomed him as if he had known him all his life. The celebrations continued for several days whilst the family invited friends and neighbours to join them in welcoming John back home. John and Harriet spent much time privately in their room where John was able to gradually relate his story to his beloved wife. Though keen to hear his history, I did not encroach on their all too precious time together and was therefore delighted when one afternoon, as John sat alone beneath the mulberry tree, he had called out to me. Intrigued, I had sped to his side and, sensing my presence, he had begun to speak.

"Mistress Jenkins, though I cannot see you, I do often sense your presence, and my wife has told me of your long existence in this beautiful house and how much you have supported her and my son during my years away. I have related some of my story to them but do not wish them to learn of the significant privations and torture I was subjected to at the hands of some of my captors. However, I feel the need to record my story in order to help exorcise the memories once and for all. I have therefore drafted my story with the thought that perhaps it might one day be published as a warning to others. I cannot bear the thought of causing further distress to my darling wife should she come across my memoir and would therefore ask that you keep it hidden away – perhaps to be published sometime in the future when it cannot cause hurt to those dearest to me."

I gently squeezed his shoulder and he held out a sheaf of papers towards me. "Feel free to read my history if you so wish, dear lady. I am sure that you will have witnessed much during your time in this place and have garnered many secrets. I trust that you will guard mine as closely."

I took the small bundle of papers and tucked them under my shawl, squeezing his shoulder once again by way of reassurance.

Leaving him enjoying the afternoon sunshine, I sped to my attic and settled to read his story. Though my reading skills were rudimentary, he wrote a fair hand and I was gradually able to discover the awful truth of his ordeal.

It transpired that John had travelled from London with a small group of men and they had been attacked soon after leaving Tonbridge. Two of his travelling companions had been killed but his assailants however, had deemed him and the other remaining travellers to be of some value and had blindfolded and trussed them and taken them to their camp in the forest. John adjudged this camp to be several miles eastwards, towards the Kent coast. Their blindfolds later removed, they had continued to be bound and kept under close guard for several nights as further such captives were added to their group. His captors had kept them surprisingly well fed, the reason for which became apparent when, after about a week they had all been loaded into a covered wagon and taken to the coast where they had been auctioned off to a motley assortment of foreign sea captains, sold as fit and healthy potential mercenaries or galley slaves.

John had been purchased, along with one other prisoner, Ben Ford, formerly a blacksmith from Hawkhurst, and they had been loaded onto a small boat and from that to a larger vessel waiting offshore.

The captain, a Spanish Moor named Amir, who usually traded off the Barbery coast, had a smattering of English and interviewed each of his new acquisitions in order to ascertain their skills and therefore their relevant value.   Ben was a large, strong fellow and he was instantly earmarked as a potential bodyguard for the Ottoman Sultan or a member of his court.   It was made clear to him that as such he would be trained to become a skilled fighter, live in a palace with food and women in abundance and would be a highly prized and powerful member of the household. In order to achieve such a position in a high-status establishment, he would also be required to convert to Islam.   He was warned that failure to convert could mean that he might then be castrated and spend his life protecting the women of the harem, or he could be relegated to the role of a galley slave where the life was extremely hard and the life expectancy short.

During John's interview, Captain Amir had become quite animated when he discovered that John was well educated and a lawyer. He saw great financial gain to be had if he could sell him as a scribe or even perhaps an advisor to the Sultan, although he again stressed that in order to achieve this highly prized role he would have to convert to Islam.

As the two captives continued their journey they discussed the options before them. Neither were happy at the thought of abandoning their Christian faith and the captain, aware of their reticence, arranged to spend a little time with them each day, to teach them the way of the Prophet so that they could make an informed decision when the time came. He had also offered John a separate cabin and the opportunity to eat at his table if he would help him improve his English. John, hopeful that he would be less closely watched and so better able to make his escape, had been happy to oblige Captain Amir. Thus, John's time aboard Captain Amir's ship had been far less arduous than that of the other prisoners. Shackled together and living in their own filth, John was sad to learn that several poor souls had died before the ship had even entered the Mediterranean sea.

Once they entered the Mediterranean a great storm had driven them off course and, needing to organise some repairs to the ship, the captain had decided to abandon his plan to sail to the Ottoman capital, Constantinople, and they had docked instead at the city of Tunis. The captives were quickly unloaded and taken to the great slave market.   John, after several weeks of a good diet and plenty of rest, had looked to be in a better physical state than his companions and, despite Captain Amir's insistence that he was an educated man, he had been purchased by an Egyptian merchant, taken aboard his ship and shackled to the oars, where he had remained for nearly four years. During those years he had worked and slept in his own excrement, had been fed only once a day on a thin tasteless gruel and stale biscuits, and had sustained many beatings and occasional sexual abuse from their captors. Only released from their posts for about 15 minutes a day, when they could stretch their legs and walk up on deck, the galley slaves knew little about where they were. Indeed, some even began to forget who or what they had been prior to their capture. Their only thoughts each day were how to avoid a beating from the vicious oars master and the direction of the wind, which eddied around them and helped to clear the miasma that filled the space below deck and thus made their environment slightly less unbearable.

After nearly four years at the oars, they were offered a brief respite when their boat docked at Alexandria and their Egyptian owner had the galley slaves taken to his estate in the country to help bring in the harvest. John, ever the alert student, had learnt a few Arabic words and phrases and had managed to attract the attention of the estate manager who, like Captain Amir before him, recognised the value in having such an educated slave. John was therefore taken from the steaming, smelly shed in which the galley slaves had been housed, into the master's clean and freshly scented palace where he was bathed and given clean clothes. It had been made clear to him that if he valued his life, or indeed his manhood, he should be honest and true to his master and would be permitted to serve as a clerk and teacher of English.

He had performed his duties diligently for many years and had been rewarded for his obedience, meticulous record keeping and sound legal advice, by being appointed as his master's chief adviser. He had his own sumptuous quarters, complete with servants, and the freedom of the house however, whilst returning to his private quarters one afternoon, his attention had been taken by the sound of music and laughter coming from the gardens at the centre of the palace. He had become entranced by the music and had followed the sound until he came to a pierced screen through which he was enamoured to see several young women playing in fountains. He instantly realised his folly and turned to retrace his steps when he was confronted by one of the eunuchs who guarded the master's harem, for that was what lay behind the screens, and marched at spearpoint to the master's suite. Despite his protestations that he had only stopped to listen to the music but had not looked through the screens, John had been unceremoniously taken to a dank cell and the next day had been ritually castrated.

I was shocked to read of this barbaric treatment, but on reading further, it appeared that John believed that this act had been the first step in his pathway home. No longer trusted by his master, once healed, he had been taken to Alexandria and sold to an Italian spice and silk merchant who, on learning of his background, treated him with respect. Though still not a freeman, he lived in relative comfort and accompanied his master around some of the great cities in Europe, marvelling at the marvellous architecture, colours, people and facilities that he witnessed. A previous student of the classics he was captivated by the wonders of ancient Rome and was intrigued at the engineering feat that enabled the spectacular city of Venice to rise above its lagoon.

Over the years he succeeded in establishing his master's trust to the extent that he was occasionally despatched to negotiate deals on his behalf. On one such occasion, when in Amsterdam, he had seized the opportunity to sound out some of the protestant merchants with regard their willingness to help him. His master's guards, having little English, watched as, having negotiated a good deal for his master, John related his own story to a particularly affable merchant who agreed to aid him. As soon as things were set in place, the merchant sent an urgent message requesting John's presence and, after arranging for a street gang to set on him and his guards, John was bustled aboard a small vessel that was bound for

England.   After a turbulent crossing deep in the hold of the rather squalid craft, John had arrived, free but penniless, on the northern coast of Kent. He had intended to walk to Rye but had collapsed with exhaustion and a fever a few miles from Canterbury. A passing carter had taken pity on him and taken him to the cathedral infirmary from whence he had eventually recovered enough to write to his brother and ask for help.

I was aghast as John's story but pleased to note that he, having written his memoir and passed it to me for safekeeping, seemed to have achieved greater equilibrium and appeared ready to move on with a new chapter in his life. He had apparently told Harriet that he had confided in me and she in turn, having also noticed an improvement in his demeanour, thanked me for my support. Indeed, the whole family noted the changes in him and welcomed the sense of peace that had at last come over their beloved John.

Matthew

On Harriet's return to Rye following her father's death, she and Matthew had had much news to impart but that had been rather overshadowed by the return of her husband. As John's health and strength improved and he began to talk optimistically about their future together, she was pleased to advise that her father's death had resulted in her becoming a very wealthy woman. Matthew too had been left sufficient means to enable him to live as a gentleman.

The family were delighted at the news, although I was perhaps alone in realising that their newfound wealth would likely mean their departure from Mulberry House. During their months in London, both Harriet and Matthew had become enamoured of the lifestyle and opportunities that the great city could offer. Harriet had suggested that she and John take a small house near to the Inns of Court and, if he so wished, John could resume his career in the law. Alternatively, they could take a small house on the periphery of the city and live a simple life just enjoying their time together.

Matthew too was keen to return to London where he had earlier become enamoured of the theatre, spending many evenings enjoying the plays of Messrs Dryden and Congreve. He most admired the work of the much acclaimed playwright Mrs Aphra Behn and had been welcomed into her intellectual circle. With much enthusiasm he acted out some of the plays to me and I could sense his desire to return to London as soon as possible where he stated he wished to live and write, both poetry and plays, perhaps even a novel. I could barely comprehend such a world, having only ever witnessed the occasional visits of groups of mummers who had visited Rye and performed their tableaux in the market square on religious feast days, and such reading as I was now able to do was mostly restricted to religious tracts and prayers. However, I was not surprised at his fervour as he had always been a bright and sensitive child, with a vivid imagination, and I was sure that he would be successful in whatever direction his enthusiasms took him.

So it was decided that John, Harriet and Matthew would take a house south of the river, near Greenwich palace, where they could enjoy the proximity of London and Matthew, but still live in relative quiet. I was sad to lose them but felt that John was never likely to regain his full strength and, given the years they had already lost, could not begrudge him quietly and comfortably spending whatever time he had left with Harriet and their son.

Prudently, before leaving for London and after much discussion between the three Bacon brothers, John drew up the necessary paperwork to ensure that Mulberry House and the printing business were gifted to Matthew, as the sole male heir, with the proviso that Samuel, Thomas, Edith, Elizabeth and their descendants could reside in the house for as long as they required to do so. Only then did John feel able to transfer to London. He had explained to Harriet that he was enormously proud of his son but recognised that Matthew's dream for success amongst the literary elite of London could come to naught and he wished to ensure that he would always have a home in Rye.

Elizabeth had grown into a fine and kind young woman and married a distant cousin of a wealthy and powerful Rye family, the Lambs. Her William however, despite his wealthy relatives, was a poor clergyman and they lived in a meagre little cottage near his church in Playden, with barely enough income to survive. He and Elizabeth were nevertheless incredibly happy, and she made an excellent parson's wife.

Sadly, when a bout of the pox hit Rye, William, never one for keeping his distance from his poorer and needier parishioners, succumbed to the dreadful disease, leaving Elizabeth and three daughters without any means of support. They were welcomed back into Mulberry House and, when her father died suddenly and unexpectedly, were well placed to care for Edith and Uncle Samuel. I was delighted at the influx of new family members into my house but was again disappointed that none paid me any heed.

Edith, determined to continue her father's business and maintain an income to support her family, decided to take on the running of the business herself. After all, she had spent many years watching her father in his print shop at the top of the garden, and she also had a good head for figures.

Unfortunately, she encountered much hostility from the other master printers of the town and quickly realised that she would need to employ a man as 'official' manager of the business if it were to survive. Uncle Samuel recommended one of his former pupils, one Charles Fletcher, as a likely candidate. Charles had worked as an apprentice under her father for several years before moving to Tenterden where he had opened up his own printshop. However, Charles, now a widower, had left his Tenterden business in the capable hands of his eldest son and had returned to Rye to enjoy his retirement. He was only too happy to oblige Edith and be the 'front' man for her printshop.

As with many small communities, gossip soon began to circulate about Charles' role in Mulberry House and it was agreed that he and Elizabeth would marry, to set the wagging tongues at rest. Theirs was a companionable union, born out of propriety but nevertheless a marriage that suited them both. Under Charles' guidance, Edith proved to be a shrewd businesswoman, and their combined input enabled them to expand their clientele much further afield. They even took on the publishing of small runs of works of poetry and literature on behalf of Matthew and some of his friends in London.

With Elizabeth's three daughters married to suitable husbands and gone to their own households, those at Mulberry House enjoyed a period of harmony and peace, albeit perhaps a bit too peaceful for me. Without any young people about to fill the days with their chatter and liveliness, the days and months seem to pass even more slowly. One by one the elderly Bacons passed away and Elizabeth and Charles lived ever more quietly and simply. The printing business continued to thrive, albeit now under the care of Charles' youngest son Francis who had joined his father and stepmother in Mulberry House.

With no direct connection with any of my residents, I again began to feel despondent of ever being able to fulfil my pledge to God and then Matthew returned and suddenly my entire world was once again turned upside down.

Matthew, now a mature man in his thirties, had lost none of his charm and good looks but arrived at his family home on the run from creditors and the wrath of the father of his young and pretty wife, Charlotte, known as Lottie.   With only minimal shame, he explained to me that life as an aspiring poet and playwright had not been easy for him and he had quickly squandered his grandfather's legacy. Several poor investments in theatre ventures had resulted him in becoming a mere copyist for some of his more successful acquaintances and occasionally playing small parts in their plays. Even the sad deaths of his parents and the proceeds from the sale of their pretty house in Greenwich, had done little to stave off his complete destitution as he admitted to have done little to alter his lifestyle, and had come to rely heavily on the regular amounts he had received from the Rye print shop.

He had hoped that marriage to Lottie, with whom he was completely besotted, would have resulted in some financial support from her father. Unfortunately, Master Bagley, Lottie's father, had not been impressed at his daughter's choice of husband and he had adamantly refused to give his blessing on their union. In fact, he had removed Lottie from their London home and sent her to a distant cousin's home in Suffolk, in the hope that she would come to forget her infatuation for the unsuitable Matthew Bacon. He had not allowed for Matthew's desperation, determination, and ability to charm however, and he had soon discovered Lottie's whereabouts and, ever the romantic, had given chase. Once he had found her it had proved easy to persuade her cousin of his honourable intent toward Lottie and they had quietly slipped away one morning and had been married quickly and privately at the first opportunity. Only then had the enormity of his actions dawned on him. Not only was he on the run from his creditors but he now had a young and inexperienced wife to support and had likely destroyed any chance of reconciliation with her father by his rash behaviour.

Without sufficient funds, their journey to Rye had been slow and exhausting. They had arrived with little more than the clothes they stood up in, having sold off anything of value to pay for only the basest of meals and accommodation when they could.

I was so pleased that my special boy was home again, despite the circumstances, and Elizabeth, who had always worshipped her fine, strapping cousin, welcomed them home warmly and genuinely. Lottie, a sweet-natured young girl was also made welcome, although I admit to feeling a little jealous of the attention and love she received from her besotted husband. It transpired that the poor girl had lost her mother when she was very young and had been a very indulged and spoilt child, doted on and waited on hand and foot by her father and his staff but she could not fail to appreciate that her role in her new home was going to be different. With Elizabeth's encouragement she endeavoured to take on some of the simpler duties within the house and her obvious efforts endeared her to them all. She proved to be a skilled needlewoman and Elizabeth was delighted to let her attend to any such mending or renewals as proved necessary. Matthew, on the other hand, apart from when he was with Lottie, seemed immersed in melancholy and became somewhat uncommunicative, even with me, to whom he complained all the while of how unfairly life had treated him. Since Charles' demise a few months earlier, Elizabeth had been concerned that Francis might struggle to manage the print shop without his father's input, particularly with the bookkeeping, and she had suggested that Matthew, who had shown an aptitude for figures when he was a boy, could work alongside Francis in the print shop. However, Matthew showed no such inclination, even though he was happy to continue to take his share of the income which he tended to spend across the street at the nearby Mermaid Inn, where he was thought to be a fine raconteur and wit, with his tales of London life.

He continued to write somewhat mediocre poetry and novellas based on his experiences in London, and when Francis was persuaded to print a short run of his latest collection, Matthew became somewhat of a local celebrity. He was thus sought out by one of Elizabeth's Lamb in-laws, as a poetry tutor for his daughters. Other similar positions followed, and his self-esteem was, in-part, restored. I continued to be concerned by his regular sojourns to the Mermaid Inn however, and, when the opportunity arose, challenged him on his thoughtlessness.

"Oh Nell, you are become quite a shrew!" he had exclaimed. "Can a man not have a break from domesticity now and then?"

I had looked sceptically at him. "And you not yet married a year." I had paused.

"What of poor Lottie? Has she not had enough to contend with having been torn from her loving father's house and dragged half across the country like a common thief in the night? Your poor mother would be ashamed of the man who stands before me now."

With as much dignity as I could muster, I left Matthew standing agog, and subsequently, on the rare occasions that he was at home and despite much personal anguish, I contrived to avoid his company for many a week after our encounter, a situation that sadly he seemed to prefer.

Matthew, as if to somehow prove his point, spent yet more hours in the Mermaid Inn and poor Lottie was often alone. She would not, however, hear a word of criticism of her darling Matthew and steadfastly supported his endeavours to establish himself locally as a man of letters and learning.

Over the ensuing months, as the seventeenth century finally ended, and with relations still strained between Matthew and I, I started to notice the appearance of some intricate lace trimming the neck and cuffs of Lottie's otherwise plain dresses. This was of a quality far and above anything that was available locally and I wondered at its origin. Surely, had they had been in possession of such fine work whilst they had made their way to Rye, Matthew would have readily sold it off in order to fund their journey, so, where had the dainty lace come from? Luckily I was not alone in my observations and Elizabeth too noticed the new additions and had bluntly asked Lottie where the fine decorative pieces had come from.

"Why from my darling husband, of course." Lottie had responded with surprise. "Think you that I would accept such fine a gift from any other?" She had smiled dreamily, "Matthew is the most generous of husbands."

Elizabeth's concerns were not allayed by Lottie's response, which had raised more questions than they had answered. Where was her profligate cousin getting the money to purchase such expensive fripperies for his wife? Tutoring around the town was unlikely to result in such a surplus of funds and, if money was suddenly in abundance, why was Matthew not making more of a contribution to the running of what was, after all, his household? I shared Elizabeth's concerns and determined to resume my former close relationship with my erstwhile golden boy, if he would let me, and establish just how he was obtaining the precious lace for dear Lottie.

I did not have to try very hard to make direct contact with Matthew who, for the first time in a very long while, seemed to actively seek me out himself. He cornered me on the upstairs landing and asked that I accompany him into the garden. I was happy to oblige, and we were soon ensconced on the bench under the luxurious spread of the mulberry tree. I looked up at the tree with pride, the luscious fruit was just beginning to ripen, and it looked to be another bumper crop this year.

"Well, Master Matthew," I enquired, "Do you have need of me?"

"Oh Nell, let us be friends again," he begged, "I regret any of the actions that have lessened your esteem of me but please, let us put all that unpleasantness to one side and become allies once more."

Whilst he tried to maintain a sombre expression, I could nevertheless see a twinkle in his eyes. What was he up to now? I nodded that he should continue, and he leant towards me as if to share a huge secret.

"She is not even aware of it herself," he began, "but my darling Lottie is with child. I entreat you to advise me of anything I can do to help her through this time." He sat back beaming, "I am to be a father and as such, I have been making contacts amongst other like-minded businessmen and we have set in motion a plan that should enable us all to live well and comfortably. The little bits of lace and other fripperies you may have noticed are just a small taste of what is to come should my plan come to fruition."

If I had still had a heart to beat, it would have surely been thrown into an erratic rhythm by his words. On the one hand I was delighted to hear of Lottie's condition – remembering only too well how sensitive Matthew had been during Edith's pregnancy and how he had had appeared to communicate with the as yet unborn Elizabeth – but equally, I was concerned at Matthew's new venture. On his disgruntled return from London, he had related stories of having been mercilessly tricked by unscrupulous associates into investing in their seemingly plausible schemes. Not once did he appear to have considered that he should have perhaps been more circumspect in his business dealings. Now he appeared to be considering a similar scheme that he believed would bring him a good return for the minimum amount of work. I was less than convinced.

I squared up to him and said gently, "I am delighted with the news of the babe – of course I will do all I can to assist Lottie to a successful outcome."

He began to interrupt but I held up my hand,

"However," I continued quickly lest he try to interrupt, "I am concerned about this new scheme of yours. Your head was ever in the clouds but now you will have responsibilities. Why can you not face the reality that you must procure a steady income, at whatever cost to your dreams of fame and fortune, in order to support your precious wife and child."

Matthew looked crestfallen. "I know you have been disappointed in me Nell and I appreciate that I did not make the most of the good fortune that had come to me in the past. However, please be assured that this time it will be different. Given the geography of our little town, great opportunities for trade are opening up as never before. However, due to the onerous taxes levied upon such trade, seen as excessive by both rich and poor alike, there is a growing market for goods that bypass these legitimate merchants and I intend to take advantage of this secret trading. Nell, I am to join forces with a band of Owlers."

"Have you lost your senses Boy!" I screeched. "I never took you for a half-wit but now, with your darling wife about to produce your heir, you are concocting some hairbrained scheme that could put you and all your family, not to mention this house and all its residents, in danger." I faltered slightly and lowered my voice a little as I snarled, "I should have thought your moonlit flit from London would have taught you to be more careful in your career choices, but it would seem not. I thank God your poor dear parents are not here to witness your further recklessness."

Matthew quickly crossed to my side and knelt before me.

"Fear not my dear friend," he pleaded, "Be assured, I have done nothing wrong and do not plan to put myself or any of my family at risk."

I shook my head sadly. "Oh but Matthew," I admonished, "what have you got yourself into now? The Owlers have become notorious for their smuggling activities over the years. They ruthlessly control the nearby Romney Marshes and I cannot see that they would have a need for an impoverished poet, actor or part-time tutor."

Matthew refused to be affronted by my comments and remained by my side.

"Please have faith my dear," he implored. "Forgive the dramatic edge to my announcement. The excitement of the scheme is quite overwhelming but I assure you I intend to do no wrong. I will be taking on one of the most challenging but potentially rewarding roles of my entire life. One that I feel I have been destined to take on since my poor dear father was abducted all those years ago."

He paused and coughed slightly. "You are the only one to whom I will tell the complete tale and for that I need some refreshment. It becomes chilly here in the garden, let me fetch a glass of ale and some bread and then we can find a warm corner indoors so that I may tell you the full story. Then, I promise, you will feel differently about me."

Once we were settled in the front parlour and Matthew had refreshed the fire and settled with a jug of ale and some bread, he began his tale.

"You may recall my young friend William Carter from my school days, son of a clothier turned smuggler catcher, also named William. Unfortunately, my friend William faced much ridicule amongst the other boys for the very public stance his father took against those who flouted the export and import laws but whose actions showed little overall success in catching any of the perpetrators. His poor father continues this fight, albeit without much support or assistance from the town or wider fiscal authorities. By chance I encountered young William the other day and we shared a companionable jug of beer at the Red Lion Inn. William joined the riding officers who help patrol the Romney Marshes under the leadership of the surveyor general, Henry Baker, and they had achieved a level of success in curtailing the activities of the Owlers. However, since the surveyor general has moved on to other duties, the Owlers are once again taking control of the marshes.

William despairs of ever being able to live up to his father's noble ideals and rid the area of the evil smugglers once and for all.

I was moved by his tale and knowing of my own family's calamity at the hands of nefarious smugglers, agreed to meet with William again, when we hoped to be able to contrive a plan to help tip the balance in favour of the customs and revenue officers.

An inkling of a plan soon manifest itself in my head and when William and I again met up at the Red Lion, I gave a broad outline of the scheme.

My plan was that I should set myself up as a legitimate merchant, dealing in the export of wool, cloth and other goods and the import of wine, brandy, tobacco and any other fine goods that my clients might request. To this end I intended to purchase a vessel that would be captained by another of our old school friends, George Clarke, lately retired from the Royal Navy. Our transactions would be wholly transparent and legitimate, with appropriate taxes paid. George would be in charge of the logistics relating to our ship's movements whilst I would concentrate on establishing trading partners across the channel and finding customers for our luxury goods, both locally and amongst my former associates in London.

Having established my business, with its totally legal status, I intend to continue my regular sojourns to the Mermaid Inn, where many of the Owlers bands meet secretly to discuss their nefarious activities, and would quietly let it be known that, providing I was appropriately recompensed, I was not averse to transporting goods on their behalf, providing the goods be off loaded before my vessel approached Rye. My vessel could thence be inspected on its arrival at Rye, with only my own dutiable goods aboard. I will pass on the details of the Owlers loading and off-loading of cargo to William who will co-ordinate their sporadic interception accordingly. Our Owler partners will understand the need for the Revenue men to have occasional successful encounters with the smugglers lest they become suspicious that they are being hoodwinked but these successes will be carefully stage managed by William to minimise Owlers' losses and not put our mutually successful collaboration at risk.

William was excited at my plan and, once George had been brought onside, we drew up an agreement outlining our individual roles in the scheme. William also procured letters from an officer at the Customs House confirming that George and I were both acting as agents for the Crown.

Now Nell, can you see, there will be negligible risk to myself or my family. Please take that disapproving look from your face and offer me a smile. Be content that I am last taking a positive step in providing for my wife and child."

I feared for the answer but could not refrain from asking, "And how will you come by the funds to purchase your fine vessel, Matthew?"

At this, Matthew did take his eyes from her face. "I have arranged to sell my one and only asset," he said simply and quietly, "my beautiful home."

I gasped a sad "Oh my dear no."

Matthew quickly continued, "Ye need not be concerned Nell for it is cousin Francis who has agreed to purchase the house and printing shop from me, on the understanding that my family and any of my descendants that may wish to do so, can continue to reside here. He is actually incredibly supportive of my new venture, albeit he is only aware of the legitimate side of the business, and I have promised to source high quality inks and paper for him if I can."

Surprisingly, I felt relieved at his answer. I had actually feared that he had taken out a loan for the purchase of the boat, with the house and printing business used for collateral. The fact that Francis had freely purchased the property did at least ensure that my dear house would be safe from the bailiffs should Matthew's scheme fail.

Over the ensuing months Matthew's demeanour and behaviour towards his family improved immeasurably and all were excited at his new venture. The news of Lottie's pregnancy also delighted everybody and although Matthew was often away making contacts with merchants in France and Holland, he always managed to bring his lovely wife a small trinket or some such for the baby.

Ever watchful of Lottie's health, I was delighted to witness her bloom and settle naturally into her new role. Matthew, also acutely aware of the development of his child, was delighted to advise me that Lottie was carrying a fine, healthy son, and sure enough, Adam John Bacon was safely delivered three months later. Matthew could not have been happier.

Business appeared to be flourishing and Matthew, who had established himself as a successful procurer of the finest goods, began to gain the reputation as one who could obtain the most scarce or bizarre items – albeit at a price. His fleet quickly increased to four vessels that regularly crisscrossed the English Channel, although it was only Captain Clarke's vessel that carried the contraband. William co-ordinated apparently random raids around the coast, some of which proved successful in intercepting the Owlers as they landed their goods, and he soon gained a reputation as having a good nose for hunting out the Owlers.

By the time little Adam was three years old he had been joined by a sister Judith, and a brother William, named after Lottie's father with whom she had recently become reconciled. Master Bagley had been surprised but delighted with his son-in-law's unexpected business acumen, although he of course, remained ignorant of the extra-curricular activities involving the Owlers, and was happy to be reunited with his daughter and her young family. He had also insisted on helping Matthew to establish a wide range of customers in the growing capital. Thus, the first decades of the new century had proved a good one for all those who resided in Mulberry House. The death of Queen Anne and the birth of the new Hanoverian dynasty opened up new avenues for trade and it was a busy and prosperous time for Matthew and his colleagues.

Only one member of the household seemed to decline during this period of prosperity and I advised Matthew of my concerns about poor Elizabeth. She appeared unable to perform many of her erstwhile duties and seemed a mere shell of her former robust self. Matthew, who had ever been aware of her health, even before her birth, confirmed that he too had sensed a rapid deterioration in her wellbeing. I suggested a few herbal remedies that could help Elizabeth regain some strength, although I feared that Elizabeth's condition was likely one that simple remedies could not address. Matthew nevertheless agreed to recommend the treatments to her.   Sadly, Elizabeth continued to decline, despite all Matthew and Lottie's attempts to bolster her health, and she passed away as quietly as she had lived.

Elizabeth's death hit Matthew hardest of them all. Being three years her senior he began to feel the strain of his age and divulged to Nell that the fine balancing act that he maintained between the legal and the illegal sides of his enterprise was taking its toll on him. He disclosed to Nell how much he feared that he had run his luck over the years and his dual role would ultimately be uncovered. Now in his mid- forties, the sense of adventure that had driven him over the years was now being supplanted by a desire to retire and spend more time with his family and enjoy the comfortable life he had earned for them all. William, who was about to retire from the Revenue service, and George were also feeling the strain of the years and shared his opinion that it was now perhaps time to sit back and enjoy the fruits of their labours.

"All in all, my dear Nell, you who are ageless are blessed that you no longer have to experience the burden of time and how it weighs heavily on those of us who inhabit frail mortal bodies."

He sighed heavily, "Why, only last week I thought all was lost when the ship on which I was returning from France, full to the gunwales with our usual mixed cargo, was boarded out in the Channel by the Revenue men. Not our William, I hasten to add, but one of the new young men of the Customs service out of Folkestone, on one of the new faster vessels. My heart was in my mouth, I can tell you, when he asked to see the manifests and inspect our cargo. He seemed impressed by the letter our dear William had had the foresight to organise all those years ago, naming me as an Agent of the Crown, and I also blessed dear George's meticulous record keeping as our books clearly showed the appropriate duties paid on all our imports over the many trips our ship had undertaken. Actually, I do not think the poor man could understand a single entry in the books and was somewhat overwhelmed at the abundance of information shown. Having initially expressed the intent to examine every inch of the ship, he only descended into the main hold where he seemingly half-heartedly compared one or two items with the manifest and declared himself satisfied that all was well. Once they had left the ship, we had not felt it safe to continue our rendezvous with the Owlers and had been forced to bring the entire cargo ashore here in Rye. The Owlers' portion of the cargo is currently stored in one of my warehouses and I am on tenterhooks lest it be identified as contraband. I am afraid that now I have been forced to bring their cargo directly to town, they may insist that we do so on a regular basis and this will likely make our involvement with them more evident."

Matthew rose and fetched himself a jug of ale from the Kitchen.   On his return he sat down stiffly, He refilled his tankard, filled his last pipe of the night and sighed once again,

"Oh Nell, how are we to extricate ourselves from our association with the Owlers?"

I pondered the situation. "You must accept that I am an uneducated old woman who may not understand the intricacies of your business world. However, would I be right in supposing that your legitimate business would not have survived long without the side income received from the Owlers and, without William in the Revenue office, you will lose any degree of protection he has been able to offer?" Matthew nodded his confirmation.

"Therefore, continuing your legitimate business but breaking your ties with the Owlers would appear not to be an option if the family is to continue to enjoy a comfortable life. Furthermore, taking into consideration all the new steps you report being encouraged by the Crown for the better policing of the coasts against the smugglers, the Romney marshes and other parts of Sussex and Kent are likely to become more dangerous for your Owler allies and potentially less profitable for your company?" Matthew nodded once more.

"Much as you enjoy the status and wealth that your venture has allowed you, I am sure you do not wish to subject your children to a less secure existence in the future?"   Not waiting for his assent I continued, "I think the answer to your predicament is clear my dear boy. You and George must be seen to withdraw from the business completely. Your own dear children are too young to take on the mantle and you must therefore sell the business, lock, stock and barrel. The income you receive from the sale of your vessels etc., should enable your families to live very comfortably for a goodly while and your children would have the resources available, when the time comes, for them to establish themselves in whatever career they so choose. Only by making a clean break from the business are you likely to enjoy the peace of mind to facilitate a reasonable retirement."

I paused for a while to let my words sink in. Matthew sat quietly nodding.

"The question will be, however, to whom can you sell your business without incriminating yourselves?" I continued. "Close scrutiny of your records will no doubt highlight the extra income you have enjoyed, although perhaps not its source, but I suggest that it would not be too big a leap of faith to come to the correct conclusion. I would therefore suggest that you need to sell to someone who has almost as much to lose as yourselves."

I sat still as stone, letting my suggestion hang in the air between us.

Matthew suddenly jumped up as if he had been sitting on a hornets' nest.

"Of course. You are most astute Mistress Nell. I will make known my intent to sell my business amongst my Owler associates. I will put it to them that they are best placed to avail themselves of my business, at the right price of course, and that having a legitimate front to their activities might keep them one step ahead of the Revenue men. I am sure George and William will be delighted with this plan. Thank you, thank you my dearest friend."

He bowed deeply to me as he swept from the room, bidding me a hasty goodnight.

Matthew wasted no time in outlining his plan with his colleagues, George and William who agreed readily that it was a sound move. Thus, within a very few short months the deal was struck and Walter Tart, the youngest son of Benjamin Tart, a successful fisherman from Lydd, took possession of Bacon and Clarke, Purveyors of fine Goods and Chattels.

The eighteenth century

Walter

Matthew's and George's choice of successor raised a few eyebrows around the townsfolk, many of whom suspected that the Tarts were one of the major Owler families that operated across the marshes, although there had never been any proof of wrongdoing by them. Benjamin Tart however, despite naming his youngest son after Queen Elizabeth's favourite privateer Sir Walter Raleigh, ran a tight ship, enjoying a fierce loyalty from those he employed, and had intentionally kept young Walter completely ignorant of the illicit side of the family business determined that at least one of his sons would live as a gentleman.

Instead of following his brothers into the family fishing fleet, Walter had been sent away to the King's school in Canterbury where he had received an education to rival that of any higher born boy. Over and above the academic learning however, Walter's most enduring lesson learned at King's was that anyone with ambition and a little money, can achieve remarkable things. Despite regular beatings by some of his fellow scholars, Walter established himself as strong, both physically and mentally, determined and yet fair-minded and kind.

After taking Walter to meet his contacts, both at home and abroad, all of whom seemed happy to continue dealing with the company and had been impressed at Walter's enthusiasm and plans for the future, Matthew invited the young man to a celebratory dinner at Mulberry House.

At this point in my tale I must advise that I was truly smitten when I first encountered the young man that was to play an enormous part in the next decades within my house. With his glossy black hair and dark eyes, he was every bit the pirate king I had imagined, based on the tales told by my dear departed husband, Arthur. Though I had become very fond of many of my former residents, when the young Walter Tart turned directly towards me and made a small bow he fair stole my heart.

Over dinner Walter expressed his disappointment that Mulberry House had not been included in the sale of the business. Conveniently positioned close to the port and with adequate storage space for the company cargo, it was a fine house and Walter wished to enjoy a similar status as the ownership of such a house had bestowed on Matthew.

Matthew explained that the property was in fact owned by his cousin's stepson, Francis Fletcher who ran a successful printing business from the premises to the rear of the site. Francis, whilst officially ignorant of Matthew's dealings with the Owlers, had often had his doubts about some of the less salubrious visitors to Mulberry House, particularly those who visited at night, and, having also heard the rumours regarding the activities of the Tart family, was not surprised when he was introduced to Walter as the new owner of the merchant enterprise.

Francis listened carefully to Walter's plans for the business, and his intent to reside locally so as to maintain the status and link to the business already so well established by Matthew. He made a generous offer for the property, even suggesting that Francis could continue to operate the printing business from the current premises at the rear of the garden, should he so wish.   He pledged that if the latter were acceptable to him, Walter would ensure that the printing of all his business documents, official documents, labels and manifests etc, would of course be offered to Francis' printing works in the first instance.

Francis was not sure that he even wanted to sell the house of which he had become very fond, particularly in light of the rumours regarding the Tart family's illegal activities.   He suggested that, like his stepmother's distant relatives, the Lambs, one of the leading families in the town, Walter might take advantage of the town's current building boom and consider building himself a new and more substantial town house in the vicinity of the church which was fast becoming *the* place to reside.

Walter had looked Francis square in the eye at that suggestion.

"Think you that the Lambs and their ilk would be happy to reside cheek by jowl to the likes of me?" he asked frankly. "My family have made the step of purchasing your cousin's successful business as a means of showing this town that we are rising above our humble beginnings. However, we are not so arrogant as to think that our presence right under the noses of those in authority would go unchallenged. Having taken on his business, the ownership of this lovely house, long associated with Master Bacon and his family, close but not too close to the grand family homes near the church, would seem the best means of establishing ourselves as the simple, honest businessmen we are."

Francis, seeing no guile in Walter's demeanour, respected Walter's awareness of the need to tread carefully if he were to achieve the desired social acceptance, and looked to Matthew for guidance.

Matthew, ever mindful that Francis had come to his aid when he needed money to commence his business, was somewhat surprised at Francis' intransigence regarding the house which, when all was said and done, had been Matthew's family home for generations and Francis had only fairly recently come to the house by virtue of his father's marriage to Elizabeth.

"This is a big decision Francis," he admitted, "I had not realised how much you had come to love the house, given your relatively short residency here. I, who was born here and whose family have enjoyed living here for several generations, would also miss the old place but can also see the logic from Walter's point of view. Perhaps Walter will give you some time to consider things?"

Walter nodded at this suggestion and had later left Mulberry House confident that Francis would accept his generous offer.

I was torn. On the one hand, I was extremely fond of Matthew and his family and would be happy to share their remaining years in my lovely house. However, that Walter was obviously able to see me promised a new era of opportunity for me. He was young and as yet unmarried, and if he were to take on Mulberry

House, perhaps his future family would offer me the chance for redemption at last.

As was so often the case, the fates intervened, and a decision was quickly made. Lottie's father, who had died a few years earlier, had left the bulk of his estate to his daughter and her two sons, Adam and William. The estate had been complex and comprised not only shares in several businesses, including banks and the rapidly growing Lloyds insurance company, but also several properties and large parcels of land on the periphery of the ever-expanding city of London that brought the estate a substantial rental income. Lawyer's acting on Lottie's behalf to assess and assimilate all the various business ventures, had written to suggest that she and Matthew visit their chambers to discuss the intricate details of her father's estate. After only a few weeks in London Lottie and Matthew came to realise the full extent of their newfound wealth and it became clear that it would require full time management. They returned to Rye and discussed the situation with Francis, explaining that they thought it best that they and the boys relocate to London to enable Adam and William to complete their education more appropriately and, more importantly, prior to their ultimate inheritance, learn how to manage what was obviously a vast business empire.

Francis saw the sense in the move and in no time at all, the Bacons had packed up their personal belongings and set off for London. I was quite bereft; how would I cope without Matthews friendship and immense enthusiasm for life.

Life in Mulberry House became rather dull with only Francis to accommodate. Fortunately he, although happy at the Bacon's immense good fortune, missed them dreadfully and recognised that Mulberry House was far too large a premises for him alone. The lovely old place warranted and deserved the presence of a large family to keep it alive. Thus, he contacted Walter and agreed to accept his offer for the property, albeit with the exception of the printing works which he intended to retain, and he made arrangements to build a modest house at the end of Watchbell street only yards from the print shop.

Despite the potential loss of the storage facilitated at the printing works, Walter was glad of the arrangement and, on completion of Francis' new home a few months later, was delighted to become the new owner of Mulberry House.

Walter initially employed only a cook/housekeeper and a gardener as his needs were simple and he travelled regularly as he sought new suppliers and customers. However, he took no time in filling the house with the finest furniture and accoutrements that money could buy, mindful of one day marrying and making this house a family home once more.

The most fascinating of his purchases, to me at least, was a beautiful long-case oak clock that stood majestically in the hall. It had the most comforting tick by which all in the household performed their duties. Indeed, it was almost as if the old house had attained a heart, the beating of which was audible to all. The mellow chiming on the hour was as comforting as it was melodic, reassuring to all that time was steadily passing and all was well.

On the rare occasions he was at home he very much enjoyed sitting with me and listening to my tales of the previous occupants of our house. He also outlined his plans for his life and his business, including the engagement of a tutor to help him improve on the basic French and Spanish he had learned at King's and to teach him the German tongue. With the accession of the Hanoverian King George, there had been an upsurge in demand for all things Germanic that he felt had yet to be fully exploited.

Sadly for me, his determination to build on the existing business meant that he was often away from home for weeks at a time and I was often lonely.   In Walter's absences and in order to pass the time, I often visited the printing works at the top of the garden to watch Francis at work. He had taken on an apprentice,   Richard Lamb, one of Elizabeth's grandsons, who, despite being a distant cousin of the affluent and influential Lambs whose impressive new home was nearing completion close to the church, lived with his widowed mother and sister in a tiny cottage on the poorer side of the churchyard. Despite being a mere clerk in his illustrious relative's household, Richard's late father had recognised an aptitude for learning in his son and had scrimped and saved in order that his son could attend the local grammar school. Francis was impressed at Richard's obvious academic prowess and had been delighted to offer him an apprenticeship. Richard proved to be a quick learner and, as a slight young man, with small, nimble fingers, mastered the art of type setting very quickly and easily. Francis was delighted with him and with his sister Sarah too, a kind and gentle girl who brought a hot meal to the print works each day for them both and who also performed any domestic duties Francis required at home.

Having inadvertently encountered Sarah on one of her daily visits to the print shop with the midday meal, I thereafter, made a point of visiting the print works around the same time, having taken an instant liking to the young lady who reminded me very much of Elizabeth when she had been young. I was convinced that Sarah could see me as she often seemed to sneak a glance in my direction when she thought nobody was watching her, however, there was never an opportunity to speak to her. After several months of watching her and witnessing her care and kindness towards Francis, the germ of a plan appeared to me. Sarah, with her albeit distant relationship with the great Lamb family, would be an ideal wife for Walter. She was no doubt a lovely looking girl, a good housekeeper and a kindly soul, but the inextricable link to the Lambs could prove enormously beneficial to Walter. As the idea blossomed further, I could hardly wait to contrive a meeting between the two.

Once again, the old house intervened to assist me and one morning, after Walter and I had spent an all too rare hour chatting in the garden, Walter went to return indoors to prepare for a meeting with a potential new customer but was unable to gain access to the house. The doors were all stuck fast and no amount of pushing or charging, even with the help of Mr Tullett the gardener, would avail. Nor was there a single window left ajar that could have afforded him access. Mrs Smith, the cook had arranged to visit her sister in Winchelsea that morning, so there was nobody inside to help Walter gain access. He was much frustrated as he had high hopes of this customer opening up many new avenues for his business.

I then had a brainwave,

"Why not exit the garden via the printing works" I suggested. "Then you can walk around to Traders Passage and up Middle Street to the front of the house. You had intended to take the man to the Mermaid for lunch so, if you are still unable to gain access to the house, you can intercept your customer and take him straight across to the Mermaid to discuss your business. By the time your meeting is concluded Mrs Smith is sure to be back and will be able to let you in."

Walter, in the absence of any real alternative, recognised the sense in my suggestion and quickly made his way back up to the top garden where he knocked on the print shop door and barged inside. In hot pursuit I was disappointed to watch him push his way through the print room without taking time to explain or apologise for his haste, barge past Sarah, who had just settled her brother and Francis to their meal, nod to the two men who were staring open-mouthed at his progress through their workshop and exit the premises onto Watchbell street.

Sarah was aghast, "Who pray was that?" she asked her uncle and then added, "What a very rude man."

I felt thoroughly disheartened; this was most certainly not the way I had hoped that Walter and Sarah would meet.

By the time Walter had returned to Mulberry House later that afternoon he had calmed and was pleased to advise me that the business meeting had shown great promise. Though I expressed my happiness at this news, I nevertheless admonished him for the unseeming way he had burst into and through the print shop.

"You nearly bowled young Miss Lamb over" I had said pointedly.

Walter seemed unashamed of his behaviour but chose to spend the rest of the evening alone. The seed had been sown however, and the next morning, after breaking his fast he had sought me out and apologised for his actions the previous day.

"It is surely not me that you should be apologising to" I had suggested. "Francis had seemed much perturbed by your use of his workshop as a thoroughfare, without so much as a Good Day or by your leave."

"I will of course make my way to the print shop and offer my apologies and explanation" Walter promised. "And, dear Nell, what was that you said about a Miss Lamb?" he asked trying to seem nonchalant.

"Why did you not know, Francis' apprentice is a distant relative of *the* Lambs who have bult the grand house just around the corner from Middle Street. His sister Sarah, a dear, dear girl, brings her uncle-by-marriage, Francis and her brother a hot meal each day and undertakes any housekeeping duties her uncle requires."

I managed to appear even more nonchalant than Walter and, saying no more, quietly left him to his deliberations. Sure enough, at around noon, I spied Walter striding up to the top garden, a flagon of beer in one hand and a bunch of freshly picked garden flowers in the other.

I could barely control my curiosity but did not rush after Walter to watch his exchanges with Francis and

Sarah. He would no doubt relate his actions to me later and, if he and Sarah were meant to be together, I knew enough of men to know that it was important that Walter be left to believe that the idea was all his own. I settled quietly in my attic room and the house around me seemed to sigh, as if in agreement.

Sure enough, Walter returned to the house and later related his story to me. Apologies and gifts had been graciously received and the four of them had laughed wholeheartedly at Walter's expense. Miss Sarah had even condescended to allowed him to escort her home from the print shop and carry her basket. She had been most civil towards him and had introduced him to her mother, who, though polite, had not deigned to invite him into their little cottage.

"From what the little I have seen of her and in spite of her humble accommodation, Sarah seems a fine young lady" I remarked.

Walter had nodded in agreement but had made no further comment.

Several frustrating months later I was disappointed that things did not appear to have moved on between Walter and Sarah.   Although nothing specific was mentioned, I understood that the two young people had occasionally met whilst about the town but Walter had made no more specific references to Sarah on the occasions that he and I enjoyed an evening together at home.   I therefore decided that a gentle nudge was in order and on one pleasant summer evening chatting to Walter in the gardens I made my move.

"Well young Walter," I began, "have you given any more thought to the acquisition of a wife? It is about time this lovely house rang with the sound of children's laughter."

Walter, who was lounging in his chair enjoying a pipe, smiled thoughtfully. "Are you a mind reader now Mistress Nell?" he asked.

"I am currently pursuing a young lady of good birth, the daughter of a local lawyer who has chambers on Longer Street. Her name is Constance Brignall and she is both comely and well born. Why, only last evening

I decided to approach her father to request his permission to ask her to become my wife."

I was aghast, "Constance?" I screeched, "What of young Sarah? I had thought you quite taken with her."

Walter had nodded, "Despite the bad first impression I made on Miss Lamb, she has ever been polite and warm towards me, and for a while, it certainly looked as if a mutual understanding had been reached. I certainly did consider an offer in that direction, but her mother made it quite clear that she would brook no such offer from one such as me. For one living so humbly, that lady certainly has a high opinion as to her standing in this town and, though I like to think that Sarah was a little disappointed by her mother's antipathy toward me, it was clear that she would not openly defy her.   Thus, I turned my attention elsewhere."

After a few long draws on his pipe he smiled rather smugly.

"As well as Constance Brignall, I have made the acquaintance of a Martha Gill, granddaughter of an apothecary whose forebears were, I believe, born in this very house; Elizabeth Slade, daughter of a former mayor of this town; and Georgiana Paine whose father owns huge swathes of the Romney marshes and virtually controls the wool trade hereabouts. Though I admit, none are as pleasing to the eye as Miss Sarah Lamb, I am confident that one of these young ladies will accept my proposal and I am hopeful, dear Mistress Nell, that I will have a wife before the year is out."

I was shocked. That he could talk so coldly about a wife saddened me.

"But Walter" I said quietly, "you make it sound like a market place. Marriage is so much more than a simple business arrangement. Surely a union based solely on social advantage will likely fail to offer either party much happiness. At least mutual respect, if not love, should be the priority? I have of course no knowledge of the others of which you speak but have grown fond of young Sarah, as I thought you had also, and oft thought what a lovely wife she would make for you. Have you thought to discuss your attraction to her with her Uncle Francis and brother Richard? They both hold you in good stead and might be able to change Mistress Lamb's attitude towards you. I would not have you condemned to a marriage without affection. If you have not already done so, please, I beg you, hold fast on asking for the hand of any of the other fine young ladies you have mentioned this evening, until you have sought out Francis' and Richard's advice."

Walter, admitting that he had been very smitten with Sarah, promised to consider my request and, sure enough, after discussing his intent with Francis and Richard, and to give her a glimpse of what her daughter's life could become as his wife, he invited Mistress Lamb, her children and Francis, to dine with him in Mulberry House. Surprisingly, Mistress Lamb accepted his invitation and Walter engaged extra staff to help make the evening a success. Sarah looked especially lovely in a blue dress that made her eyes seem even more lustrous, but when Walter complimented her on her attire, she blushed and admitted that the dress had been passed down to her, like so many of her clothes, by one of her Lamb cousins. Her mother was obviously furious that Sarah had so openly admitted to their receipt of charity, and Walter was afraid that this would overshadow the whole evening, but he said he applauded Sarah for her honesty.

The rest of the evening seemed to go to plan, and Mistress Lamb appeared impressed at the sumptuous fare served at the table, and the fine furnishings of the dining room. However, when they retired to the front parlour, sitting near the great fireplace, with its gleaming copper hood, and Walter formally asked for Sarah's hand in marriage, Mistress Lamb stated that the decision did not rest with her. Her late husband's cousin, Master James Lamb, was legally Sarah's guardian and she made it clear that she thought it unlikely that he would wish his niece married to Walter, no matter the fine trappings that his money afforded him.

Walter stood and pressed his case nevertheless. "Mistress Lamb, Master Fletcher and your own son Richard will attest to my endeavours to better myself. I have not and would not deny my humble beginnings but would point out that, from my birth, my father was adamant that I would be a gentleman. I never worked alongside my brothers and was educated alongside the sons of many a fine gentleman at King's School in Canterbury. Yes, my father invested a large amount of capital with which to establish me as a reputable merchant and businessman, but in the year or so since taking over Bacon and Bourne, I have seen his investment tripled."

His indignation drove him to add, "I paid a fair price for this lovely old house and my wife will live here as a queen. I mean no disrespect but would suggest that your connections to the Lamb family do not appear to have assisted you or your children to a similar standard of abode. That Richard and Sarah have become such worthy and kind people is to your credit but without good Francis Fletcher's benevolence where would Sarah and Richard be now? Sarah might have aspired to become a companion to one of her wealthy aunts, forever dressed in hand-me-downs and Richard might, if he was lucky, have been taken on as a clerk, like his late father. As my wife, however, I make you this solemn pledge, Sarah will take her rightful place in society and never have to wear someone else's cast offs, no matter how alluring they make her look."   At this he gazed approvingly at Sarah who beamed in response.

He then continued, "I would also see your good self, living as befits one of your connections madam and pledge that, with Francis' blessing, if the printing works prove insufficient to satisfy Richard's talents, I would welcome him into my business, at a status befitting to the brother of the owner's wife."

He paused for a while to catch his breath and allow for his words to strike home before concluding, "I am a simple man, madam, and do not need to flaunt my wealth in order to achieve respect. I would never see a member of my family live in squalor and poverty or treated with the disdain such as you obviously enjoy from your Lamb relations. As a mother, madam, can you deny your children the opportunities I offer them and condemn them to lives of hardship on the fringes of society?"

Mistress Lamb stood and gestured to her children that it was time to leave but, as she reached the door she turned to Walter.

"You have given me much food for thought Master Tart. I thank you for your frankness but wonder if you give too much credence to your wealth and marriage being able to open doors for you in society. My own dear husband failed to enter such echelons, despite his birth, and, as you so rightly stated, the Lambs have done little to assist me and mine since his death. Theirs is a closed world and I would not wish for my children to be further spurned by their own family simply due to their close association with yours. I thank you sincerely for a splendid meal and ask that you give me time to consider your words."

After they had all gone Walter slumped in a chair and looked across at me as I sat in my corner by the great fire, "Well Mistress Nell, I have played my cards. Now we must wait."

One morning, a few weeks later, I was most excited to see a liveried messenger come to the house and request that Master Tart attend his master, James

Lamb, at his convenience. Walter was pleased, for surely the summons would suggest that Sarah's mother was considering his offer for Sarah's hand. I would have had him running up the hill, hot on the heels of the messenger, but Walter, determined to maintain his dignity, had advised the messenger that unfortunately he had some pressing engagements for the rest of that day but that he would be free to attend Lamb House at ten o'clock the following morning if that would please Master Lamb.

I was appalled. "Do you not fear that your seeming apathy to his invitation will be seen as indicating poor intent on your part?" she asked.

"Madam, will you have me beggar myself to him?" Walter had almost snarled. "I am most enamoured of Sarah and yes, I admit, I do very much wish her to be my wife, and not simply because of her connections, but I will not go running to the 'mighty' Lambs at the first call. Nor will I be made to feel subservient."

He paced around the front parlour and seemed quite animated but spoke calmly.

"I have been making enquiries around the area and believe me, though they preen and strut about the town and have monopolised the Mayoralty for generations as if by right, the building of their fine house has all but bankrupted them and I understand there are still some traders awaiting settlement of their fees. They may well have accommodated the King during his impromptu visit to the town last winter, but having the monarch stand godfather to your son does not put food on the table. The Lamb's business ventures, such as they are, are doing little to restore the family finances. They are desperate for capital, and I would suggest that this summons has as much to do with my financial dealings as with my suitability as a husband for Sarah.

Master Lamb will have no doubt made enquiries about my background and business acumen, not to mention my pursuit of other young ladies of the town who would be happy to call me husband, and this invitation to meet, I would accept, indicates an interest in my proposal at the very least."

I nodded and was impressed at the maturity and calm with which Walter faced the future.

"You are wiser than your years give you credit for, my dear boy" I said. "I will pray that your proposal is met kindly as I know with all my being that Sarah is the right wife for you."

The following morning, at precisely 10 o'clock, Walter presented himself at the imposing door of Lamb House and was promptly ushered inside. A little less than two hours later he exited the house and on his return to Mulberry House, it was clear to me that all had gone well.

He beamed at me as he called for food and wine with which to celebrate his betrothal. Mrs Smith, delighted at the news, bustled in with a platter of cold meats and relishes and a large flagon of wine, and expressed her congratulations to her young master. Mr Tullett too came in from the garden to offer his congratulations at the news.

I looked on smiling as Walter attacked his meal with gusto.

"It is done," he grinned. "Darling Sarah is to be my wife. Oh, he tried to talk down to me and 'put me in my place' but, as I have lately discovered, Master James Lamb's needs are greater than my own.

He began by pontificating about his grand house and the high social status that the Lambs and their extended family had enjoyed in Rye for generations. He then showed his true colours and started to rant about young upstarts with money who thought they could buy status. At that point I stood and made as if to take my leave.

That stopped him in his tracks I can tell you. How I wish you could have seen him Nell.

I calmly and quietly made it clear to him that I had not accepted his invitation to the meeting just so that he could list his credentials and bolster his own sense of worth. I advised that if he were not prepared to act in a gentlemanly fashion and discuss my perfectly reasonable proposal to wed his niece, I would take my leave.

He opened and closed his mouth like a fish and then slumped into a chair and waved his hand, that I might continue. I knew at that moment that I was to be victor in this battle.

I stated that having recently purchased a couple of businesses in the town who were facing collapse, I had become aware of his current financial status. I also showed him several letters that I had obtained that outlined some decidedly shady deals that he and his father before him had been party to. Deals that, as magistrates of the town, had altered the outcome of certain legal cases that had come up before them. After he had seen the documents he visibly paled whilst I slowly folded them and placed them securely in my pocket but remained silent.

Giving him a minute to regain his composure, I indicated that, as a relative by marriage, I would be happy to provide him a substantial personal loan, at a modest interest of course, to help him repay his debts and restore his family coffers, without which, I pointed out, he would likely be unable to continue as Mayor of this town.

He rang for a servant to bring us some refreshments and I was served a very average glass of sack and some dainty but stale, biscuits.

Once the servant withdrew, I continued and reassured him that I wanted nothing more from him than his public blessing on my marriage to Sarah and his undertaking to furnish her mother and brother with accommodation more fitting to their position within his extended family. Despite the tradition of the bride's family holding a lavish wedding breakfast to celebrate the occasion, I also proposed that I fund the whole wedding, to include anything Sarah and her mother desired by way of attire, jewellery, flowers or other accoutrements, determined as I am to ensure that my bride has a memorable and joyful day.

He continued to puff and blow like a landed fish but ultimately held up his hands in defeat. He begrudgingly accepted my offer of financial assistance but did request that my funding of the wedding should be not made public and that the wedding breakfast be held at Lamb House. I agreed to his conditions as I do not want anything to cloud Sarah's day or our future life together. We then shook hands, if not as equals, with a clear understanding as to who was the better man, and now I am come home."

He stared dreamily into space and then concluded his meal.

"I was feeling curiously light-headed whilst returning home and felt a need for some sustenance before I attend my beautiful Sarah to advise her of her uncle's blessing on our union.   I also wished to place the aforementioned papers outlining his magisterial misconduct in a safe place. I would not want dearest Sarah to inadvertently come across them Do you know of any such hidey hole?"

I smiled and nodded as I held out my hand. "I know of exactly the right place," I said simply, "one in which I have many such treasures hidden away and that this dear old house guards most effectively. Your papers will be quite safe in our care."

He handed me the papers but before I could whisk them away to my attic, he put his hand in the pocket of his waistcoat and pulled out an exquisite but simple diamond ring which he held out for me to admire. "Think you that this will suffice to convince Sarah of my sincerity?"

I had never seen such a jewel and nodded emphatically.

Leaving me to hide the damning paperwork, Walter made haste to Sarah's cottage to formally offer himself as her husband.

Thus it was that just three months later, after a wedding ceremony in St Mary's, all the great and good of the district had strolled amicably through the churchyard and along to the great gardens of Lamb House where they enjoyed a sumptuous wedding breakfast under a gloriously blue sky. Music and entertainments were laid on and even Master Lamb seemed to enjoy the occasion and condescended to partner Walter's mother in a genteel dance. His pleasure was made complete after one or two of the guests praised the wonderful venue and feast and thanked him for his exceptional hospitality.

Walter and Sarah were heralded as a perfect couple and Walter's chest swelled with pride as he escorted his beautiful bride down Middle Street to their new home. In the arms of her new husband, Sarah entered Mulberry House as its new mistress, where a bevy of staff stood in the hall to welcome her and assure her of their best wishes for the future. Walter stood by proudly and beamed at me as I stood on the stairs full of love and hope for them both.

For several weeks the young couple stayed at home simply enjoying each other's company.   However, business matters began to accrue and Walter was all too soon forced to leave his bride and travel to France to consolidate a particularly intricate deal.   He had suggested that Sarah might like to accompany him on his travels but, much as she did not want to be apart from Walter, she recognised that she needed to get used to his absences and consolidate her own new role as well.

Whilst he was away Sarah, with the new housekeeper (Mrs Smith having given up that side of her duties in preference to continuing as cook) did a full inventory of goods and set about adding some more feminine furnishings and fittings as she saw fit. On one or two occasions I had thought that Sarah was about to address me, and I had smiled encouragingly, but to no avail, she remained quiet.

On his return from his first trip, Walter was delighted to see that Sarah was making the house her own. He praised Sarah's new additions, which had certainly made the house more homely, and the kitchen improvements that made things easier for Mrs Smith to run her kitchen ever more smoothly and efficiently.

The upstairs garden room, ever my favourite room in the house, became Sarah's sitting room where she entertained her mother, mother-in-law and other friends who became regular visitors to her home.

Sarah delighted in her new life but never forgot how hard things had been for her family in the past. After discussion with Walter, who gave his unequivocable support, she determined to set up a soup kitchen for the poor of the town. I was most impressed when he told me of Sarah's plan and suggested to Walter that with my input Sarah could also offer basic health care and advice.

"Although she will have to overcome her fear and talk to me" I had stressed, "I feel sure that she can see me. Can you not tell her of our relationship so that she does not see herself as deranged?" Walter agreed to confide about our friendship to his young wife but try as both he might, Sarah was adamant that she could neither see nor hear me.

Still keen that the poor be offered help with health issues, I had subsequently suggested to Walter that Sarah contact the Gill family, local apothecaries whose forebears had resided in Mulberry House, to enquire if they would join her in the charitable venture. Sure enough, Master Edward Gill, the third of that name, was delighted to offer his services and, to this end, his daughter Martha, who worked alongside him in their apothecary shop in the town, came to visit Sarah to discuss things.   The girls were eager to meet one another, both being aware that Walter had previously considered Martha, amongst others, as a prospective wife, and they took an instant liking for one another.

They teased Walter mercilessly about his previous dalliances which he took with good humour.

Another reason Martha had desired to visit Mulberry House was that her family had long talked of Nell, a lost soul who inhabited the house, and she wished most strongly to see if Nell was still in residence. When I entered the garden room during Martha's visit, being as curious to see the visitor as she was to find me, I felt an instant connection as Martha turned quickly and smiled at me.

"You must be Mistress Nell" she had stated simply, "Your name is spoken of so fondly in our household – I am honoured to make your acquaintance." I was moved at the warmth of the greeting and smiled at the young girl.

"You do me an honour Miss Gill" I said. "How well I remember your forebears Jack and Catherine and what a happy house it was when they were here."

Martha had turned to Sarah and apologised to her for any confusion or distress. "I have not lost my senses dear Sarah" she had reassured, "Nell was an integral part of my family back at the time of old Queen Elizabeth. It was Nell who first encouraged my ancestor Jacques to consider becoming an apothecary and helped his grandson Jack and his wife Catherine when they later took up residence in this dear house. She was also involved in the adoption of their first son, Henry and she assisted and advised Catherine during the birth of their second son, my great grandfather Edward. As a family, we have much to be grateful to her for. Do you not see her Sarah?"

Sarah sadly shook her head, "No; Walter can and does converse with her on a regular basis and has mentioned her presence to me but, though I am aware of a cold sensation which I believe heralds her presence, I can neither see nor hear her."

Martha, sensing her new friend's discomfort, smiled and went on, "There will be plenty of occasions for me to indulge my curiosity about Mistress Nell in the future, so, for now, let us concentrate on the matter in hand. Our first priority in establishing the soup kitchen cum apothecary shop must be to acquire a suitable premises, yes?"

Sarah seemed relieved at the change of subject and asked,

"Have you anywhere in mind? There are a number of vacant premises on Longer Street but I do not think the tradespeople of the area would wish to conduct their business alongside the poor and needy of the town. Perhaps down by the quay or up by the castle?"

As the conversation progressed as to the size, position and basic amenities of the future soup kitchen and medical centre, my involvement was neither sought nor offered and I slipped silently from the room offering my thanks that I had been granted yet another opportunity to befriend and assist a member of dear Jacques' family.

Over the ensuing weeks, Sarah and Martha viewed several unsatisfactory sites and were beginning to feel that their charitable venture would fall at the first hurdle. Then, quite out of the blue, the most appropriate property became available to them.

In keeping with Walter's request prior to his wedding, Master Lamb had indeed offered Sarah's mother and

Richard a more comfortable home in the town, but they had declined his offer, having already been invited to move into Francis' comfortable home in Watchbell Street, an arrangement that suited all three. Francis, now approaching the age of sixty, and glad to be no longer living alone, had, after much debate with nephew Richard, decided to retire and give up the printing business. A rival print works, much larger and with more modern presses etc., had been established at the top of Conduit Hill and the struggle to compete in a shrinking market was becoming ever more difficult. Richard, although grateful for the opportunity his uncle had given him when his future had seemed at its most bleak, had turned to his brother-in-law for advice regarding his future career. Walter was delighted to offer him a partnership in his company, nowadays so much more than a simple mercantile business, and before very long, Richard joined the company as General Manager and was quickly capable of managing the business on the occasions that Walter was away.

Thus, the print works, easily approached from the garden of Mulberry

House, and equally accessible to the poor of the town from Watchbell Street, became vacant. Francis was happy to make over the ownership of the premises to Sarah where she and Martha were delighted to turn their dreams into a reality.

From its first day, however, the demand far exceeded expectations and, whilst initially Sarah, Mrs Smith and their team had prepared the food at Mulberry House and it had been conveyed up to the former print works via the garden, it soon became clear that a separate team of cooks, and a small kitchen, would be necessary to ensure that all who needed sustenance went fed. A small extension was added to the premises, that included a small kitchen and a still room for the preparations of medicines, and a large awning was suspended at the front of the building so that more could shelter and be fed at each sitting. The upstairs, former storerooms, were cleaned and set up as a modest dispensary.

A head cook and an assistant cook were employed to prepare and serve meals every day and upstairs, Martha or her father, with an apprentice, supervised the dispensing of medicaments each morning. Suffice to say, their efforts were in great demand and were gratefully received by the poor of the town.

I took enormous pleasure in spending time in the dispensing rooms where I could often discuss remedies and treatments with Martha. We soon became firm friends and it was to Martha therefore that I suggested that Sarah might be pregnant. Sure enough, this proved to be the case and both Walter and Sarah were delighted with the news and it was with a fine celebration that they welcomed their son, James Benjamin later that year.

Sarah, most keen that her brother and her friend should enjoy the sort of happy life she had herself, suggested that Richard and Martha should stand as godparents to their son. Walter agreed that this was a splendid idea, although teasing his wife at her blatant attempt at matchmaking and suggested that her Uncle James should also be a godfather. All three were delighted to be so nominated and, following the simple but dignified christening, Richard and Martha's former friendship blossomed further and their wedding followed within six months.

It was with a heavy heart, when Sarah was expecting their second child a few years later, that Walter advised me that he was considering moving out of Mulberry House. Middle Street, now commonly being referred to as Mermaid Street due to the ever popular Mermaid Inn across the street, was declining as a residential area. The proximity to the busy inn and the port at the bottom of the hill, made it a clear favourite for the less savoury aspects of port life, and, following a vicious murder of a member of the extended Lamb family, (Sarah's uncle having been the intended victim) Walter was keen to remove his wife and growing family to a more respectable part of town, or even out of town. I was most upset to hear that they might be leaving but recognised that, having worked so hard to establish himself as a worthy gentleman of the town, remaining a resident of Middle Street could ultimately count against him. I knew that both Walter and Sarah loved the old house and God knew, I would miss them dreadfully, but I recognised that it was the right time for them to move on.

Whilst his new house was being constructed and his business empire continued to expand and flourish; Walter confessed to me his disappointment that his link with the Lamb family had afforded him no further acceptance into the higher echelons of the town elite. He seemed to become rather bitter about this and mentioned that he desired to establish a lasting memorial so that all would know of his contribution to the prosperity of the town. I was able to offer him little succour as my suggestion that his legacy would be that his heirs would enjoy a more privileged life than he, seemed only to fuel his determination to achieve personal recognition.

After one of his many trips to the continent to secure new and existing contracts, he returned home in high spirits.

"I have a plan Nell," he announced to me excitedly as we sat in the garden enjoying the freshness of the evening air. "I have seen some marvellous automated clocks on my travels and intend to install a similar function to augment the old church clock at St Mary's. It will be a resplendent automaton that will ring out the quarters throughout the day and night. It will be the envy of many a town in the area and will stand testament to the wealth and benevolence of the house of Tart. What think you of that?" He sat back in satisfaction.

I, who had for years enjoyed hearing the church clock ringing out the hours stated that I did not really see the need for a quarterly reminder of how slowly time could often pass but Walter was adamant.

"Time is so fleeting," he insisted, perhaps becoming aware of his own mortality, "It's alright for you Nell, you who are ageless and count your time here in centuries. People are just tiny specks in time and should make each precious minute count."

He jumped up. "In fact I think the automaton should be accompanied by a tract to warn of the dangers of ignoring the passage of time. Nell you are a genius."

Walter lost no time in sourcing a craftsman worthy of his plan and I was proud to learn that the successful artist was a Master Arthur Playford, whose fine work was highly praised locally and who was the descendant of one of the poor young boys who had, more than a century before, learned their craft under a certain Master Jacob Capsey, a former resident of Mulberry House.

The automaton was to feature two gilded cherubs who would bring a hammer to bear on two small bells — once for the first quarter, twice for the second and three times for the third. They would remain silent on the hour when it was deemed that the clock chiming was adequate. In between the cherubs was an ornate, bescrolled, plaque on which was inscribed a passage from the bible *"For our time is a very shadow that passeth away."*

Walter was apparently much fêted at the grand unveiling that took place later that year and, though I was never able to see the final automaton in situ, Walter presented me with one of the preliminary sketches of it which I was delighted to add to my secret cache of treasures. I had to admit to him too, that despite my reservations, it had not taken long for their regular little chimes to become familiar and precious to me.

Sarah was subsequently safely delivered of a daughter who they called Edith, and, by the time she was a year old, the family had relocated to their new home, built to Walter's exacting specifications, on the hillside just above Rye, off the London Road.

"The house is splendid, Nell," Walter had announced proudly when he came to take his leave of her, "I have incorporated many modern features and acquired fine new furnishings and fixtures. The house and gardens enjoy extensive views across the town, neighbouring marshes and the sea beyond and I have had a special observation room at the top of the house constructed where I have positioned a large telescope to enable me to watch the passage of ships in and out of the port and where, on a clear day, I can still hear the distant chiming of my precious quarter boys."

His face darkened as he continued,

"I will miss you most dreadfully my friend and would that I could pop you into my pocket and take you with me to the new house. Your friendship and guidance has been invaluable to me and I offer you my most heartfelt thanks. Though you have never explained your continued presence in Mulberry House, I pledge that if ever I, or a member of my family, are in a position to offer you help to achieve your release, you have only to ask. The strength of our bond will surely transcend any distance or time that separates us and ensure that our assistance reaches you. In the meantime, I will pray that another will soon enter this house and offer you the companionship you deserve."

Neither he nor I could speak as he turned and left the house. I watched him until he was out of sight and then returned to my attic room to pray that he and his family lived long, happy and healthy lives.

The nineteenth century
Hettie and George

Walter did not simply abandon Mulberry House;   it had been a crucial part of his life, and he could not see it empty or ill-used. One of his nieces, Judith Cutting, who had ably taken over the management of the soup kitchen from Sarah,   and her husband, Joseph, a fisherman working in the Tart family fleet, moved into Mulberry House with their two children, Henry and newborn Hettie. Judith had been relieved that Walter had seen fit to leave much of the furniture and fittings so that they should live comfortably. Even the much-admired long case oak clock remained in situ, keeping the pulse of the house alive,   as Walter had commissioned a fine mahogany clock to be made that better suited his new abode.

On his death a few months later, Francis left his house on Watchbell Street to   Richard and Martha on the understanding that Richard's mother could remain in the house until her demise. Richard and Martha, who had resided in a small house on Longer Street since their wedding, had been delighted to join his mother in the pleasant house and their son, Edward was born there the following year. From the business point of view, Richard still maintained his office in Mulberry House and the Watchbell Street house was ideal for Martha to continue her regular shifts at the nearby dispensary.

Martha continued to visit Mulberry House, ostensibly to share lunch with Richard, to liaise with Judith regarding the soup kitchen and to take advantage of the bounties of the herb garden, but chiefly to maintain our close friendship and pass on news of the family. The family business continued to thrive and Walter and Richard's sons, James and Edward, were educated and trained to take over the company as and when their fathers decided to retire.

Unfortunately for Nell, however, when the boys did ultimately take over the reins from their fathers, they considered Mulberry House an ill-placed and out-dated premises from which to conduct their business and thus, once more appropriate offices had been acquired on Longer Street.

Mulberry House was made over to Judith and Joseph Cutting who lived somewhat humdrum lives and, with Martha struggling with inflammation of the joints and only able to make intermittent visits to the gardens to gather herbs, I had only these brief moments of respite from an otherwise dull existence.

I saw little of Joseph who came and went according to the tides, but he, Judith and Henry seemed quite oblivious to my presence. However, I had high hopes of being able to communicate with baby Hettie in the future as the infant often turned her large dark eyes towards me whenever I entered the room.

It was perhaps inevitable that Joseph's connection with the Tart fleet would involve some illicit cargoes and Mulberry House once again became involved in smuggling activities.   With the former storage at the old printing works being unavailable due to its current incarnation as soup kitchen and dispensary, the secret cellar below the front parlour that I had revealed to Walter in case he should need to hide any contraband, was soon put to good use. Judith and Joseph entertained several of her uncles after they had stowed away their stocks and enjoyed a celebratory drink across the street at the Mermaid Inn and, much to my shameful delight the house often rang late into the night with their drink-driven sea shanties and bawdy songs.

The fruitful trade with France, both legal and illegal, had been possible due to a prolonged period of peace between the two nations. Thus, the town defensive gates and wall fell into disrepair and ultimately all bar the main Landgate, albeit without its portcullis, and the castle, were dismantled. Stones from the old walls were utilised to encircle the ever-expanding churchyard with an enclosing wall and Joseph, with a decline in the fishing industry and despite the extra income he derived from the family's illegal activities, was happy to take advantage of the extra days labouring when the weather prevented him being able to put to sea.

There had long been a shortage of able young men in the town as many had been coerced into the army and taken to fight in the American colonies where rebels were fighting for independence. It was with much surprise that I later learnt of the defeat of the mighty English army at the hands of the colonists, and I remembered the Bournes, only short-term residents of Mulberry House, who had migrated to the American colony in order to enjoy greater religious freedom. Whilst I had not been overly fond of them, I had admired the strength of their beliefs of a better and fairer world and I prayed that their descendants, if any, had remained safe during the insurrection and would thrive in the newly independent country.

Mulberry House at present, lacking the income and status of Walter and Sarah, was fast becoming a shadow of its former self and I marvelled at how, over the four hundred years or so of my purgatory, the house and its residents' lives, and most likely those of all the people of the town and beyond, had waxed and waned according to the prosperity of the nation. Whilst people had their own individual troubles, they also had so much more opportunity to learn about, travel and experience different places and new ideas. They seemed so much better informed about local and national events, not to mention those from further afield. I too had become more knowledgeable, taking advantage of the books and broadsheets I found in the house, and listening to the day-to-day chatter of the residents and their visitors, and I began to feel that purgatory was not actually the hardship I had expected it to be. Indeed, apart from the almost physical need to save the life of an otherwise doomed baby or its mother, I was content to exist in this half-world. Whilst I would always regret my actions, I felt almost blessed to have met, and tried to assist, some interesting and warm-hearted people throughout the centuries. I had learned of new ideas and innovations and had in turn used my own thoughts and experiences with the hope of doing good.

As we entered the last decade of the eighteenth century, I pondered on yet another hundred years of purgatory. This last had passed so quickly, having started under the ill-fated Stuarts and then proceeded with significant social, political, industrial and cultural changes under the subsequent three Hanoverian Georges. Despite the loss of the American colony, Britain was enjoying a period of expansionism and world dominance, although, as in previous centuries, she was once again at war with the newly formed French republic.

Having previously given thanks to God for the loving atmosphere I had witnessed over the centuries, I was sad to notice a strained atmosphere develop between Judith and Joseph. Life was indeed hard for them. Joseph appeared to resent the risks he was expected to take to support Judith's family's smuggling activities for what he considered to be a meagre return when compared to her uncles' cuts. The extra labouring work did not pay well and was exhausting, coupled as it was between equally demanding trips to sea for an all-too little return. He was often too tired for civility and pleasantries on the rare occasion he was able to spend time at home. Judith too felt overwhelmed with the running of the house as well as the soup kitchen, the latter offering a small wage which became all too vital to the family's wellbeing. They often snapped and nagged at one another, and I feared that Joseph might become physically aggressive towards his wife. On those occasions I contrived to slam a door or tip something over in order to distract the warring couple. Thankfully, their antagonism towards each other seemed to go unnoticed by their children.

Henry had grown into a fine young man and had been apprenticed to a local carpenter and cabinet maker as Joseph was adamant that his son would not become embroiled in the activities of his Tart relatives. Hettie too was a lovely young girl, although she lacked any spark or vitality and made little attempt to communicate with anyone, although she was well able to speak if she deemed it necessary. She still made no attempt to communicate with me however, although she never ceased to look straight at me when she encountered me around the house or in the garden.

I was keen to establish contact with the poor girl, without scaring her to death, and also wanted to ensure that she was kept safe from the possible effects of her parents' ill-feeling towards one another. I therefore decided to ask Martha to help the poor girl. Knowing that Martha, now sadly widowed, still attended the dispensary one morning a week, I visited the dispensary in order to ask for her help.

Martha was thrilled to see me and after hearing of my concerns, promised to help poor little Hettie if she could and advised that she had planned to visit Mulberry House later that week with news that would further add to the family's problems; the soup kitchen and dispensary were to close.

She explained that on Sarah's demise, (Walter having died a few years earlier), James Tart and her son Edward, now sole proprietors of the solid business empire their fathers had built up, had decided that they could no longer support the soup kitchen and dispensary. They had kept it going whilst Sarah was alive, in deference to her vision, but Martha advised that their business had been adversely affected by the political unrest in France. When this had developed into open revolution and the executions of not only the royal family but also many other aristocrats and noble members of the elite, many of their wealthy business associates in France, fearing further backlash and reprisals, had abandoned their businesses and fled. Without this very lucrative side of their business, James and Edward felt unable to continue to support the soup kitchen.

Martha had expressed her abhorrence at the murder of the French King, his family and the other nobles, but was surprised when I did not seem overly outraged or upset.

"Why Nell, I did not think you the rebellious sort" she challenged, "surely you do not approve of the people taking such action against their monarch?"

I had smiled at my friend, "Remember dear Martha, I have resided here a long time and I am no longer easily shocked by the behaviour of folk, be they lords or paupers. I remember the execution of the first King Charles – a shocking event for many at the time, despite it being sanctioned by parliament – but which ultimately did little to change things for the ordinary people. What I do believe will have a far-reaching effect are the ideas coming from the Americas. There they see no need for a monarch and seem to have embraced the idea that the power should rest with the people rather than a hereditary elite. It was only a matter of time before these ideas take hold across the rest of the world. You mark my words, France is surely just the beginning, a possibility that both shocks and delights me."

Martha, having lived a comfortable life and been happy to do her part in helping the poor of her little town, could not countenance the idea of Britain without a King and hoped that my prophesy would come to nought. Putting her fears to one side, she duly visited Mulberry House a few days later to inform Judith of the closure of the soup kitchen.

Martha had apologised that she could not support the venture alone and was saddened that it had to close. She thanked Judith for her support over the years and, in an attempt to lift Judith's spirits, asked after the children. Henry, just home after a long day at the workshop, was happy to join them and entertain Martha with tales of his work, colleagues and customers. He was a great raconteur and reminded me of his great Uncle Walter. Hettie, however, merely sat quietly to one side, happy to let her brother entertain their visitor. Henry, his stories at last exhausted, and Judith, left the room in search of refreshments and Martha was able to turn her attention to Hettie.

"And how are you, young lady?" she asked kindly, "you seem incredibly quiet. You must have a bevy of young men after you, affairs of the heart troubling you?"

Hettie blushed and stammered, "Oh no, Mistress Lamb, nothing of the sort. I am quite content."

Martha had noticed Hettie watching me from the corner of her eye and turned towards me now, "Well Nell my dear," she said as she sat back firmly against a cushion, "I cannot see how we can be of service to this young lady if she will deny that there is anything troubling her."

Hettie's mouth opened wide and she cried, "Who do you address Mistress Lamb? Who is Nell?"

Martha smiled, "Why my old friend Mistress Nell Jenkins, a long-term resident of this house and one of your great Uncle Walter's biggest allies and friends. I believe that you can see her as well but why you do not admit to that and speak to her, I cannot comprehend."

I smiled at Hettie, "I mean you no harm at all. I have watched you since you were a babe and wondered if we should ever become friends. Will you not confide in me?   Not everyone has the ability to see or hear me, sadly neither your brother, father or mother are able to do so, but it is such a waste to deny such a gift."

"You spoke to my Uncle Walter?" Hettie asked falteringly.

"Oh yes, and many more before him," I boasted. "I have resided in this house for over four hundred years now and it is always pleasing when people are able to see me and converse with me. I have known since you were a babe that you could see me but wondered why you did not attempt to speak."

"I usually have little to say" Hettie confessed but Martha suggested that this was perhaps because her brother and other family members filled the house with their own voices, leaving little room for her to speak.   Hettie nodded thoughtfully and smiled, "Perhaps you are correct."

As Judith was heard returning from the kitchen, the girl fell silent.

"If you so wish," I said quietly, "We can continue to become acquainted later. I am usually to be found in the front attic room but if you prefer, you have only to whisper my name and I will come to you wherever you are."

From then on Hettie could hardly keep away from me, appearing at odd times in my attic or in the garden, and she became quite a chatterbox. Judith also noticed a change in her daughter and in a rare peaceful exchange with her husband, stated that she was pleased that at long last their daughter had come out from behind her brother's shadow and was becoming the person she had always had the right to be.

The closure of the soup kitchen and dispensary had necessitated a change in direction for the occupants of Mulberry House and a new source of income had to be found.   As the turmoil in France appeared to settle, the new Republic sought to spread its ideas of social and political reform and expand its boundaries and once again turned its attentions to its neighbour across the narrow channel that divided them. Following the revolution, one Napoleon Bonaparte had swiftly risen to power in the army and taken control of the new Republic, only to then style himself as Emperor. With the army under his control he was attempting to sweep across Europe to incorporate other states within his empire and once again the southeast of England, which included Rye and its environs, faced the risk of invasion.

As a response to the threat across the sea, many soldiers were moved to the area around Rye, and this gave Judith the opportunity she so desperately needed. She decided to establish Mulberry House as a lodging house for the many army officers who would require such accommodation locally, little knowing that the dear old place had been so used in the past.

At Martha's insistence, James and Edward had given Judith a substantial bonus on the closure of the soup kitchen, by way of compensation for her future loss of earnings.   Martha too had made over the ownership of the soup kitchen premises to Judith who had wasted no time in converting the building back into stables, with comfortable living accommodation above. Henry, having become betrothed to a young lady who lived close by the carpenter's shop where he worked, opted to take a room over the workshop until such time as he wed and could move in with his bride and her widowed mother. Thus, it was that Judith, Joseph and Hettie took up residence above the stables, thereby enabling Judith to maximise the number of rooms/beds she could let out in Mulberry House. Word soon spread of the respectable, clean, homely rooms and excellent fare available at the house and it soon became the lodging of choice for the locally based officers of the King's army.

I was pleased to see that things were improving greatly for the Cuttings. Judith and Hettie worked hard to maintain a high standard at Mulberry House and were soon able to take on a housemaid and a kitchen maid to ease the burden. Joseph too, tired of the erratic nature of life as a fisherman, had turned his back on his Tart in-laws and was currently employed as a labourer on the construction of the military canal that, it was hoped, should an invasion be launched against England from France, would enable the quick movement of troops along the coast from the Pett levels in the west to Hythe in the east. He had no wish to continue as a labourer however, and following long discussion with some of the army officers who stayed at Mulberry House, he had gained an introduction to the engineers in charge of the canal project and, with his quick eye and strong arm, was soon appointed as a supervisor. So keen and quick to learn was he that he further rose to become an assistant to one of the engineers in charge of the project, from whom he was able to learn much about building and construction. When one of the senior army engineers was subsequently charged with the construction of a chain of Martello towers along the coast that were to further bolster the protection of the southeast corner of England, he requested that Joseph be employed as his assistant, to aid him in this new project.

Thus the Cuttings' fortunes improved markedly, and I was glad to see a renewed harmony develop between

Judith and Joseph. Though they no longer actively participated in their Owler relatives' more dubious practices, the secret cellar under the front parlour was very occasionally still utilised for the urgent and short-term storage of their goods. One dark night however, when they were bringing in such a cache, I was concerned to witness one of the resident army officers, disturbed by a noise whilst visiting the privy, watching as they had brought their goods down the garden and in through the dining room doors.

The next morning the officer had mentioned his observations to Hettie as she served the breakfasts. I had warned the girl of his unfortunate observations the previous night, so she managed to stay quite calm, suggesting with a laugh that he had perhaps witnessed the activities of the ghostly smugglers who had used the premises many decades earlier. She told him that the house had long had a reputation for being haunted – this said with a wry smile in my direction. However, he was not convinced by her response and stated that what he had seen had been only too real. Thus, later that morning, after he had passed on his information to his superior officer, the Revenue men arrived at the door of Mulberry House with orders to conduct a search.

Judith, completely unaware of the accusations at breakfast, but only too aware of the contraband that currently resided in her cellar, was visibly shaken by the presence of the Revenue men. They made a token gesture of searching the front parlour, and one of the search party received a large clod of soot directly in his face as he attempted to inspect the chimney, but it became clear that their goal was the dining room. Judith and Mary stood nervously as they checked out every inch of the room and both held their breaths as the searchers neared the panels that gave access to the secret storeroom. Once again, the house came to the rescue of its residents as, try as they might, the Revenue men were unable to gain access to the secret store, although they seemed convinced that some sort of storage facility lay behind. Hammers and levers were applied but the panels held fast. When lumps of plaster started to fall on them from above, Judith reminded them of the age of the house and said that she was afraid that they would bring the whole building down on top of them if they did not cease their assault on the wall. To add credence to her words, the timbers holding up the ceiling and floors above started to creak and groan, and a couple of large pewter chargers fell from the large dresser in the corner. I watched in amusement as the Revenue men, not wishing to risk damage to themselves or the house and having found no evidence to support the information they had been given, withdrew from Mulberry House empty handed.

That night, in the safety of their quarters above the stables, Hettie told her father of the visit of the Revenue men. They all agreed that they had been lucky on this occasion but that the presence of the army officers in the house made it too dangerous for the Owlers to continue bringing their cargoes to Mulberry House. Judith sent a message to her uncles to indicate that the house had come under the scrutiny of the Revenue men and that she would no longer be prepared to offer them the storage facility. Arrangements were made for the contraband to be removed and, over a period of a week or so, the goods were moved from the cellar piecemeal - during the daytime when the residents were mostly out on manoeuvres – and taken to the stable from whence they were collected. Only once the last barrel had been removed did the family breath easily again.

Life returned to normal once again and Hettie and I engaged in many pleasant conversations. Hettie was enthralled by the stories of the former occupants of the house but never questioned why I had been condemned to such an existence. We had become close and it was to me that she turned for advice when she admitted to being enamoured of one of the young military men who regularly frequented the lodging house, one Captain George Ellis who originally haled from Suffolk.

Following Hettie's admission I made a point of watching the young man and listening as he interacted with his fellow officers. I found him to be a popular fellow amongst his peers and was therefore happy to assure Hettie of my good opinion of his character. She had also learned that he had no immediate family, his parents having died when he was quite young. He had been raised by an elderly uncle, himself a retired military man, and educated well. When his uncle too had subsequently died, George had been left alone but with a modest property in Suffolk. It had been his uncle's wish that George follow him into the military and, having nobody to consider but himself and a desire for adventure, he had sold off the property and availed himself of a commission in the army. He had acquitted himself well and was apparently held in high esteem by his commanding officers. When he subsequently approached Joseph and Judith for Hettie's hand there was great celebration in the house. The happy pair were duly married in St Mary's, complete with a military guard of honour.

George, having no family of his own, and aware that he would soon be spending considerable amounts of time away in the service of his King, had no wish to uproot Hettie from her family. However, he did not wish his wife to be working in a lodging house, albeit one as fine as Mulberry House. He suggested that he purchase the house from Judith and Joseph, which would enable them to enjoy a comfortable retirement, and he and Hettie would make Mulberry House their family home. Although invited to move into the main house with their daughter, Judith and Joseph were happy to continue living above the stables in companionable retirement.

Life was good for George and Hettie and when their first child, a daughter called Katherine, was born they felt their lives complete. Although George was often away on manoeuvres, he had only been called away to fight once, at the Battle of Roliça where he had first came under the command of Arthur Wellesley, the Duke of Wellington. George had returned home a decorated hero and much in awe of his commanding officer. Needless to say, when their second child was born, a son, he was named Arthur. George, now a senior officer in the army, was primarily involved in ensuring that the southeast coast of England was well protected against potential invasion by Bonaparte and his forces. However, in 1815, when the British army joined with other European nations to face the French at Waterloo, George had ensured that he saw further action under his former hero. The battle, an unrivalled success that brought an end to the Napoleonic wars, saw George return home relatively unscathed and promoted to the rank of Colonel.

The period of peace that followed the triumph of Waterloo saw a huge increase in population across the nation which unfortunately led to elevated levels of unemployment and hardship, particularly in rural areas.   Trade routes were re-opened, and Rye prospered once more, but the poor flocked to the town in search of work, putting a strain on the town's coffers. George, who had resigned his commission in order to spend more time with his wife and young family, was horrified at the imbalance of power in Rye and, like many others in the town, despaired of the control that the Lamb family and their cronies had enjoyed for generations. I often joined Hettie and the children when George subjected them to many a lecture on the subject of rotten boroughs and the need for social reform, although he was most insistent that he wanted change by legal means and was not one for taking up arms against his own leaders.

As the years passed and his children grew up, George became rather despondent about the chances of reform.   He had to be content to live in quiet retirement with Hettie in their lovely old house. Their daughter Katherine was happily married to a former

Army surgeon and had settled in Brighton where her husband had established a small hospital. Their son Arthur had followed his father into the Army and was fast making a name for himself with the British Army in India. Communication was sporadic but whenever a letter arrived from either of their children, Hettie, on the pretext of being a slow reader, insisted that George read their letters aloud to her, thereby ensuring that I could also hear of the family's progress.

As I listened to the letters I could only wonder at the way the world had changed over the centuries. During my own lifetime, I had barely travelled more than a few miles from Rye, and then only to assist at the birth of a baby. My life and the lives of many others across the country, had been governed by the seasons and had changed little over the centuries, the whims of Kings, Queens and Parliament, having had little direct impact on our mundane daily lives. Since my death however, change had come; slow at first but gaining momentum as each decade passed. That a family from my house had emigrated to the colony of America had been rather beyond my comprehension at the time. As a port, Rye had ever interacted with those from other lands and I had learned much of the world when I had sat in on the lessons of the young Bacon brothers, entranced by strange looking maps of the world. That the ancient civilizations of China and India still existed, albeit no longer in such isolation, whilst others, such as the Greeks, Romans and Egyptians, had long since foundered, was beyond my comprehension, and shocking though his experiences had been, John Bacon's experiences around the Mediterranean Sea, so far removed from all that I had known or could have imagined, had seemed somewhat unreal. Since then, families from my house had traded across Europe and beyond and now a son of the house was forging a career for himself in the East and his exploits were causing him to become thought of as quite a hero in the town. I felt enormously proud.

George was also justly proud of his son's achievements but hankered for a more meaningful occupation for himself. His former interest in reform became reignited when, in 1832, the Reform Act was passed, enfranchising a much broader range of men, and legislating that towns were to be administered by elected representative councils. He was optimistic that these changes would herald a more egalitarian administration in the town that would ultimately be to the benefit of all. I had been most interested when George entertained like-minded gentleman of the town and was proud to hear them encourage George to stand for election to the new local council. Given his successful career in the army they felt confident that he would be of enormous benefit to the new administration of the town. However, whilst the Lambs and their ilk had lost their control over the administration of Rye, it was to be many decades before similar levels of corruption and control were overcome.

Powerful banking families and successful businessmen contrived to manipulate and control both parliamentary and local elections and, despite their best efforts, George and his friends, lacking any substantial financial backing and George personally having no familial support, limitless financial resources or local history to call on, once again became frustrated and disillusioned at ever witnessing any meaningful reform.

As the Georgian era came to an end and the country was once again under the rule of a young Queen, Victoria, I shared my residents' anticipation of further innovations and successes of the British Empire. I was pleased to hear that the young Queen had married, remembering only too well the struggles that had ensued during the reign of a previous queen, Elizabeth, who had remained unmarried and childless. There had been no cause for concern, however, as the young Queen proved fecund in the extreme, ultimately bearing nine healthy children. She and her husband, Albert, came to epitomise the stable, loving family and were much admired. Prince Albert, being excluded from any political responsibility, took great interest in his children's welfare and education and proved a great enthusiast for the sciences and social reform, and the industrialisation and reforms of the previous century gathered momentum under his patronage.

There was a sense of optimism emanating around the country but George, whilst fast approaching his sixtieth year, and ever an avid student of new innovations, both social and industrial, still desired to leave his mark on his now beloved adopted hometown. Having been thwarted at his attempts at social reform, it was to the sciences and industrial developments that he turned his attention, desperate that Rye should not fall behind when it came to modern innovations. Not that he sought personal acclamation; he simply wanted to end his residency of the town in the knowledge that he had perhaps made a difference to its future wellbeing. Hettie had been quick to point out that he had served both King and Country against the despotic Napoleon, but this was not enough for George, and he busied himself in seeking ways in which he could be effective.

Of all the recent innovations, the one that most sparked George's interest was that of the steam locomotive. Railways were being established up and down the country and George was most keen that Rye would benefit from what he espoused as the finest invention since the wheel. When it became clear that the newly established railway network might be extended from Hastings to Ashford, via Rye, he saw an opportunity to make his mark. He was so excited at the prospect and explained to Hettie that the railway could open up huge opportunities for the town, with London becoming accessible in a matter of hours rather than days.

His excitement was short-lived however, as the two rival railway companies that operated in Kent and Sussex were somewhat apathetic towards the extension of the line that would cross county boundaries. It seemed that they had reached a stalemate, with neither side wanting the other to take overall control of the scheme. George despaired; how to overcome the petty squabbles of such short-sighted businessmen? He spent much time writing letters to the railway companies and to local dignitaries and landowners who would ultimately benefit from the extension of the railway, but to little avail.

Hettie watched poor George fall into despondency and acutely felt that perhaps it was the inadequacies of her humble background and education that were somehow limiting his success. She had mentioned this to me one afternoon but I did not agree.

"Your love and support for George has given him the thing he most craved, a home and family." I had stated bluntly. "I have never seen him belittle you with regard to your 'lowly' birth as you describe it. In fact I would say he is enormously proud of the wife and homemaker you have become. He genuinely loves you and the children, and your own perceptions of your apparent humble background are just that – yours alone."

Chastened, Hettie nodded, "You are probably right my dear, he is the kindest and most loving of husbands. I count myself blessed. If only I were better educated I would be able to help him in his ambitions," she had added.

Though neither she nor I could completely understand his desire for being hurtled around the countryside behind a hot, steaming metal machine, we agreed to give thought to any way of helping poor George achieve his goal.

Sitting in the garden one gloriously sunny afternoon I mused on George's predicament. I put aside my fears that London, previously two to three days of hard travel away, would suddenly become accessible within a couple of hours, and focussed on how to help George fulfil his desire to get the railway line extended. Then the germ of an idea came to me and I quickly went indoors to find Hettie.

"Does George have any contacts with anyone with a bit of power?" I asked, "perhaps from his army days?"

Hettie thought for a while and then leapt up suddenly, "Of course, dear Nell," she exclaimed, "You have hit the nail on the head. I know just the man," and with that she had rushed from the room to find George.

I caught up with them in the front parlour locked in a firm embrace. When they at last drew apart George beamed at his wife.

"I thank God every day that I am blessed with you as my wife, my very dear Hettie. I know that you believe yourself inferior to me and some of my associates, but to me you are the best wife a man could wish for and the evidence, if any were needed, is here and now. Whilst I have been racking my brains at trying to resolve the issue of the planned railway for Rye, you have quietly given the matter some thought and arrived at the obvious answer. You are quite a marvel," and with that he kissed her hands exuberantly and strode to his desk. "I will write to him straight away. Come help me compose the letter."

Hettie, looking somewhat overcome by George's excitement and abashed at being given the credit for what was, after all, my suggestion, joined him at the desk, giving me a half-smile and mouthed a 'thank you.' Pleased that my idea had so invigorated George, I had merely smiled warmly and nodded.

Together the couple constructed the letter, and I watched and read as George wrote:

His Grace the Duke of Wellington
Lord Warden of the Cinque Ports
Walmer Castle
Deal
Kent

My Lord Duke,
I remain your Grace's obedient servant, having enjoyed the thrill and honour of serving under your command at the

glorious battles of Rolica and Waterloo. I was also fortunate to have had the pleasure of meeting you personally on two occasions though realise that you are hardly likely to remember me at all.

Having retired from active service, I am now a resident in the ancient town of Rye, part of the Cinque Ports Federation, and it is in your capacity as Lord Warden of this esteemed federation that I write to you now to request your assistance with what I am sure you will agree is an important matter with regard to the defence of this realm.

It has been suggested that the prosperity and, dare I say it, safety, of this southeast corner of our blessed country could benefit enormously from the rapid deployment of troops on the new steam locomotive network should there be a risk of further invasion of this great nation from the continent. However, the line is not yet linked between Hastings in the west and Ashford in the east due to arguments over the management of the linking line which would cross the existing operating boundaries of the Sussex and Kent Railway Companies. I am sorely frustrated at their short-sightedness, but they appear intransigent.

Knowing you to be a man of great vision and influence, I am sure you will appreciate the potential benefits that this rail link would mean, not just to Rye but the area as a whole. As well as the aforementioned troop movement, the new line would also offer our town opportunities for trade, both agricultural and industrial.

I am confident that any support for the scheme from yourself, not only in your capacity as the Lord Warden but also as a former Prime Minister and, more importantly, the hero of Waterloo, would counter any petty squabbling between the two factions and enable the railway link to be approved and built.

I would be happy to renew our acquaintance should you require any further information.

I remain your Grace's humble servant

George Ellis (Colonel, rtd)
Mulberry House
Mermaid Street
Rye
Sussex

Well, m'dear," George had boomed, "Will that do, d'ya think?" Hettie and I had nodded our approval.

Sure enough, a few days later, George received a letter from the great Duke himself in which he thanked George for his missive and acknowledging the merits of the extension of the railway. He did, however counsel caution, explaining that he had often found that a subtle approach to a problem often resulted in the desired outcome. He asked that George leave the matter in his hands and thanked him again for bringing the matter to his attention. George was ecstatic at his hero's response and was hard pressed not to run around the town brandishing the precious letter. Hettie gently took it from his hand and said he must respect the Duke's wishes to keep his involvement a secret. She promised to keep the letter safe and asked that George be patient and let the Duke work his subtle magic. The letter from the Duke was later passed to me for safekeeping.

The exact reason for the capitulation of the two rail companies over the rail link was never fully explained and, despite several who speculated as to the involvement of the Duke of Wellington, George maintained his silence on the matter. When the line was duly opened, with much aplomb, in 1851, George attended the ceremony and was one of the first to ride on the train and gave a silent thanks to his military hero for achieving that which he himself had been unable to affect.

He returned home somewhat dishevelled and smutty but exhilarated and wasted no time in regaling Hettie of his adventure and, sitting by his wife's side I could only wonder at his excitement.

Later, that same year, George and Hetty travelled to London on the train and spent an exciting few days visiting the great Empire Exhibition, organised by the Queen's husband Prince Albert. This showed the enormous diversity of arts, crafts and industrial innovations of the mighty British Empire and they returned home to regale me with all the fine things they had seen, many of which were beyond my comprehension.

That night, once George and Hettie had retired, I completed my regular prayers with a thanks to the dear Lord for enabling me to bear witness to the amazing developments that were taking place in and beyond my little town.

<u>Victoria and Anu</u>

Time passed slowly for the three elderly residents of Mulberry House and the house became a quiet and sombre place, particularly when the realm was plunged into a prolonged period of mourning after the sudden and unexpected death of the Queen's beloved husband. Katherine visited occasionally with her only child Harold, and George and Hettie delighted in their visits, prompting George to express his desire to meet his other grandchildren. Whilst away serving with the army in Calcutta, Arthur had met and married Victoria, the daughter of one of the leading officers of the East India Company.   Having tired of the constant movement associated with army life and wishing to spend more time with his new wife, Arthur had resigned his commission and had joined his father-in-law in the renowned company.   He and Victoria now had two sons and a daughter, Albert, George and Alice.

George suggested that he and Hettie might travel to India to visit Arthur in Calcutta. I listened with interest as he advised Hettie that work had recently begun on a canal that would link the Mediterranean Sea with the Red Sea and thus the Indian Ocean, cutting by half the journey time between Britain and her eastern colonies. He purchased a fine globe to adorn his office and proudly showed his wife (and me) the proposed journey they would take.

"It will be a great adventure my dear," he had enthused, unaware of his wife's terror at such an undertaking.

"Oh Nell," she said to me later, "How can I support my dear husband in this plan? I, who am exhausted after a simple train ride to Hastings. He is so excited at the prospect, his 'Last Great Adventure' but I fear that his health is not as it was and the journey would be too much for him."

I understood her fear but could offer little in the way of comfort.

George was most certainly invigorated at the thought of their trip to the Indian sub-continent however, one evening, whilst walking home from a dinner at the

Gentleman's Club near the Landgate, he stumbled and fell when half way up West Street. He was found unconscious by the Night Watchman who, recognising him, carried him home.

Hettie wasted no time in calling the doctor who advised that George, who by then had regained consciousness but who could barely speak, had most likely suffered an apoplexy.

His recovery was slow, despite Hettie's untiring nursing and encouragement and, though thankfully his speech was restored, he was left with a weakness down his left side. It became obvious that the long journey to Calcutta was beyond George's capability and he therefore asked Hettie to write to their son to advise of his ill health and to ask that Arthur bring his family visit them in Rye. Much to her surprise and pleasure, Arthur wrote back to say that he had been planning such a visit for a little while and had intended to surprise his parents. He had intended to wait a year or so, until the marvellous new Suez Canal was completed but, due to his father's failing health, was happy to embark sooner, even though the journey would take much longer. He anticipated arriving in Rye within six months.

Hettie discussed her son's visit with some of her lady friends who also had family members out serving in India and later confessed to me that she   was overwhelmed at their stories of the grand palaces, the many servants and luxurious lifestyles enjoyed by the British Officers, Administrators and the 'Company Men' and their families. She feared that Arthur and his wife would deem Mulberry House very lowly. When George heard of her fears he dismissed them as nonsense.

"This is Arthur's home, my dear" he had tried to reassure, "and he is his mother's son and unlikely to have acquired any such affectations of grandeur."

Hettie, however, was unconvinced and, to George's amusement, undertook a   complete room by room overhaul of the house and the staff, anxious that her home would prove acceptable for her daughter-in-law. George contented himself with the planning of a series of excursions that he and his grandchildren could undertake during their visit.

I was excited at the prospect of hearing about life in India and was eager for the family's arrival. The months seemed to pass slowly but eventually the greatly anticipated arrival time drew close. George scoured the daily newspaper for any announcements regarding ships arriving from Calcutta and, allowing for their travel from Southampton, advised Hettie of the likely date of their arrival. After three false alarms they began to despair of ever being reunited with their family when one warm July afternoon a carriage pulled up outside Mulberry House and discharged its passengers at the door.

George, who relied on a stick to move around the house, threw open the door and bade the visitors enter.

"Welcome, welcome, one and all," he cried cheerfully shaking his son's hand most enthusiastically and then slapping him on the back. "Welcome home, m'boy!"

"It is good to see you father," Arthur responded, "and looking better than I had envisaged. Now, where is mother?"

Hettie barely had time to check that her hair was neat and tidy before she entered the hall and was swept off her feet and spun around like a doll.

"Oh Mother, it is so good to see you looking well. I am glad to be home at last. Come, let me introduce my family."

Arthur put her down gently but whilst still holding her hands, he turned to the slight woman at his side. "Mother, this is my darling wife Victoria, named for our own blessed Queen. Is she not the most beautiful of girls? And these fine lads are our sons, Albert, who is twelve, and George who is ten, and last, but by no means least, is Alice, my beautiful daughter who is just five years old. Victoria, children, come meet your grandmama." Arthur finally stopped to draw breath.

Hettie turned to Victoria, the tiniest woman she had ever seen, much younger than her husband, with luscious dark hair, large eyes and a small smiling mouth, who bobbed a quick curtsey and then threw her arms around her mother-in-law. "I am so pleased to finally make your acquaintance Mother Hettie. Arthur has long told us stories of you and dear Father

George and this lovely old house, and I am so happy to finally join you in your lovely home. It is as beautiful as Arthur described."

"I hope you will all be comfortable here my dear," Hetty began

As she welcomed each of her grandchildren, who were also quick to embrace her, Hettie's fears of her own inadequacy and that of her house, quickly dissipated. Arthur was the same dear boy who had marched off to adventure in the army and his family seemed to share his unbridled pleasure at coming home. Certainly, there did not appear to be any affectations of grandeur amongst them, and Hettie was relieved and grinned at the 'told-you-so expression on her husband's happy face. Finally, after much hugging and laughter, Hettie turned to lead them upstairs to their rooms and suddenly noticed, standing quietly to one side, another member of the entourage. A slight dark-skinned woman, dressed in a simple tunic and pantaloons and bedecked with bangles, placed her hands together as if in prayer, and bowed slightly to Hettie.

Hettie bowed her head in reply and looked to Victoria for an explanation.

"Oh, how could we forget my dearest Anu" she explained, "my old ayah, and my mother's before me, who now cares for my children. I hope it will not be an inconvenience but she is so dear to us all and we could not leave her behind. She speaks a little English and will be no bother."

Hettie bowed towards the nursemaid. "You are also most welcome here" she said, "I will have another room made up for you."

"Oh no Madame" Anu spoke quietly with a soft lilt to her voice, "a mattress in the room with the children will suffice. Please do not go to any trouble."

Hettie led them upstairs to their rooms and announced that she would organise for refreshments to be served in the garden and added,

"You must be exhausted after your long journey. I will have hot water sent up for you to freshen up. Please join us in the garden when you are ready."

Once settled in the garden and flushed with excitement, Hettie was eager to discuss the first impressions of her family with me. I shared her excitement and relief that the family had arrived safely. Victoria was the first to arrive in the garden and explained that dear Arthur had been side-lined by his father and they were now ensconced in the front parlour. As she settled in the chair beside Hettie she looked straight at me and gave a smile. "Good day Madame," she said simply.

I was delighted, "A good day to you too Madame."

"This is Nell," explained Hettie, "I am so pleased that you are able to see and converse with her.   She has been a blessing to me throughout my life in this house and I am sure you will be good friends."

"It will be my immense pleasure to become better acquainted with you Nell," Victoria said, "and with you too Mother Hettie."

Just then the children arrived, noisily jostling to be near their grandmother. Anu followed quietly behind and took a seat behind Victoria. She too looked straight at me but with none of the friendly interest her young mistress had shown.   In fact, I was disappointed to see fear in her eyes. I nodded and smiled at her, but she turned away quickly and went to help the children with their tea.

Thereafter there was hardly a quiet moment in Mulberry House. The excitement of the reunion and the ensuing bustle of the house, often exhausted poor George but he endeavoured to spend as much time with his grandchildren as he could.   When Hettie chastised him for doing too much, he simply held her close and begged her leave him to enjoy whatever time he had left.

Arthur, aware of his father's deteriorating health, spent many hours with him engaged in frank discussion about the future. He made it known that, after a few months, he had to return to his duties in Calcutta but he had planned that Victoria and the children would remain in England so that the boys could enrol at a good school and complete their education. Arthur further stated that he had initially intended to take a house in London but, seeing how comfortable his family was at Mulberry House, and seeing how much pleasure his parents enjoyed at their presence, he asked that Victoria and the children remain there when he left for India. George, Hettie and Victoria were thrilled with this plan and George quickly suggested that the boys first join the local Grammar school so that their academic progress to date could be assessed and appropriate schools selected for their future education. The boys would have to board whichever school they went to, which they would have done had the family remained in India, but could return to Rye for their holidays. So it was agreed and all relaxed into a comfortable co-existence in the lovely old house.

All that is, apart from Anu, who maintained a frostiness towards me and refused to engage in any conversation. Even the children noticed her sudden stiffness or swift change of direction if she spied me, although they remained ignorant of the cause of their nursemaid's strange behaviour, not being able to see me themselves. Despite Victoria's encouragement, Anu remained hostile towards me and I felt rather cheated. Victoria had told me that Anu had skills as a healer and I had been keen to discuss and perhaps share our mutual knowledge but sadly, this did not seem likely to happen.

Apart from the obvious distain Anu felt toward me, I was also concerned about a small shrine that had been set up in the children's room, at which Anu, occasionally accompanied by little Alice, performed her prayers twice a day, with small offerings and the burning of pungent smelling sticks. I was worried that these heathen practices would offend my God, on whose benevolence I relied upon to ultimately free me from purgatory. I mentioned my fears to Victoria who tried to reassure me that if I believed in one true God, as all good Christians did, then just because Anu called Him by a different name and worshipped him in a different way, did not make her wrong. I was not completely convinced of this argument and offered extra prayers to *my* God that he would make allowances for the heathen practices taking place within my house.

The summer months passed quickly and one afternoon, following an assessment at the Grammar

School in which the boys had excelled, they returned excitedly to advise that the headmaster, after discussion with their father, had agreed to write a recommendation for them both to the King's School in Canterbury.

Over a celebratory tea, James expressed interest in the history of the quarter boys that adorned the church clock on St Mary's tower. He had been told that they were about one hundred years' old but that little was known of their history. George admitted ignorance of the origin of the familiar and popular pair of figures and suggested that he and James could investigate this further. With James' assistance George was able to walk up to the church and Town Hall nearby and they spent many an hour perusing the archives in an attempt to solve the mystery.

George returned home and expressed to being baffled at the lack of information regarding the source of the quarter boys.

"They are of such fine workmanship and must have cost a pretty penny but we can find no record of why they were installed or who commissioned what must have been a costly gift to the town. There is much information on the origins of the clock and other additions to the church but of the quarter boys there is no word. All we can say for certain is that they were present in 1760 as there is an engraving that shows them in situ. The archives in the church and Town Hall are meticulous and show such minute details as the fines imposed for the theft of a pig, or the names of labourers involved in the maintenance of the walls that surround the churchyard but of the generous benefactor or benefactors who installed the quarter boys, there is no direct mention. It seems widely believed that that they were installed as part of the substantial embellishments to the church that were being undertaken by the Lamb family during the eighteenth century, although no actual evidence of this is recorded."

I was most distressed to learn that Walter's efforts to leave his mark on the history of this town had come to nought. I fled up to my attic and was little surprised to find the preliminary sketches for the mechanical marvels already lying on a box.

"Thank you dear house," I whispered.

Later that evening I passed the papers to Hettie and explained that the Walter Tart mentioned on the sketches had been a successful merchant and former resident of this fine house and it had been he who had endowed the town with the now famous church automatons, having seen similar machines on his travels around Europe.

Hettie wasted no time in showing the papers to her husband, stating that she had come across them whilst she had been clearing space in the attics for the family's trunks but had simply tucked them inside a book until she found time to show them to her husband. She admitted to having completely forgotten all about them till now.

"No matter my dearest," George boomed with a vigour that belied his frailty. "I will take them to my friend Harold, the Archivist. I am sure he will be delighted that the mystery benefactor has been identified."

George and James returned to the Town Hall a few day later and were pleased to advise Hettie that

Harold Playford, the archivist was thrilled with their find.   Walter Tart did not appear to have held any office within the town, nor had he appeared in court, as plaintiff or defendant.   Of his successes as a merchant and philanthropist, there was also no mention.

In fact, the only record of the name that was found was in the church records that showed a Walter Tart, identified merely as a gentleman, marrying Sarah, the distant cousin of the incumbent mayor, James Lamb. Where Walter had originated or how he had come to Rye was unrecorded.   "Master Playford was much excited M'dear," George reported.

"Apparently, the Tart family were an infamous smuggling family at that time," he added in a half whisper, "they controlled several of the Owler groups who operated along the coast and across the Marsh and were rumoured to have many a government official in their employ. That one of their ilk would marry into the higher echelons of society such as the Lamb family is intriguing to say the least. Harold intends to dig further to ascertain how a member of this notorious family might have risen to such a height but unfortunately, he will need more evidence of Walter's precise involvement, such as a bill of sale or receipt for the work before he is able to update the records with regard to the quarter boys."

I was bitterly disappointed that Walter's generosity had been so blatantly overlooked by the town and furious that the Lamb family had somehow managed to take the credit for Walter's gift. It was small comfort to me that neither Walter nor any of his immediate descendants were likely aware of this heinous calumny.

George had the precious sketches framed and hung in his office. He proudly showed them to any of his associates who visited but sadly the enthusiasm for the mysterious town benefactor that had so invigorated him was short lived and indeed seemed to have taken all of his reserves of energy. His health deteriorated quickly, particularly when Arthur returned to India and the time came for his grandsons to leave for school, and he fell into a decline. Though he tried to put on a brave face for his wife, I could tell that he was suffering and I warned Hettie that his end was nigh. Katherine was called home from Brighton and, along with her mother, Victoria and young Alice, they ensured that George's last few months were filled with love. When he finally took to his bed, even Anu helped with his care, massaging his tired and painful limbs and head with aromatic oils and instructing the cook in the preparation of light, sweet, milk-based confections with which to tempt him to eat. When I expressed a keen interest in learning of Anu's techniques and herbal oils I was once again shunned and had to remain a simple spectator.

George slowly slipped away but Hettie, although obviously sad at the loss of her husband, found contentment in the knowledge of a life honourably and honestly lived that had ended in the presence of his loving family. She was proud to inform me that a large throng of local dignitaries had attended George's funeral service, though they had been caught in a heavy deluge during the interment and only a few had returned to the house for refreshments, preferring instead to return to their homes to get dry clothes.

I chided myself for not having revealed Ned's document to dear George who, I admitted with hindsight, would have been the ideal candidate for bringing the information to the nation's attention. The dear Queen's long reign and extensive family ties around Europe had surely made her position and that of her dynasty secure and the revelation of the innocence of Richard III in his nephews' demise would have done little to besmirch or unsettle the current regime. How George would have loved being the instrument of such a sensation and I prayed for forgiveness at having denied him that pleasure.

Autumn took its hold on the town, with persistent rain and strong winds, and Victoria and Alice began to complain of feeling unwell. Although Arthur had had ensured that their wardrobes included plenty of warm clothing for their stay in England, neither were prepared for the dampness that seemed to reach to their very bones. Fires were lit in all rooms of the house, but they could find no comfort in them. Their joints and heads ached, and they suffered from bouts of severe coughing. Anu's treatments did little to ease their symptoms and when Hettie sought my advice on herbal remedies, Anu accompanied her.

Overcoming her fear and distrust of me she looked directly into my eyes and, with hands pressed together in supplication, she pleaded, "Please help my babies."

Of course, I was only too happy to assist and instructed Hettie in the preparation of herbal tinctures, infusions and balms that I hoped would help the two patients. Alice seemed to rally fairly quickly but poor Victoria remained frail, beset with a persistent, rattling cough, particularly at night, which was of concern to me. The use of steam inhalations helped slightly but I felt that there was a need for a more sustained treatment to enable Victoria to breath more easily through the night. After much debate it was agreed that we should construct a sort of tent over Victoria's bed inside which we would maintain a constant supply of herbal scented steam throughout the night. A small bowl containing an infusion of balsam would sit atop a candle lamp and keep the air within the tent moist and facilitate easier breathing. The infusion would need to be replenished throughout the night and Anu insisted that she would facilitate this. I offered to sit with her for mutual support and she gratefully accepted my presence.

Thus it was, that for four nights we sat in vigil over our beloved patient, as unlikely a pair of nurses as ever toiled in this house.

Over the long nights Anu opened her heart to me and explained that she had been one of fourteen children of a peasant farmer. Without any dowry but being pleasant to look at, her poor father had sold her to Victoria's grandfather when she was just 13 years of age. In most circumstances girls like her would have become concubines, ending up discarded on the streets when their bodies had ceased to please their owners. However, Victoria's grandfather had not approved of such practices and he had appointed Anu as nursemaid to his newly born daughter Isabella, Victoria's mother. Isabella's own mother took little interest in the baby and it was to Anu that the child turned for affection. Anu could not have loved the child any more had she had been her own. When Isabella grew up and was married, there was no question that Anu, now a valued companion, would accompany her to her new home. Victoria's father, much older than Isabella and a busy officer in the East India Company, was happy to indulge his pretty young wife and, when Victoria was born, it was into Anu's loving and nurturing hands they placed their precious daughter.

Now that her initial fear and hostility towards me had abated, we exchanged receipts for medications and treatments and, once we had exhausted that topic, Anu talked freely and enthusiastically about her life in India. She described the grand houses and lifestyles of the British settlers in Calcutta and the intense heat that brought so many of them to their knees. She also described the exotic food and spices used for their delectation, though so many people outside their sumptuous residences were starving. She mentioned that the men often went hunting, riding on the backs of elephants, returning with the skins of magnificent and beautiful tigers which they had made into rugs or had the heads mounted on plaques that they hung on the walls of their palaces. On the occasions that the British women left their homes, to attend church or soirees in each other's homes, they travelled in closed carriages, not only to shield themselves from the sun and the inquisitive eyes of the native people but to protect their sensibilities from the great poverty and degradation that existed all around them.

I too related my history to Anu, albeit omitting to describe the heinous crime for which I had been condemned to purgatory. Unlike many Christians, Anu seemed perfectly able to comprehend the concept of purgatory, perhaps because she believed in the reincarnation of the spirit and therefore accepted that there could be somewhere the soul might reside whilst awaiting rebirth, and she delighted in the tales of my previous residents and friends.

After our long nights of maintaining the steam tent and watching over Victoria, we each gave thanks to God that her symptoms started to improve. She was soon able to leave her bed for short periods and engage in games with Alice once again and Anu and I had become firm friends.

It took a while for Victoria to feel fully restored but by Christmas all in the household were well, and with the boys back from school, they all enjoyed a jolly feast.

As spring approached a letter arrived from Arthur advising them of his advancement within the company. He was to be the Chief Logistic Officer of the company's operation in the quickly growing British colony of Hong Kong. Whilst he appreciated that his wife and daughter were safely ensconced back in England, he missed them both and humbly requested that they join him on his new venture in Hong Kong.

Victoria was distraught. She so loved her life in England and had come to love Rye and the precious old house, not to mention her dear mother-in-law Hettie. However, she also missed her husband and the life they had led together in India. The thought of joining him and starting a new chapter of their lives together was very appealing, as was the opportunity of enjoying a warmer climate. I had made it clear to her that she had been extremely ill that winter and she was likely to experience similar or perhaps worse episodes each winter. She could not bear the thought of such a situation and was fearful of dying without seeing her dear Arthur once more. It was the latter that ultimately helped make her decision and she and Alice, with Anu of course, were soon booked for passage to Hong Kong. The boys would remain at boarding school and reside with their grandmother during the holidays.

The night before they left for Southampton and the long voyage to Hong Kong, Anu came up to my attic to make her farewell. She apologised for her initial antagonism toward me and thanked me for my patience. She also thanked me for saving her previous babies and placed in my hand, an intricately cast gold bangle. I protested that she need not give me such a gift which, she had advised had been a present to her from Victoria's father on the event of her marriage, as thanks for her care of his daughter. She was most insistent that I should have the bangle as a mark of her great respect for me and our newly established friendship. I thanked her most profusely and expressed my sadness at our parting, promising that I would continue to care for Hettie, and the boys when they were at home and, though we both expressed the wish to meet again in the future, we were aware that this was the last time we would be together.

With many tears and much jostling of baggage, Victoria, Alice and Anu left Mulberry House for the station and the start of their long journey. Katherine's son Harold, now a bright, intelligent young man of twenty, had been offered a post within the British administration of the new colony and was to accompany his aunt on the voyage. He would join their train at Brighton.

The sense of emptiness in the dear house seemed almost palpable and I joined Hettie as she inspected every room, looking for any small job that might require attention and help fill her time. Having been so immersed in the bustle and noise of their visitors, George's absence was more acutely felt and Hettie struggled to achieve any sense of contentment in her home. Even the boys' first trip home in the holidays did little to raise her spirit and, after a short visit from Katherine it was agreed that Hettie, and the boys at holiday times, would in future reside in Brighton.

So it was, after nearly 500 years of purgatory, following an emotional farewell from Hettie, I was once again alone in my dear old house. I took to retrieving all my secret treasures, including the beautiful Indian bangle, from their hiding place and reminiscing about those who had been so dear to me and had entrusted the items to my care. So involved had I become in my residents' lives and so interested in the amazing developments I had learned of, I had almost come to forget the reason for my long association with this place. Was God testing my resilience and resolve? Did He still have a plan in place for me?

On reflection, I conceded that I had very much enjoyed my years of purgatory and, if God had indeed changed His plan for me, I did not fear spending eternity in this dear old house.

My years of purgatory continued slowly and the house remained empty for nearly five years. I had learned from Hettie prior to her departure that the house had been purchased by a Mister Charles Buss, an engineer who worked abroad. He required a ready home for when he stopped chasing foreign contracts and thus the house had been simply furnished and equipped so as to be ready whenever he returned to live in England.   A cleaner visited each week to open windows and shake out dust sheets but there was never any indication that the arrival of the proprietor of the property was imminent.

No family had been mentioned and I thought it unlikely that Mister Buss would provide me with any opportunity to achieve redemption.   To my surprise, however, this thought did not cause me any undue distress.   I pondered on the past centuries and acknowledged that I was inordinately lucky for all that I had witnessed in this house. I had not yet entrusted King Edward V's declaration with any of my residents, nor had I had the opportunity to save the life of an otherwise doomed babe and I was therefore content to remain in Mulberry House and share in the lives of any future residents until such time as these pledges were honoured and I was permitted to join my Lord in Heaven.

Eleanor and Charles

One afternoon, a few minutes after the weekly visit of the cleaner, I became aware of a frantic knocking at the main door. It was securely locked but I could see from the side window a young woman, heavily pregnant and looking exceedingly weary, knocking desperately on the unyielding door. As the woman pulled back to look up at the house she pushed some locks of unruly auburn hair up under her hat, a gesture that was vaguely familiar to me. To my surprise she looked directly at me.

"Ah Madame," she said with relief in her voice, "Would you please let me enter, I have need of assistance."

I was nonplussed; how could this young woman see me? The window flew open, leaving me no option but to explain, "I am sorry, but I am unable to open the door madame. I have no key."

"Then I am come to the right place at last," she said with a sigh, "You must be Mistress Nell Jenkins of whom I have heard much."

At my surprised nod of ascent, she continued, "My time is near Mistress Nell, and I am in need of your help. Is there no other way into this noble house?"

At her words, the two women heard the grating of a lock and the large door slowly opened.

"I believe the house wishes you to enter Madame," I said with a laugh. "I bid you come in, come in."

As the woman entered she looked intrigued and a little scared and jumped with fright as the door quickly closed behind her and the lock was once again secured. Although not really understanding what had just happened, she quickly gathered her wits however and said,

"My thanks, dear house."

I ushered her into the kitchen, and we sat at the large table.

"Who are you and what brings you here at such a time?" I asked.

"My name is Eleanor Astley, and I believe my forebears lived in this lovely house many centuries ago. The legend of Mistress Nell Jenkins of Oak House in Rye has long been passed down from mother to daughter and it has always been impressed on us that if we ever find ourselves in challenging times and in need of assistance, particularly midwifery, we should avail ourselves of your aid. It has been most difficult for me to find you, as I understand this fine house has had a number of different incarnations, but at last you are found."

She slumped in the chair and gazed around the kitchen.

I was amazed and thrilled, imagine my story being relayed in such a way. Who could Eleanor's forebears have been?

I studied the weary woman and then started to recognise certain features and mannerisms I had thought long forgotten.

"You are one of Meggie's I think?" I asked.

Eleanor nodded, "Yes, my many times great grandmother was Eleanor, daughter of Meggie Southerden who I believe resided here and counted you amongst one of her most cherished friends. In Meggie's name, dear Nell, will you now help me?"

My eyes filled with tears.

"Of course I will do all in my power to help you, but I fear you cannot remain here. The new owner could arrive at any time, and, though I do not believe we will be disturbed this night, I fear we would not be able to explain your presence in this house, particularly given the strongly locked door," I laughed.

"I have an idea but need to check things." I continued.

"You see if you can get a small fire going in the grate, I see you shiver, and if the house will come to our aid once again, go out to the well and draw some water. I will pick some herbs from the garden to make you a restorative tea. I shall be back very soon."

The kitchen door duly opened silently and as I left in the direction of the garden. Eleanor found a small pail and followed me out to fetch the water.

I sped up to the top garden and entered the old stable block. Now unused and partially derelict, there was still enough left standing to offer Eleanor a temporary refuge. I returned to the garden and gathering some herbs and some gnarled vegetables from Hettie's erstwhile kitchen garden, entered the kitchen to find Eleanor fast asleep in the chair that she had dragged across in front of a small fire. The small pail of water was bubbling above the meagre flames and to this I added the herbs.

In her sleep, Eleanor smiled, and a sense of happiness bubbled in my chest; that sweet smile was unmistakeable. This poor young thing was most definitely one of Meggie's. So many generations must have passed since Meggie had been my friend but that she had passed on her story and ensured that our friendship would never be forgotten, awakened a deep sense of love in me. I said a prayer of thanks and asked that God would give me the ability to help this dear girl when the time came.

When Eleanor awoke sometime later she drank the herbal tea and seemed slightly restored.

"Are you now able to tell me what brings you to my door?" I enquired.

Eleanor's eyes filled with tears as she handed me an old, crumpled package, sealed with a familiar seal. "I bid you take this first."

The letter was addressed to me in person and when I broke the seal and unfolded it, several other sheets of parchment fell to the floor. I scrambled to retrieve them and then, as I commenced to read the faint script, I could almost hear the author's voice in my head.

My dear Mistress Nell, I read, *I know not how many years have passed since we last met but as you read this missive I must accept that one of my descendants is in dire need. I have instructed that this packet be passed down through the eldest child, with instructions that any of my family who find themselves with no* other course, should seek you out for assistance. I know that you will never turn anyone away if you are able to offer sanctuary and succour.

Though I know you will need no further encouragement to assist the carrier of this letter, I enclose further documents, recently found amongst my adopted father's papers, from my aunt, Margaret. These clearly refer to my escape from captivity and her desire that I should reclaim that which was rightfully mine. Perhaps I should have destroyed these documents. However, as you well know, it is ever my wish that the true history of my escape and the role my dear uncle played to keep my brother and I safe, will one day be made public so that he can be exonerated of the crime of nepoticide. I therefore ask that you deposit these documents alongside the other items I left in your care.

I close by assuring you of our deepest affection and to advise that Eleanor and I have enjoyed a long and happy married life. We currently have five fine granddaughters; all of whom will learn of your existence and the strong affection we have for you. I am occasionally saddened at the lack of a male heir *but, when I look back at my early life, I give thanks that none of my girls and their descendants are likely to face the turmoil and risk to life that my poor brother and I were subjected to by dint of our birth.*

I remain your friend

Ned

I sat back in amazement at what I had read.   Tucking the papers inside my shawl, I turned to the slight, pale girl who sat patiently at my side.

"This is merely a note from one of your forebears confirming your familial link with this dear house and asking for my assistance. Will you now tell me your story?"

Eleanor nodded and, taking a deep breath and holding her tears at bay, she began.

 "My darling Winston and I were married but one week when he left to join his uncle on his tea plantation in India. Winston was the youngest of four sons and with no likelihood of any significant inheritance, was keen to make his mark in the world. His uncle in India, himself childless, suggested that he join him with a view to taking over the plantation one day. He left full of high hopes, and it was agreed that he would send for me as soon as the opportunity arose."

It transpired that as Meggie had for her own Eleanor, the women in her family had all striven to arrange marriages for the further betterment of their daughters, and to this end this young woman's mother had not been happy at her decision to wed poor Winston. Despite coming from a minor aristocratic family in Norfolk, she had deemed that his prospects did not match up to his lineage and she had therefore sought a husband for Eleanor elsewhere. Likewise, Winston's mother had also been against the match as she had hoped that he would snare himself a wealthy heiress rather than the simple daughter of a prosperous farmer.

"We were not to be deterred however," the girl continued, "and Winston and I were married in secret. Just before leaving for India, he took me to his family home in Norfolk, announced that we were legally wed and left me in the care of his father and elder brother. The Astleys were none too pleased at their boy's actions and I was not made at all welcome. They were not physically hostile but allowed their low opinion of me to show so that even the servants began to treat me with disdain.

After a few months of unhappiness my world was shattered into pieces when the news came that my darling husband had died during a cholera epidemic shortly after arriving at his uncle's plantation. I was distraught, but instead of succour, the Astleys became even more unpleasant toward me. When it also became obvious that I was pregnant, instead of celebrating, they refused to accept that Winston was the father, preferring instead to insinuate that I, as a person of low birth, must have lain with another following my husband's departure. Winston's brothers all had heirs so there was no need for any son of mine to be accredited as a legitimate Astley, thus they encouraged me to denounce my claim on the Astley name and leave their home. Not wishing to remain with such unpleasant and cruel people and not wishing to bring my child into their hostile world, I agreed to depart. They gave me a small amount of money with which to travel home and I was rather ignominiously despatched from their house.

In anticipation of support from my mother in Kent, I returned home only to be shunned once again. My mother failed to believe that Winston and I had wed, despite the papers to support the fact, and did not wish to be seen to harbour me in my current condition. She would not let me speak to my father who, I believe, would have taken me in with open arms and offer me support and love, and would not countenance my presence in her house and bade me leave at once and not return, with or without my bastard child. She did however, give me the package of letters I have passed to you and bade me remember the tales told by my grandmother. Having nowhere else to go and nobody else to whom to turn, I have made my way here. I am entirely at your mercy."

The telling of her story seemed to have exhausted the poor girl and she once again slumped in the chair in despair.

"It is a sad tale indeed," I responded, wishing that I could at least hold the poor girl's hand to comfort her.

"Rest for a while, and we can discuss a plan later. For tonight at least, take yourself upstairs to one of the beds and rest comfortably."

Once Eleanor was sleeping, I pondered on how best to help the poor girl. Once more I was frustrated at not being able to leave the boundaries of Mulberry House. Was there anyone in Rye to whom I could direct Eleanor?

Whilst I pondered the issue I attempted to envisage and examine Eleanor and her baby. Sadly I could discern no heartbeat and there was no sense of a burgeoning life. On top of everything else this poor girl had endured, had her baby also died? Was there anything I could do to affect a miracle and enable this baby to draw breath and live? Was this to be my chance at redemption? I implored God to give me the skills to bring this babe to life.

When Eleanor awoke the next morning I instructed her to take a blanket and some basic kitchen pots and follow me to the relative safety of the old stable block. Once Eleanor was settled beside a small fire, I explained my concerns about the baby. Eleanor admitted that she had not been aware of any movement for a few days and she dissolved into tears. I tried to reassure her that babies often go through a quiet phase just before the birth and suggested that if she were to deliver the babe soon, we might, with God's help, be able to bring forth a living babe. Eleanor was despondent but agreed to try. I brought some herbs from the garden and we made an infusion. I encouraged Eleanor to walk around the gardens and sure enough, the following day, her labour began. Pains wracked the frail girl's body and I was frustrated at not being able to offer any physical support. All I could do was offer words of encouragement and prayers to God for assistance. When Eleanor could walk no more and lay exhausted near the fire, I attempted to show her how to massage her belly whilst pushing gently downwards. To my surprise, whilst demonstrating the technique to her, I was able to feel Eleanor's belly under my hands and Eleanor confirmed that she could feel my hands upon her. Giving thanks to God, I continued to massage and became excited when I was able to see the baby's crown appearing. As the baby's head was delivered I attempted an examination to ensure the cord was not restricting the baby's neck and was delighted to find the neck free. A few minutes later, after one last effort from the exhausted mother, a baby girl was delivered. I was able to touch and massage the baby in an attempt to encourage her to draw breath, but to no avail, the tiny baby remained still and lifeless.

"Hold her up by her feet and swing her gently," Eleanor suggested, "I saw my father do that many times with stillborn lambs," she explained.

I did as she bid but sadly the small form remained lifeless. I therefore wrapped it in a piece of sheeting and handed the bundle to its mother. I then pressed hard on Eleanor's abdomen and soon the placenta was passed. It was as shrivelled and lifeless as the baby, indicating that the poor mite had been dead for some days prior to her delivery, but was intact.

"Why do you treat me so," I screamed to the heavens, "you enabled me to touch Eleanor and the baby even though you had already taken its life. Why did you let me hope that I might help her to live? What would you have had me do?"

I slumped down beside Eleanor and took her hand. Though surprised at my outburst she said nothing and we sat for several hours in silent contemplation. Eleanor dozed still clutching her little bundle and I merely sat benumbed. I had been so confident that this was to have been my opportunity for redemption and now felt completely abandoned.

Over the ensuing days Eleanor recovered from her ordeal and sought to plan her future. She dug a small grave under the vast mulberry tree and we buried the poor little girl, who Eleanor named Margaret, and said prayers for the repose of her innocent soul.

With her dwindling resources, Eleanor, now fit and willing to work, took a room in a small house in Watchbell Street. That she was educated and a lady was evident by her dress and demeanour and she let it be known that she was a young widow in need of work as a housekeeper or companion. She did not turn her back on me however, and we met up regularly in the old stable block so that she could keep me informed of her wellbeing and progress.

I was once again in a pit of despondency and despair, wandering aimlessly around the old house, finding fault in every floorboard and beam. Even the rustlings of the mice, once so reassuringly homely, did little to improve my humour. I berated God for having allowed me to hope and for prolonging my purgatory. The intermittent meetings with Eleanor were the only highlight in my humdrum existence and, though delighted to see how well the poor girl had recovered from her ordeal, I was concerned that there remained a pall of sadness in her.

Some months later, the sudden appearance of some large packing cases and tea chests in the house did little to pique my interest, but when I heard the carters talking about the imminent arrival of 'the gentleman' I remained to listen. It would appear that the long absent owner of the house was to return shortly. There was no mention of a wife or family and the opportunist in me wondered if Mr Buss would be in need of a housekeeper. At our next meeting I mentioned this to Eleanor and suggested she write a note outlining her association with the house and her current circumstances and offering her services as housekeeper. This she did and I promised to ensure that the note was given prime position in the hall so as to not go unnoticed as and when Mister Charles Buss arrived home.

Weeks later I was disturbed by a cacophony of voices out in the street. Watching from an upstairs window, I saw a fine carriage pull up outside my house and from it an impressive looking gentleman descended. He was dressed in a fine woollen coat, top hat and shiny black boots, although, with his full dark beard and moustache, I saw a vague resemblance to the many smugglers of old who had frequented this location.   Brandishing a large brass key,   he approached Mulberry House and, as he entered the hall he stood admiring the grand staircase.

"Home at last" he boomed in a deep voice.

As he passed the table by the front parlour door, I contrived to make Eleanor's letter fall to the floor. Mr Buss, for of course it was he who had arrived at last, picked up the letter and stuffed it into a coat pocket. He strode through to the front parlour and began pulling the dust sheets from the furniture.

"Splendid, splendid" he announced with satisfaction. Having then inspected the dining room and kitchen he moved on up the house, discovering each room in turn with obvious pleasure. The garden room in particular seemed a favourite and he tried several of the chairs in turn before moving one nearer to the doors that led onto the garden. There he sat for a while, contemplating the now overgrown garden that confronted him.

"Soon get things ship-shape" he said with glee.

He did not sit still for long as there was a fuss and bother downstairs as more boxes and crates were being unloaded from his carriage. He busied himself in advising of the ultimate destination of each box and gave off an air of excitement such as of a child with a new toy. I could not but be endeared by his obvious joy at taking ownership of my house, and my humour began to lift.

If I could only get him to read Eleanor's letter.

Twice I managed to pull the letter from his pocket and twice he simply thrust it back inside, too immersed was he in discovering all the nooks and crannies of his new home.

When at last all the packages had been unloaded and the carriage had been dismissed. Charles Buss closed the door behind the last of the carters with a large sigh. He returned to the garden room and the comfortable chair to gaze out at his new domain. There he remained for several hours, occasionally muttering to himself about where things were to go within the house and what plants he would introduce to the garden, but generally content to sit in quiet solitude in his own home.

It was only as he stood, with the intent of visiting the Mermaid Inn across the street to avail himself of some supper, that he at last remembered the letter in his pocket. He opened the note and read it quickly and, as he rushed down the stairs and out of the door, I heard him cry out 'perfect' and I smiled.

The next morning, having set the old house shaking with his resounding snores, Mr Buss set off up the street with Eleanor's note in his hand. He returned an hour or so later, with Eleanor at his side. They were followed by a young lad bringing Eleanor's meagre belongings and some basic provisions on a handcart. As Mr Buss ushered her into the front parlour he gave a small bow.

"Welcome to your new abode Mrs Astley, I trust you will be as comfortable here as your predecessors."

Eleanor smiled shyly at Mr Buss and nodded as I joined them in the parlour,

"I am happy to be returned to the house sir," she said, "though young and relatively inexperienced, I hope that I will prove a satisfactory housekeeper for you. Shall I start by making us some tea?"

When she returned with the tray, Mr Buss had lit a fire in the hearth, and they sat either side of its welcoming warmth whilst they enjoyed their tea. I remarked at what a fine couple they made, and Eleanor frowned at me but also blushed.

The next few weeks were a complete bustle as Eleanor interviewed staff to assist her in the smooth running of the house. A cook, kitchen maid and housemaid were employed, as was a gardener/handyman. Mr

Buss, appalled at the condition of the stable block, made enquiries as to the current ownership of the site and, there being none on record, assumed control of the building and had it restored to his former glory. Though he had no intention of keeping horses or indeed a carriage, he had a considerable number of boxes and equipment relating to his work as a marine engineer and designer and these he had stored on the ground floor. He had the windows of the upper rooms enlarged to bring in more light as he planned to establish a drawing office cum artist studio there as he wished to continue his work as a marine engineer, albeit only from a design point of view, and was also a keen amateur artist.

He was not a difficult employer, and the household soon settled into an efficient routine. His only real demand was that Eleanor join him for tea every day; initially this was to enable them to discuss any issues that may have arisen with regard to the house or staff but over time he admitted to himself that he looked forward to their meeting simply because he enjoyed her company. Eleanor too came to look forward to their afternoon chats at which he had insisted she call him Charles and he in turn asked for permission to address her as Eleanor.

On one such afternoon, Charles had spent the morning out on the marshes where he had been sketching. He was showing Eleanor his drawings and she had been very impressed and had offered her appreciation of his use of colour and tone. Charles was much impressed with her comments and, blushing, she explained that she had very much enjoyed her lessons in drawing and watercolours as a girl and had very much missed the opportunity since. Thereafter, whenever her duties allowed, he invited her to accompany him on his sketching trips. He also provided her with a splendid array of paints, brushes and her own easel in the studio and they spent many a companionable hour together painting.

Rye had long attracted artists, writers and poets and the like, and Charles, keen to make friends amongst such like-minded men and women, often hosted soirées for this burgeoning artistic society. At Charles' insistence, Eleanor acted as hostess for these occasions and she marvelled at the open exchange and sharing of ideas, sometimes leading to quite heated debate, that the evenings proffered.

I also very much enjoyed sitting in on these soirées and listened to the exchange of ideas, particularly when the talk turned to social reform. Several of Charles' associates seemed to believe that the factory workers, so vital to the world-leading industrial British Empire, were held in a bondage perhaps comparable to that of the slaves of earlier times. Long hours, grim and often dangerous working conditions, poor accommodation, and wages that often ended up back in the coffers of the employers, were deemed iniquitous and radical changes proscribed.

Charles did not agree however, and explained that having travelled extensively, he felt that the plight of the workers in Britain paled into insignificance when compared to the treatment and lifestyle of working people oversees, particularly in the less industrially developed lands, although he accepted that not all employers in Britain treated their workers fairly.

Conversely, Eleanor, appalled at some of the working and living conditions described and having also experienced significant hardship in her life, became wholeheartedly committed to social reform.

I became concerned at the opposing ideas Charles and Eleanor embraced. It was nearly a year since I had helped contrive Eleanor's presence in Charles' life and, despite the difference in their ages, he being nearing forty and Eleanor being not yet thirty, I had watched with pleasure as a close relationship had developed between them. Now though, finding themselves at odds with regard the question of social reform, I was concerned that their paths might diverge and take them on different paths.   I need not have worried however as Eleanor, with a quiet determination so reminiscent of my own Meggie, gently and gradually persuaded Charles that by leading the way with regard the treatment of the poor and needy, Britain could by example, initiate reforms to which those in need around the world might eventually benefit.

Charles, greatly impressed by Eleanor's generosity of spirit and kindness, was encouraged to take more interest in social reform and, with some of his associates in the local ship building industry, initiated some changes to improve the safety and wellbeing of their employees.   At the same time he acquired two of the new houses being built between the south cliff and the River Brede that he offered to some of the poorer shipworkers at peppercorn rents.

Much to his surprise, Charles derived much pleasure in being involved in measures to improve the lives of some needy local people and for this he acknowledged Eleanor's quiet influence. He recognised that Eleanor had become an integral part of his life and as such he wished to make her his wife.   During one of their pleasant sessions painting in the studio,   Charles decided to act.

He coughed and turned to Eleanor, "My dear Eleanor, you must be aware of the pleasure you have afforded me since you entered this house. You have managed this house with efficiency and kindness and your friendship is very precious to me. However,"   he paused.

Eleanor looked at Nell with a scared expression, was Charles about to announce that he had become tired of his uneventful life in Rye and was to leave Mulberry House?

Seeing her pale, he crossed the small room quickly and took her hands.

"No, you need not be afeared dear lady" he continued, his words coming quickly, "You must make allowances for my bluff, unmannerly ways. I had long felt myself a confirmed bachelor and was contented as such. On my travels around the empire, many mothers have, less than subtly, encouraged my interest in their daughters but there were none who were able to persuade me to change my comfortable solo status. However, your quiet and undemanding presence in my life here has made me reconsider my future. I cannot imagine a life without you by my side and I would very much hope that you would consider becoming my wife. I do not ask that you admit to an undying love for me; I am fully aware of how much you loved your poor late husband. I am much older than you and have no right to expect you to accept me, but I hereby pledge to you that as my wife, you will have my enduring affection and, if it is in my power to provide it, you will want for nothing."

At this he went down on one knee and looked up at her, his eyes shining with love.

"Oh Charles" Eleanor smiled. "You are a dear, sweet man and you brought me peace and stability at a time when I despaired of ever finding such again. That you also offer me your love is beyond all I could have wished for as I too have come to hold you in great affection. There is nothing that would give me more pleasure than becoming your wife."

And she smiled down at him and encouraged him to stand. I sat back smiling as they embraced.

The ensuing months passed in a frenzy of activity and Eleanor, swept along by Charles' enthusiasm, enjoyed a hectic week in Tunbridge Wells where they visited fine dressmakers, milliners, shoemakers and jewellers. Charles was determined that Eleanor was to have the trousseau he felt she deserved. When the packages began to arrive and the fine garments and accessories were displayed, I was amazed at the luxurious fabrics and designs and delighted that young Eleanor was at last enjoying the finer things of life that would have seemed impossible when we had first met.

When the day arrived for the ceremony Eleanor, resplendent in a pale brocade gown, with matching parasol, was taken by open carriage to the doors of St Mary's where Charles, who had spent the night at the George Inn, awaited.

The ceremony was a small affair. Charles had no family to speak of, just an elderly aunt who resided in Bath and for whom the journey would have been too arduous, but Eleanor, much to Charles' surprise, as she had told him of her mother's callousness in the past, had notified her parents of the event and they duly took their place in the church amongst the small cohort of Charles' friends and neighbours

After a lavish wedding breakfast in the garden of Mulberry House, Eleanor's mother took her to one side and congratulated her on her marriage. She made no reference to Eleanor's condition at the time of their last meeting and stated coldly that she was happy to see that she was now settled appropriately. I had been delighted to see Eleanor's father proudly declaring that he was the father of the bride and I was therefore much disappointed to witness the disdain toward their daughter that his wife portrayed. I need not have been concerned however as Eleanor, determined that her mother's cold words would not spoil her day, politely offered her mother her forgiveness, thanked her for attending the wedding and wished her a safe journey home.

Quickly turning her back on her stunned mother, she smiled at me.

"It is done" she said, "now I have put the past behind me and feel free to enjoy my new life." So saying she ran daintily across the garden and, threading her slight hand under his arm, smiled up at her new husband

After a month or so visiting the major cities of Europe, Charles and Eleanor returned to Rye and started their lives together. Charles continued to seek new commissions for his ships and marine machinery, and Eleanor, now with a new housekeeper in situ to take control of the day-to-day needs of the house, was free to immerse herself in charitable works in the town.

She learned that there had once been a soup kitchen and infirmary in Watchbell street and was instrumental in establishing a similar operation, albeit at the opposite corner of the town, near the workhouse by the gun gardens and castle. With the implementation of compulsory education, a school had been opened further down Mermaid Street (as Middle Street was now most commonly called). Initially co-educational but, as numbers increased, the girls and youngest boys were moved to new premises in Lion Street, where Eleanor volunteered to tutor the young girls on hygiene, household management and basic needlework, whilst the older boys remained in Mermaid Street.

In the evenings Eleanor would tell Charles of her experiences in the little school, particularly with the youngest children, and he delighted in her obvious pleasure.   When she soon advised him that they were to have a little one of their own, their happiness knew no bounds and Charles wasted no time in devising plans for the nursery. Nell too was delighted at the news and was quick to reassure Eleanor that, provided she was sensible in her diet and exercise and avoided any stressful situations, the pregnancy was likely to have a successful outcome.

xXx

It is here, dear Robbie, that my recollections start to feature some people with whom you have become acquainted. Though you may have heard several of the ensuing tales, I make no apology for regaling you with my detailed recollections of the histories of our dear Lexie and Kit, both of whom have endeared themselves to us and indeed, to all those who have known them.

Isabeau

One afternoon, as Eleanor and I were sitting in the garden room chatting about baby names, Charles entered the room and looked around keenly.

"Who are you were talking to my dear?" he enquired of Eleanor. "I have oft seen you, apparently alone but deep in conversation. Are you quite well?"

"Dear husband, you must not fear, I am better than well." She looked at me and I nodded encouragingly.

"You must not be alarmed or shocked, I am quite sane, but I converse with the spirit that resides in this dear house, one Mistress Nell Jenkins, a former midwife who has been in residence since my family built this house back in the fifteenth century. My forebears passed down Nell's history to all the girls in the family that they would know to whom they could turn at times of need. It was to Nell that I came when my first husband died and I found myself pregnant and abandoned. She has become my dearest friend." With this she gestured toward me.

Unexpectedly to us both,   Charles turned in the direction Eleanor had indicated and bowed deeply.

"My warmest felicitations Mistress Jenkins" he said, "I thank you for your past kindnesses to my dear wife and would like to also thank you for allowing us to share this beautiful house with you."

With that he sat down whilst Eleanor looked on dumbfounded. Seeing his wife's astonishment Charles laughed.

"If you had travelled the world as I have, my dear one, you would have encountered much that it is inexplicable. The world is a wondrous place; with many mysteries we are yet to understand. That this dear old place has a resident ghost with whom you are able to conduct conversations is indeed a wonder but not one I would question or decry. Would that I could so engage with her – the questions I would ask."   He sank back against the cushions deep in thought.

A few minutes later he jumped up.

"A midwife you say. Is there aught amiss?"

"No, no, my dear husband. I am quite well, Nell is taking diligent care of me, I promise."

Thereafter, the three often sat in the garden room exchanging stories; Charles of his travels and the exotic things he had seen, and myself telling of the former occupants of the house and their antics. Eleanor was pleased to act as intermediary between the two people she held most dear.

Once or twice I almost confided in them about the precious documents I had hidden in the attic, after all, dear Ned was an antecedent of this latest Eleanor. How would they react to the revelation? Charles, she was confident, had an abiding love for his country and respect for the monarchy and would do nothing that might jeopardise its stability or status. I was also sure that the empire, with its ties to many of the royal households of Europe, would be unlikely to feel threatened by the documents but, for reasons I could not fathom, I kept my counsel.

Having followed my dictates to the letter, on a sunny May afternoon, Eleanor was safely delivered of a healthy daughter whom they named Alexandra (after the much loved and long-suffering wife of the Prince of Wales), who became fondly known as Lexie. Sadly Lexie showed no awareness of my presence, although as she grew up Eleanor maintained the family tradition of telling her daughter my story. Despite Eleanor's confirmation that I continued to reside in Mulberry House and that she was able to converse with me, Lexie seemed completely disinterested in my existence. She preferred instead to spend time with her dear papa who regaled her with tales of his travels to exotic lands and showed her some of the marvellous artefacts he had collected.

"One day, my precious girl," he had said to her one cosy winter afternoon as they sat by the fire, " you and I will travel to far off lands and you can discover the world's mysteries for yourself. Meanwhile, do not dismiss your mama's tales of Nell and this wonderful old house. Without Nell's support many years ago, your dear mama would most probably have died. We both, therefore, have much to be grateful to her for and should treat her with respect, even though we cannot see or hear her ourselves."

Chastened, Lexie endeavoured to respond to her mama's tales more enthusiastically however, as she grew older she became increasingly frustrated that she could not share her mama's ability to communicate with me. I shared her frustrations as I had a deep but inexplicable feeling that somehow her presence in this house was linked to my potential redemption.

Lexie grew to be a beautiful child and all who encountered her were entranced. She was as clever as she was beautiful, though without any airs or artifice. Charles, though happy to be involved in his daughter's education with regard her knowledge of the world, world history and the exciting trends in science and technology, employed a governess for her to provide a more rounded education. She proved to be an able student, as adept at mathematics as she was in French and needlework, with an inexhaustible appetite for reading.

She had also inherited her parents' talents for sketching and painting and, by the turn of the century, at the age of ten, she became a firm favourite at the monthly artistic soirées that Charles and Eleanor continued to host. Their friends delighted in Lexie's intellect, and, where her artistic leaning was concerned, they were all pleased to find that she seemed to combine her father's precision with her mother's flair for colour and light. Some of their friends even went as far as to say that with the right tuition, she could far exceed her parents' abilities.

The death of the old queen saddened the household of Mulberry House but, after decades of mourning and Victoria's almost total withdrawal from public life, they all anticipated a less sombre tone of life under the new King Edward and so it came to pass. An era of expansion and innovation swept the nation and, whilst many of their business associates and friends opted to build more modern homes on the outskirts of Rye, Charles and Eleanor, who could not bear the thought of leaving Mulberry House, opted to stay put and modernise the old house instead.

Charles, fast approaching his sixties, and beginning to experience intermittent bouts of ill health, recognised that he was likely approaching the end of his life. His aunt in Bath, had recently passed away and had left him a significant inheritance, including her large house and its contents. He, Eleanor and Lexie took a trip to Bath so that they could enjoy the sights and also decide what to do with the property. They all agreed that, whilst it was a lovely house, it was not as beautiful as their home in Rye, and it was decided that, with the exception of one or two fine pieces of furniture and the odd painting, which would fit well into Mulberry House, both house and remaining contents would be sold.

On their return home, Charles, determined to ensure that his wife and daughter would live comfortably once he was no longer with them, arranged to have a coal-fired boiler and modern plumbing installed, to supply hot and cold water to hand basins and a bath, not to mention the latest in flushing lavatories, and to heat strategically positioned radiators to make life more comfortable for them all during the cold winters. Once he had completed his domestic modernisations Charles began to set his financial affairs in order, calling on the expertise of local solicitor and friend, Stanley Woodall.

The years passed and were kind to the family, although Charles' health deteriorated and he was greatly saddened at the thought that he would not live to see Lexie, by now a lovely, intelligent and articulate fifteen-year-old, grow up to make a life for herself. That she continued to enjoy her painting gave him such pleasure, although he could see that there was still a certain amateurish aspect to her work. At one of their art soirées he therefore resurrected the idea of her having an art tutor.

One otherwise ordinary autumn afternoon, after weeks of interviewing many unsavoury and unsatisfactory applicants for the post of art tutor, a Madame Isabeau Mûrier, dressed in a loose, flamboyantly coloured tunic over harem pants, arrived at the door of Mulberry House complete with what was later established as her entire worldly goods, in three packing cases. On entering the house she swept up both Charles and Eleanor in a strongly perfumed embrace and announced. *"J'arrive enfin."*

Charles was somewhat discomfited by the lady but Eleanor inexplicably and immediately felt a rapport with her and ushered her into the parlour enthusiastically.

It appeared that Isabeau, as she insisted they address her, and who addressed them in heavily accented English, had been recently widowed and left penniless. She had heard of their need for an art tutor from a close mutual friend with whom Charles had dealt in Paris and had set off post haste for Rye rather than let her friend send a letter of recommendation. Isabeau had been confident of being accepted for the position as she advised that it was fate that brought her to them as her surname meant mulberry in English. Charles and Eleanor were little able to get a word in as she continued to explain that her poor dear husband Pierre had been an artist and, as was typical of one of his talents, had cared little for the mundane issues of finances and subsistence, and had thus left her with scarce more than the clothes on her back. Their only son Paul, also a painter, was away studying art in Florence and, as a student, and sharing his father's lack of interest in monetary matters, was not in a position to assist or support his mother.

Charles, attempting to rein in their visitor's exuberance, tried to explain that his daughter required lessons from one who could actually paint and help her develop a more mature style.

"Précisément" Isabeau had cried and continued her diatribe. It appeared that she had been recognised as an accomplished artist prior to her marriage but, as with so many women of the time, her work had ceased to be of any interest once she had become a wife. She retrieved a large canvas bag from her cases and, with a flourish, excitedly showed Charles and Eleanor examples of her early work, much influenced by the impressionist movement, and then some of her more recent pieces which were much looser and freer in style, in keeping with the more modern styles that were taking Paris by storm at that time.

Charles, whose engineering background called for precision and accuracy, was not a fan of the 'French' influences, preferring instead the realism and storytelling of the 'British' Pre-Raphaelite movement, but Eleanor was entranced with Isabeau's work and when Lexie joined them from her studies, she too was enthralled at the paintings. In spite of Charles' misgivings, Eleanor had been captivated by the vitality that seemed to emanate from Isabeau and announced that she was happy to offer her the position as tutor. Moreover, she would make arrangements for the old studio and stable block to be cleared of all Charles' boxes and made into a comfortable residence for her, with a studio in which she could instruct dear Lexie. In the meantime, she could reside in a comfortable room here in Mulberry House.

Charles, slightly discomfited at the thought of losing his workshop/studio expressed some misgivings at the sudden arrival of the ebullient Madame Mûrier and quietly asked Eleanor if she were quite sure of the engagement and would it not be wise to think on the decision before unleashing the flamboyant whirlwind on her family and household. I expressed a similar reticence when the subject of my concern threw up her arms in horror and exclaimed,

"*Mon Dieu, Elle peut parler!*" and with that she collapsed in a swoon on top of poor Charles.

Eleanor and I stifled a laugh as Lexie helped her father to extricate himself from beneath the barely conscious French woman.

"She can see Nell," Eleanor exclaimed with pleasure. "Perhaps she is right, and she was fated to come to us."

Charles, whilst not overly enthusiastic at the idea, fetched some sal volatile and brandy from the housekeeper and within a few minutes Isabeau was restored and sitting in the armchair waving her glass for more medicinal brandy.

Eleanor, indicating towards me as I sat across the room, faced Isabeau and stated simply, "This is Mistress Nell Jenkins, a long-term resident of this house and a much respected and beloved friend to this family. If her presence here unsettles you then I am afraid we will be unable to proceed with our offer of the position as previously discussed."

She then sat quietly beside Charles, and they all awaited a response.

Lexie, who had been first startled and then intrigued and finally excited at the prospect of becoming Isabeau's pupil, said prettily,

"Oh please do stay Madame Isabeau, Although I can neither see nor hear Mistress Nell, her presence in this household appears to be one of benevolence and love. I assure you that there is nothing to fear."

Eleanor beamed at Lexie and I was warmed by her kind words.

After a sizeable number of mumbled '*mon Dieus*' and '*sacré bleus,*' and with sideways glances in my direction, Isabeau took a few deep breaths and finally nodded.

"I will accept your kind offer Madame Buss and I apologise for my outburst."

She turned to me, "Madame Nell*, je m'excuse*, in my country such '*fantômes*' as yourself, whilst often seen, are seldom heard and are usually thought to be malevolent spirits - servants of '*le diable*' *if you will.* I mean you no disrespect and look forward to becoming your friend."

Over the ensuing months Isabeau became such an integral part of the household that it was soon difficult for them to remember a time when she had not been a part of the family. As Charles' health declined further, he was grateful to the effusive French woman for offering support and succour to his darling Eleanor, who was trying so hard to be brave at the thought of losing her precious husband. When he ultimately peacefully passed away, I was happy to join Isabeau in support of Eleanor who found it difficult to cope without him.

It proved impossible to organise the quiet funeral he had requested, as so many from his beloved little town wished to pay their respects. Charles had touched so many lives with his kindness and generosity and it was a large throng of people that joined Eleanor and Lexie on their way up the hill to the new cemetery on a snowy and windy February morning. They emanated such a warmth towards Charles' memory that Eleanor felt uplifted at having been married to such a good man. The epitaph on his headstone simply read, *'Here lies Charles Buss, a good man who travelled the world only to find his perfect home in Rye.'*

Eleanor immersed herself in her charity work in order to fill the void she felt at Charles' loss. As well as helping out at the school in Lion Street, she became a member of the committee that managed the continuously full workhouse in the gun gardens, even helping to serve the traditional Christmas dinner which was presided over by the town Mayor. The demands on the town soup kitchen far outweighed the capabilities of the small premises near the workhouse and in 1907 a new soup kitchen was opened at the top of the Rope Walk that had long since ceased to provide ropes to the now dwindling ship building industry that had formally been so important to the town.

Eleanor took a turn in distributing the tickets for bread and soup amongst the throng of poor and unemployed people who came to the Town Hall for help and I warned her of the risk of overtiring herself. She dismissed my concerns, adamant that where she saw a need that she could fill, she was content to do her part.

Isabeau and I had become good friends over the months and I had come to admire her determination and independent spirit. However, when I voiced my concerns over all Eleanor's exertions, Isabeau counselled me to let her be.

"We all grieve in diverse ways *'ma cherie Nell.'*

Eleanor needs to feel needed and if she goes to her bed exhausted each night, so be it. At least she is able to sleep instead of lying awake thinking of her loss."

Recognising the wisdom of Isabeau's words I ceased to challenge Eleanor on her activities. I did, however, given her close proximity to the poor and needy of the town, endeavour to keep a close eye on her physical condition, looking for any signs of disease or illness. She often retired early, leaving Isabeau and I to while away the evenings.

During one such evening Isabeau confided that she had been forced to leave her beloved Paris following a short but intense affair with a fellow artist, a young Spaniard named Pablo. She had become completely obsessed with the young artist whose talent, she was sure, would change the art world for ever. He had greatly influenced her style and, though she was much older than he, she had hoped to marry him and legitimize their relationship. He, however, had different ideas, and, when she had learned of several other women in the artistic community who shared her obsession as well as Pablo's bed, she had felt ashamed and decided to distance herself from the hurtful gossip and ridicule. During their all too brief affair, Pablo had undertaken several sketches of her in varying stages of undress and she had carefully hidden these amongst her clothes as she left Paris. She firmly believed that Pablo's work would become much sought after in the future and, if she ever had the need, they would be worth selling. She produced the sketches and even I could see that they had been produced by a skilful hand.

"I could never show these to Eleanor," the embarrassed Frenchwoman had admitted. "Though she undoubtedly loved dear Charles, I somehow doubt that she would understand or condone the intense passion and abandon that I had shared with my Pablo – emotions that are so well reflected in the sketches. I would ask that you hide these dear Nell, so that dear Eleanor need never set eyes on them. I fear that our close friendship would falter if she were to inadvertently see these images."

I thanked her for her trust in me and duly added her sketches to my growing hoard in the attic.

Meanwhile, Lexie, under Isabeau's careful and knowledgeable eye, was developing her own artistic skills and , at her insistence, Eleanor had continued to hold the regular evening soirées for the artistic clique of the town. It was following the recommendation of one of the attendees at such a soiree that Lexie, at just seventeen years of age, received her first commission, the portrait of the wife of her late father's solicitor, Caroline Woodall.

Woodall Hall was situated a mile or so outside the town and Lexie was invited to attend regularly for several weeks to make sketches of Caroline as she worked in the house or walked around its beautiful gardens. She prepared a series of sketches that Isabeau and Eleanor agreed captured the sitters liveliness, quick wit and humour. Lexie however, feared that Stanley would expect a more traditional depiction of his wife as befitting of the wife of a country solicitor.   When Stanley came to the studio to assess the preliminary sketches, she was surprised, delighted and not a little relieved when he expressed his relief that they showed his wife's loving, happy character and liveliness.

"I don't want some stiff formal pose gazing down on me in my chambers," he admitted. "When faced with a legal dilemma or the like, it is Caroline's lively spark of humour that always helps see me through."

A sketch in which Caroline was playing with her wriggling puppy, Roly, whilst sitting in her beloved rose garden and with Woodall Hall in the background, was selected and Lexie could hardly wait to get started on the actual painting.

During her visits to Woodall House Lexie had been introduced to Caroline's son, Christopher, known as Kit, recently returned from his studies in London and who was to join his father's chambers in Rye. He had been most impressed at Lexie's quick but charming sketches of his mother and he took to walking back to Rye with her, ostensibly to help carry her equipment, on his way to visit his father's chambers.

A comfortable and easy friendship developed between them and, once Lexie had ceased to visit Woodall Hall in order to commence the painting of his mother's portrait, he contrived to visit her in her studio in the old stable block. He very much approved of the chosen sketch and it was he alone that Lexie allowed to view the portrait as it developed. Though he claimed an inability to draw even a stick man, he had a good eye for composition and the use of light and colour and was full of praise for the painting.

After several months the portrait was unveiled at a lavish garden party at Woodall Hall and it was praised most vociferously by all who attended. Many commented on the vibrancy of the sitter and complimented Lexie on how well she had captured Caroline's sense of fun and love of life. Eleanor, who had not been allowed into the studio whilst her daughter had been working on the portrait, was overwhelmed at how significantly Lexie's skill had developed, and Isabeau too was enormously proud of her young student.

Many commissions followed and Lexie was kept very busy. By the time she was twenty, she had produced a vast quantity of work for the great and the good of the area and continued to be much in demand. Eleanor worried that she did not take care of herself, as she often worked through the night and only occasionally attended the main house for meals but I reassured her that Lexie often visited the kitchen during the night to raid the pantry and was certainly not going hungry. I also stressed that she was strong and healthy and that the work was not taxing her, rather the opposite, it invigorated her.

As Lexie's star continued to rise, Isabeau realised that she could do no more to guide her and she announced her intention to return to her beloved France. Lexie, Eleanor and I were all aghast at the thought of her departure, so integral had she become in our lives but we respected her right to return to her homeland. A small legacy from Charles would enable her to set up a studio on the very outskirts of Paris where she could paint and teach. She sought the tranquillity of the countryside but within easy reach of the artistic culture of the city and she had hopes that her son would join her.

On the eve of her departure she beckoned to me and whispered that she wished to leave the secret sketches in my care.

"I have left my old life far behind me and have no need for such reminders of my foolishness," she had sighed. "I have accrued sufficient funds for my new venture, thus would be pleased to leave the sketches in your hands so that they might be used to further Lexie's career should it prove necessary."

I was touched by her generosity and trust and assured her of their safe keeping.

The next morning, with far more packing cases than when she had arrived, she embraced Eleanor and Lexie in a bear-like grip.

"*Mes cheries*, you gave me a purpose when fate had turned its back on me, and I have felt both welcomed and loved in this place. '*Alors*' you have been most generous whilst I was in your employ, a task I would have been happy to perform for far less, and I can now return to my beloved Paris and resume my life. Rest assured, I will never forget your kindness and I will follow young Lexie's career with interest and not a little pride. Now I must away."

She turned towards me as I stood on the stairs and blew me a kiss. "Madame Nell, I will remember you always and in my prayers I will ask that your purgatory may soon come to an end. '*Eh bien, Au revoir mes trois amies et la maison précieuse,*" and with tears in her eyes, she swept out of the house and into the waiting carriage.

Without Isabeau's boundless energy for life, the old house seemed overwhelmingly empty but Eleanor and I gradually settled to enjoy a period of peace and quiet.

It was Lexie who felt Isabeau's absence most keenly and Kit's frequent visits to her studio became even more precious to her. He had now completed his formal training in the chambers and was a junior partner in the firm. Lexie was delighted at his progress and, on the occasion of her twentieth birthday, when I was sitting watching her paint a simple but beautiful watercolour of the rear of the house seen from her studio window, he asked her to become his wife. I was delighted that she had had no hesitation in accepting and I smiled as I watched them run across the garden to inform her mother of their news. I was a little perturbed when Lexie stopped suddenly near the pond and seemed to hesitate.

"Oh, but I cannot leave this house my dearest," she said, "Apart from not wishing to leave my mother alone, I have a deeply held belief that my presence here is inextricably linked to this dear place. I will be proud to become your wife but request that Mulberry House become our family home."

She hardly dared to look at Kit whilst she awaited his response. I too was anxious to hear his response.

"Oh my darling girl, as long as your mother has no objections, of course we can reside here" he responded, "This old place has its own charm and will make a wonderful family home for us. It is convenient for me too, being close to my chambers in Watchbell Street. If that is your only concern about our future life together then let us delay no further."

With that he laughed, picked her up and carried her towards the house.

Eleanor greeted their news with pleasure but little surprise. She was also delighted when they announced that they wished to make their home with her in Mulberry House. The Woodall's too expressed no surprise at the news and were happy that Lexie and Eleanor would become part of their family. From then on, both households were consumed in a whirl of activity as arrangements were made.

It   had been agreed that Woodall Hall could more easily accommodate the large number of guests the couple wished to include in their happy day and thus, a few weeks before the bride's twenty-first birthday, after a ceremony at St Mary's, a cavalcade of carriages and other guests, dressed in their finery and following on foot, made its way up Rye Hill to Woodall Hall where a fine wedding breakfast was laid on.

A few days later, Eleanor returned home alone and wasted no time in describing the whole event to me in detail.

"We did our girl proud Nell," she said with pleasure, "she looked so beautiful and happy. Charles would have been so proud."

Due to Kit's work commitments, the couple could not manage a proper honeymoon and, after only a very brief visit to Isabeau in Paris, they returned to Mulberry House to begin their new life. At her own insistence, Eleanor had moved her belongings to the old nursery rooms above the garden room, next to my attic, where she had established a comfortable bedroom and a small sitting room to which she could retire and thus allow the young couple to enjoy their new life pas deux.

On their return to Rye, the newlyweds quickly settled into an affable routine. Kit continued with his commitments in chambers and Lexie spent most of the day in her studio. She still accepted the occasional commission, if the sitter interested her, but was now concentrating on putting together a collection of local landscapes through the seasons. Having seen some of her commissioned works, a small London gallery had agreed to stage an exhibition for her and she was excited at the prospect of reaching an even wider circle of followers.

Following their days work, the couple would spend the evenings in domestic harmony, sometimes entertaining friends or, more usually, simply enjoying each other's company. Lexie had often played chess with her father and, though he had usually allowed her to win, she had become a good strategist and she and Kit, as I looked on in amusement, had whiled away many an evening in fierce competition.

The young couple filled the old house with their love and Eleanor and I agreed that we were blessed to be able to witness their happiness.

The Twentieth Century

The Trip of a Lifetime?

Life for the extended Woodall/Buss family settled into an amicable and informal routine, with Sunday lunches and afternoon teas alternating between Woodall Hall and Mulberry House. It was on one such Sunday afternoon at Mulberry House, as summer was giving way to autumn, that Kit's father, Stanley, asked to speak to Lexie alone. Being a fairly pleasant afternoon albeit with a faint chill in the air, Lexie had grabbed a shawl and suggested they sit in the garden.

Always curious about anything that could affect my precious girl, I accompanied them and was astounded to hear Stanley explaining that dear Charles, who had always expressed the wish that Lexie experience for herself some of the far off lands he had enthused about during her childhood, had left a considerable sum of money for this purpose, with instructions that the funds were to be made available to her following her marriage.   Lexie was stunned and excited at the prospect of travelling to some of the places her dearest papa had talked so lovingly about.

I was overcome with jealousy that Lexie would have the opportunity to see some of the world whilst I remained trapped. I was also a little afraid that she might not return to Mulberry House, through accident or design, a situation that filled me with dread.

No! I admonished myself, you wicked woman; how selfish you have become. This is a wonderful opportunity for the precious girl, and you must not dwell on such ill thoughts. She and Kit love this dear house and will certainly return home with tales of their experiences and they will surely write to Eleanor who will share their stories with you.

Whilst I was lost in my reverie, Lexie started to head indoors to tell Kit the exciting news, when Stanley laid a gentle hand on her arm.

"There is more my dear. Again, as per your papa's instructions, I have made enquiries about a potential world tour for you and Kit, that includes some of the places he remembered so fondly. I am hopeful that, if you so wish and we act quickly,   the first leg of the journey could be aboard the new luxury liner that has recently been launched and is due to make its maiden voyage across the Atlantic to New York   in April. Knowing your dear papa as well as I did, I am sure that he would have loved to have sailed on board the RMS Titanic, as she has been named, as she has been heralded as not only the most luxurious and the fastest ship ever built, but also as being unsinkable. I thought it could be like a belated honeymoon for you both. What do you think of this idea?"

Lexie had smiled at the idea of her papa planning this wonderful trip and sailing on this new wonder-ship.

"He would have had his shirt sleeves rolled up and badgered his way into the engine room before the ship had left the port," she had laughed. "It is an excellent plan, dear father-in-law. Let us hurry indoors to discuss things with the family."

Like me, Kit and the family were amazed and delighted with the news; the potential world tour was beyond anything they had ever dreamed of. Lexie's obvious excitement at the trip was contagious and, once Stanley was able to confirm that first class passage had indeed been booked on the maiden voyage of the RMS Titanic planned for April, she and Kit were both thrown into a frenzy of preparation for their tour.

Due to her papa's overwhelming generosity, it was an itinerary to surpass all expectations. From New York they would take ship to the Caribbean islands and Mexico, where they could visit the ancient Mayan ruins that were currently under excavation and whose discovery in the last century had so excited her dear papa. From Mexico they would set sail up the west coast of America, visiting San Francisco and Los Angeles before spending a week in British Colombia, meeting up with one of her father's very distant relatives who had migrated to Canada and made a fortune during the Yukon gold rush. Another ship would then take them from Canada to Japan and from there to Hong Kong, Singapore and Calcutta. From Calcutta they would take a train to Delhi and thence to Agra and Jaipur, before continuing to Bombay for a ship that would take them across the Indian Ocean and via the wonder that was the Suez canal to Egypt. A week exploring the temples and tombs of Luxor and the Valley of the Kings, would then see them sailing back up the Nile to Cairo to visit the pyramids before they embarked on a ship that would take them to the ancient sites of Greece, Italy and Spain and then home to England. They were to be away approximately eight months and I could only wonder at the amazing sights they would enjoy.

Lexie, with only five months to go until their departure, turned her attention to her forthcoming exhibition in London. She worked tirelessly to complete the dozen or so paintings she had promised the gallery, often working through the nights. By the end of November the collection was completed and she and Kit accompanied the paintings to the gallery in Bond Street, staying at nearby Claridges. Whilst awaiting the opening of the exhibition they completed their shopping for all the clothes and paraphernalia they would require on their world trip.

Eleanor, with Isabeau, who had been the guest of honour at the exhibition and who was to remain as company for Eleanor whilst the young couple were abroad, then returned to Rye and took great delight in teasing me with the story of their scary rail journeys to and from London. They reassured me of the overwhelming success of the exhibition, with all the paintings sold to both private and corporate buyers, and that a further exhibition had been discussed. However, both expressed concern at Lexie's seeming lack of sparkle. I too had noticed a change in the girl and expressed the hope that it had been the strain of completing her collection ready for the exhibition that had taken its toll on her. We were confident that now it was completed and a success and the preparations for their wonderful trip were also confirmed, she would recover her former enthusiasm for life.

As Mulberry House was in a tumult of preparations for the forthcoming world tour, it was agreed that Christmas that year would be enjoyed at Woodall Hall and Eleanor, Isabeau, Lexie and Kit spent four days with the extended Woodall family, enjoying much good food and wine, plus hours of fun and fiercely competitive games. They returned to Mulberry House much exhausted but full of joy.

Lexie had given Kit a camera for Christmas, so that he could keep a pictorial record of their forthcoming trip. Kit had often assisted her with suggestions for the composition of her paintings, positioning of characters and manipulating the light source to good effect and she felt sure that this would stand him in good stead when it came to capturing the many events, places and people they would encounter on their wonderful trip, some of which might otherwise be quickly forgotten so full was the itinerary.

He was instantly smitten with the art of photography and quickly availed himself of the necessary equipment to set up a dark room adjacent to Lexie's studio where he spent several weeks developing the reels of film he had used over Christmas. Not satisfied with some of the results he attempted to hone his technique by snapping many more photographs, some formal poses and other more impromptu studies of members of the household whilst they went about their daily routines.

Lexie, having not taken on any new commissions prior to their trip, was pleased to indulge him by posing around the house, although, with only a few months left before their trip, Kit was concerned to see that she had still failed to regain her usual colour and energy. He asked that she see a physician so that should she require any treatment, it could be initiated forthwith so she might be completely restored prior to their departure.

Declaring that she was simply overtired, Lexie nevertheless obliged, and much to her surprise, was informed by her doctor that she was pregnant. She returned home in a state of much confusion. Kit, naturally delighted at her announcement called excitedly for Eleanor to come quickly. It was only once they were settled in the front parlour and Lexie had advised her mother of her condition, confirming that the doctor had calculated that her baby would likely be born in mid-July, that the significance of the news sank in. According to their meticulously planned world tour, at the time of the baby's birth, she and Kit would be hurtling across India by train.

Though thrilled at the prospect of becoming parents, Lexie and Kit looked at each other with sadness. Their trip, their wonderful, much anticipated and precisely planned trip would have to be postponed.

After much debate Lexie suggested that Eleanor and Isabeau travel in their stead. Eleanor however, advised that they were much too old to go galivanting around the world, although she did express an interest in sailing on the RMS Titanic's maiden voyage which she knew would have greatly enthralled her dear Charles. Thus it was agreed and the next morning Kit called on his father in his chambers and advised him of the joyous but slightly clouded news.

Kit returned home to advise that his father was ecstatic at the prospect of becoming a grandfather and would make sure all was arranged for the comfort of Eleanor and Isabeau's return trip to New York. He had also reassured Lexie that when the opportunity arose in the future, perhaps with their child or children accompanying them, they would be able to re-organise their trip of a lifetime.

As Lexie became used to the idea of motherhood, Eleanor and Isabeau prepared for their voyage, trying hard to contain their enthusiasm in front of Lexie and

Kit. When the day came that they were to set off on their journey, Lexie and Kit accompanied them to the station to wave them off. They duly posed alongside their splendid new trunks and then again whilst boarding the train, so that Kit could take photographs of them setting off on their adventure. The first part of the journey was to Hastings where they would change trains for Brighton and then to Southampton. Eleanor and Isabeau waved madly as the train drew slowly out of the station and, once they were out of sight, Lexie and Kit walked slowly back to Mulberry House, each deep in thought at what might have been. As they arrived home the old house seemed to encompass them in a warm embrace and, as Kit placed his hand on his wife's abdomen, they smiled at each other and felt immediately at peace.

A week after the intrepid sailors had set forth for their historic trip across the Atlantic, Kit returned early from his chambers and sought out his wife who was enjoying some spring sunshine in the garden.

"My dearest one," he said, "I have some shocking news and pray that you can contain your pain, for the sake of our baby."

Lexie, looking alarmed, nodded tentatively.

Kit handed her a newspaper on which the headline read, 'DISTASTER, RMS Titanic Lost, Many Missing.' Her hand flew to her mouth as she gasped, "Mama…….Isabeau?"

Having read the headlines across Lexie's shoulder I felt a sense of loss such as I had not experienced for centuries for I realised that my dear friend Eleanor was lost.

"How could this have happened?" Lexie cried in anguish. "Did your father not mention that the ship was unsinkable? It must surely be a mistake!"

"I fear there is no mistake my darling," Kit advised gently, "There is mention of some passengers being rescued but details are scant," he added. "We must be strong dearest and pray for good news."

The two sat for some minutes, each in silent prayer, before Lexie reached for her husband's hand and led him indoors. They alerted the staff to the tragic news and asked that they too pray for good news. Lexie then retired to her bedroom to rest and, frustrated at not being able to directly comfort the poor girl, I simply sat by her side whilst she sobbed herself to sleep. When she did sleep, however, she was racked with nightmares and called out several times for her mother to forgive her.

Some two days later a telegram arrived from Isabeau.

I AM SAFE. MUCH CONFUSION. AWAIT NEWS OF ELEANOR.

BE BRAVE MA CHERIE. ISABEAU.

It became obvious to Kit that Lexie blamed herself for her mother's presence on the ill-fated voyage and he was concerned for her mental well-being and for the health of their baby. The doctor was called and counselled bed rest and prescribed a mild sedative to enable Lexie to sleep peacefully. So racked with guilt was she that she could barely muster the energy to leave her bed, let alone her room, and as the days passed with no further news, Kit engaged the help of his mother to try to distract his poor wife.

Caroline visited Mulberry House regularly to engage Lexie in discussions about the baby or local gossip whilst they worked on items for the layette. On one afternoon, Lexie had been persuaded into an armchair by the window of her bedroom and she and Caroline were looking at some of Kit's photographs. Lexie was only half-heartedly looking at the pictures when suddenly Caroline called out in surprise, "Who or what is that?"

Curiosity piqued, Lexie leant across and looked at the photograph. There, standing to one side of her mama, was a blurry image of a woman dressed in old-fashioned-looking shirt over the top of a long skirt, with a shawl around her shoulders and a close-fitting coif. On close inspection, the figure appeared in several other photographs taken inside Mulberry House.

Lexie had stiffened, had her mama been speaking true all these years? Was this perhaps Mistress Nell?

Not daring to mention her suspicions to her mother-in-law, Lexie simply suggested that perhaps Kit had forgotten to wind on the camera and superimposed one image atop another. Caroline appeared to be about to speak but remained silent whilst Lexie placed the photographs to one side and they concentrated their attention on the remaining pictures, many of which had been taken at Woodall House at Christmas. For a brief while their anxiety was forgotten as they laughed at the memories that the images evoked. However, feeling guilty at even such a brief moment of mirth, Lexie feigned tiredness and retired to her bed to rest.

As soon as Caroline left to return home, Lexie had whispered quietly,

"Mistress Nell, are you here? Forgive my previous ambivalence, I thought you merely a figment of my mama's imagination. Can you somehow let me know if you are here."

I had been somewhat discomfited to see my image on the photographs and looked around desperately for a means of communicating with Lexie. Spotting her sketchpad on a side table, I wondered if I might be able to write something. I had mastered reading long ago but writing - I had so rarely had the means or need to practice. Concentrating hard I managed to manoeuvre the pencil and a shaky NELL appeared on the page.

Lexie had gasped, "Oh thank you Nell."

Realising the limitations of such a means of communication, Lexie, who had many questions she wished to ask me, simply wrote Yes and No on two sheets of paper and suggested that I raise one or the other as appropriate. I instantly lifted the YES page.

By the time Kit returned from chambers, Lexie and I had spent a very pleasurable few hours in simple communication. Once or twice, when there was no simple yes or no answer, I had managed to write simple words, and we were both exhausted at our afternoon's work. That night, the first since the terrible news, Lexie felt no need for her mild sedative and enjoyed a good night's sleep undisturbed by nightmares.

One of her questions to me had been 'should I tell Kit?' to which I had responded a definite 'Yes.' Thus, the following morning, armed with the telltale photographs and with Nell's response sheets, Lexie told Nell's story to her incredulous husband. At first he despaired that his wife's mind had become deranged due to her grief at the likely loss of her mother. However, the photographs did suggest the presence of some vague being with Eleanor, although Kit swore that there had been nobody else present when he had taken the pictures. Lexie asked me a few simple questions that I was able to answer with the Yes/No sheets and Kit's disbelief began to waver.

"My dearest, the surest way to prove Nell's presence is for you to photograph her on purpose" Lexie suggested.

"Fetch your camera and then you can instruct Nell where to stand for her picture."

Kit did as he was bid and asked that I stand beside Lexie in front of the fireplace, perhaps holding her hand. Lexie stood as instructed and held out her hand. To our joint delight, she and I could both feel one another's hands and I offered an instant prayer to God for enabling me this physical contact, such as I had enjoyed previously with Eleanor. Kit took the photograph and a few days later, was reassured to learn that his wife was indeed perfectly sane as the photograph showed her standing and holding hands with a shadowy form that was her mother's friend Nell.

Having made his apologies to us both, Kit warned of mentioning his photographs beyond their threesome, fearing that such images would unleash unprecedented and unwanted attention on them. Lexie and I, so pleased to be at last able to communicate, were happy to comply with his suggestion and I picked up the precious photographs and later stowed them with my other precious treasures in the attic.

Weeks passed with no official communication as to the plight of poor dear Eleanor and then a letter arrived, addressed in Isabeau's elaborate hand. Lexie's hands shook as she opened the letter, and her eyes swam with tears so she passed the letter to Kit to read it to her.

Isabeau wrote that the splendid and luxurious ship had hit an iceberg and had sunk very quickly. Many were saved in the lifeboats but still more were washed into the freezing water from where few would have survived. She had exhausted all channels to determine if her dear friend had survived the shipwreck but had received no positive news. It had to be accepted by them all that Eleanor was gone but Isabeau counselled against too much sadness. She explained that Eleanor had died as she had lived, helping those less fortunate than herself.

She explained that Eleanor had befriended a number of the third-class passengers whom she had encountered when they were permitted to walk on deck for short spells early in the mornings and very late at nights. Having learned of the cramped and unpleasant conditions under which they lived, she had ventured deep within the bowels of the ship with food and medicines. She had been distraught at the conditions of the third-class accommodation and had raised the issue with the purser who promised to mention her concerns to the captain. Receiving little communication that anything would be done to help the poorest passengers, she continued to visit the lower decks, administering such medications as she could purchase from the physicians on board and personally organising the distribution of any left-over food from the first-class dining room.

After the initial impact with the iceberg, women and children had been loaded into lifeboats but as Isabeau clambered into one such boat, clutching her lifejacket to her, Eleanor had turned and run back along the deck, calling out that she had friends on the third-class decks who she would bring up to the higher level. Though Isabeau had insisted they must wait for her friend's return, the lifeboat was soon filled to capacity and they were forced to leave the ship. She had been distraught and, as soon as they arrived at New York, had made frantic enquiries amongst the all-too-few survivors for any news of her dear friend but nobody seemed to have seen Eleanor during the chaos.

She hoped that Lexie would come to accept that her dear mama was gone and prayed that she would try to put this tragedy behind her and remember her dear mama as she had always been, generous to a fault and with such kindness as to put them all to shame. She wished them well with the baby and advised that she could not as yet bring herself to attempt another trans-Atlantic voyage and would be remaining in New York for the foreseeable future. She would let them know an address in due course and would welcome any correspondence from them. She signed off as their forever friend, Isabeau.

Lexie and Kit eventually received official communication from the White Star line that Eleanor was on the list of those confirmed to have been lost with the sinking of the RMS Titanic. No body had been recovered but it was assumed that she had gone down with the great ship. There being no option but to accept the sad news, on an overcast June morning, a small private memorial service was held in St Mary's. In the absence of a body to inter, Lexie simply had an inscription added to her father's headstone. It read,

'And in memory of his beloved wife Eleanor, who sailed off for an adventure and never returned home.'

Mulberry House remained a somewhat forlorn place for some weeks until one afternoon, with a sudden and unexpected burst of energy, Lexie announced that she would paint a picture of her dearest mama to serve as reminder to all of her lifelong kindness and joy of life. Kit thought this a splendid idea and even suggested that she incorporate the suggestion of a ghostly presence at her side, as Nell had been a presence through so much of her adult life.

"Although I do not wish to overly exert yourself my dearest" he admonished. "Before you commence, please let Mistress Nell examine you if she is able for our reassurance that all is well with the baby."

I was happy to oblige, and Lexie stated how strange it was to be examined by hands she could feel but not see. Nevertheless, she was pleased when I reassured her that all was well. She was also surprised when the word TWINS appeared on her sketchpad. She had certainly been expanding at an alarming rate and had been feeling more tired of late and was therefore not surprised when, at her next antenatal visit, her doctor had confirmed that she was indeed carrying twins. He advised more rest and she promised to follow the doctor's orders. Thus, it was agreed that the portrait of Eleanor could perhaps wait until after the babies' delivery, although Kit was happy for Eleanor to put together some preparatory sketches whilst she rested.

The fast-approaching arrival of the twins did much to allay the intense grief and sadness of the household and, on my advice, a midwife was engaged to be on hand when the time came. Despite the deep sadness at her mother's demise, Lexie had maintained a healthy regime during her pregnancy, exercising regularly and eating little and often, as per my instructions and she ultimately required little intervention from the midwife when, on 12 July 1912, Master Charles Stanley and Miss Adelaide Caroline Woodall, were safely delivered.

Lexie and Kit were instantly bewitched by their offspring and their happiness was only slightly overshadowed by the sadness that Eleanor was not there to meet and enjoy her grandchildren. A nursemaid was engaged to assist with the twins' care and they quickly became the talk of the town when they were paraded about in their perambulator.

Lexie, quickly restored to her normal energetic and lively self, began work on her mother's portrait when the twins were about three months' old. As her mama had advocated before her, Lexie insisted that the twins be exposed to as much fresh air as possible and, duly swaddled and protected from any draft, they spent many an afternoon asleep in their perambulator under the shade of the glorious old mulberry tree in the top garden. There is really nothing so gloriously calming as watching a sleeping baby and I was happy to sit alongside them, with Lexie regularly glancing down from her studio to ensure all was well. Once or twice I thought that the little girl opened her eyes and looked straight at me but it was all too brief a glance and I was not totally convinced.

To avoid too much disruption for the twins, now affectionately known as Charlie and Della, it was agreed that Christmas that year would be held at Mulberry House. Lexie was determined that the occasion, despite being the first without her mother, would not be marred by any sadness, and the presence of Stanley, Caroline and some of their extended family, ensured that it was almost as much fun as the previous year.

Life returned to a gentle routine in the new year and Lexie, determined to complete her mother's portrait whilst the twins were still relatively immobile, spent most of her time in the studio. One afternoon, as she worked on the picture, Caroline came to call to ask for a favour.

Intrigued, Lexie pushed some sketches off a chair and bid Caroline sit. After sitting quietly for a few minutes Caroline, gazing at the portrait of Eleanor had said,

"Oh, so you *do* know about Eleanor's ghost. You didn't mention her when we saw her in Kit's photographs and so I assumed you did not know about her."

Lexie was rendered speechless as Caroline continued,

"Your dear mother was always mentioning her ghostly friend Nell" Caroline stated simply, "and at first I thought she had created Nell as a means of compensating for the loss of your dear papa. Eventually, however, I came to realise that Nell was as real to Eleanor as I was, perhaps even a part of her, so I went along with anything she told me about her. Sadly, I was never able to see or hear Nell for myself. Are you able to see her as well then?"

Lexie, unsure whether to confirm that Nell was actually more than just a figment of her mother's imagination, merely stated that Eleanor had told her of Mistress Nell's presence in this house since she was a child. She explained that there had long been stories of a house ghost and Eleanor had sought to reassure her daughter that there was nothing to fear from such a phenomenon should the idea frighten her. A gentle squeeze of her shoulder prompted her to say,

"Nell has befriended many previous residents of this house, including two of my many great grandmothers, Meggie and a previous Eleanor and, though I can often sense her presence, sadly I have never been able to see or converse with her directly. In view of her significance to my family, particularly my darling

Mama, I thought her ghostly presence in the portrait would be a fitting testament."

She raised her hand and placed it on top of mine as Caroline nodded her approval of the inclusion.

"But enough of ghosts, that is not why you have come visiting this afternoon dearest mother-in-law, what is the favour you wished to ask of me?"

Caroline looked a little embarrassed as she spoke,

"I know how time consuming your painting is my dear, and I know that the twins will soon start to take up even more of your time but would you be able to paint a portrait of my dear Stanley without his knowledge?" she looked at Lexie hopefully, "He will be sixty next year and I would love to be able to present him with the portrait as a surprise. Could you do it?"

Lexie was surprised at the request but found herself relishing the challenge that such a commission would provide.

"I would be delighted to attempt the portrait," she said quickly, "If I may embroil Kit into our scheme?"

Caroline nodded, "Of course, but why and how?"

"Clearly I cannot ask Stanley to sit for any preliminary sketches so I will ask Kit to contrive a reason for taking lots of photographs of his father. Perhaps he could suggest taking photographs of all the partners of the firm to hang in their chambers. I am confident of being able to construct a portrait of Stanley from the photographs and I certainly have enough sketches of your lovely home and gardens to provide an appropriate backdrop. Yes, I really do think that would work. Do you wish for something very formal or less so?"

"Perhaps a slightly more formal study than your portrait of me, beautiful though that is," Caroline responded eagerly, "but certainly a picture that shows his lighter and more loving side as well. If that is possible," she added.

Later that evening, once the twins had been bathed and put to bed, Lexie mentioned Caroline's comments about me to Kit and advised of her response, asking if he felt that she should remove my image from the painting. He was surprised that his mother had known of my presence in Eleanor's life and was both relieved and a little disappointed to learn that his mother had confirmed that she could neither see nor hear me. After a short discussion he and Lexie agreed not to remove me from the painting.

Lexie then outlined Caroline's special request to Kit and he was happy to assist in their subterfuge.

In February the twins were christened and it was at the subsequent party at Mulberry House that Lexie decided to unveil the portrait of her mother. The full-length portrait was hung at the top of the first flight of stairs, so that all who entered the house could see it and be aware of her ongoing presence, in their hearts, if not physically in the house. I was thrilled to see myself featured in the painting, albeit obliquely, and moved that Lexie had thought to include me. I smiled to myself when some of the visitors whispered of a vague ghostly presence at Eleanor's right hand whilst others dismissed this as a trick of the light. I was however even more thrilled when, as the twins were taken up to bed that evening, Della stretched out an arm toward the painting, pointed at the blurry image and smiled.

The War to end all Wars

Kit fast acquired a reputation for his photography around the district and, when he suggested to his father that a series of formal prints of the senior partners would be an appropriate adornment to the waiting room of the chambers of Messrs. Woodall, Howard and Bartholomew, Stanley was happy to support him. Several formal and informal poses were captured and the final portraits looked very professional when displayed in chambers. The photographs led to a number of similar commissions for Kit amongst other professionals of the town and some of his less formal work, such as the scrabbling of the children for hot pennies being thrown out of the town hall window by the newly installed Mayor, and the annual bonfire boys torchlit procession through the narrow town streets in November, were eagerly snapped up and appeared in the local newspaper, the Hastings
Observer.

Kit, with the formal, professional shots and the family shots taken at Woodall Hall and Mulberry House, had a plethora of photographs of Stanley from which Lexie could contrive a portrait. Lexie was particularly fond of one photograph of Stanley, taken the previous Christmas in which he was bedecked in his wife's fur coat, on all fours and stalking his two small nieces around the hall of Mulberry House. Though attempting a snarl or a growl, the sparkle in his eyes could not hide the delight of the chase. Caroline had also loved the picture but expressed the wish for something a little more formal. Kit, with his clever eye for composition, suggested a meeting of the two. Stanley in a formal stance, perhaps at the foot of the grand staircase at Woodall Hall, his eyes sparkling as his hands reached for the fur coat that was draped across the newel post. Gazing up at him through the uprights of the banisters and beside a table on which was the photograph of them being chased by 'a bear,' were two of his young nieces, faces shining with anticipation. Both wife and mother were delighted with his suggestion and the sketches were made.

When she was not busy with the portrait, and to take full advantage of a glorious summer, Lexie and the nurse Louisa, often took the twins for a short stroll around the town, usually returning via Watchbell Street and through the studio block for a picnic tea in the gardens. They were often stopped by many of the area's residents who had known, been assisted by and had loved Eleanor. They all spoke fondly of her and were delighted to witness her fine, strong and beautiful grandchildren. Lexie felt enormously proud and moved by their kind words and invited many of them to the twins' first birthday party at which they both took their first wobbly steps.

As they became more and more confident on their feet, it became difficult for the nursemaid to manage them both and Lexie spent many pleasurable hours in the nursery helping to keep her offspring entertained. They were bright children and often up to mischief, Della being very much the ringleader and Charlie her reluctant assistant, but they were both charming little people who were much beloved by all who knew them.

One afternoon, following their leisurely stroll, Lexie and the twins were enjoying a picnic tea under the mulberry tree when the nursemaid started to choke. Lexie, frantically trying to aid the poor girl, did not notice that the twins had toddled off together and were fast approaching the pond. By the time the blockage had been cleared and Louisa could breathe once again, Lexie watched as Charlie who had been watching the fish swim lazily between the lily pads seemed poised to launch himself into the inviting water to join them. Della stood unsure beside him.

"NO!" screamed Lexie and abandoned the by then snuffling nursemaid, to run towards her children.

I was there before her and called to Della, "Make your brother stop. He endangers himself."

Della duly grabbed Charlie's arm and pulled him backwards. As he fell on top of his sister yelling crossly, Lexie arrived and swept them both up her arms.

"Oh my darling babies" she cried, "You must never go near the pond my dear ones." She hugged them so tightly and her voice was so shrill that they both became frightened and started to cry. She carried them carefully into the house, followed by the equally shaken nursemaid, and took them up to the nursery. Once safely in their playroom, they ceased their tears and Lexie was able to relax. She kissed them both gently and reassured them of her love, whilst Louisa offered them the remains of the picnic which they set upon with gusto.

Della looked around at me, seeming confused, and I smiled. "You did well little one," I said, "My name is Nell."

Della seemed to understand my words and smiled shyly at me before quickly returning to her tea, lest her greedy brother ate her share.

Later, once the twins were asleep and Lexie had told Kit of Charlie's near dip in the pond, they discussed how to twin-proof the pond. After much debate at their offspring's curiosity and recognising that a fence around the pond's perimeter would be unsightly and likely only offer a short-term solution, perhaps even offering a greater challenge to the twins as they got older, they agreed that the pond would be filled in.

A few days later I watched in sadness as the golden fish that had so often mesmerised me over the years were removed for careful transportation to the small lake in the grounds of Woodall Hall and the pond was filled in. The already large lawned area, much overshadowed by the mulberry tree, was then extended to cover the newly filled-in pond and a small summer house erected to one side where it was hoped the children would enjoy a game or two as they got older.

The family again joined together at Woodall Hall for Christmas 1913 and it took the combined resources of all the family members, young and old, to keep the twins fully entertained and out of mischief. Now eighteen months old, having always seemed to be able to communicate silently with each other, they were starting to communicate with their parents and other members of the household. 'Mama' and 'Papa' were soon mastered, as was 'Lulu' which is what they called their nursemaid Louisa. Lexie and Kit were surprised and pleased when Della's next word was 'Nell.'

A few months later, at Stanley's sixtieth birthday party, the surprise portrait was unveiled and he was rendered almost speechless.

"How? When?" he spluttered and then feigned indignation at the thought of the plotting and subterfuge that had been perpetrated right under his nose by those he trusted most in all the world. He could not maintain such high dudgeon for long however, particularly when he saw how much pleasure the surprise had given his dear wife. He thanked her most warmly and paid tribute to Lexie's skill at her masterful combination of the professional and the private man.

All the guests at the party agreed that the portrait had skilfully hinted at the lively character of its sitter whilst maintaining Stanley as the undoubted man of substance he was. Lexie, delighting in the praise for her work, was quick to point out that it was Kit who had suggested the composition, and together they basked in the shared glory.

Many commissions poured in for both Lexie and Kit, and as the spring was supplanted by a glorious summer and the twins approached their second birthday, Kit suggested to his wife that he could perhaps give up the law and commit himself full time to photography. She gave her full support to his idea and, with his father's reluctant blessings on the venture, Kit took a small premises in the Landgate approach and set up a photographic studio. Thereafter he was never seen without his precious camera and soon the window of his little studio was filled with varied examples of his work.

The twin's birthday party was a great success, with a large birthday tea served in the garden. As well as all the family, many of their friends from their walks around the town also called in to offer their love and best wishes and to bring small gifts. Charlie and Della were delighted with all the attention and the new toys and sweetmeats, and solemnly but sincerely went round the numerous guests, shaking hands and offering their thanks. Watching the festivities from the summer house, I was a little sad that Eleanor had not lived to see these fascinating little people and prayed most fervently that their lives would continue to be filled with such obvious love.

Unfortunately, barely a month from the twin's birthday, the news reached Rye of the assassination of an Archduke in eastern Europe. The consensus of those present was that this event could escalate into something much more dangerous and so it transpired. Within a month or so it was declared that Great Britain was at war with Germany.

Not really understanding the intricacies of international politics and having lived through so many wars between the European nations, I was not overly concerned at the thought of yet another war. However, as Lexie and Kit discussed the war and the likely ramifications for their little family and the wider community, I came to realise that this war was going to be quite unlike any that had gone before.

There was much speculation that it would all be over by Christmas but Kit was keen to enlist and 'do his bit for King and country' before it was too late. Lexie, concerned at the possible horrors her gentle, kind husband could face, saw his excitement and enthusiasm and tried hard to hide her anxiety. When the recruitment stall was set up in the town, Kit was amongst the first in line, laughing and joking with the other young townsmen, all desperate not to miss out on the adventure. As they marched to the station to be taken away for basic training, the townsfolk lined the streets, cheering and waving flags in support of their brave young men. Lexie could not bring herself to join the throng, although she did permit Louisa to take the twins so that they could wave at their brave papa. When they returned home Charlie was full of enthusiasm and excitement at having seen the soldiers marching but Della, though she joined her brother as he marched up and down the hall, seemed less enthusiastic. When Charlie eventually tired of his marching and made his way to the kitchen to wheedle a treat from the cook, Della made her way upstairs to the garden room where Lexie was sitting, gazing out at but not seeing the garden. She slipped her little hand into her mother's and simply said

"Papa will come back."

Kit, ever thoughtful of his family, wrote to keep them informed of his progress, and advised that on his enlistment papers he had simply listed his occupation as 'photographer', however, one of the former clerks in chambers had offered his name as a reference. Once his university education and former life as a solicitor was entered onto his record, Kit had been put forward for officer training. He had expressed much disappointment at this promotion, as he would have preferred to have served alongside his fellow townsmen as equals, but Lexie, when she replied to his letter, said how proud she was of him and that she was sure the men would feel safer in his care, knowing that he was 'one of them.'

Despite her brave words and encouragement she slipped into a pit of despair at his absence and fear for his safety. I could only sit and watch, occasionally taking her hand to remind her of my presence and love. The twins offered some diversion for their mother, but Lexie certainly lost some of her sense of life and liveliness.

Following his officer training Kit returned to Rye for 48 hours leave and all agreed that he looked exceptionally fine in his captain's uniform. Lexie was, of course, enormously proud of him, as were Stanley and Caroline who joined them for supper on his first night home, but she could not shrug off the sense of doom that had settled in her chest.

That night, before he was to join his men at Folkestone before they crossed to France, Kit came to my attic room and whispered my name. Sensing my presence he produced a letter addressed to Lexie.

"I would leave this in your safekeeping dear Nell," he said solemnly. "Should I not return from this war I beg that you give it to my darling wife. Within are written the words that must go unsaid at this time lest I find myself unable to leave her. She is the light that makes my journey into the darkness possible and I implore you to help her maintain that lightness of spirit which will most assuredly guide me home."

He turned quickly, leaving the letter on a nearby box, and left as quietly has he had come.

The next morning, gently prising himself from her grip, he had stared intently into Lexie's eyes as if to absorb her spirit and light.

"I will come back to you my dear one. I promise," he had said softly and, turning quickly so that she would not see the tears in his eyes, he had left the house.

Christmas that year was a rather sombre event, although they tried to emulate previous years' festivities for the sake of the twins. The war certainly did not appear to be nearing its conclusion, as had been the expectations back in August, and even Stanley, usually so optimistic about life, seemed to be shrouded in despondency.

Over the ensuing months, whilst others pored over the newspapers for news of their brave boys' progress, Lexie could not bring herself to read of the war. Instead, after sharing breakfast with the twins, she would take herself off to her studio where she was working on a collection of stormy sea and landscapes.

These dark and oppressive paintings, unlike anything she had produced before, were a visible outpouring of her pent-up anxiety and rage.

One evening, after a particularly tempestuous session in the studio, she had returned to the house exhausted. Whilst she enjoyed a nightcap in the last glow from the fire in the front parlour, I took her hand and, leaning across her, I wrote on her sketchpad,

HAVE FAITH.

She tried so hard to smile but I could see only despair in her eyes so I added

YOU ARE NOT ALONE.

She had nodded and slowly thereafter I was relieved to see the shadow that engulfed her gradually began to lift.

Not one to sit idle but having seemingly exorcised her inner daemons via the turbulent paintings, Lexie decided to attempt a miniature painting of her darling husband, utilising, probably for the first time, the eye for minute detail and precision she had inherited from her dear papa.   The miniature was one of her finest works and, when she had it set into a locket to wear around her neck, her mother-in-law admired it greatly and requested a copy for herself, perhaps as a brooch. Mr Woolger, the local jeweller who had made the items for Lexie, asked if she would be happy to accept commissions for similar portraits and she was soon inundated with requests for similar miniatures of husbands, sons and brothers who were away at war. In some small way these pieces helped soothe her anxiety and calm her rage at the futility of war, part of her reasoning being that all the while these men were loved and remembered, they would live on forever.

Despite her reticence at reading the newspapers, Lexie could not but be aware that the war was going badly for Britain although Kit's letters, as and when they did arrive, were short on many details of his experiences and mostly filled with love for his family.

Taking her husband's lead, Lexie insisted that life in Mulberry House continue without any reference to the war and its horrors. She implied that this was to protect the twins from any fears about their papa but, in truth, it was because she could not risk falling back into the pit of despair.

Slowly the months passed, and the twins celebrated their third birthday. For some time they had appeared to be able to communicate between themselves in an almost silent and imperceptible code but were now able to converse easily with others, although Charlie's favourite words still appeared to be 'why?' and 'no!' Della, the more affable of the pair, enjoyed telling occasional stories of her dear papa and Lexie wondered at her daughter's vivid imagination. Della's stories, in marked contrast to her own fears of danger and death, helped lift her spirits.

I was intrigued at Della's stories, wondering if they were more than simple wishful imaginings. As time passed her stories became more detailed and I began to believe that she did perhaps have a deep link with her papa via which she could 'see' or 'feel' his experiences. It appeared that Lexie shared my suspicions as one evening she raised the question with me and asked if I thought Della mad.

I had written

SHE JUST MISSES HER PAPA

on the omnipresent notepad, though I was not completely convinced that it was that simple, and for the time being Lexie seemed reassured.

One sunny autumn afternoon, three years since Kit had marched away to war, I was sitting in the summer house listening to the birds singing and the bees busily humming, when Della climbed onto the seat beside me and slipped her little hand into mine. It was soft and warm and once again I said a quick prayer of thanks for the ability to physically feel this child's love.

"Hello Nell" she said quietly.

"Hello, sweet Della" I replied and smiled down at her.

We had sat thus in companionable silence for several minutes before Della spoke again, her sentences almost running into one another,

"Why can't mama see you, or Charlie, or papa, or Grandma Caroline? Mama says she knows when you are close to her, as she can feel your touch, but she cannot see or hear you. She says you are *incredibly old* and have seen many things. How old are you?" She eventually stopped to take a breath.

"Well young lady" I laughed, "I have resided here for nearly six hundred years and yes, I have seen many interesting things and known many people who lived in this lovely old house. In particular, three of your grannies, Meggie, her daughter Eleanor and then your Mama's mama, another Eleanor, were my special friends, but there have been many others and not only women."

I closed my eyes as I brought to mind the many people whose lives I had watched and aided and I felt blessed.

"I don't know why some people can see and hear me when so many cannot, but it makes it all the more special for me when people can do so. I have come to learn that there are many things in this world that cannot be easily explained. I hope you will allow me to share your life. You need never have any fear of me. I will help and guide you should you ever need me."

Della sat quietly, seeming to digest my words. Eventually she nodded as if to confirm her decision to confide in me.

"When I told him that I would tell Charlie and Mama that he was safe, Papa warned me not to mention our conversations to anyone but you. He said nobody else would understand that I see him in my dreams, even speak to him, if he is not too busy." She added indignantly. "He said that they would think I was just making up stories."

"Oh you dear girl. It is kind that you want to reassure your Mama and Charlie but your papa is quite right, it would be better not to mention your conversations with him to anyone else for the time being. I will always be here to listen if you need me."

Della sat thinking for a while and then nodded seriously. Having seemingly expunged her fears, she slipped from the bench and wandered off in search of her brother.

"Thank you dear Lord," I said out loud.

Life continued slowly and another Christmas passed, this time at Mulberry House, with only scant information and irregular letters from Kit. Stanley and Caroline, now beginning to look frail at the strain of the past years, had given thanks for Kit's continuing safety at Christmas dinner and the children had solemnly joined the adults in raising a glass to toast their absent papa. As well as the commissioned miniatures, Lexie had painted a miniature portrait of each of the twins, as a Christmas present for the absent Kit. Mounted as a diptych that could stand on his desk, it awaited his return from war. Surely it could not go on for much longer.

The children were now under the care of Nanny Burke, a jolly soul who the children adored. Their former nursemaid Louisa, having left to marry a local fisherman, had not abandoned them completely and visited once a week when she came into town from the harbour, for the weekly general market. She and Nanny would share a cup of tea whilst the children regaled 'Lulu' with all the comings and goings of the previous week.

On one such occasion, both Louisa and Nanny Burke, although used to her quaint stories about her papa, were slightly discomfited when Della let slip that she had recently spoken to her dear papa and that he had been in Hospital. She reassured them that he was well now, although he seemed to have three legs, and that he would be home soon.

Rather than make an issue of her tale, they nodded to each other and simply laughed at her funny story, but Nanny did relate the story to Lexie later on. She also suggested that perhaps Della's imagination needed to be channelled and that both she and her brother would benefit from having a tutor so that their energy and intellect could be challenged and encouraged more appropriately.

Lexie, realising that the twins were no longer babies, promised to discuss the question of a tutor with her father-in-law. The next morning she strolled along to Stanley's chambers and, without mentioning Della's remarkable tales, discussed the twins' education with her father-in-law. He wholeheartedly agreed that they could benefit from greater stimulation than Nanny and she could provide. However, he suggested that the twins should attend the local schools rather than have a tutor at home. He maintained that mixing with other children was just as important as the twins learning their ABCs. It was thus arranged that in September Charlie and Della would join the infants' class at the school in Lion Street.

Kit returns and Della reveals a secret

On a cold wet morning in January 1918, one which Lexie had dreaded for so long, a small buff envelope was delivered to Mulberry House. Feeling quite faint with fear, she could hardly bear to open the envelope lest the telegram announce that which she dreaded most. I led her gently into the parlour and pushed her gently down into a chair in case she did actually faint. I squeezed her shoulder to reassure her that she was not alone and, with a trembling hand and tremulous voice Lexie drew out the telegram and read,

SLIGHT INJURY TO LEG. HOPE TO BE HOME SOON. MUCH LOVE KIT.

"He's coming home Nell," she whispered.

After a few precious moments of peaceful contemplation of a happier future all together, Lexie rose and called upstairs to the children. Whilst they made their way down from the nursery,   she despatched the kitchen boy to Woodall Hall to advise Stanley and Caroline of the good news.

Day by day she waited on tenterhooks for a further message from Kit. The whole household, and indeed the house itself, seemed to be in a state of high expectation and finally, four weeks after the telegram, Kit arrived home. Though thinner and looking tired and wan, his eyes still sparkled at the sight of his beloved wife and their children.

As he stood in the hall, with the sunlight pouring in through the window behind him, his shadow was thrown across the floor and I gasped; the shadow did seem to show a three-legged man as Kit, with a quantity of shrapnel still embedded in his right leg, now walked with the support of a stout walking stick. I smiled at Della - so she had indeed been able to see her papa. How remarkable.

Kit walked across the hall with a pronounced limp but nothing could prevent him from enfolding Lexie in a firm embrace whilst the children and I looked on with tears in our eyes.   Eventually they reluctantly separated and she led him gently into the parlour where he settled in a large armchair.   Charlie and Della quickly threw themselves into his outstretched arms and, with Lexie perched on the arm of the chair, the tableau was complete and one that I have never tired of bringing to mind.

Stanley and Caroline arrived shortly afterwards and a sumptuous tea was served whilst Kit distributed the gifts he had bought for everyone.

Bombarding him with questions, Kit explained that he had been hit in his lower right leg by shrapnel that had shattered the bone. He had been lucky to have been taken quickly to the field hospital where the wonderful doctors had fought to save his leg, though some small fragments remained in situ and he would likely have a limp for the rest of his life. He had been shipped back to a London Hospital for assessment and had only received his discharge papers two days earlier. He had then spent a day in town selecting presents for them all; Liberty scarves for all the female staff and soft Morocco leather tobacco pouches for the men, a Noah's ark, complete with 100 lead animals for Charlie and a doll's house, with furniture for Della. For Caroline and his mother, he had purchased two exquisite, enamelled brooches and matching bracelets and for his father, a fine Morocco leather briefcase with his initials embossed in gold leaf. His eyes brimmed with tears as he handed each precious gift over.

Once tea was over he seemed to tire, so Lexie escorted him upstairs to rest. They could still hear the excited chatter from the parlour, but Kit was pleased to sink onto his old bed and close his eyes in bliss. Lexie kissed his closed eyelids and said softly, "Welcome home my darling boy. Sleep now. We have the rest of our lives to talk, laugh and love." As she rose from his side, he smiled and took her hand but did not open his eyes.

"I told you I would return to you, my darling. Your love, and that of the children, kept me strong throughout it all. I may never be able to talk of it all but give me time. Now I will sleep, a sleep such as I have not enjoyed for years."

Lexie watched over him until he started to snore gently and then left the room. Unlike so many other families, her man was home, and she determined that they would never be parted again. Watching from the door,

I gave thanks to God for Kit's safe return. My very precious family was complete once more and I was content.

Kit spent the next few months resting and doggedly undertaking the daily exercise regime the doctors had recommended to help him regain the strength in his damaged leg. Lexie was concerned at the way he was pushing himself physically and was quick to reassure him that his limp was soon barely in evidence. She was also worried about his daily perusal of the newspapers, which he scrutinised closely for details of the war.

"I do not crave the excitement of battle my dearest wife," he had smiled fondly at Lexie when she had mentioned her concerns,

"I merely check for the names of members of my regiment who might have fallen and, you will be relieved to learn, the consensus appears to be that the war is drawing to a close at last so it is to be hoped that many of my Rye comrades will be returning home soon. As for the exercises, the leg is stronger and I feel much more stable these days and may be able to forgo the use of my trusty cane before long. The intermittent pain from the residual shrapnel is also becoming more bearable and I hope to be able to resume my photography career ere long."

"No need to rush things," his wife admonished. "Let us enjoy having you to ourselves for a while longer."

When it later became obvious that Kit was in need of activity to further improve his rehabilitation, Lexie accompanied him as he visited the families of some of the men under his command who had already fallen. She could see that as well as offering them a personal account of their loved one's demise, which provided them with great comfort, each visit also seemed to lift Kit's spirits as his sense of guilt at surviving seemed less burdensome.

By easter, Kit announced himself almost fully restored and determined to resume his photographic career. Stanley, who was looking to his retirement, tried to persuade his son to return to the law, which would less physically exacting for him, but Kit firmly declined his father's generous offer. With the promise that he would engage an assistant to do all the heavy lifting, he returned to his premises in Landgate approach and set about cleaning and renewing his former studio and shop. On his desk sat Lexie's beautiful miniatures of his dear children and their smiling faces did much to restore his optimism about the future.

He took several reels of used film to the studio which he locked away in a drawer. I later learned that these comprised photographs that he had taken whilst he was away at the front and which he intended to develop and publish when he felt the time was right. Thus far he had not been able to talk in detail about his experiences during the war, save to say that it was 'pretty grim.' Though there were a few images that showed some of the rare lighter moments of his experiences, the pictures, in the main, would show the appalling conditions under which he and his men, along with countless others, had had to live and fight. His hope was that their eventual publication would help ensure that there was never such a devastating conflict again.

Commissions for his photographs soon started to trickle in, and as promised, he engaged a young apprentice, Albert Boreham, who proved a willing and able assistant. Much to his parent's horror and his wife's amusement, he also purchased a motorbike and sidecar to enable him to reach a wider range of clientele.

To everyone's great relief, the 'War to end all Wars' came to an end in November 1918 and the Christmas festivities, to be held at Woodall Hall again that year, were being carefully and meticulously planned by Caroline so as to be the best ever. Prior to the celebrations, Kit, accompanied by Della, delivered food, fuel and gift hampers to the widows and families of his fallen men, to help them through what was likely to be an especially tough time of year for them all. Whilst they were away from the rest of the family, the two talked freely of their special communications during his time at the front. Kit told Della how much strength he had derived from her talk of home, and she too reassured him that seeing him had helped overcome her anxieties about his safety. She told him that only Charlie and I had really believed her when she told of their chats and that I had counselled against repeating them, lest people think she was becoming too fanciful. Kit said he was pleased that she could communicate with me, and he agreed that my advice had probably been wise.

Christmas, with everyone shedding the anxieties of the previous war years, exceeded all Caroline's expectations and all who attended confirmed that it was the best Christmas ever.

Kit's business continued to grow over the next year and Lexie too, enjoyed ongoing success with her paintings, securing a second London exhibition, this time a mix of both landscapes and portraits, plus a selection of her exquisite miniatures. The children continued to do well in their lessons, Charlie moved up to the boys' school and it was hoped that he would soon be able to join the grammar school and in due course follow his father's footsteps and go to King's in Canterbury. Della remained at the Lion Street school and often sought me out on her return to discuss the lessons and events of the day.

Isabeau, now well into her sixties, wrote to advise that she was planning to return to France and would visit 'ma famille en Rye,' on her way to her homeland.

Several weeks later, much as she had on her first arrival at Mulberry House, she burst into the house, a rainbow of colours and a cacophony of noise as she offered endearments to them all. She remained with them for only two weeks and her visit was filled with equal amounts of laughter and tears. She very much enjoyed hurtling around the countryside in Kit's sidecar, something Lexie consistently declined, and also enjoyed renewing her acquaintance with me and hearing of all the happenings in the house since that fateful day she and Eleanor had left for their trip to New York.

Isabeau told us all of life in New York; the fast pace and the freedom to live the American dream and be what you will. However, she had, she was loathe to admit, started to feel too old for the razzmatazz of the lifestyle and had yearned for her homeland, although she had been happy to wait until the end of the war so that it was safe to embark on an Atlantic crossing. Having learned of the death of her son, yet another casualty of the devastating war, she had briefly considered remaining in New York but the thought of the imminent prohibition of the consumption of alcoholic beverages had swayed her decision.

"Imagine," she had shrieked, " *La vie sans vin*! - *C'est impossible.*"

We had all smiled in agreement and expressed joy at seeing our friend once again. Tears were shed for the loss of dear Eleanor and I was reassured that her death, as her life, had been in the service of others and would have surely ensured her a place in heaven alongside her darling Charles.

Isabeau had inspected Lexie's studio and expressed surprise at the dark paintings she found hidden in a corner. She suggested that Lexie exhibit the paintings as a reflection of the horrors of war, an idea Kit wholeheartedly supported, and a small private exhibition was arranged at a new gallery that had recently opened in Rye. Surprisingly, given their gloomy nature, the pictures were enthusiastically received and sold very quickly.

Isabeau, also spent many hours in the nursery getting to know the children and she later advised Lexie and

Kit that she saw a great artistic future for young Charles suggesting that he had his father's eye and his mother's flair. The proud parents promised to ensure that Charlie received the encouragement and support he would need to help him realise his dreams, in whatever direction they lay. Isabeau also praised Della's uncanny maturity and capacity for caring for others.

"Your children do you credit *ma cherie Lexie*," she advised, "like their mother, they are as talented as they are beautiful."

All too soon, Isabeau left Mulberry House, to continue her journey to Paris, there to reopen her house in the suburbs and resume painting, teaching and dealing in fine art. With an open invitation to them all to visit her whenever they liked, she left them as she had arrived, a wonderful, colourful whirlwind. The house had seemed unnaturally still and quiet for some weeks after her departure.

As the country entered a new decade, plans were discussed for an appropriate memorial for all those who had fallen during the War. Ultimately, two projects were planned and Kit was invited to sit on the committee that sought to raise the necessary funds for them.

As in so many towns, a memorial cross was to be erected on which the names of the fallen would be listed. Secondly, a cottage hospital would be built at the top of Rye Hill that would serve all the people of Rye and the surrounding area, so that the sacrifices of those gallant men would ultimately benefit their families and all the people of their hometown.

Kit, along with Lexie and many of her artist friends, held regular charity events to raise money for the two schemes and, with other donations and bequests, the two memorials were soon completed.

One evening as we sat quietly in the parlour, Lexie sketching and Kit pouring over some photographs that he planned to send to the local paper, Lexie suggested that, as he had seemingly enjoyed being involved with the fund raising for the memorials, he might get further pleasure if he were to take an active interest in local politics, perhaps even standing for election as a councillor. Kit concurred that he had very much enjoyed working on the memorial projects but, ever modest about his abilities, he stated that he did not feel that he was cut out for politicking. He was ever happy to work behind the scenes for the good of his community but he did not crave recognition, praise or self-gratification for his efforts.

"I do have another project in mind though," he admitted mysteriously. "Now that the memorials are completed and people are moving on with their lives, I think that it might be an appropriate time to begin work on the publication of the photographs I took whilst at the front. I will print off a selection and bring them home to see if you agree,"

A week later, when he brought home the newly developed photographs, both Lexie and I were horrified at the images laid out before us. I wondered if all wars had been so barbaric. I had never really considered the inhuman conditions and personal dangers faced daily by those directly involved in the conflicts. That weapons of war had evolved, was of little surprise to me when I considered how much else had changed during my long purgatory, but wars were now being fought closer to home, in the air as well as on land and sea, and also, so Kit had advised, with the deployment of poisonous gases and missiles fired from miles away from the frontline. It seemed to me that the more 'efficient' the weaponry, the more inhuman and hellish war had become, and I prayed that this had indeed been the war to end all wars.

Lexie sat benumbed by the images before her and, recognising her distress, Kit gathered the offending items together and placed them back in their box.

"Too soon my darling?" he enquired quietly and his wife had nodded, too engulfed in horror, anger and sadness at what her darling husband had faced to speak.

As they later retired for the night, Kit brought the box of photographs to my attic.

"I leave these in your safe-keeping Nell," he announced. "I never again wish to see such horror and fear reflected in my lovely wife's face and feel that these images must not enter the public domain until there are none left who can be so personally affected by them."

As he spoke, his letter to Lexie fell from its hiding place and he picked it up. Tucking it safely away in a pocket he left the box of photographs on a shelf.

He patted his pocket.

"Now that I am come home, there is nothing therein that I cannot now say in person. I thank you for keeping this letter for me and for all you have done to support me and mine."

I followed him as he returned downstairs and watched him throw the unopened letter on to the dying embers of the fire where it smouldered slowly before turning to ash.

Life in Mulberry House continued at a relatively slow pace, with Kit, Lexie and their children, able to enjoy a period of peace and domestic harmony, safe from the world's hardships in the comfort of their dear old house.

As the world experienced a financial downturn, with the decadence and profligacy of the upper classes a stark contrast to the poverty and deprivation of the working people, Kit continued to support the families of his fallen comrades with regular supplies of food, fuel and other basic necessities. Della, who sorely missed the companionship of her brother who had gone off to boarding school at the age of twelve, often accompanied her father on his rounds and, after begging me to teach her some basic first aid and herbal remedies, soon became adept at offering help and advice on hygiene and diet to those who needed it.

Kit became quite animated when the Labour Party came to power and he had high hopes that the plight of the poor would be addressed once and for all. Though they did introduce some significant reforms during their brief time at the helm, these made only small inroads into the overall issue of poor pay, poor working conditions and a lack of empathy amongst the ruling classes.

Lexie too became more politically aware, having never been very interested in social reform but, when Della returned from a day trip to London with the Girl Guides and showed her a leaflet that she had been given in London, she began to recognise that the world beyond her cocoon was indeed changing. The leaflet was in support of women's suffrage, a movement that had sadly lost some of its momentum when war had given people more pressing needs and concerns.

Lexie was interested to read that many women, with so many of the previous male incumbents failing to return, had been able to continue in the jobs they had taken on during the war.   With their newfound financial independence and commercial status, the fight for women's suffrage was once again finding a voice.

Due to the examples of both her parents and Kit's, Lexie had never considered herself subservient, or indeed superior, to anyone, be they man or woman, although she was not so naïve as to think that all women enjoyed the same freedoms to think and act that she took for granted. She and Kit tried to treat all people with respect and empathy and, thus far in her life, had never felt any adverse attitudes or constraints on their way of life. However, though a small number of women had qualified for a vote in the new bill of 1918, now she was the mother of a daughter she recognised that the reforms had not gone far enough and choices for women outside her comfortable home were often very different and she wanted Della to be able to avail herself of any opportunities that came her way, regardless of her gender.

Having learned of some of the more extreme activities of the suffragettes in the past, Lexie had not felt the need to ally herself with such a movement however now, swept along by Della's obvious enthusiasm and support for their ideals, she decided to take a more active interest in the campaign.

She and Della attended meetings and rallies in Rye and the surrounding area and on one occasion, they even travelled to London to attend a great rally in Hyde Park where they joined a throng of many thousands of women from all walks of life and all parts of the country.

Lexie was asked to speak at local meetings where she espoused that, if the Great War had taught the world nothing else, it had shown clearly that women could step up to a challenge as well as any man. Many heads nodded as she further declaimed that their daughters deserved to grow up in a country where women had the right to take control of their own lives and play a part in how the country was governed. As Della later told of me of the resounding success of her mother's speech, her eyes glowed with pride.

Although actively supporting the women's movement, Della, like her strong-minded mother before her, had already decided on her future path. She asked me if I felt that she had what it takes to become a professional nurse. Like Isabeau before me, I had long recognised Della's enormous capacity to care for others and wholeheartedly supported her ambition, remembering fondly many of my former residents who had taken on similar roles.

When Della later mentioned her idea to her parents, they were very enthusiastic about the suggestion and, as a first step, Kit suggested that she must continue to study hard at school and, as soon as she was old enough, he would arrange for Della to assist as a volunteer at the local memorial hospital. She was delighted with this plan and, in the meantime, spent many hours badgering me to further her knowledge of the healing arts. I showed her the now very fragile and faded copy of Meggie's herbal compendium which she showed to her parents. They were all rightly proud that one of their antecedents had produced such a fine piece, from which Della took copious notes, but Kit cautioned her that medicine had surely moved on significantly since Meggie's time and she must keep an open mind to any new methods and treatments. A sentiment I completely endorsed.

Charlie continued to do well at school, particularly in languages and art, and when he returned for the holidays often brought home friends whose parents were abroad. Kit and Lexie were delighted to welcome the boys into their home and pleased to see that Charlie seemed well-liked by his peers at school.

I basked in the lives of the loving family of which I was a small part and I had begun to think of entrusting Kit with dear Ned's secret as I was confident that he would ensure that the facts were made public in a respectful manner. However, the murder of the Russian Royal Family and the anti-royal sentiments expressed against the King during the war (that prompted him to change the family name to Windsor as a means of foregoing their German roots) and the subsequent wave of socialism that appeared to be gaining strength across Europe made me hold back. Also, from a purely selfish point of view, I was sure that the ultimate reparation for my sin would involve a member of Kit's and Lexie's family and so I decided not to do anything that might cause them potential harm or upset.

Whilst I deliberated over this dilemma, I became alarmed to learn that Kit had signed up to have electricity installed in the house. The Hastings Electric Company was to extend its supply capacity to Rye and he wanted to be amongst the first to embrace the modern technology.

Lexie shared my lack of enthusiasm for Kit's proposal, both of us fearful of a power hidden within walls and under floors, but Kit, always one to embrace new ideas, was not to be thwarted. He rationalised that the use of oil lamps and candles was far more of a risk in houses such as theirs and electricity was thus a much safer option. Della, also intrigued by the innovative technology, supported her father and between them they persuaded Lexie to accompany them to Hastings to see for herself how electricity was transforming the streets, shops and homes. On their return she had seemed amazed at what she had witnessed but, no matter how impressive it had been, she remained resolute that she would not have electric lights in her studio.

"It will distort the colours, my dear," she had informed her husband when they were discussing things at home, "Though I have often worked by candlelight, natural light is so much better for my work. The new electric lighting is simply too harsh and unforgiving."

Kit was not to be deterred however and towards the end of 1925, Mulberry House, along with many others in Rye, embraced the potential benefits of electricity. I was amazed that light could be produced at the flick of a switch but remained convinced that I could hear a buzzing from the unseen cables that transmitted the power around the house. Della delighted in making me jump with surprise as she switched on a light whenever she came across me enjoying some quiet contemplation in the dark, and, whilst I was gladdened to see her enjoying such a childish prank, I was enormously pleased when the novelty eventually wore off.

With their children growing up and requiring to be taken hither and thither, Kit reluctantly gave up his beloved motorcycle and sidecar and purchased a new Morris Oxford car. Lexie, with her distrust of speed, had managed to avoid being hurled around the countryside in the sidecar, but had been overruled by her family with regards the car and, following a few trips around the marshes and to Hastings, she admitted to me that she had found it a comfortable ride.

One afternoon, whilst Kit and Charlie were off watching a football match, Della and I were relaxing in the summer house enjoying an all too rare period of peace and quiet. Suddenly she gave a huge sigh.

"Dear Nell, you know of my ability to communicate with Charlie and my father from afar."

"Of course my dear one," I said, "You are indeed blessed with such a gift."

"I am not so sure Nell," she had countered quickly, "I have occasionally 'seen' things that do not involve anyone I know or love. Things that have yet to occur."

She looked at me, fearful that I might laugh at her words.

"Initially these images were fairly vague and as they did not involve anyone known to me I largely dismissed them as mere dreams. However, as time has passed the images have become clearer and I have learned that the some of the events did subsequently occur as I had foreseen them. Am I going mad?"

"You are certainly not mad, my dearest," I reassured the girl. "You have a maturity and wisdom seldom seen in one so young but I understand how this 'sight' may seem like a madness. Many with such a gift have been deemed 'mad' or 'possessed' in the past and I counsel against you revealing it to anyone else at this time."

I paused and she nodded.

"I sincerely believe that we are given skills for a purpose and that we should always use them to help those around us and keep them from harm. You are blessed with an usual gift and I am sure that in time you will come to trust your own instincts and use the knowledge you attain wisely."

We sat quietly for a while, each considering the enormity of Della's ability. She really was a special girl and I prayed that the 'sight' would not overwhelm and darken her otherwise sunny disposition.

Over the months following our discussion, Della advised that her 'sightings or visions' were becoming less frequent and I was relieved to note that she seemed to relax into the normal trials of growing up.

The next couple of years sped by, with Lexie, Kit and Della immersed in their own personal causes and activities. Della had started as a volunteer at the local hospital and had loudly proclaimed, within a very few weeks, that she felt very much at home there and intended to enrol on a nursing training programme as soon as she was able. I was amazed and impressed at the strength of her commitment and proud that she was continuing Meggie's legacy.

All in all, there was a general air of contentment around the house which made me happy too, and, when, in July 1928, the act was finally passed giving women voting parity with men, Lexie threw a lavish garden party to celebrate the momentous occasion. The house and garden were full of people and rang with much laughter. Kit took many photographs and the local paper featured several pictures of the event which, it was agreed by all who attended, was the party of the decade.

Once again I gave thanks to God that I had been able to witness such a momentous event. I had been a fairly independent woman in my time, lucky that my skills enabled me to earn enough to support my children after the death of my husband, albeit within the constraints that the narrow social parameters imposed on me as a woman. The laws and social norms at that time were mostly church led, a wholly patriarchal system, which thankfully, over time, lost much of its power. As elected parliaments had taken over the mantle, although these too had comprised only men, I had long marvelled at the strength of character shown by some of the women who had resided at Mulberry House, who, when the need arose had taken control of their lives in order to survive and protect their families, in spite of not having a say in how their town or country was managed. No indeed, I was delighted that at last the voices of women were to be heard.

As the festivities of the summer dwindled into a memory, Della returned from the hospital in a very agitated state and called me to her in the garden room. It was a blustery, grey November day and she anxiously explained that she had one of her 'visions.'

"There is a great storm coming" she had announced, "and there will be a tragedy that will affect our little town," she had continued.   "A ship will get into difficulties out in the bay and the Rye Harbour lifeboat will be launched. However, the conditions will be too severe and the entire crew will be lost. Nell, Lulu's husband is a lifeboat man, I cannot sit back and let him die. I must warn them." Her eyes grew large and tears fell down her cheeks.

I gently held her hand whilst she sobbed. "I do not think you can change things my dear one" I said simply, "Nor perhaps should you try" she warned.

The distraught girl jumped up in anger, "I knew you would say that" she cried, "but why has God given me this ability if I cannot save the ones I love?"

She fell back into her chair, frustration bringing forth more tears.

I could offer no answers to the poor girl who, at the age of sixteen was still transitioning from child to woman and I prayed hard for some guidance. With nothing forthcoming, I could only repeat my earlier warning to Della.

"How are you to convince people to heed your warning?" I asked, perhaps a tad sharply but keen to make the girl see her predicament. "They are likely to dismiss your warnings as a fantasy at best or a girlish desire for attention at worst."

Della eventually got her tears under control and looked sadly at me.

"But I cannot just sit and do nothing" she said quietly.

After a few minutes I took her hand.

"Let us tell your mama," I suggested, "She will know what to do."

We sped up to the studio and burst in on Lexie who was working on a sketch.

"Good gracious Della!" she exclaimed, "Is the house on fire?" she added flippantly.

Seeing her daughter's obvious distress, she suppressed her mirth and put her arms around Della who, determined not to be prevented from her mission, remained rigid.

"I have had a vision, Mama. There is to be a dreadful storm tonight and the lifeboat will be called out. All hands will be lost and I must warn Lulu so that her husband does not go out with the lifeboat tonight. I have to warn them."

"A vision?" Lexie questioned, her brain in a whirl. In an instant she recalled several times when Della had insisted that they should change their plans at the last minute, for no logical reason, only to find that they had avoided being involved in some predicament or other unpleasantness. She also recalled how Della had often mentioned having spoken to her father when he was away at war. Did her daughter have hidden powers? Having been brought up learning of Nell and her influences on her family in the past, Lexie was hardly surprised at her daughter's revelation.

As these thoughts whirled around her head, she continued to hold her reluctant daughter in a warm embrace.

"We must think carefully about this my dearest one," she said softly, "you cannot simply burst in on poor Lulu with tales of doom – she will think you possessed."

Realising that her mother believed her and was not about to lock her away as one deranged, Della relaxed into Lexie's arms.   Gesturing towards the rattling skylight and the howling of the wind outside, "Oh Mama, this wind is just the precursor of the fierce storm that will hit tonight."

She jumped up, "We cannot let the lifeboat be launched knowing that the crew will be lost. What can we do?"

Lexie held out her hand to her daughter and led her back to the house. Once securely enwrapped in warm waterproof coats they set off towards the harbour village.

Lexie called out, "Nell, if you are able, please send Kit to retrieve us from Lulu's."   She turned to Della, "Come dearest one. I am not sure that we will be able to save all souls tonight but at least let us try to ensure that dear Lulu's husband Daniel is not amongst those who lose their lives."

I was in a state of agitation as I waited for Kit to return home. Would Lexie and Della be able to prevent a tragedy this night?   Surely Lulu would remember Della's odd stories as a child and recognise the truth in the girl's warning?   The wind was certainly getting stronger as I waited anxiously.   When Kit and the Charlie arrived home from a hike, windswept and hungry, I made sure that my hasty note was the first thing Kit saw as he entered the kitchen

DELLA AND LEXIE GONE TO LULU'S .   GREAT DANGER. PLEASE FOLLOW THEM.

Alarmed at my message, Kit left Charlie to eat and wasted no time in retreating from the house. As I heard his car hurtling back down the cobbled street I retreated to my attic to pray.

It was several hours later that the trio returned home ashen-faced and bone weary. After Della had had a warm bath and a therapeutic brandy-laced hot drink to aid her sleep, Lexie and Kit had collapsed into chairs, each clutching a whisky.

"Are you here Nell?"   Lexie asked and I offered a reassuring squeeze of her shoulder.

"Well, that was an experience," the younger woman said sighing, as she described her visit to her former nursery maid..

"Poor Lulu was much confused at our unexpected arrival, particularly given that I was hardly dressed for socialising, dressed as I was for painting, in Kit's trousers and paint-spattered shirt. She had nevertheless bustled around and prepared a cup of tea for us. She listened intently as Della related her vision and warning of what was likely to happen this night but Lulu assured us that the Mary Stanford was a sound and unsinkable boat and the crew were very experienced so she should not worry. I reminded Lulu of Della's unusual predictions when she was a child and begged her to take this warning seriously.

She had seemed to hesitate but then agreed to let us tell her husband of the prediction, though she advised that it would be unlikely to prevent the lifeboat from being launched if the call came. She sent one of her son's to collect his father who had spent the day working on his boat.

Della and I had sat anxiously sipping our tea and it seemed ages before a bedraggled Daniel entered the small parlour. Once he had peeled off his wet coat Lulu had given him a large cup of tea and, took her son through to the kitchen for dry clothes, and bade us repeat our forebodings to her husband.

I asked Daniel if Lulu had ever mentioned Della's unusual gift and he had nodded warily. I then relayed her vision to him and warned of the potential loss of the lifeboat crew if it were to launch tonight. I entreated him to try to prevent the lifeboat from answering any such call suggesting that his little village had already lost enough of its young men to war.

I had said no more, allowing my words to take effect.

After a while Daniel had stood and formally thanked us both for the warning. With a sad but proud expression he reminded me that the lifeboat men were dedicated to saving lives at sea and as such they could no more ignore a request for assistance than fly to the moon. He had added that they were all seasoned sailors, well able to put to sea in the worst of storms and with extensive knowledge of the waters out in the bay. He ended by repeating his wife's words about the soundness of the Mary Stanford and its history of withstanding many a storm and turbulent sea.

Louisa had entered as he had finished his response and stood nodding proudly at his side.

It was a strained atmosphere that Kit encountered when he arrived a short while later.   Della and I, having begged Daniel to reconsider putting out with the lifeboat this night if called to do so, could do no more but return home.

So here we are now, safely home and fearful of what this night is to bring."

Kit had looked fondly across at his exhausted wife. "You did all you could my dearest."

He hesitated slightly before adding, "Though you will not want to hear it, I have to endorse Daniel's comments. Let us hope that he does not relay Della's warning to his colleagues, particularly its source, lest she be thought a harbinger of doom should the worst occur."

We three then sat in silence, each saddened at the thought of how many might die that night, simply because they would not heed the warnings. I was proud that my two girls had tried so hard to alter the course of things, although deep down I believed that what would be would be, regardless of how much one wished it to be different.

Despite her nightcap, Della slept only fitfully and I remained with her through the night chatting to her when she woke about anything apart from the howling gale and driving rain that were battering the poor old house.

At a subdued breakfast the next morning, we heard the bell on St Mary's start to toll and realised that Della's prediction had come true. Kit hurried off to the harbour to offer such help as he were able and Lexie and Della sat sadly and quietly in the front sitting room, unable to put their feelings into words.

When Kit returned an hour or so later he confirmed that the Mary Stanford had indeed been called out during the night and that all hands, including Daniel, had indeed been lost. What was even more tragic was that the crew of the beleaguered ship that had put out the call for assistance, had already been rescued by the time the Mary Stanford had been launched.

A few days later, Lulu and her girls visited Mulberry House. Kit ushered them into the sitting room before going into the kitchen to order refreshments and to ask that Lexie be fetched from her studio. As the tea arrived, so did Lexie, looking very much how she had looked when she had turned up on Louisa's doorstep only a few days before – wearing Kit's paint spattered clothes and with her hair in disarray.   One glance at Louisa's face told the story. Lexie threw herself at the former nursemaid and the two women wept in each other's arms.

Eventually their sobs subsided and Louisa, sitting herself primly on the edge of a chair said,

"I thank you wholeheartedly for your attempts to save my Daniel and the other crewmen on the night of the big storm. However, Daniel's last words to me were that he would rather be a lost hero than live long having turned his back on someone in need. My heart is both broken and full of pride at his sacrifice, though only we are aware of how he could have remained back and let another take his place. I have told none of Della's vision, not even my children, and promise you that her amazing ability will remain known only to me."

She wiped away her tears.

"I fear that the village will surely die now. Not only was one generation of men lost during the Great War, but we have now lost their sons and some of their grandsons. Such sorrow hangs over us all and I can see no likelihood of our community ever recovering from this."

She sat forlornly whilst Lexie stroked her hand. "Be brave my dear, we did what we could but," she opened her arms wide, "who are we to challenge God's will?"

They then sat in silence whilst they drank their tea and half-heartedly nibbled on a few biscuits.

When Louisa finally made to leave, Lexie once again enfolded her in a hug. "Thank you for keeping Della's secret," she whispered. "It is a gift she did not seek and I fear it is perhaps more of a burden than a benefit."

Ever mindful of the needs of others, Kit had arranged for a retired fisherman from Hastings to come and skipper Daniel's boat for a year or so whilst he trained Louisa's two boys so that they could take over the boat in due course. Kit sometimes accompanied them out on the boat and told Lexie of his respect for those who battled to eke out a living from the unpredictable and unforgiving sea. He also admitted to a sense of vulnerability being out on the open sea, whilst at the same time feeling empowered by the enormity and beauty around him. The photographs taken during these fishing trips formed the basis of an extraordinarily successful exhibition, the proceeds of which Kit gave to the fund set up to help the families of those lost on the Mary Stanford.

xXx

I mention this tragic event dear Robbie, to merely bring your mother-in-law's unique ability to your attention. She has, I am convinced, since the loss of the Mary Stanford, tried hard to suppress her visions rather than experience the disappointment at her inability to prevent such tragedies. I will later relate a more positive outcome from such a vision but would like to advise you at this point that if Della should, at any time, advise you against doing something, or indeed recommending that you do something extraordinary, you should heed her words, safe in the knowledge that she will only ever have your wellbeing at heart.

xXx

The 1930's passed intolerably slowly for us all in Mulberry House and Rye was not immune from the effects of the recession that was spreading its tentacles around the world. With unemployment hitting the poorest of the local community, the town, being the central marketplace for the surrounding area, remained fairly self-contained in terms of food production and the provision of most people's basic needs. Kit, Lexie, Della and Charlie when he was at home, hit less hard by the recession due to some fortuitous investments of their capital by Kit's father Stanley, did not turn their backs on those less fortunate and volunteered for several shifts at the local soup kitchen in Rope Walk. Kit's regular visits to his poor war comrades' families, with what Lexie fondly referred to as 'Kit's red-cross parcels' now included other needy families and Lexie too, a long-term supporter of the Red Cross organisation, also volunteered to work at their newly established Thrift Shop in the High Street, where second hand clothes and household goods could be exchanged for similar items or purchased for pennies. She also offered free, after-school painting lessons at Mulberry House for those children whose mothers were out at work and provided a light meal and a hot drink for all those who attended.

At Della's insistence, presumably following another of her visions, Kit and Caroline turned a larger part of their garden into a vegetable plot and converted the summer house into a hencoop where twelve hens and a noisy cockerel were soon ensconced. Two handsome piglets also joined the menagerie after part of the ground floor of the former wormery/printshop/studio had been converted into a grand pig sty.

Kit's parents, first Stanley and shortly afterwards, Caroline, both passed away and Charlie, enjoying a post-graduate sojourn in Florence, studying the Renaissance school, inherited the bulk of the Woodall estate. Della, now a nurse and who had married Stephen, one of Charlie's old schoolfriends who had visited Mulberry House regularly during their holidays and who was now a successful doctor, was left a substantial sum of money by her grandparents and, whilst her husband forged a successful career as a Surgeon, opened a free health centre in the East End of London.

After many months of politicking, war was inevitably declared in the autumn of 1939 and, when your dear mother who had worked for Della in the clinic, was killed along with your father, when London was hit by its first wave of bombings in early 1940, it was Della who alerted Kit and Lexie of your plight and they were happy to welcome you, aged four, and your brothers and sister into their home where you remained for the duration

Della's daughter, your delightful wife Susie, was born only a few months after your own arrival at Mulberry House and it has been my enormous pleasure to watch you both grow into the fine young people you are today.

Kit and Lexie maintained a seeming unwavering air of optimism for you children, though they often shared their fears with me once you little ones were abed. They never let their concerns filter down to you, not even when you were all squashed up in the erstwhile secret storeroom, (by then reinforced and equipped as an air-raid shelter) and the old house shook and groaned as enemy planes flew overhead. I hope you look back on those times with contentment.

When the war finally ended, you and your siblings were able to join your aunt and uncle in Hertfordshire and we were all sad to see you go. Stephen returned from his naval duties and, recognising the immense needs of his wife's medical centre, now reaching a wider patient base due to the acquisition of an old ambulance in which Della sped to all corners of East London, joined her to work amongst London's poorest residents. Susie also left Mulberry House, to join her parents in London, leaving her grandparents and I alone once more.

x X x

You alone know of the journey that ultimately brought you back to Rye and that it was the recent birth of your much longed-for twins that has offered me the opportunity for redemption. You will understand the significance of this later, once I have related my own story, but first there is one more treasure that I must pass on to you.

x X x

Charlie's War

You may have heard only scant details of Charlie's wartime experiences and Della's subsequent years of tireless searching for her brother. That he is now able to live a happy and fulfilling life is due to the love and support of his family and his own strength of mind but I would not have his current equilibrium upset by my action this day.   I would therefore ask that you leave untouched my last and perhaps most unprepossessing treasure, at the very least whilst Charlie is still alive.

As you probably know, Charlie, as Stephen had done before him, had enlisted soon after the outbreak of war. He returned for a brief furlong that Christmas and, as he and his father enjoyed cigars after a sumptuous lunch on Christmas Day, he asked his father to draw up the necessary papers to set his affairs in order in case he should not return. I watched on as the two most dear men in my life discussed quietly and dispassionately about the risks Charlie was to face, risks, the younger man explained, were to be kept secret, even from his darling Mama.

"I could not say anything earlier, papa," he began, "and this must remain entirely between you and me." He stared hard at his father who looked a little scared but nodded.

"With my proficiency in languages, particularly French and Italian, I have been approached to join a specialised branch of the armed services. I can tell you no more than that I received a phone call on Christmas eve ordering me to present to my commanding officer in two days' time to be advised of my assignment." He paused.

"You are to be spy." Kit stated simply and I gasped. Surely spies were traitorous, deceitful agents of the enemy, whom nobody could trust. It had never before occurred to me that such heinous operatives could be employed by both sides of a conflict. Moreover, I pondered, how could my own dear Charlie, who had such an open face, be a spy?

"I can say no more about it, Papa," Charlie sighed. "Other than that, it will be dangerous work and I will not be able to communicate with you and Mama."

He paused to let his words sink in.

"Will you wish me luck, Papa?" Charlie added, holding out his hand.

"Of course, my boy," Kit stood and taking his son's hand, shaking it vigorously before enfolding him in an embrace.

"I am so proud of the man you have become. Promise me you will take all reasonable care and come back to us."

Charlie nodded, tears in his eyes. "I'll do my best, I promise.

That evening, whilst the others were preparing for supper, Charlie entered my attic room and called my name. I was not able to touch him but he seemed to sense my presence and turned toward me.

"You must know that I was most envious of Della's relationship with you Nell. It was small comfort to know that Mama could also neither see nor hear you but I understand that over the years she has been able to develop a deep friendship and degree of communication with you." He paused, seeming afraid to speak and then he turned back and looked intently in my general direction.

"I was hoping we could establish a similar friendship?"

I quickly drew   MY PLEASURE   in the dust atop an old box and he smiled broadly.

"I ask that you keep this safe for me, dear Nell," he said quietly, holding out a tatty blue and white knitted bear that he had loved as a child. "Mr Perkins has been my special companion for as long as I can remember. I even took him with me to Art college and to Italy and, even when darling Susie was born, I could not bring myself to part with him. I like to think of him as my lucky talisman and I would ask you to keep him safe as I feel his presence in this dear old place will ensure my return."

He half-turned to leave and then said rather hesitantly,

"Thank you, thank you, my friend," he said and, still smiling, left his special toy on the box and went back downstairs. I picked up the tatty old bear and hid it carefully behind my special beam.

I remembered well when Mr Perkins had arrived at Mulberry House. One of Eleanor's regulars at the soup kitchen who often stopped to admire the twins on their perambulations around the town, Hilda Polley, who supplemented her family's income by knitting basic items of clothing, scarves, mittens, blankets etc., that she sold locally, presented the twins with a stripey bear each on the occasion of their second birthday. Charlie's, of course was blue and white, and Della's pink. Della had quickly discarded her bear in favour of more fashionable, shop-bought toys but Charlie had loved his bear, named Mr Perkins for a reason even he was unable to explain.

Over the ensuing years of the war, despite not receiving even sporadic communications from their son, Kit and Lexie somehow managed to retain the hope that he was alive and well. However, when the war finally ended, with much ringing of bells and celebrations around the nation, Kit and Lexie became anxious when their son did not return and they did not receive any information about his whereabouts. Months later, when Stephen had been demobbed and returned home and there had still not been any information received regarding Charlie,   Della, who was convinced that her twin still lived, made it her mission to find her brother.

Kit's army contacts from the Great War, had eventually been able to advise him that Charlie had been seconded to the Special Operations Executive and he had been sent to do undercover work with the French Resistance.   Understandably, for the safety of such agents, files showing their locations and activities were limited, where they existed at all.   Unofficially, that he had not returned home once hostilities ended, was accepted as indication that he had either been killed whilst actively assisting his Resistance colleagues or as was thought most likely, he had been arrested by the Germans and had most probably been executed as a spy.   When Kit sadly relayed this information to his wife and daughter, Della would have none of it.

"No, no, no," she had said vehemently. "I would know if he were dead."

Neither of her parents could challenge the intensity of her words but it was very hard for them to share in her optimism that she would find him.

Never one to sit on her laurels, Della spent much of her spare time sending out photographs and a description of her brother to the Red Cross and other such organisations in the hope that this would help them find him. Months passed and, with no communication from Charlie or any confirmation of his whereabouts she began to consider that he was most likely suffering from a physical or mental condition that prevented him from returning home. She vowed not to leave any stone unturned until she had established his whereabouts. When she visited her parents with little Susie, they were concerned at the effect the search was having on her.

In response to their words of caution she had repeated a mantra that continuously buzzed around her head and kept her searching and with which they could not argue.

"I would know if he were gone."

There were some occasions when a potential candidate for Charlie was proffered but, when Della's dashed off to meet these poor individuals who then turned out not to be her brother, Lexie's already frail hopes began to fail her and Kit became concerned about his wife's health.

Many a night, once the family had retired, I sat watching the fire as it dwindled in the sitting room.

"Times are a-changing dear house." I whispered. "Hopefully, we have seen the last of wars now and we can enjoy watching as our dear residents rebuild their lives. I believe that it is this family who will provide me with the opportunity to atone for my great sin and take my leave of you at last, although before I am released it would please me to know that Charlie is safe."

The house seemed to sigh in agreement and, though I was not often given to fanciful thoughts, I thought I heard a soft voice whispering, "Be patient. He will come home" as the house creaked and settled for the night.

Della continued the hunt for her brother, spending many hours scouring the newspapers for reports of the many unfortunate souls who, for whatever reason, had been left nameless and unwanted after the cessation of hostilities.   At her father's request, she ceased to tell them of the many wild goose chases she had pursued, when she set off to meet the poor men with a renewed wave of optimism, only to have her hopes dashed.

On one of her rare visits to Mulberry House she had admitted to me that the previous night she had 'seen' Charlie. He had not spoken to her and she had initially only seen his image reflected in the glass of a window, but she had strongly believed that he had been aware of her presence and when he turned from the window, there had been a glimmer of recognition in his face. The window at which he sat was in a rather grand room, with views over the countryside but there were no clues as to where the grand room could be.

"I admire your determination my darling girl," I had encouraged.

"But you must also look to your own health. Your parents cannot lose you both."

She had assured me that she would not do anything to jeopardise her own health or the future of her own family and, though her actions thus far had exhausted her, the 'sighting' of Charlie now filled her with renewed energy and hope. When she returned to London the following day Kit and Lexie both remarked that she had seemed in much better spirits.

Meanwhile, Kit, in an attempt to lift Lexie from her malaise, suggested that she paint a portrait of their beloved son, one that could hang alongside those of his grandparents in Woodall Hall.   He looked out several photographs of Charlie from which she could work.   He was surprised and concerned when Lexie had seemed apathetic towards the idea and Kit began to wonder if he had made things worse for her. He called to me and begged for my assistance in encouraging Lexie to cast off her malaise.

One afternoon as she sat in her studio half-heartedly trying to sketch her son's face, I grabbed her hand and took the charcoal from her. I wrote on her sketchpad

PAINTING HIM WILL KEEP HIM ALIVE FOR YOU.

Tears sprang from Lexie's eyes and she sobbed, the like of which I had not heard since dear Harriet had mourned the loss of her darling husband John.. Recognising Lexie's need to let out her pent-up fears, I sat quietly and patiently beside her until all tears were spent.

It was quite a while before she could speak and she softly said,

"I felt so blessed when Kit returned to me from the first war."

She paused and wiped away a tear before reaching out a hand towards me which I took.

"I don't feel as though I have any right to expect that my son will come home too. Why should my son be spared when so many others have lost sons, husbands, fathers… Oh Nell, how my heart is breaking at the thought."

I pulled my hand from hers and wrote on the sketchpad:

HAVE FAITH

BE BRAVE FOR KIT

Lexie nodded and leant back in her chair. Eventually she shook her shoulders and ran her fingers through her untidy hair, a gesture I had seen so often replicated by her darling son.

"How selfish you must think me," she bemoaned, "Kit and Della are surely suffering as well."

NOT SELFISH

JUST SAD   I wrote.

She nodded and blew out a long hard breath as she reached for a photograph, picked up her charcoal, turned to a new page in her pad and began to sketch with more of a sense of purpose in her strokes.

I sighed with relief. Hopefully the old Lexie was at least partially restored and I prayed that soon we would receive word about our own dear boy.

Two months later, after many recent and unsuccessful trips in pursuit of her brother, Della arrived at Mulberry House in a state of agitation.

"This time I really think I have found him Papa," she said excitedly. "In France. See this photograph, does this not look like our darling Charlie?"

Kit and Lexie both examined the photograph and agreed that it did indeed look like their son.

"His details match Charlie in all but one – this chap appears to be French and does not respond to English nor Italian. After the war he was discovered in a cell in a semi-derelict Gestapo prison block outside Paris and had no documentation to suggest who he was or where he had come from. He had been badly tortured and still does not speak but is otherwise physically healed. He is currently being looked after in an old chateau on the outskirts of Paris."

She let her information sink in before continuing,

"I am so convinced that this is Charlie that the need to see him is causing a physical pain inside me and, for the first time, I am scared to go alone. Will you come with me Papa? If I am once again mistaken, I fear that the disappointment will be too hard to bear."

Before Kit could respond, Lexie spoke, "We will all three go. There is no need for you to carry the burden alone my darling girl. The photograph is indeed encouraging but I need to see this man for myself. And, should it prove not to be our boy, springtime in Paris will help us cope with the disappointment."

So it was agreed. The trio would travel to Paris where the Red Cross team would take them to the chateau to meet this poor as yet unidentified soul. No time was lost; train tickets were purchased and suitcases packed. The evening before they were to set off for France I was in my attic praying that Charlie would accompany them on their return, when a scruffy blue and white teddy fell to the floor beside me.

"Of course," I said, "Thank you dear house," and I made my way downstairs.

As they prepared to leave Mulberry House the following day, I stood anxiously at the bottom of the stairs.

"Fear not dear Nell, we will be back before Christmas," Della smiled, "and I have carefully packed that which you advised me to take," she added conspiratorially.

The following weeks seemed to be the longest of the hundreds of previous weeks of my purgatory. Surely, I reasoned, this is more in-keeping with what purgatory should be about. Waiting for something that you want most ardently, but which is totally beyond your own control. Having become so accustomed to participating in my residents' busy and interesting lives, I now found the time dragging. I spent the weeks praying most vehemently that they would find dear Charlie and bring him home.

Nearly three weeks had passed and Stephen and Susie had come to Mulberry House for the weekend when, on the Sunday afternoon, the recently installed telephone rang. An excited Stephen returned to the front parlour and said tearfully, "It *is* Charlie, it is Charlie. They are bringing him home and should be back within the week."

He and Susie danced around the room laughing and crying at the same time.

Sure enough, late in the afternoon some four days later, Kit and Lexie arrived home with Della gently leading a very much changed but smiling Charlie into the parlour.

"Here we are then, my dearest boy," Kit announced. "Home at last."

Stephen and Susie, not wanting to miss the momentous event, had remained at Mulberry House and now stood smiling at the returning hero. Charlie looked around him and smiling said, "Susie?" as he held out a gloved hand to his niece.

"Welcome home Uncle Charlie," she smiled back at him and, though she had been only an infant when he had headed off to war, instantly felt a sense familiarity as she took his hand.

"And Stephen" Charlie added, trying to stand to shake his friend's hand.

"No, no, you stay seated old man," Stephen said firmly whilst squeezing his friend's shoulder. "It's so good to have you home at last."

It was a subdued celebration that evening, as all were exhausted by the emotional strain of the previous weeks. Charlie soon retired to his old room and Kit and Lexie also decided on an early night. Stephen took Susie up to bed and Della settled in the parlour with me to recount Charlie's story.

They had visited the old chateau with representatives of the Red Cross. The old house was home to fifteen amnesiac patients, all presumed French. The man who was thought might be Charlie had been informed that people were coming to see him but not who they were. They had been warned not to give him their names or mention any specific people or places, for fear that he would latch on to them and thus convince himself that he remembered. The nurse had insisted that he must be the one to proffer any names so that they could be sure that it was memory and not suggestion that was triggering him. It had seemed so cruel, but they had agreed.

They were shown into a room by one of the nurses and Della had gasped. This was the room in which she had seen Charlie in her vision. However, the man who sat at the small table in front of the window, concentrating on a chess board before him, was most definitely not the man she had seen and was most definitely not her brother.

Della described almost collapsing with disappointment and thought she might have even cried out in despair. Disappointment had been etched on the faces of her parents and they had turned to leave the room when a nurse had rushed into the room and rapidly admonished the poor man in French.

"What are you doing in here?" she had cried. "This is not your room!" and with that she had grabbed the poor chap and ushered him out of the room apologising to the English visitors as she went.

A minute of two later another nurse arrived and apologised to them again for the error and urged them to wait whilst 'Monsieur Jacques' was located.

After what had seemed like hours but was probably only about ten minutes, the original nurse had returned with a different man, and this was indeed the man Della had 'seen'. Being so close to him now, they were all convinced that he was their own dear Charlie. Oh, he was much thinner of course, and his hair was snow white, not the luscious and unruly auburn locks he had inherited from his mother and of which Della had always been so jealous. There were multiple scars across his face, making him look so much older than his thirty-seven years, but there was something about his eyes and the way he held his head that were so familiar. He had walked across the room with a slight limp and, without appearing to look at them, had sat down on the bed. His hands, which he held clasped in his lap to ease their trembling, were twisted and scarred.

He sat on the edge of his bed and did not speak. Apparently, he had hardly uttered a word since he had been taken from the gestapo prison.

Della had moved forward and knelt on the floor at his feet and asked if he recognised her.

He had remained silent but had looked down at her seeming to examine her features most carefully. He had then turned to look at Kit and Lexie but his face remained blank, though sitting close to Della, the similarities between them were obvious to the older couple.

The silence in the room had become unbearable and Lexie had buried her face in Kit's shoulder, not wishing to let her distress show.

Della, convinced that this poor man was their own dear Charlie, realised how distressing it must have been for her parents to see him so broken. She realised that the search had been an entirely selfish one on her part. It had never occurred to her that the brother she sought, though still alive, might never be fully restored to her. Looking at the broken man before her she was racked with a doubt that perhaps it might have been better for them all if she had not persevered with her search.

She had stood and returned to her parents' side, offering her apologies for being the cause of their obvious distress.

Kit had then passed Charlie an envelope containing photographs of the family, Woodall Hall, Mulberry House and other Rye views, and though he had examined each one carefully, he had shown no obvious signs of recognition.

"And then, dear Nell, I remembered the item you had encouraged me to take with me." Della had said her eyes shining.

She had asked her parents to give me one last chance and had reached into her handbag and pulled out the saggy old blue and white bear. Placing it in the man's hand she had and asked if he remembered it.

He had looked carefully at the bear and gently turned it over and over in his twisted hands before holding it to his nose as if to divine the scent of home. After several long minutes that had seemed like hours, he had shaken his shoulders and, in a manner only too familiar, ran his mangled fingers through his now white hair. He looked up at his sister and then at his mama and papa and as tears trickled down his cheeks, he had said slowly and in English, "Mr Perkins."

They had been euphoric. Nobody but their own Charlie could have known the name of that tatty little bear, but, for fear of overwhelming him, they did not all go rushing to embrace him.

Della had sat down beside him on the bed and taken one of his mangled hands in hers. "Oh yes, my dearest, dearest brother, it is Mr Perkins, and here we are too, come to take you home. Your ordeal is over."

He had eventually looked up at her and said quietly, "Della?"

At her tearful nod and warm embrace, the floodgates had opened and he, once he was able to speak, had tentatively asked if the war was really over. She had reassured him that yes, England and her allies had been victorious and the Nazi regime was no more. His whole body had started to shake at the news but then he suddenly stood up and limped across the room and taken his parents by the hands. "Mama, Papa, I am so happy to see you. Please take me home to Rye."

"So now, here we are, home at last," Della slumped back in her chair, her tale completed.

It was several months before Charlie felt restored enough to give his concerned family more details of his experiences. Looking tired but much stronger than when he had arrived home, he sat in a chair in the garden room, looking out across the pleasant garden, his family around him.

"There is lots to relate, and lots that must remain untold, but be assured, it was my memories of you all that kept me from breaking completely. Oh, they could and did break my body, but never my resolve or my spirit."

Taking a deep breath, he began.

"I was attached to a brigade of the French Resistance who were active in and around Paris and whose sole purpose was to disrupt and interfere with the activities of the Nazi invaders. My new persona was that of Jacques Dupont, not very original I know, a part-time artist and curator at a small town museum a few miles from Paris. I was often to be seen cycling around the countryside with my sketchpad but my extracurricular activities included the bombing of Nazi barracks and depots, the rescue of captured allied airmen and soldiers and the facilitation of their safe return home. Within the brigade I was familiar with only a handful of my co-fighters and, though I never knew their real identities, there was enormous trust and camaraderie between us.

After years of successful raids and assaults on Nazi held positions our luck ran out and my associates and I were captured. I never saw any of them again."

Charlie paused to wipe a tear from his cheek.

"I was told that my friends had all been shot as traitors, though this begged the question as to why I had been singled out from the group. It can only have been that my captors must have seen through my disguise and anticipated being able to force me to reveal important information regarding my mission. Despite being tortured both physically and mentally I managed to hold fast. Perhaps too well."

He grimaced around at his family whose expressions reflected the horror at what they were learning of his treatment.

"Once the war was over and I was freed you may wonder why I failed to announce my true identity and return to you sooner. This was entirely due to my own cowardice and for that I sincerely apologise, particularly now I realise the extra anguish this has caused you.

Having been kept in dark, windowless cells, I had lost all sense of time and could not have said whether I had been incarcerated for weeks, months or even years. When I was taken from the cells and assured that the war was over, despite being housed in better accommodation and being fed well and treated with kindness, I convinced myself that it was all a clever ploy. My captors had been physically brutal but also psychologically clever in their attempts to make me talk and I came to believe that the change in my environment and care were simply a way to trick me into letting down my guard and talking freely of my mission and associates within the resistance. I feared that if I showed any sign of such a lapse I would be returned to my previous hellhole for further torture. I therefore maintained my identity as a feeble-minded Frenchman, not responding to any words spoken in English or comments about England and her allies. Ultimately my fear of torture resulted in my being fearful of my memories and I ceased to allow myself to remember my life before the war until ultimately I could no longer recall any life prior to my capture. I apologise for having been so weak."

Lexie shook her head.

"My dearest boy, you have no need to apologise to us and cowardice and weakness are the last words anyone would use to describe your actions."

Charlie smiled across at his mother.

"At this point I must convey my very great thanks to my darling sister who, I understand, remained convinced of my ongoing existence and spent the last four years scouring the continent for information regarding my whereabouts. This must have been an enormous strain on you my dearest and I feel ashamed that my self-imposed mental barriers prevented me from being able to sense your struggle and despair and spare you such a prolonged hunt. Words will never be adequate to express my love and appreciation for you dear Della."

He rose and embraced his sister.

When he resumed his seat he gazed around the room.

"At this stage I must also offer my very great thanks to our friend Nell. Without her support to Della and her insightful intervention, (here he held up his scruffy blue and white bear) I might never have been able to break through the self-imposed mental barriers. You have given me back my life Mistress Nell and I will be forever in your debt."

"Just so, just so," Kit agreed. "We are all in your debt. Thank you dear Nell."

He coughed slightly before turning back to his son.

"I thank you for sharing your history with us Charlie. That you withstood horrors such as we could never imagine and remained true to your country and your family, makes us immensely proud.   We are overjoyed to have you home at last and keen to assist you in any way with regard the restoration of your physical and spiritual strength.

Though the war has left its mark on us all, our experiences are nothing when compared to your own ordeal but let us move forward together, with the strength that comes from knowing that we love and are loved."

Charlie smiled lovingly at his parents.

"You are right Papa," he acknowledged. "We are all changed."

There was a moment of quiet as they all reflected on the past years or war.

Wishing to lighten the atmosphere in the room Charlie then continued,

"With regards to the changes here at home, Della has advised me that you have become an accomplished cook Mama," he said with a hint of the old Charlie twinkling in his eyes.

"Despite the ongoing privations of the war, I am looking forward to sampling your fare. I would beg to remain here in this dear old place whilst I regain my strength. Just being with you all within its precious walls is like a tonic in itself. However, I am keen to take over the custodianship and management of Woodall Hall as soon as I am physically able. Since returning home and in an attempt to replace the memories of my darkest hours with more optimistic thoughts, I have been making plans for the future of the estate and I have much to discuss with my tenants."

"No need to talk of that now my dear boy. You must not rush things. The estate will manage just fine until you are fully restored," his mother protested but Kit laid a hand on his wife's arm.

"I share your concern my dear," he said gently, "but Charlie will know when he is ready to move on. Not that I compare my own experiences with those of our own dear boy but you will remember that when I came home from my own war, as well the loving environment I returned to, it was my work that helped me to ultimately lay my ghosts and learn to live with the burden of sadness and feelings of guilt.

Though he is our boy, he is now a man who must be allowed to determine his own future, Only then will be truly restored."

Charlie nodded and stood.

"Thank you Papa. Let there be no more talk of what is past. Let me take some rest now and tomorrow we can start planning our futures."

Charlie then left the room whilst all in the parlour sat in an uncomfortable silence.   Tears were evident on most faces, a mixture of anger and joy. Anger at the brutality Charlie had had to face coupled with the joy that he was at last restored to them.

Lexie, eyes swimming with tears, said quietly, "His beautiful hands, so broken and twisted. Will he be able to paint again do you think? How can one human being inflict such torture on another? It truly breaks my heart." She looked up at her husband, "I will also take a short nap, my dear, I feel quite drained."

Despite his resolve to be both mentally and physically restored,   Charlie made slow progress.   I had recommended some herbal teas to help him control the tremors in his poor twisted hands and to ease the persistent nightmares that troubled him at night, and a balm to rub into the scarred skin of his face and hands to ease the tightening.

"You must be patient," I advised Della on one of her regular visits. "The longer it takes the more complete will be the recovery."

Realising the wisdom of my words, Della nodded. "I will try," she promised, "though patience has never come easily to me."

Christmas 1949 was a joyous occasion. As ever, though rationing continued, Lexie produced a sumptuous meal for all the family, after which they listened to the King's broadcast on the radio before exchanging the presents that had accrued around the tree.

On New Year's Eve, as the family gathered, glasses filled, ready for a rendition of Auld Lang Syne, the church bells, began their muffled toll. The church clock struck twelve and the muffles were removed enabling the bells to ring out boldly and cheerfully. I could not remember them ever having sounded so beautiful. A good omen for 1950 I thought as the family, together again at last, raised their glasses in a toast to the new year and then joined hands to sing.

A weariness came over me as I realised that it was nigh on six hundred years that I had dwelt here. This precious family, with whom I had shared the last four generations and several more at the start of my purgatory, would surely offer me the chance of redemption, likely little Susie I thought, though she was young yet.

xXx

Little did I know at that stage, the part that you would also play in my redemption, young Robbie.

xXx

When the family eventually began to retire for the night, I heard several whispered, 'Goodnights and God blessings on you too dearest Nell' and I began to realise that if I were forced to make a choice regarding the safety of these most precious of my friends or my redemption, it would be a harder decision than anything I had ever had to face before.

As Charlie's physical health improved he remained troubled with nightmares. Though he could neither see or hear me, he seemed aware of my presence and would often whisper things to me that he did not feel able to say to any of his family. I responded with my brief notes, as I did when communicating with his dear parents.

When sleep refused to offer him any peace he would often creep from his room and make his way silently to his mother's studio. There, with much frustration at his twisted fingers, he attempted to sketch. Initially he produced little more than scribbles and scratches but, as his fingers began to gradually remember their earlier prowess, he started to create some remarkable images that he hid away in a dark corner of the studio lest his mother see them.

When at last he felt ready to turn his sketches into paintings they were dark indeed, both in tone and subject manner, and even my untutored eye could see the terrors and fears expressed therein. He completed six such paintings, each representing elements of his experiences of war, including the torture, and all featuring the same demonic face. When he added his signature to the last one, he sat back and seemed to finally relax.

WHO   I wrote on his sketch pad.

"I will never name him, Nell," Charlie had said bluntly. " I recall having seen him hanging from a second-floor window as I was settled into an ambulance on my release from the Gestapo prison but had not believed that he was dead at that time. I had convinced myself that the image had been either the wishful thinking of my weakened mind or, perhaps had been yet another somewhat twisted ploy by my captors to trick me into letting down my guard. Since being restored home I have made surreptitious enquiries as to his whereabouts and have learned that he had indeed, like so many of his kind who could not face up to the consequences of their inhuman and criminal activities, taken the coward's way out.   It was indeed his body that I had seen hanging from that window as the prison was being stormed and its residents liberated and he will therefore never be held to account for his crimes. To name him now would, I feel, afford him a notoriety and infamy that many of his ilk seem to be enjoying. I do not wish that. It is better that his name be forgotten."

JUSTICE FOR OTHERS   I scrawled

Charlie sat back and ran his now stronger fingers through his hair.

"You may have a point Nell," he said quietly.

After a long time spent in contemplation, he reached for a blank page. Turning it so that I could not see, he began to write.   I watched his anguished expression begin to ease as he wrote and finally, he settled back in his chair and smiled. Folding the paper and placing it into an envelope, he sealed it and pushed it away from him across his work table.

"Please take this and hide it Nell," he pleaded. "Should the need arise in the future I will ask for it or, if I am gone, you can release it if you think it might help to bring justice for any of his many victims. Until then, please let his name go unspoken."

I lightly touched his hand and took the envelope for safe keeping.

Having now revealed all the secrets and precious items that have been entrusted to me over the years, dear Robbie, I am ready to reveal my own dreadful secret. You may so abhor my revelation that you turn away and distance yourself from my story but I entreat you to put any prejudices against me to one side and read on.

Though I ask no judgement or forgiveness from you - this is most surely in the hands of the Lord - I do ask that you note my immediate and continuous sense of contrition following my dreadful crime and that I would not have considered such an act had I not feared for the future safety of the child concerned and for that of my own family.

Now, in the year of our Lord 1969, I will perhaps explain my recent actions on behalf of Susie and your children. That you are reading this suggests that my actions have proven beneficial and that I have now been released from my purgatory.

xXx

My secret

My own story begins in the year of our Lord 1335 in the small town of Rye. I, like my mother and grandmother before her, was a well-respected midwife in the town, ready and willing to assist any woman who might have need of me. My own daughter, Agnes, desirous of learning from me, often accompanied me in my work.

One dark, October night there was a knock at the door of our cottage.

"Mistress Jenkins, Mistress Jenkins," came a shrill voice, "You are needed at once."

As a midwife, I was accustomed to being disturbed during the night, although, as I entered my fourth decade, it was becoming more difficult to wake as quickly as I had in the past.

I splashed water over my face and donned a shirt and rough woollen skirt over my shift. On top of this, an old tabard, belted firmly around my thickening waist, thick hose and stout wooden clogs completed my garb. Fastening my loosely plaited greying hair around my head, I firmly tucked this and as many errant wisps of hair as I could, inside my wimple.

The knocking continued and I opened the door a crack, "I come," I said quietly into the dark night so as not to wake Agnes, with whom I shared the large truckle bed across from the hearth. Whilst Agnes often accompanied me to birthings, this night I let her sleep. I smiled down at my daughter who slept as sound as any babe under our threadbare quilt.

Time enough for disturbed nights in the future I thought as I completed my preparations.

Stretching to loosen my stiff joints, I reached above the fire and selected some of the drying herbs that I often used during my administrations. Bay leaves, betony, borage, chamomile and feverfew could often ease the trials of childbirth and hasten the arrival of a stubborn babe and I never left the house without them.

With the herbs safely stowed away in my mother's old leather scrip, I grabbed a shawl and cap from their usual peg and re-opened the door. Who was in need of me tonight, I wondered? Lady Mathilde, on her fourth babe, was near her time, as were young Mrs Breeds, the Mayor's new wife, with her first, and Fanny Haffenden, a fisherman's wife who was awaiting the arrival of her eighth.

There stood the pot boy from Capel House, "You are needed Mistress Jenkins, Milady Alard has need of you."

My heart sank but I nodded and pulled the door firmly shut behind me. It was good that I had left Agnes to sleep. Tonight, it was important that I attend the delivery alone. Following an uneventful pregnancy, this would likely be a straightforward delivery. However, both Milady and Milord Alard, with three fine, healthy daughters, were desperate for a son, and I was fearful of what this night would bring, should Lady Mathilde bring forth another girl.

As we made our way between the tightly packed cottages and past the partially constructed Castle, I was glad to have grabbed my shawl as the autumn night was chilly and there was a dampness in the air that heralded rain. Clouds sped past the moon which gave scant light, and I was glad of the lantern that the boy carried as he ran ahead, bidding me to hurry. I struggled to keep up with him and almost stumbled as my clogs clattered across the cobbled churchyard and I heard a faint and eerie chanting emanating from the old friary. Though it had been long since abandoned by the friars and remained empty, I glanced over at the old building; was that a faint light flickering inside? I shivered and crossed myself as I continued on.

"Do you hear that?" I asked the boy.

" 'Tis just the wind in the trees Mistress," he responded impatiently, "Do hurry, Milady awaits."

As we reached the top of Middle Street, I shivered again, although this had little to do with the fear of any ghostly activity at the friary or the damp weather. I recalled my meeting with Sir Gerald when I had visited Capel House a few weeks' earlier. After examining Lady Mathilde, I had been ushered into his private office at the front of the house. He had looked weary but gazed fondly at the three little girls playing on sheepskins strewn on top of the rushes, in front of a cheery fire. I had assisted at the births of all three girls, Katherine, now six, Isabelle four and little Marie, who was little more than one year old.

"Are they not as beautiful as their mother," he had stated with immense pride and affection, "My precious, precious girls." He had sighed. "Come closer Mistress Jenkins."

Smiling at the girls as I stepped around them. "Precious indeed," I had agreed.

He had sat back in his chair, "Mistress midwife, how fares my Lady wife this time?" he had enquired formally.

"She is blooming as ever, Milord," I had sought to reassure, "The babe has not yet turned but this can often happen late. I am confident that Lady Mathilde will be delivered of another healthy child within a few weeks."

"I cannot have another daughter, Mistress," he had said quietly.

I gasped, "Oh sir, that is of course in God's hands, not mine, but rest assured, I will do all I can to ensure that both mother and babe survive the delivery. Lady Mathilde is strong, and the babe feels to be a decent size. May it please God to give you a fine healthy boy."

Sir Gerald stared grimly at me and despite the warmth coming from the fire, I had felt a chill down my spine. From the knowledge of Lady Mathilde's previous pregnancies and the position of the babe, my instinct and experience suggested that this was to be yet another daughter. I feared that my face would betray my thoughts but I did not dare mention this to Sir Gerald.

"You misunderstand Mistress," Sir Gerald had said icily, "I do not require your platitudes about God's will. It *must* not be another daughter."

He had paused, "My family has been prominent in this town since my ancestor came across from Normandy with the Conqueror. Ironically, nearly 300 years on, my elder brother, as yet unmarried, is now in charge of the Channel Fleet, dedicated to protecting this realm from a French invasion. With his continued commitment to the defence of our town, I foresee a great expansion of our port which will bring much wealth for all and it is therefore imperative that I have an heir to ensure that our family line continues."

He paused again and sighed as if he carried the weight of the world.

"It *must not* be another daughter Mistress Jenkins," he had repeated, slowly and firmly.

He had been unable to meet my eyes as he spoke but had reached into a box on his desk. I had heard the clink of coins, and his message had been clear.

"Milord Alard, I cannot …" I had begun, but he held up his hand to silence me.

"I understand you lost your husband at sea fighting against the French, and that your son, George I think, is likewise aboard one of the town's Cinque Ports' ships under the command of my brother?" I had nodded.

"Life at sea can oft be hazardous and it would be unfortunate indeed if you were to lose your only son, having already suffered the loss of your husband."

He waited to allow his thinly veiled threat to sink in and then he coughed and stared coldly into my eyes

"As well as a generous bonus for your excellent midwifery skills and care of my dear wife, I would be happy to have your son restored to you and offered safe and secure work locally."

I was shocked and even the gentle murmurs of the nearby children at play failed to offer any solace. Before I could speak I heard a further chink of coin as Sir Gerald held my glaze.

"So it is agreed."

He had taken my silence as affirmation and had then simply waved his hand at me in dismissal.

As I had turned to leave, Sir Gerald had stood and had swept up the two youngest girls in his arms.

"Come girls, let us see if cook has any sweetmeats that we can take upstairs to your mother." With Katherine skipping on ahead, he had made a slight bow in my direction and had left the room. I followed behind and was quickly ushered from the house. I trudged slowly back up the hill, my chest filled with an icy fear at what had been asked of me.

Now, just a few weeks later I was hurrying to Lady Mathilde's lying-in and, for the first time in my lengthy career as a midwife, I was dreading what was to come.

Capel House was a well-proportioned house built approximately a third of the way down Middle Street which led to the prosperous port where merchant ships docked, and Sir Gerald had his warehouses. Set back from the street and enclosed in its own fine gardens, Capel House was the epitome of wealth and status. Today, instead of the usual entry via the kitchens, I was admitted via the main door and escorted straight up the stairs to Lady Mathilde's suite of rooms that overlooked the gardens. The main room was large, with substantial leaded windows that, despite the darkness and the promise of rain on the wind, had been opened wide to bring fresh air to Lady Mathilde who, dressed only in her shift, was sweating profusely as she paced the room, supported by two of her ladies. As I entered, she let forth a loud growl as a pain racked her body.

As the pain eased she smiled, "Ah Nell, you are come. All will be well now ladies," she had reassured her attendants.

I bade her lie down briefly to enable an examination and was pleased to feel that the baby had turned. However, as with her other babies, it was lying back-to-back with its mother, and in my experience, this was further indication that it was likely to be another daughter.

"Not long to go now Milady," I had reassured and had helped Lady Mathilde to sit up. Offering her an arm I suggested we walk some more until she was ready for the stool. Whilst we continued our perambulations around the room I bade the ladies pull the windows closed so that Milady did not become over chilled and instructed them to warm some sheets before the fire.

"We need to ensure that this young babe has a warm welcome." I had said enthusiastically.

After several circuits of the lavishly appointed room, Milady's pains became more frequent and intense, and she indicated towards the stool.

"Please God let this be a son," she had cried as a strong pain coursed through her.

As she settled herself on the birthing stool, I knelt before it and a sheet was laid over my head and held against Lady Mathilde's midriff to protect her modesty and that of her ladies, who were as yet unmarried. I massaged Lady Mathilde's lower abdomen, pressing gently downwards.

After several fierce contractions the babe's head was clearly visible.

"I can see the head Milady," I said loudly and encouragingly. "He has a thick mop of hair just like Lady Isabelle."

Sure enough, with two further waves of pain, the baby slithered out – a beautiful baby girl once again. Without allowing any time for sense to stay my hand, I placed my hand over the baby's mouth and pinched at her nose, whilst my other hand looped the cord around the baby's neck and I pulled hard.

I wept silently as the babe's body became limp in my arms. I sat back on my heels, murmuring a short prayer for the poor, innocent soul.

"Why does he not wail, Nell? Is aught amiss? Give me my son," Lady Mathilde had cried.

After a short pause I mumbled from beneath the sheet, "Milady, it is another daughter."

As the babe's mother let out a wild cry of distress I added, " sadly the poor mite has not drawn breath."

After making the sign of the cross on the tiny forehead, I gently wrapped the lifeless body in the waiting cloth before emerging from under the sheet. I handed the little bundle to its mother.

"It would appear that she turned too late, Milady, and the cord became entangled around her neck thus strangling the poor mite before she had a chance at life. She would not have suffered any pain."

Lady Mathilde gave another cry and gazed sadly at the tiny face of her fourth daughter. One of the ladies in waiting had been sent to summon Sir Gerald who now entered and rushed to his wife's bedside.

"I have failed you," Mathilde said flatly, "another daughter, although God has seen fit to take her from us. Perhaps He is displeased with us."

Tears fell silently down her cheeks, "I should have liked her named Alys for my mother," she said sadly, "hopefully she will not wait long in limbo before taking her place in heaven."

"My dear, do not berate yourself," Sir Gerald's voice was gentle and full of emotion as he attempted to comfort his wife. I was amazed at how calm and loving he appeared, given that he had brought about this sorry situation himself.

He continued, "You could never fail me, my dearest. We will have masses said for the soul of our dear little Alys so that she may make her way straight to heaven."

He turned towards me with eyebrows raised. "Mistress Jenkins?"

I did not respond straight away, so fraught with guilt was I, but busied myself with the inspection of the afterbirth. Once I was completely happy that it was intact and healthy, I slowly wrapped it a soiled sheet ready to be burned. I then turned towards him, eyes lowered.

"Sadly stillborn, Milord, strangled by the cord which had become wrapped around the poor babe's neck as she turned in the womb. She never drew breath," I had said with tears in my eyes. Then I raised my eyes to meet his, "She would have been a bonny girl, just like her sisters."

"Is my wife undamaged?" he asked abruptly.

"Yes Milord, she is strong and healthy. She should make a good recovery and be able to carry more children, God willing."

Sir Gerald turned to his wife,

"When you are quite recovered my dear, let us take a pilgrimage to Walsingham and pray for the intervention of Our Lady to give us a healthy son next time. We could perhaps visit the shrine at Canterbury as well."

Mathilde had smiled weakly at him. "If you so wish my dear. Here Nell, take the poor lamb away. I would sleep a while."

As the sky began to lighten, Sir Gerald left the room and asked that I attend him in his office when I had completed the care of his wife. As I checked my patient for any signs of a fever, I experienced a sense of weariness such as I had never felt before. I stumbled against the bed post and slumped to my knees. God was punishing me for what I had done that night. He had given me the skills to help women with the trials of pregnancy and childbirth and I had completely turned my back on His benevolence and taken things into my own hands. I felt truly damned.

"Nell, are you unwell?" Mathilde asked with concern, "Ladies, quickly, attend Mistress Jenkins." The ladies helped me to my feet.

"I have failed you Milady," I said as I struggled to keep myself upright. "I should have saved the poor babe."

"It was God's will Nell and who are you or I to challenge that." Mathilde had sighed and forced a smile. "I will go to Walsingham with my husband and pray for the safe delivery of a son, and I expect you to attend me and share my joy when the time comes. Now, I must sleep and so must you; I will see you in six weeks' time as usual."

Having left Mathilde drinking a decoction of sage that would help minimise her milk production, I was led to Sir Gerald's office where he was waiting with a bag of silver.

"My thanks Mistress Jenkins," he had said simply as he passed me the purse. "I will write to my brother and your son will be restored to you as promised."

I could not speak and simply tucked the purse inside my tabard as I left the room.

Dawn was almost breaking as I retraced my steps up Middle Street and the anticipated rain started to lash down.   Though homeward bound, as I crossed the churchyard, I decided to enter the church to confess my sin and seek the solace of His presence.   Kneeling on the cold, hard, stone floor before the altar rail, I felt no need for any priestly intermediary,   preferring instead to open my heart directly to God and beg forgiveness for my action that night and to pray that the innocent babe would find her way straight to His side.

In the cold, lofty confessional, my wet hair and clothing added to the intense sense of chill that engulfed me as I listened to the wind and rain bludgeoning its stout walls. So long did I kneel, that any who had entered the church at that hour might have thought me one of the stone effigies that adorned the tombs and recesses of the hallowed place. Indeed, my heart felt as stone, so weighed down was it by the enormity of my actions. Guilt filled me and I knew that my life was forfeit.

I prayed fervently that God would acknowledge and accept my remorse and offer me a means of making amends for my dreadful transgression. As my prayers continued, a watery light slowly filtered through the fine tracery of the east window, and I felt my soul begin to lift. The first hint of the day to come illuminated the altar and I truly felt God's presence. Realising that what had been done that night could not be undone, nor indeed forgiven, in my soul I knew that He understood that it had been fear of Sir Gerald's actions towards his new daughter and fear for my own family that had prompted my actions. As the light increased and sought out even the darkest corners of the church, I gave thanks that He would one day give me the means to make amends for my weakness.

I bowed my head in recognition and acceptance of His compassion, pledging that with His help I would continue to assist at the births of both high and low born babes and would one day atone for my sin by ensuring that a babe who should otherwise have died, would be allowed to live a long and healthy life.

Raising my eyes to the strengthening light shining through the windows I said a quiet "Amen."

I rose stiffly and before making my exit, lit two candles, one for the soul of little Alys Alard and one for the safe repose of my dear husband. I then deposited the entire contents of Sir Gerald's purse into the poor box and left the church.

With no expectation that it will alter your condemnation of my actions, I hereby advise that Lady Mathilde did undertake the pilgrimages to Walsingham and Canterbury, as suggested by her husband, and my daughter, Agnes, and I were summoned to Capel House on numerous occasions during what proved to be a difficult fifth pregnancy for Milady. Despite our best efforts, she died shortly after the birth of her long-prayed for son, Edwyn.

Much to his surprise, my son, George was discharged from service with the Portsmen and was appointed Seargeant at Arms of the Town Watch. A post he held with pride for many years.

Some fifteen years later, in spite of attending many births, the opportunity to atone for my sin had not presented itself. I had told none of my crime, not even when I was close to death, preferring instead to let my contrition show through my actions and prayers. Once or twice I did consider telling my story to my daughter, to serve as a warning to her, lest she be asked to perform such a heinous act in her role as my successor. However, I was too cowardly to risk her loss of respect. You are therefore the first to receive my confession. Do with it what you will.

xXx

So there you have it – my own dreadful secret. Infanticide. For six hundred years I have remained here, witnessing with growing interest, the lives of the many residents that have passed through and offering succour and assistance when required. My guilt and shame have prevented me from ever sharing my secret with anybody, though there were times when I was sorely tempted to unburden myself. However, the fear of losing hard-won respect and affection always stayed my hand.

I could not tell you of my tale before, else you might have thought my advice to you and Susie lay in my own self-interest. I had watched with dismay each time Susie had suffered her devastating miscarriages and berated myself for not being able to have changed the outcomes for her. Thus, when she at last passed into the second trimester for the first time, I was as excited and optimistic as you both and as equally distressed when she contracted the pertussis that was to affect her so severely.

I watched in disbelief as you were advised of the likelihood that your baby would be mentally or physically disabled, perhaps both, and was aghast that the medical experts of today, with all the knowledge and modern equipment and medicines at their disposal, could so glibly suggest that the pregnancy be terminated. That Della and Stephen, so excited at the prospect of becoming grandparents but fearing that proceeding with the pregnancy would put their daughter at risk, had accepted their medical colleagues' advice was also disappointing.

At Lexie's request, though my own knowledge was limited, as compared to these modern men of science, you put your faith in me and allowed me to examine Susie and offer my own verdict on the outcome of her pregnancy.   I felt God's power during my examination and was able to ascertain, with utmost surety, that your baby, a daughter, was whole and healthy. I could also detect a faint second heartbeat and suggested that your daughter was accompanied by a twin brother.   That you accepted my clinical findings and despite the warnings of the risks, decided to proceed with the pregnancy, filled me with such joy.   As I watched over Susie through the rest of her pregnancy I knew that it would be your children's birth that was to offer me redemption.   As I write this letter it is with the great hope that you and Susie are now the proud parents of twins.

I was saddened that our dear friend Kit did not live to meet his great grandchildren but I look forward to meeting him again as he, of all my acquaintances over the centuries, was surely destined to ascend quickly to heaven. Though you are not related by blood, you share many of his characteristics and I know he will be reassured to know that his family is safe in your hands.

I know not if I will have time to bid you farewell when my time comes but please be assured that your friendship has enriched my stay in this place beyond all measure. I wish you and yours many decades of happiness. Use my secrets and treasures wisely, out of respect for the original owners. This old place has offered a sanctuary and opportunity to many who have come to its door and I know that you and Susie will continue to offer such to anyone in the future.

When at last your time on earth is done, I look forward to renewing our friendship in heaven and to hearing about the lives of those who have dwelt in my dear old house since I was permitted to leave it.

xXx

Robbie turned the final page with a sigh. The historian in him recognised the immense opportunity that he had been bequeathed but he was also aware of the great responsibility Nell had placed on him. He gazed at the papers and precious items that surrounded him and tingled with excitement at the prospect of bringing some of the secret items into the public domain however, he could hear both Nell's and Kit's voices in his head warning of utilising the items for his own benefit and aggrandisement.

He slowly replaced the treasures in their hiding place along with Nell's letter and histories. For now he would let the secrets and treasures rest in situ.   On reflection, he was content, the birth of his children completing his happiness.   He and Susie lived comfortably, had careers they loved and, like so many of the house's residents before them, they would never turn their backs on anyone who came to them in need of help.   Nell's treasures would not change that.

Over a quiet supper with Susie that evening, Rob showed his wife Nell's letter and described some of the letters and treasures that had accompanied it.

She was astounded and moved by the obvious affection Nell had expressed towards her husband.

"What do you intend to do?" she asked. "Publication of such stories would make you famous."

Rob acknowledged that possibility but stressed that he had no such ambition.

"Fame carries its own issues and problems," he said simply, "and what need have I to change the world?"

"Then I think you have your answer," came the sage response.

Rob nodded and later made his way back to the attic. Tapping on the beam he once more looked upon the package of documents and the precious artefacts. Satisfied that they were secure he added a new letter to the pile in which he had explained the role Nell had played in the birth of his children and, as such, had earned her redemption.

"Keep them safe, dear house. It is you who are the true custodian of these items. Let them remain in your safekeeping. I know you will offer up any that might offer assistance to someone in the future but for now let them remain undisturbed."

594

Author's note

Though set in Rye, Mulberry House itself is an invention that incorporates features of similar houses I lived in or visited within the old town.   I spent many happy hours wondering who had lived in these homes, often inventing stories with which to entertain my family.

I have utilised many old local surnames in my tale but all the characters therein are of my own making, apart from those historical characters that helped give the story structure and chronology, and if there is any similarity to any real former Ryers, it is purely a coincidence. Any historical errors are my own – for which I apologise.

If you have enjoyed my tale please tell your friends and also submit a rating on Amazon. As a self-publishing author it is gratifying and helpful to receive favourable comments.

Bibliography

A New History of Rye by Leopold Amon Vidler
:Combridges, Hove, 1934

Culpeper's Complete Herbal by Nicholas Culpeper
Edited by Steven Foster   :Union
Square & Co, 2019

Rye, A Short History by Kenneth Clark   :Rye
Museum, 2023